HIDDEN
AGENDAS

CLAIRE RIDDICK

Copyright © 2015 Claire Riddick
All rights reserved.
ISBN-13: 978-0986096204
ISBN-10: 0986096202

Library of Congress Control Number: 2015942952

OLD CASTLE PRESS, LLC

Cover Design and Interior format by The Killion Group
http://thekilliongroupinc.com

This book is dedicated to Rita —
We will play cards again in Heaven someday,
And we will still beat the guys

ACKNOWLEDGMENTS

My warmest gratitude and love to my husband Jeff and daughters, Cassie and Hailey, who believed in me, braved firsthand critiques, and put up with my typing day and night,

To Mom and Dad for giving me life and instilling in me the morals that kept me out of trouble (most of the time),

To Patty, Wendy, Nancy, and Kathy for helping me with research, offering vital critique, and urging me onward,

To Doug for the military information, and to Mom S. for the stories about Atlanta,

To Lori, Andrea, and Carla for their helpful edits and advice,

To Doc H. for teaching me how to *boldly* stop splitting infinitives,

To my dear friend Colleen, who always believes in me,

To Terri and Brian for blazing the trail and teaching the rest of us, to Jackie and Ane for broadening my horizons, to Cec M. and Patricia D. for showing me that my unique stories are a calling,

To all my wonderful friends and critique partners—
Lisa, Patricia, Tigner, Joyce, Barbara, Martha, Jeff, Leigh, Cindi, Grace, Beth—and so many others who have encouraged me, each one special,

To all the conference speakers and volunteer manuscript editors whose tutelage has been priceless, and will continue to be,

And to Robyn Q. for being a candle in the darkness.

I thank you all from the bottom of my heart.

GLOSSARY OF VHURRUH LANGUAGE

Amvezu – Vhurruh drone term of endearment for a young queen
Arragall – Captain of the mother ship, *Farrekhren*
Genahm – A drone past mating years
Gherrenfae – The Gray mother ship (1 of 2 in the original mission)
Ghissella – Gray queen who traveled in the third mother ship with *Nekkai* members
Farrekhren – The third mother ship transporting the *Nekkai* queens
Hahmah – A queen's selected harem of drones
Hahmurent – Queenless drones
Hovuret – The Blue mother ship (1 of 2 in the original mission)
Herrengae – Blue Commander linked to Vince Mansfield
Himenta – Laser
Hmraay – Gray *surranenn* assisting *Wysstangrr*
Hurratt – Vhurruh home planet
Khram – A Vhurruh metal
Khrennam – A *kurnistarr* (guard) linked to Rapunzel
Kurnistarr – Guard caste, with dragon-like dorsal ridges, clawed forearms, and walrus-like tusks
Linked – Human term for being telepathically linked to a Vhurruh through a *M'hye* connection
M'hye – An unbreakable telepathic link that Vhurruh form with each other, and with humans
Mahyen nde-dehye – Interdimensional electromagnetic field generator used for bypassing distances in space
Manarenen – One of 3 known orders of *Nemeygenyah*
Mazak – A Captain of a mother ship
Mekrenzett – A Gray Drone Commander, part of the faction
Mhetrrian – Young Blue drone linked to Caffrey
Mrennah – Gray queen that died
Nekkai – Social reform movement led by elders and queens to unify races and hives
Nemeygenyah – Spiritual sect led by wise elders

Rahzukai – One of several names for God

Rezefhen – Battalion of Vhurruh led by a drone

Rhemerett – Captain of the mother ship *Hovuret*, killed by *Vrenenjurr*

Rinuut and Zinzamey – Friend and Brother

Sahmaen – Nursery aid caste (smallest Vhurruh)

Sozuul – Young, unmated queen (aka princess)

Surranenn – Worker caste

Tarrek(en) – Commander(s), leadership title granted to drones who lead battalions

Tay-nuniz – In 3 Vhurruh time segments, equal to 5 Earth hours

Tmeerah – Gray *surranenn* assisting *Wysstangrr*

Teknaht – Thought wave augmentation device

Umurrgnn – 1 of 3 Gray *surranenn* linked to Caffrey

Varraay – The Blue Vhurruh race

Veerinay Hodzu – The new planet where Zgeyyans originally housed abducted humans

Vrenenjurr – Gray Captain and leader of the faction

Vrreemeh – 1 of 3 Gray *surranenn* linked to Caffrey

Vinrrahi – Blue queen who traveled in the third mother ship with *Nekkai* members

Wennatt – The Gray Vhurruh race

Wuvena – Vhurruh greeting similar to hello

Wrrynatt – 1 of 3 Gray surranenn linked to Caffrey

Wysstangrr – A Gray Commander who appeared part of the faction, but was secretly linked to a sect of *Nemeygenyah* elders who remain part of *Nekkai*

Zinzamey – Brother

Zizza netae – Information disc

1

MERE COINCIDENCE

Caffrey Hanson grimaced at the odor of burnt rubber and acrid smoke that blew into her face. Placing a hand over her mouth and nose, she abandoned the safety of her office building, and stepped into the chaotic street. Beyond the manicured shrubs and black marble Peachtree Towers sign, vehicles lay frozen across all six lanes of the Atlanta street in bizarre, twisted positions, hissing and billowing smoke. Fire blazed from nearby vehicles, making it difficult for her to ascertain where the explosion had originated.

Panicked faces whirled by her like a disturbed fire ant nest. Shouting, screaming and sobbing filled the air and tore at her heart. Occupants of wrecked vehicles were still exiting their cars, disoriented, as though awakening from a deep sleep with no idea of how they had arrived there.

Good Samaritans were courageously opening car doors and checking for injured, while others furiously dialed cell phones for help. Caffrey reached for her cell phone and realized it was in her purse, still under her desk.

Green fluid burst suddenly from a crumpled red sports car, and she side-stepped to avoid the spray. Glass and metal debris crunched under her high heels, turning her ankles. With an odd sense of foreboding, she dodged mangled vehicles and frightened people, hoping to be of some assistance.

"It's okay, it's okay," crooned a young woman leaning into the backseat of her car trying to comfort two crying children, their faces streaked with tears. The dark green car appeared to have suffered only a dented fender and a smashed headlight.

Caffrey approached, but a man arrived before her at the open car door. "Hey, are you okay?" he asked the woman.

"Yes, we're just shaken up." The young woman's brown face was lined with stress and fear as she looked up at the man. "Did you see what happened?"

The man gestured with his hand and shook his head, exasperated. "Somebody said there was a police chase. Everyone started swerving everywhere. My car just stopped working. I had no brakes." He glanced at the calm blue Atlanta skyline. "Do you think it was...?"

"I could swear I saw a scout ship above me." The woman's cell phone rang, and she answered it. She burst into tears as she relayed her situation to the caller.

Caffrey turned in a circle several times, wringing her hands, anxious to reach out and assist someone. So many people were in the street now, helping or comforting, that she began to feel useless. Soon she would be in the way of the newly arriving firefighters and paramedics.

Visualizing the indignation of her boss for leaving the front desk unattended, she reluctantly shuffled back toward the tall building.

Low movement caught her eye, and she gasped at the shadow of a child crawling between cars. She darted toward the shadow, her heart thumping wildly at the thought that he might have become separated from his parents. Dodging debris and vehicles, she closed in on the figure and recoiled in surprise when the hunched shadow rose to become a middle-aged man covered in blood. From a gash in his head, blood dripped onto his disheveled white lab coat. Red words—Telenex—were emblazoned across the left pocket.

"Are you okay?" she asked. "Do you...?"

The man lunged forward, grabbed her sleeve and pulled her down to a crouched position, nearly toppling her over. She let out a cry of shock and fear.

"Get this to the Underground!" he ordered in a raspy voice. A deep cut on his lip was depositing blood onto his teeth. Caffrey pulled back in fright, but the man's grip had the strength of desperation. With a trembling hand, he forced a quarter-sized object into her palm and closed her fingers over it. "Hide it. Now." His widened eyes flicked in all directions. "Hurry!"

Caffrey dutifully examined her clothing. There were no pockets in her dress. The inch-wide belt was too thin to hide anything underneath. She reached for her neckline and remembered the dress was designed with lace and a high collar up to her throat. She could not get into her bra without unzipping the dress. "I...I don't have any place to...."

With an odd, strangled noise, the man winced and clutched his chest.

Alarmed, Caffrey pulled free of his grasp. "Help! Anybody!" Her call evaporated over the roar of fire engines, water hoses, and sirens. She jumped up and waved an arm to signal for help, but her 5' 3" frame barely rose above the darkened windows of the sport utility vehicle behind the man, the crumpled van to the right, and the back of the pickup truck wedged against them in a triangle.

From the rise of the street to the North, she caught a glimpse of sunlight glinting off the badge of an officer running zigzag through the maze of mangled cars and people, his gun drawn. The black shirt and gold shoulder bands were unmistakable. SAAF. Special Allied & Alien Forces.

Caffrey lowered her arm. If his gun was out, then someone in this horrific scene was his target. She glanced back at the injured man. The man's mouth hung open as he gasped for breath. His eyes were shut tight in pain. He was in no shape to hurt anyone.

"*Please*," the man begged, his voice weak.

Caffrey stooped beside him. "It's going to be okay. Everything's going to be okay. I'll just hide it in one of these cars."

"No. No. Take it with you. Go." A single tear dripped from his left eye.

"I'm not leaving you here." Caffrey reached toward her sandals and stopped. The crisscross straps exposed most of her feet. She considered pushing the disc under her toes.

Voices caught her attention and she turned, hoping to catch the eye of someone returning to their vehicle.

"No." The man shook his head and reached out a hand. "You," he managed to say, before his eyes closed.

She watched for movement in his face, praying he would keep breathing. It was an older, kind face, with soft laugh lines imbedded in plump, walnut-brown skin. His ebony hair was close-cropped and silvering. Somehow, Caffrey knew this was not the face of a criminal. It was a shy, intelligent face, free of violence and selfish ambition. She decided she would find out who he was—later, when she gave the disc to the police.

With a labored gasp, his eyes widened as if realizing she was still there. "Go. Hide it!"

"Look, I'm going to go find a paramedic, okay?"

"No," he begged. "You must leave. Now."

"Okay. Okay. I'm just going to...uh...." Caffrey licked her lips and popped the tiny disc into her mouth. She raised her eyebrows and opened both hands to show she had complied—sort of.

Though she tried to hold her facial muscles completely still, her tongue involuntarily curled around the smooth, slightly convex surface. It was cold, the feel of it a metal or hard plastic with no apparent seams.

As if given permission, the man collapsed like a rag doll against the bumper of the sport utility vehicle behind him. A gurgle emanated from his throat. Caffrey shook the man's arm, then his shoulders.

His eyelids fluttered, then widened. "Run," he whispered, his voice barely audible.

"Hands up! Hands up where I can see 'em!" commanded an officer sliding to a stop.

Caffrey threw up her hands and held her breath. The officer's arm shook slightly as he aimed a curiously thick, long-nosed weapon. Caffrey had never seen an officer's arm shake when holding a gun, which caused her alarm to rise higher.

Daunting in his black and gold SAAF uniform, the officer was oddly disheveled and drenched with sweat. A quick shift of his wild eyes to the injured man determined his true target.

Caffrey stole a side glance at the injured man as he labored to breathe. What could he have done to evoke such behavior from an officer of the elite division?

A deafening roar vibrated through Caffrey's bones as a helicopter hovered directly above her. Sand whipped into her face as she searched for news station emblems, but discovered the side of the helicopter was completely black. The officer took a careful step closer.

With calm resolve, the injured man opened his sad, brown eyes and reached into his shirt.

Without hesitation, the officer fired his weapon.

Bright, laser-like blasts hit the injured man in the chest, spattering warm blood across Caffrey's blue dress.

Caffrey tumbled backward and gagged as the object lodged in her throat.

"Caffrey!" a familiar, high-pitched voice screamed from behind.

Desperate to breathe and escape the grisly scene, Caffrey flailed against the bumper of the pickup truck behind her. She slid along it, and fell against her co-worker, Kimberly.

Kimberly squealed in alarm. "Are you okay?"

With the stench of burnt flesh in her nostrils and the object denying her air, Caffrey clawed at Kimberly's shirt sleeves, impeded by two bags from the corner sub shop.

Comprehension dawning, Caffrey tore into one and ripped the plastic cap off of a tall fountain cup. Diet soda splashed everywhere as Caffrey swallowed hard. Even colder than the frothy liquid was the chill of the disc moving slowly down into her body.

"You okay? You okay?" Kimberly begged with tear-filled eyes. Caffrey gasped for air as Kimberly frantically tried to drag her between the vehicles.

Fearing the officer would come after her, Caffrey reluctantly turned to find him roughly examining the man's clothing. Her stomach churned as the officer ripped off the man's bloody shoes and stuck his hands into them.

A raspy military voice issued from the officer's shoulder com unit. "Status of the target. Status of the target."

The flustered officer stood and pressed a button. "Target is secure. Negative on the package." He threw down a bloody shoe in disgust. "Request secure ambulance for transport."

"Is the vehicle secure?" came another stiff voice from the unit.

"Vehicle is secure," replied a different voice in the exchange.

Satisfied, the officer turned back toward the dead man; then his eyes and weapon rose menacingly toward Caffrey.

Gasps from behind told Caffrey a crowd had gathered.

In three long strides, the officer was beside Caffrey and had clenched her arm. His voice was low and fierce; his lips barely moved as he spoke. "Did he *say* anything to you? Or *give* you anything?" The officer's crazed eyes flashed back and forth, warning he would detect a lie.

"No," Caffrey replied, answering his fierce glare with one of sheer terror. "He...he just said, 'Help me.'" She stole a piteous gaze toward the dead man and held her breath, certain her stomach would reverse itself at the gory sight of charred flesh, oozing blood, and the now-vacant, staring eyes.

To her surprise, the officer holstered his gun, grabbed both of her wrists, and turned up her hands, which forced the remaining drink to crash onto the street.

"Hey!" Kimberly protested, stepping forward.

"Stay back!" he warned through gritted teeth. "Everybody, stay back. Nothing to see here."

"Oh, yeah," drawled a dark-skinned woman who raised her eyebrows. "Like we got dead people layin' all over the street *every* day." Several bystanders backed her up with angry comments, including Kimberly.

Ignoring them, the officer whirled Caffrey about, pressed his palms blatantly over the back of her dress, down her backside and hips, and jabbed fingers into her belt. Seeing the high collar, he grabbed at her breasts. She recoiled and tried to thrust his arms away.

"Hey, this girl *works* with me!" shouted Kimberly. "She came out here to *help!*"

"Take off your shoes," the officer ordered. Murmurs from the restless crowd grew louder. Phones were flashing. Caffrey stepped out of her heels obediently, too terrified to protest. He stuck his fingers in them and dropped them to the street.

His jaw jutting forward in disappointment, he raised the cover of his wrist phone and snapped a photo inches from Caffrey's face, the flash making her flinch. "Let me see some I.D."

"I...I don't have anything with me," Caffrey squeaked and rubbed invisible pockets at her hips. "It's back at the office."

Kimberly leaned forward and in a sarcastic tone said: "Caffrey Hanson, age twenty-one, 1025 Avery Street, Alpharetta, Georgia."

Caffrey froze, certain the officer would take offence at Kimberly's tone. Instead, he took a close-up of Kimberly's angry face.

"You two...." He added a stiff, pointed finger. "Do not leave. We'll need to question you further."

Dismissing the suspicious onlookers with a glance, the officer stiffened at site of a wide-eyed man and woman clinging to the doors of their SUV where the man's body remained slumped against the back bumper.

"You two, out of the vehicle. Hands where I can see them!"

Another SAAF officer joined him and spoke in a low voice, the same strange weapon held tightly in one hand.

As the officers began examining the man and woman, Kimberly yanked Caffrey by her shoulders through the crowd and over to the silver-black building that housed their firm, Property Resources.

"What happened, Caff? What the heck was he after? Who was that poor guy? Did he, like, rob something or what? I was in the sub shop when I heard everything hit—whoa, *what* a *sound!* Bam-bam-bam. All those cars hittin' everywhere. Never seen anything like it. But, when I saw you sittin' down there, and he *shot....* Oh, my gosh! I thought you were dead. And where does that SAAF get off? That guy did *not* have a gun— or *anything.*"

"Kim...."

"Geez, is this street a mess or what? Hey, look, a fourth ambulance. And more fire engines coming over that way. I mean, like, seriously, there's nowhere for the cars to go...." She waved a hand expressively.

"Kimberly, I've got to get inside."

"Oh, sorry, kid. Let me help you. Don't faint on me for crying out...! Sheesh, here's the door."

Bystanders observing the scene from the safety of the lobby stared and whispered at the blood and cola stains on Caffrey's dress. Kimberly pushed her way through to the first office on the left and triumphantly shouted.

"'Scuse me, please! Make way. Injured lady here."

"I'm not injured!" Caffrey hissed. A wave of nausea rushed over her, followed by a stabbing pain in her stomach.

"Whatever," Kimberly spat, unwilling to be denied such rapt attention.

"Kim, what about the SAAF?" Caffrey shivered at the thought of seeing his wild-eyed face again. "He said not to...."

"Oh, I don't care about him." Kimberly added a curt wave of her hand. "I know who you are."

2

AMVEZU

Caffrey crossed the foyer of their office suite to peer out the giant floor-to-ceiling windows. She felt irresponsible for having left the man there, though he was surely dead.

Mary Parker, the office manager, burst from her office and yelled in a sharp New York accent. "Why am I the only person answering the phone?"

"Oh, my gosh, you are *so* not going to believe what just happened." Kimberly ignored Mary's frosty glare.

"Is that blood?" Mary glared at Caffrey's dress.

"Yes! It's *blood*," blurted Kimberly with excitement. "A guy was shot *right* in front of us." She pointed to the window, her straight blonde hair flying in a circle. "He's out there now, dead as a doornail."

"*Kim....*" Caffrey pressed a hand to her heart.

"Oh, sorry." Kim continued with her graphic explanation in a lower voice to Mary, as if Caffrey could somehow not hear.

"Is that a wreck outside?" Mary stepped closer to the window, her mouth falling open.

"Didn't you hear all the cars crashing?"

"I had my head-phones on. And I *thought* somebody was here answering the phones. The whole staff's not back from lunch yet. Where's your shoes?" Mary's eyes flashed with disapproval at site of Caffrey's feet.

"Uh...." Caffrey began, but she could not continue. A sudden drip on her arm made her realize tears were falling down her cheeks. The dull throb in her stomach grew into a snarling beast. She began to shake, not knowing what to do.

Mary ignored Kimberly and put an arm around Caffrey, a rare motion of concern. "Honey, let's go to the ladies' room, get you washed up."

Kimberly rushed behind them, desperate to continue whispering events to Mary. In the restroom, Caffrey tried to rinse the stains from her dress, but hot tears blurred her vision so that she could not see what she was doing.

"A SAAF?" Mary interrupted Kim's monologue. "Well, it's got to have something to do with the Alliance, then. Maybe the guy tried to get into a Vhurruh embassy or something."

"But, that's miles from here, at that Fort near Savannah," argued Kimberly.

"Not necessarily." Mary arched one thick black eyebrow. "They can drop those quarandomes anywhere. They probably have one at the airport, right under our noses."

"Eeuuw, I don't wanna see it, if it is." Kimberly grimaced. "Don says they get slime all over 'em, and it steams up, and you can't see through them."

"Oh, what does Don know?" Mary snorted, adding a toss of her short black hair. "He's never been to one."

"Well, he heard it from somebody." Kimberly sniffed. "Caffrey wants to visit one, don't you, Caff? She thinks the slugs are...." Kimberly waved her arms in mocking ballerina motions. "*Graceful.*"

"You okay, girl?" Mary asked.

Caffrey nodded out of habit, but more tears spilled from her eyes. She glanced up at the mirror to whisk them away. Her face was ashen against disheveled locks of red hair, her eyes gray instead of their usual bright blue. Muddy black circles of running mascara did not help alleviate the ghostly effect. With shaking hands, she unzipped her dress and pulled it off. She shoved the stained spots under the faucet. Reddened water splashed everywhere.

"It's all right, honey. It's all right," Mary crooned, and pumped soap from the dispenser. "We'll sponge it with paper towels and hold it under the hand dryer, okay?"

"Oh, my gosh, it's *on* you!" Kimberly pointed at Caffrey's chest and waved her hands in disgust.

Caffrey grabbed at paper towels. She could hear herself gasping but could only think of getting the blood off her skin where it had seeped through the lace.

"Just calm down. We'll get it off." Mary wet more towels and applied soap to Caffrey's skin while Kimberly backed away.

All three women squealed as someone knocked sharply on the door. "Mary? You in there?" called a muffled voice. Mary rushed to the door and opened it an inch.

"What?"

"Where're the girls?" Jim Brockett sounded worried. "We thought you were outside at the wreck or...."

"They're in here. Caffrey's...had a little accident."

"Is she okay?" The concern in his voice warmed Caffrey's heart. During the past ten months, she and Jim had developed a platonic fondness for each other that neither had ever mentioned and probably never would, since Jim was married. Jim often laughed off the office whispers as the two boldly went out to lunch together to renew their debates over the most recent Alliance news, proposed alien life forms, and government conspiracy theories.

"Jim, you're not going to believe it!" Kimberly pressed her face to the crack of the door. "This guy got zapped right in front of...."

"Shush." Mary pushed her back. Then to Jim, Mary said in her commanding voice, "Caffrey's fine. I'll explain later."

"Uh...okay." Jim was hesitant. "Well, see Martin when you get back. We've got two new addenda just came in."

"Geez," Mary complained. "How can anybody pass a law that fast? Wouldn't have happened in my day, buddy. Took an act of God for Congress to pass anything. It's gettin' weirder by the day."

"Yeah. Tell me about it."

Caffrey could hear Jim whispering low before Mary closed the door.

"What's going on?" Alarmed that her voice shook, Caffrey swallowed to gain composure.

Mary shot a glance at the four stall doors to be sure they were all open. "Two suspected *liftings* have been reported, off the record."

A cold chill seeped up Caffrey's spine. Her chest tightened and her lip trembled. The memory of her fiancé's disappearance a year earlier threatened to make her vomit. She wondered if that wasn't a bad idea.

As if on cue, her brain replayed with crystal clarity the hysterical voice of her friend, Tami, calling to announce that she had reported their boyfriends as missing from their hiking trip in the North Georgia Mountains. Caffrey felt the same sensation of something heavy falling onto her chest, as she had that night. She had left five voicemail messages that he would never hear. She squeezed the repulsive memory from her mind.

"Maybe somebody's just late reporting it." Kimberly's eyes widened. "You know, lots of isolated people didn't get reported for a long time while the Zgeyyans were sucking them up."

Caffrey dropped her dress. "Kim, for heaven's sake."

"Sorry, sorry." Kim held up her hands in surrender.

Mary lowered her chin, and her voice. "Word is, one month ago."

Kimberly was speechless—a first, Caffrey was certain.

"And that's not all," said Mary with reservation. She pressed paper towels against Caffrey's dress to absorb the water. "We all have to get Secret clearances next week."

Kimberly gasped. "Are you serious? Wow, Top Secret. Cool."

"Is it?" asked Mary. "And it's not 'Top Secret.' It's just 'Secret' right now. There are levels. Martin and I have to apply for 'Top Secret.'"

"Whoa."

Caffrey helped Mary hold the dress up to the hand dryer. Part of her found the prestige of a Secret clearance tantalizing. But, with rumors of more disappearances and cover ups, it felt like the offer of a new wool coat that was going to itch around the neck.

After applying several cold, wet paper towels against her flushed face, Caffrey reluctantly squeezed back into the semi-dry dress. She, Mary and Kimberly returned to the office to find their colleagues swarming the windows of the foyer. Everyone clamored to hear Kimberly's excited rendition of the accident. Several of them confirmed for themselves that Caffrey was okay, which caused a lump to form in her throat.

Returning to her desk to answer phones was a welcomed distraction, although keeping her voice steady proved difficult with Kimberly continuing to embellish on the story for anyone who would listen.

A sharp pain in Caffrey's side made her groan, and she looked over the colleagues she had worked with for the last year. Most of them she was not sure whether to trust. Jim, however, would know what to do. It would have to be before his next client at three o'clock. Mary was a possibility. She would keep a level head.

Breaking from the crowd, Martin White, the firm's portly, gray-haired business manager, loudly conveyed his sympathies for Caffrey's difficult afternoon and mumbled that she might need to go home and change. He glanced over her stained dress and shoeless feet. Caffrey knew her boss well enough to know the suggestion was for the benefit of everyone listening. Her apartment in Alpharetta was 45 minutes away, north of Atlanta. The afternoon would be gone by the time she drove home, dressed, and returned.

Caffrey watched Jim engrossed in a conversation with Don Harper at the window. Emergency lights blinked through the heavy glass and created a pale halo of red and blue around them.

"Yes, I *should* go home. But, I think I'm just going to sit here for a few minutes first, Martin."

"Okay, hon. Let me know what you're gonna do." He laid a supposedly comforting hand on her shoulder and offered a flat smile as he headed toward his office. The switchboard rang, and Caffrey picked up a line.

"Jim," Valerie Webb called out, "we've got to prepare for your three o'clock. I changed that last paragraph of Attachment A. You need to look at it."

Caffrey talked faster, but the female caller continued asking strange questions, obviously mistaken as to what type of firm this was.

"And you handle the front desk?" the caller asked.

"Yes. Do you need to speak with our Office Manager?"

"No. First office on the left, correct?"

"Yes, that's correct, but...."

"Thank you." The caller hung up.

"Mary, you got those new addenda?" Jim called out.

"They're on the share drive." Mary replied as she headed to her office.

"Mary, would you make sure I'm not disturbed before my three o'clock?"

"Sure thing. Hear that, ladies? Jim's a hermit 'til three!"

Kimberly rolled her eyes at Caffrey and returned to her office.

"All right, people! We got work to do!" Martin bellowed, closing his door loud enough to make a point.

Two more lines rang while the staff disappeared. Caffrey fumbled to put the callers on hold and called out for Kimberly's help. Painful cramps knotted the ride side of her abdomen.

Jim's door slammed shut, and Caffrey closed her eyes. It would have to be Mary. Wasn't her son-in-law a county police officer? He could at least give advice. Mary's line glowed orange. Caffrey's shoulders sagged.

She knew her parents were out of the question the moment they came to mind. The credo of the Underground would pale in comparison to her health. They would insist she go straight to the hospital.

Joey, her younger brother, lived with them 300 miles away in Maryland, and was in his last two months of high school. He would not be much help, but he could keep a secret.

Her cousin, Rhonda, was a thought. She had recently moved to South Carolina, which was only a four hour drive. They had experienced many wild adventures together as children, and Rhonda was one of toughest women she knew. She would at least consider both sides of the issue, and assist her in finding a connection to the Underground. Caffrey reached for her phone, but a light jingle at the front door arrested the motion.

A tall, obese man, his jet-black hair pulled back into a clip, squeezed through the doorway and tottered across the foyer without taking his eyes off hers. She wondered if he was diseased from the labored way in which his torso swayed unsteady in the curtains of black material covering everything except his head and hands. The collar and cuffs of the robe were embroidered in brilliant yellow. His pallid, expressionless face was so swollen it seemed ready to burst.

The red hair on Caffrey's arms rose as he leaned his enormous frame toward her. Before she had finished her usual greeting, the man reached out and touched her cheek.

"*Wuvena*, my brave *amvezu*," he purred.

An electric sensation raced through Caffrey's brain and spread through her limbs. The shock was uncomfortable but left an odd, pleasant sensation. Wide black eyes with yellow rims swam before her, glistening, as if under a layer of plastic. Dreamy and relaxed, in a distant region of her brain Caffrey knew she should be saying something, but a response would not formulate. A deep voice whispered and vibrated within her soul, creating a strange euphoria she did not want to lose.

"Yesss. I believe he chose wisssely." The man sounded far away. "Though it would seemmm fate left himmm no choiccce at aaall."

A deathly pale hand passed over Caffrey's eyes. Abruptly alert, she blinked, then nearly doubled over with nausea. She grabbed the edge of her desk. Only practiced professionalism kept her upright and standing.

"I'm...I'm sorry, what did you say again?" she managed to ask. Acid roiled up her esophagus and burned her throat. Lights in the office were suddenly too bright to endure, the onset of one of her migraines.

"No problemmm, I believe I haff wrong officcce. I mmmeant to step to jewelersss nnnext doorrr." There was an airy, purring quality to the man's voice, and his mouth moved unevenly as though damaged by a stroke. Odd bulges, like tumors, protruded from various places under his waxen cheeks. He attempted a crooked smile, but the muscles around his eyes drooped and did not move at all. With great effort he turned, retreated awkwardly through the door, and headed toward the lobby entrance instead of the jewelers. Caffrey collapsed into a chair.

"Oh—my—gosh. Who was *that*?" Kimberly exploded in comical amazement, after slapping a handful of legal folders onto Caffrey's overflowing "IN" box.

"I don't know." Caffrey steadied her pounding head with both hands. "I think he had the wrong office. Wow, have I got a headache. I think I'm going to be sick. You got any ibuprofen? I need a diet soda and something sweet and bready into my stomach."

"There's two donuts left in the break room. It took him *that* long to figure out he had the wrong office? Sheesh! Was he huge or what?"

"Yeah, he was. I think he's ill. He wasn't here long, only a second."

Kimberly's eyes widened. "Caff, he's been here for like five minutes talking to you. I mean touching your face and all. I got worried, but...you were smiling. I thought, *whoa, she's gettin' it on with a real, live sumo dude.*" Kimberly guffawed, though she hastily cleared her throat at Caffrey's alarmed expression. "Seriously, I looked out my door twice 'cause the phones kept ringing. But, he was talking so low and all.... Don't look at me like that. It was really weird. I mean.... Look, I'll get you the meds, okay? You just...just sit there. You look kinda pale." Kimberly disappeared down the window-lined corridor.

Caffrey sat with her mouth suspended open, then propped both elbows onto the desk to balance her throbbing head. This was going to need more than ibuprofen. She reached into her desk to see if any headache powders were left. The electronic bell atop the glass doorframe chimed again. She groaned.

One upward glance at the handsome face and her heart sank. Evan Parchek. A more greedy, conceited, and absurdly rich vulture the office had yet to acquire as a client. Attempting to prove only charitable purposes for the *'compromised and/or abandoned'* properties he petitioned for seemed a mere hobby to him.

Everyone in the office saw a dashing, wealthy humanitarian, an active state senator for the Alpharetta district, but to Caffrey his intelligent green eyes yearned for insatiable power and admiration. Still, he was ruggedly handsome in a California beach kind of way, with sandy-blond hair, tanned skin, and a surfboard-lean profile from his broad shoulders to his well-muscled thighs.

Flashing a bleached-white smile, he leaned his long frame over the counter with ease. "Well, Caffrey, looking a bit piqued today, sweetheart." His spicy cologne wafted over her with enticing allure, and she breathed deeply in spite of herself. "Some good loving would take care of that, you know. Put color in your cheeks." Both blond eyebrows flitted rapidly. How he managed to do that, she never knew. She had actually attempted it, in private.

"I am not in the mood, Evan."

"Oooo, we are *touchy* today." He pressed a hand to his heart to cover the wound. "Is that any way to treat your favorite client?"

"Hi, Evan!" Kimberly bounded in breathlessly with a bottle of ibuprofen and a frosty can of soda. Nearly tripping on the carpet, she amended her stride and tried to appear nonchalant.

"Well, Senator Parchek." Mary strolled out of her office to fumble through mail, which she normally never picked up.

"Mary, Mary, quite contrary, how does your garden grow? And did you grow me some corn yet?"

"Yeah. Yeah." Mary chuckled sarcastically. "Right off my balcony."

"Oh!" Evan slapped his hand again to his heart. "And she takes the shot. That's two."

"Ha! Be nice to me, and I'll make you some cornbread."

"Really?" Evan's tanned face brightened like a child on Christmas morning.

"Yeah." Mary snorted. "Right outta the box."

"Oh." Evan placed his other hand on his heart. "And she goes for the kill."

Mary giggled like a teenager and continued to flip through the same four envelopes.

"Hey, what's with our receptionist today?" Evan's eyes held Caffrey's. Caffrey could feel her cheeks flush. "Ten months I've been coming here, and she still doesn't like me."

Caffrey tilted her chin down and rolled her eyes up to glare up at him. The motion made the back of her eyeballs throb.

"Well, that's probably because she doesn't," Kimberly offered, with a flip of her thin, hip-length blonde hair over her shoulder, an irritating habit to everyone around her, since it fell relentlessly into everything, including lunch. "We can't fix her." Kimberly shrugged and clunked the pill bottle and soda can onto Caffrey's desk without taking her eyes off Evan.

"Got a headache?" Evan frowned with concern.

"It's been a really bad day." Caffrey squinted as the office lights grew brighter, and her head threatened to explode.

"I'm sorry," Evan cooed. His furrowed brows and mournful green eyes resembled a sad-eyed Beagle. "What happened?"

Caffrey knew this act, knew that he had absolute confidence in his ability to charm her, and could not help being moved by it.

"You are *so* not gonna believe the accident we saw," Kimberly blurted. "Totally gross! We were right there. And...."

"You saw what started this mess?" Evan asked. "I had to pay fifteen bucks to park in that gravel pit four blocks down. It's the worst I've ever seen on Peachtree Street."

"Well...." Kimberly faltered. "Um, you know, Jim said his three o'clock called to re-schedule, so since you're early, why don't I go ahead and get Jim for you? I've *got* to get back to this O'Connor project." She glanced expectantly at Caffrey.

"Oh, that's okay, Kim," Caffrey responded, knowing how desperately Kimberly hoped for a moment alone with Evan. "I'll tell Jim." Caffrey watched Evan's shoulders stiffen and knew he sensed her fondness for Jim. Evan's eyes flicked to the damp stains on her dress and the absence of her shoes. Halfway down the hall, she overheard Evan question Kimberly. Kimberly smoothly evaded the subject, and instead, inflated her own involvement at the accident scene.

Just as well, Caffrey thought, as she rapped on Jim's door before entering. Jim glanced up while rustling paperwork and folders. Short and lean, with perfectly combed brown hair and a booming voice as though to compensate for his size, Jim was sometimes impatient but always fair. He often executed administrative tasks for himself when he knew Caffrey was busy.

"Is that Evan already?" Jim's brow was furrowed with stress. "Wow, he's way early."

"He wanted time to bother me." Caffrey grimaced.

Jim smiled. "Still trying to get you to go out?"

"Sort of. Um, Jim, I need to talk to you about something…serious."

"Oh, okay." His smile dropped as he read the concern on her face. Caffrey realized that he assumed she wanted to discuss some of their secret fears concerning continued reports of missing people and the mysterious laws that kept passing before journalists had time to debate them.

"Jim." Caffrey reached out to touch his arm as he strode past. Jim stopped immediately. She had never touched him before. "Jim, I *really* need to talk to you." She lowered her voice. "Now. Before you see Evan."

"Yo! Jim-Bob!" called Evan as he emerged in the doorway beside her.

Caffrey whirled to put space between her and Jim, but she ran right into Evan's rock hard frame as he entered the room with an easy stride.

"Whoa," Evan exclaimed as he grasped her shoulders and pivoted her body as if the two of them had walked in together. His strong arm forced her against his side as he reached for Jim's hand. Caffrey stood wide-eyed with forearms and hands flattened against her chest like a confused praying mantis.

"How are you, Evan?" Jim cheerfully returned the firm handshake.

"*Wonderful!* How 'bout you, Jim? Been out boating yet?"

"No, no. Still need to get the boat ready. It's a little cool yet."

Caffrey stood mute, unable to back out of the room without pushing further against Evan in the narrow, angled doorway. Jim gestured toward the hallway. 'Let's go in the conference room. I've got my files if you want to get started."

"Sounds good," Evan replied. Caffrey tried to break his blatant embrace, but his long-fingers slid up and down one silky blue sleeve. "Are you okay?"

Caffrey swallowed and added a nervous smile. "I'm…fine."

"Caffrey's had a harrowing day." Jim raised his eyebrows. "She *needs* to go *home*." When Caffrey's eyes widened, he quickly added,

"Caffrey, uh, if you're still here after our meeting, I've got something I need you to look over."

"Okay, sure." Caffrey sighed with relief. Evan pressed a hand to her back as if to indicate she should exit first. Caffrey's heart pumped fast, and her skin tingled—a not altogether unpleasant feeling, she noted with unease. The supply room beside Jim's office was a quick escape. She grabbed several items and breathed deeply before returning to her desk.

Martin White came out of his office, swinging his glasses. "Caffrey, I'll need the Brown contract. Are you done with that one?"

Caffrey bristled and held her breath. They both knew the document was not needed until the next afternoon.

"Well...I can get to it. It's almost done. I'm not feeling well, Martin. I may need to leave a few minutes earl...."

"Sure, sure," he interrupted. "No problem." He glanced at all the paperwork spread across her desk, heaved a sigh, then replaced his glasses and slipped back into his office.

Fine. Caffrey plopped down to finish the document. To her surprise, she pulled open the desk drawer and placed a hand on her purse. The desire to pick it up and walk out nearly overwhelmed her. She frowned, then spied the tiny red light that indicated Kimberly had transferred the phones and was answering them for her.

Yes! Thank you, Kim. Once the Brown contract was finished, she could get out of there, Jim or no Jim.

She pounded away at the keyboard, but instead of endless lines of legal script, the computer screen replayed gruesome scenes of the man in the lab coat handing her the disc and being shot. Questions and options danced across her throbbing brain. Taking responsibility for the disc would mean an impossible search for people even the government could not find.

She snorted, realizing she was actually considering trying to meet the dead man's last request—to contact a member of the elusive Underground. What she needed to do was go straight to the hospital and have the disc removed. No, she should probably call the FBI. No, she should find some kind of watchdog group that would be more interested in what the disc was, someone who would not immediately report it. Someone like the Underground. She sighed sharply and rolled her eyes.

Pressing her lips tight with resolve, she attempted to focus on the text before her. The cold-hearted officer's crazed eyes appeared. Special Allied & Alien Forces was supposed to contain the most highly trained officers from every nation. No local police, not even federal agents, had jurisdiction over a SAAF officer. She would have to find someone higher than that. But who was higher?

She groaned. Of all groups, why did it have to be the Underground? Ignoring the document, she searched for the email Jim had sent her weeks before containing a news link: *Leader of AllianceWatch.org Found Dead*. She bypassed the media clips of Vince Mansfield's death, and the tearful interview of Thashan Kumar, friend and founder of *We-The-Humans.org*, both of which she had already seen, and clicked on Vince Mansfield's secret interview with prime-time reporter Holly Dunn, whom Vince Mansfield had surprised by showing up in her office and taking off his disguise.

Allowing Holly Dunn one trusted cameraman, he made the declaration that *AllianceWatch.org, We-The-Humans.org* and *Earth-Sentinels.org* were all going *underground* together, due to the "unstable infiltration of the government and military leadership by alien factions."

His sky-blue eyes glistened as he spoke of his late father, Senator Richard Mansfield, who died suddenly of a heart attack after speaking out about inconsistencies in the Earth-Hurratt Alliance, calling for "thoughtful consideration" of the findings of the AW movement; it had been a surprising recommendation for a group accused of being tree huggers and UFO watchers. Mr. Mansfield added that, though We-The-Humans was created to represent all countries, and Earth-Sentinels was more concerned with the preservation of natural resources, they had all come to the same conclusion and agreed to join forces, as well as getting off the radar. Holly Dunn had dubbed them *the Underground*. The name stuck.

Caffrey stared at Vince Mansfield's striking blue eyes as the film clip ended. It took a moment to realize she was still staring and her back was hurting. Reluctantly, she clicked out of the link.

An audible *tick* from the brass wall clock caught her attention. Four thirty. She breathed faster. How could an hour and a half disappear? Why didn't she hear the phones? Had any customers walked in and found her zombied out?

As if on cue, her stomach growled. Tonight would be an impossible meal. Thoughts of the disc slowly dissolving, spreading poison throughout her body.... *What is taking Jim so long?*

A shadow flickered across the window front. Caffrey smiled and waved back at the leather-skinned face. Ignoring the expensive shrubbery, Monte stepped up to the window and waved to her every day after he closed up his mobile jewelry and souvenir stand. Caffrey had made friends with him by stopping often to chat on her way to lunch, even though he usually smelled of stale cigarettes and liquor. He and five others now shared a rehab house together, donated for them by Evan after he had observed her and Monte's daily ritual.

Caffrey tilted her head in thought. Street people. Drug addicts. Panhandlers. They knew the dark places where people hid when they did not want to be found. She chuckled with sarcasm. She, who had never taken street drugs, or been drunk, or homeless, would not have a clue which wily street people to ask.

"Kimberly?" Caffrey tapped on Kimberly's office door. "What were you planning on doing tonight?"

"Me?" Kimberly grabbed her brown coat and flung a gaudy, red and gold-sequined purse over her shoulder. "Uh, watch *Vegas Nights*, and hope my phone rings. Why?"

"Kim, I've got a serious problem. I mean... I have to find someone. And, I kind of need to talk to you, too. Could we... how 'bout if we go over to that club you've been talking about? I feel like I need to go... somewhere, I don't know."

"The Brim?" Kimberly threw her hands into the air. "I can't believe it. You finally want to go, and it's *Thursday* night. All the wild stuff happens on Fridays and Saturdays."

"Well, its Ladies' Night, isn't it? I saw an ad for free drinks until eleven."

"But you don't hardly drink."

"So. Besides, I hear it's positively life-threatening on Friday and Saturday night. You said you wanted to ride around Buckhead again, so...?" She mustered a daring smile, knowing Kimberly could not resist one of the hottest "see and be seen" spots in Atlanta.

"Okay." Kimberly brightened. "But I just called. My car's still in the shop."

"That's okay. We'll take my...."

Evan burst from the conference room, exultant. Caffrey pretended to fumble for keys. It meant he won the Harvey mansion petition. The young owners, two brothers, had disappeared on a cruise the year before, along with several hundred unfortunate people. Litigation over it had been endless until Evan jumped into the fight.

"We're going out to The Brim tonight." Kimberly grinned at Evan with glowing invite in her eyes as she flipped her hair over her shoulder.

"Oh, *without* escorts, I hope." His eyes were on Caffrey. She started to protest but caught herself. Rumors that Evan sometimes used questionable means to accomplish his "missions and acquisitions" were often whispered by Martin and Don, though they laughingly approved of him in the same breath.

Kimberly answered for her. "Well, not so far. You never know, though, we might get lucky!" She was giddy with anticipation and sent pleading glances in Caffrey's direction.

"Well, girls, I think you're in luck tonight. Just the place I had in mind to celebrate." He placed well-muscled arms across their shoulders and led them to the door. "Got the old Harvey place, Caffrey. Love for you to come see it."

"Oh, we'd love to!" Kimberly squeaked. Evan threw Kimberly an icy glare, parted his lips for a tart comment, then changed his mind. "Kim, if you can get our cautious Caffrey out there, we'll make a night of it. Food, fun, and friends. I'm having it worked on this weekend, but I'm sure we could get around them. How about it?"

On Caffrey's left shoulder, his fingertips rubbed small seductive circles into the silky material of her dress. To her surprise, the touch sent warmth through every starved nerve of her body. *I have really been away from guys too long*, she decided, thinking of the past empty year since Brian's disappearance. She slithered from beneath Evan's arm to open the heavy door, which he quickly grabbed, placing his broad chest for a moment nearly against hers.

"I...I'm sure I'm busy this weekend, actually," she stammered, but then she made the mistake of looking up at his eyes. They were handsome, golden green, and hungry.

"Ride with me." His voice was a soft, sensual command.

She swallowed. "I've got to change first, Evan. This dress...."

"Oh, just change at my place," offered Kim from behind. She waved a hand and gyrated on her toes behind Evan's tall frame. "It's only fifteen minutes away, and we *do* wear the same size, you know."

Caffrey opened her mouth but halted and smiled. Kimberly was taller, with wider hips and a smaller chest, but she had an odd way of advertising at any opportunity that she and Caffrey were somehow the *same* when Evan was around.

As Evan's freshly waxed red convertible and Caffrey's practical navy blue sedan met in front of Riverton Estates, Caffrey was certain she had never seen Kimberly so ecstatic. During the drive to Kimberly's apartment, Caffrey had watched Kimberly's arm darting and exploring every button on the expansive dashboard of Evan's car. When the roof began opening and closing, Evan's arm shot out to block her. Kimberly had whipped her head around and grinned back at Caffrey like an ill-behaved child. Caffrey snorted with laughter.

Inside the apartment, after trying on several of Kim's gaudy dresses, Caffrey chose a short-sleeved, green shirt with a pattern of golden threads, which offset her thick mane of red hair, a present of her father's Irish lineage. Kimberly rolled her eyes and tried to coax

Caffrey into a shimmering purple dress, but finally gave up and tossed her a pair of black designer jeans that had shrunk, and a pair of brown, high-heeled boots with silver fringe.

Caffrey dabbed powder on her nose in front of Kimberly's necklace-covered mirror. Kimberly sighed behind her. "I wish I had your red eyebrows."

"What?"

"They have this cute arch, makes your eyes look bright. Mine are so thick they'd be a unibrow if I didn't pluck them. I have to put color on, too, or you wouldn't see them."

"Well, *you* make them look good." Caffrey smiled, determine to convince Kimberly she was pretty and did not need to compete with her. "My dad used to say I looked like a mischievous Irish faerie."

"You? Mischievous? Ha! *That* I'd like to see. Cool earrings, by the way."

Caffrey's smile dropped. She had been in such a hurry that morning, she had forgotten earrings. She pulled her hair out of the way, puzzled. "Aaugh!" She grabbed her head at sight of thin silver swirls.

"What is it?"

Caffrey held her head for a moment. "I've had a headache for hours. It felt like someone stabbed me with a knife. This is one migraine that won't quit. Come on, let's go."

When they emerged from the bedroom, Caffrey threw Evan a fierce glare of promised retribution as he opened his mouth. Reading the look correctly, he spread his arms wide.

"Well, you both look *hot*. I'm going to have to fight off the wolves tonight." They each threw him comments of sarcastic ridicule, but Caffrey passed him a special "thank you" smile for not mentioning Kimberly's outfit.

Kimberly shimmered and flashed in her neon orange miniskirt and candy-apple-red, see-through blouse covered in gaudy blue and silver dangling beads that made tinkling noises as the trio walked out to the car.

Kimberly raced for the passenger side in order to sit in the middle where the console converted to an extension of the front seat. Evan slipped his hands around Caffrey's waist, hoisted her up as though she were weightless, and deposited her neatly onto the center seat.

Kimberly's face paled, but she screeched with raucous laughter and overzealous declarations of admiration—enough to turn the heads of several balcony occupants—in an effort to disguise her disappointment. Caffrey mockingly slapped Evan for scaring her and for risking Kimberly's mood. Secretly, she was pleased that she was slim enough, and that Evan was strong enough, to do it.

Evan sported a boyish smile as he leapt into the car without opening the door. Kimberly's riotous laughter rose several decibels. Caffrey silently rolled her eyes.

Shortly into the drive, Kimberly's continued exclamations of delight over Evan's antics were silenced when Evan began interesting tales of his travels and accomplishments, clearly enjoying so rapt, and captive, an audience. Caffrey had heard other colleagues talk about this, and now she knew why. Not only was his voice charming and magnetic, but he used it like an artist would brush and paints, creating magic on an audible canvas with every pause and exclamation.

Caffrey eyed him with genuine amazement and began to notice his side glances to her as well. His muscled arm rested across the back of the seat, giving him the opportunity to nestle close in the snug accommodations. She fought the warmth and delight of his firm body against hers and found herself entertaining possibilities she had promised herself never to consider.

3

THE BRIM

The Brim swarmed with partiers huddled across two spacious balconies outlined in tiny white lights. Hopefuls waited in a line below, the glow of cigarettes and cell phones giving their locations away. Dark clouds hovered, and the sky rumbled with threats of a storm. Evan was admitted with a mere greeting, his long arms cuddling Caffrey and Kimberly against the cool wind.

Once inside, the driving beat was so loud Caffrey was not sure how long she would be able to take it. Soon she found herself smiling for no reason and walking with a bounce to the familiar pop tune. A slight argument ensued when Kimberly wanted a table near the dance floor, but Caffrey pushed them, to Evan's amusement, to sit near the back wall in the dark. She felt so underworldish the shadows felt safer.

After Evan ordered a round of drinks and fries to claim the table, Caffrey steered the conversation to Evan's connections with movers and shakers in Atlanta while Kimberly attempted to interject comments concerning her favorite rock bands. Blatantly ignoring Kimberly, Evan answered Caffrey's queries with a twinkle in his eyes.

When the waitress arrived with their order, Kimberly yanked Evan into the whirl of dancers with half a fry still in his hand. His lingering glance to Caffrey promised time later for the two of them.

Caffrey sighed and her shoulders dropped. She was about to pose questions concerning the Underground to see what Evan knew. She stirred the ice in her drink, her emotions at odds with themselves. She considered brazenly going out onto the dance floor and grabbing someone looking for a partner, but she lost her nerve and began to evaluate each dim face around her instead, not sure what sign she was looking for.

The whirling crowd resembled a strobe-lighted pool of salmon, each tensed for the right "chemistry" to signal some kind of spawning. Many wallflowers decorated the edges of the pond.

Caffrey felt a twinge for the lonely, hopeful expressions and wondered if she looked as obvious as they.

Weeks before, she awoke in tears on the one-year anniversary of Brian's disappearance, March 19th. She had been a fiancée for only one month. On Valentine's Day, in the official *Year of Contact*, Brian had asked her to marry him. She had been so happy then.

Thank God she hadn't bought her dress. She sighed deeply to herself, as she had many times before. The memory of planning attendants, guests, and colors still evoked a twinge in her heart, but the deep loss of Brian and their friends still ached in a dismal chasm of her soul. Her circle of girlfriends never recouped the loss of the men; several drifted away and formed new relationships. Caffrey's engagement ring rested in its black satin box, where she had finally placed it last fall.

Spying a terminal imbedded in the center of the table, Caffrey pressed the Internet icon. A quick search of "Underground" and "AllianceWatch" brought up numerous sites, blogs and commentaries. She opted for the official AllianceWatch.org site, only to find a message across a white page that read: "This site is temporarily unavailable." *Big surprise there.*

She clicked into several links that hinted of Alliance conspiracy theories, hoping to find one with a "Contact Us" link, knowing it was probably futile. Most of the sites were forums discussing everything from "Vhurruh planning a one-world order" to "Vhurruh impregnating humans." Visualizing half-human, half-walrus, half sea-slug creatures made Caffrey grimace. A line caught her attention.

ALLIANCETALK.COM – ARE THEY TALKING ABOUT YOUR ISSUES? JOIN ALLIANCETALK, CHAT NOW...

This Week's Question: Visions of Utopia – Is the Alliance too much of a good thing?

chrisganter – The economy is better, jobs are easier to get, and all the countries seem to be getting along. I love the changes, but makes you wonder if AllianceWatch and We-The-Humans have a point. What if the Alliance is making things better so they can announce the Vhurruh want a piece of our planet, and we'll be so complacent we'll say, "Sure, you can have this little spot right here." The Native Americans did that, and look what happened to them. Just saying....

Stantheman43 – Yesterday, claims that Vince Mansfield of the AW was spotted in Atlanta were all over the Internet but didn't make any of the major news networks. The guy's been dead for over four weeks and

granted I've heard about sightings before, but still, did our
fire-breathing journalists suddenly become wusses? Since
when is the Underground old news? I thought my uncle
was crazy for believing in news subversion. Who is pulling
the Pleasantville strings at the top?

ricky459 – Wasn't Utopia all about controlled
perfection by force? Two of you suggested that the heart-
attack weapon the CIA created in the '70s was used on
Senator Mansfield last year. Didn't he have a physical
stating he was in perfect health right before? I say they
iced him to shut him up. If it's true, we won't find out until
forty years from now when all the people involved are
dead and nobody cares if we know.

bjandcj – Forget Utopia, anybody know who's running
AllianceWatch now? I was hoping Thashan Kumar would
take it on, but there's been no announcement, and nobody
can find him. Then I heard MAP, the Texas militia group,
took over. Hope not. Those guys are whacked. Wish Vince
Mansfield had a brother. 'Course, I have a brother, but
he's crazy, so that's no guarantee.

alwaysask22 – For those of you who have been
following us, ALTERNATEAWSITE4 was our fourth
attempt to continue the forums of the AllianceWatch. Shut
down again. No official word yet from Thashan Kumar,
Vince Mansfield's good friend and founder of We-The-
Humans, on whether he will become the spokesperson for
AW. He hasn't been heard from since Vince's death. We'll
try to get the word out about an official leader soon. Keep
asking questions people.

jonesygirl33 – Just wanted to comment on last week's
question: *Recent Disappearances – Could They Be True?* I
came across reports of liftings in isolated areas of
Wyoming and Kentucky. Government officials are
mocking any rumors stating they are simply late reports
from the yearlong Zgeyyan invasion. But, what if they are
true? Could the Vhurruh and Zgeyyans be working
together, right under our noses?

We accepted help from the Vhurruh, and the Earth-
Hurratt Alliance was formed. Life's been good. No one else
has disappeared. Or have they? Has our generation
become the luckiest in history, or have we become the
proud, the brave, the uber-naïve?

We skeptics have to acknowledge that the historical
Alliance has resulted in a détente between earth's nations
of which the world has never dreamed. Imagined slights

and unresolved wars were easy to forget in light of planetwide annihilation, but never has there been peace among 95% of all nations like there is now.

Not to mention the Vhurruh hive mentality changed the way our lawmakers think. I don't know a single person who does not have a job now. Why? Because in a Vhurruh hive everybody has a job. Nobody sits at home watching cable while collecting unemployment. (Granted, the Vhurruh don't have cable TV, and they don't use money, but still.)

Vhurruh are obsessed with order and cleanliness. I saw a report yesterday that several streams in Colorado are almost clean enough to drink. That hasn't been true since the 1960's. All the new laws banning chemicals, pesticides, and sewage dumps in our environment have made a difference. *Earth-Sentinels.org* is ecstatic but still claims a conspiracy in the Alliance. Too much of a good thing?

As always, I welcome your comments. Here's the latest video of a Vhurruh I found.

Caffrey anxiously clicked on the blue link entitled, *Commander Wysstangrr with Senate Committee members.* She turned up the sound but realized nothing verbal issued from the walrus-like, silver-gray Vhurruh in the steamy quarandome except for the journalist giving the report. Presumably the Vhurruh was communicating telepathically with the Senate members who stood outside the dome and nodded at unheard comments.

"Buy you a drink?"

Startled, Caffrey regretted her quick denial as the hazel eyes and chocolate-brown hair politely moved on. She reprimanded herself, embarrassed at her own shyness.

A thin busboy with curly black hair and pale skin passed by, carrying a tray of used dishes.

Caffrey took a deep breath. "Hey! Um, have you...do you ever get strange people, like, from the Underground here?" Caffrey felt her cheeks blush as the young man's disdainful cackle turned several heads close by.

"*Underground*? Why?" He smirked. "You wanna join up?"

Caffrey threw him a sarcastic glare. "Why not? Who's to say they're not right?"

"Yeah, but do you know the secret symbol?" He cocked his head but his side grin belied his seriousness.

"What secret symbol?"

He flashed a handsome smile.

She rolled her eyes. "Very funny."

He leaned close. "Hey, we get *all* types around midnight. Conspiracy stuff, talk about the Underground and mind control and all that. Maybe you'll get lucky."

A silver necklace swung free of his shirt. From it hung an oval circle with a rhombus diamond in the center. Caffrey felt a cold chill run over her arms.

"With a little drink in 'em, people boast about anything," he continued. "But," he lowered his voice, "the owner doesn't like 'em, so...if I hear anybody talkin' I'll send you over, okay? Just don't say it was me." He winked and headed for the kitchen.

"Hey, Caff, are you actually flirting?"

Caffrey whirled to find Kimberly approaching the table, a hopeful glint in her brown eyes. "I thought I saw a nice-looking guy over here. What happened?"

"She pushed him away like all the others." Evan waved his arm. "Hey, Frank!"

"There he is, the next President," declared a wiry, dark-haired man sporting a thin mustache and a confident grin. Heavy gold chains glistened around his neck and his hands were adorned with flashy gold rings and bracelets. He sauntered over to take Evan's hand in both of his. Evan introduced him simply as "Frank."

At first Caffrey thought Frank interesting, until she realized that serious, political talk was reserved for Evan and silly, nonsensical questions were directed toward her and Kimberly, which set her blood boiling. She snatched Kimberly's arm and excused them both to wander past tables and hip-thumping bodies before finding the ladies' room, which was barely visible through the smoke, laser lights, and confetti.

Kimberly whistled and commented that the real party must have been in there. Water, tissues, paper towels, even plastic cups so littered the floor that both women had to step gingerly for solid footing on the dingy black and white tile beneath.

"Kim?"

"Yeah?" Kimberly began to giggle, then wobbled as she lost her footing.

"I need to talk to you tonight, okay?" Caffrey whispered, reaching for a stall door.

Kimberly paused to take in Caffrey's expression. "Why, what's up? Is it that guy?"

"No, it's about..." Caffrey detected movement from another closed stall and lowered her voice. "It's about...." Her throat closed of its own accord. She coughed until she was able to swallow. "I can't talk here. We'll talk when we get back to your place, okay? After Evan's gone. I need your help making a decision. It's really, *really* important. It's got to be tonight."

"Okay." Kimberly half-grinned with intrigue. Then she promptly slipped on a wet paper towel and slammed into an open stall door, which sent both women into snorts of laughter.

When they returned, adoring fans had enveloped the table, most of them female. Frank snatched a chair from a nearby table and offered a hand to Kimberly, which she took, releasing a giggle as she sat. Though Caffrey disliked Frank and his demeaning questions, she had to admit he was similar to Evan in his enviable talent of making each person he spoke to feel that he or she was, in that moment of time, the most important person in the world.

Surprised that Evan would let anyone have as much attention as he usually commanded, Caffrey found herself dealing with Evan in a way she had previously been able to avoid. Fending off his amazingly discrete touches turned out to be a battle in itself, since his hand periodically alighted on her shoulder, arm, leg, and was withdrawn, making it difficult to fault him. All the while Evan, and alternately Frank, charmed and wooed the growing crowd with a finesse that would put a dozen used car salesmen to shame.

Aware that she was Evan's assumed partner, Caffrey found it disconcerting to have women bristling with open hostility, all the while smiling as if they were not. After meeting so many of Evan's "friends," Caffrey realized his attraction for her was not merely physical. Though one or two admirers were confident and sincere, the majority appeared shallow and jealous and did not hesitate for a moment to sacrifice their dignity for attention. Caffrey wondered why she neither wanted nor needed attention from any of these people.

"Dance with me." Evan stood, holding out his hand.

It was a typical Evan command, but Caffrey was more concerned with her ineptitude at dancing. Having done so only twice in her life, with the exception of the ballroom dance class Mary Parker had badgered her and Kimberly into taking months before, rock and roll called for a release of inhibitions Caffrey did not have practice with.

When she hesitated, Evan snatched her hand and pulled her to her feet. The irresistible beat seemed to call her, coupled with a strange, growing sense of urgency. As they wove between tables, Evan stopped to whisper to a somber man in a suit. By the time they reached the dance floor, the music had changed to a slow, romantic ballad.

"How do you like it? This one's for you," he purred in his most persuasive voice, smooth as the calming assurance of a hypnotist.

Caffrey smiled with sarcasm as she locked her hand into his and loosely draped an arm around his firm body. Evan encircled her small waist with eager anticipation.

"And how is this one for me?"

"I know the owner."

Caffrey squinted with suspicion. "Oh, right, Evan."

"You never believe me. For your information, I'm good friends with the owner of this little establishment. Well, more so with his son. But, he's doing me a favor." A confident smile spread across his tanned face.

"Sounds like a favor I wouldn't want to owe."

Evan chuckled, unthwarted. "Caffrey, have you ever heard of a place called Papua New Guinea?"

Caffrey nodded.

"Well," he continued, "I visited there with my father years ago. Native people there have a wonderful outlook on life. They give away much of the wealth they acquire and in doing so build up the favors owed to them. A man is measured not by what he owns, but by the debts *owed* him. A wonderful way to live, isn't it?"

Caffrey opened her mouth to agree, but something in Evan's greedy emerald eyes made the whole idea seem twisted. He drew the pair of hands they had locked together against his chest.

Caffrey averted her gaze to his broad neck and glanced further down to the sandy blond chest hair escaping from his unbuttoned shirt. She swallowed and leaned her head toward his shoulder. His lean, muscled arms tightened around her. To her surprise, his body felt incredibly inviting against hers.

His lips lingered against her temple. He planted a soft kiss. The sensation sparked fire throughout her limbs. She swallowed and mentally forced her body to react the opposite as they swayed to the seductive music. She found her thoughts reassessing, her cautious nature out-voiced by loneliness and long-suppressed desire.

His lips brushed her cheek. She pulled back.

"Caffrey, why do you avoid me?" Evan whispered, sounding baffled. His thick, sun-bleached brows were knitted together. "Am I so terrible?"

Caffrey felt a stab of guilt as she looked into his eyes. "No, you're not terrible. It's just... something about the way you...." she faltered, at a loss to describe her misgivings. "I guess I don't want to be anybody's flavor of the month, Evan."

"Caffrey!" Evan looked as if he'd been struck. "Is that what you think? That you're just...."

"You're always in the news. Always with a different woman, at this event, or that event. Look at that table back there. Women are drooling to be on your arm."

He shook his head in disbelief. "They aren't you."

"But they will always be there."

"So what? You think you won't be turning the head of every man who walks by you?"

Caffrey blinked in surprise. "I don't turn the head of...."

"Yes, you do. You're just so lost in yourself you never notice."

Stunned, Caffrey examined the sincerity in his face, still unable to accept his words.

Evan smiled as if she were a child. "I can see you don't believe me, but, I promise you, that goes both ways."

"Okay, but, I'm not that kind of girl."

"I know you're not. That's what I like about you."

Caffrey felt a slight flutter in her chest. "I hope that's not the only thing you like about me."

"Oh, trust me, it's not. Everything about you is different from that crowd over there."

Caffrey started to smile, but the sensation felt so foreign, she worked to get her face back under control.

"Now, will you enjoy yourself for once?" Evan asked. "You never do that, you know." Long fingers caressed the side of her face and gently forced her chin upward. His breath was hot against her skin.

"You know, you didn't actually say you *weren't* attracted to me. Maybe you do avoid me because you don't believe my feelings are real. And maybe you avoid me because...you want me." Their eyes locked. "Don't you?"

The warmth she was beginning to feel toward him faltered. His version of "want" was not the same as hers. She tried to pull away, which became little more than a lean since she did not break his firm hold. "Pretty sure of yourself, aren't you?"

"Sometimes. But, you haven't answered my question, have you?" Instead of his words being accusatory, they were pleading, which diffused her. He moved his hand sensuously down the curve of her spine. Caffrey inhaled as every nerve tingled under his touch.

"Evan, we are not discussing this. And it's time for you to take me home, anyway. *Some* people have to work in the morning."

"Already?" He chuckled in disbelief. "Are you crazy? It's not yet the *witching* hour. We have to wait for that. This place is famous for all sorts of things happening come midnight. Everyone says the place is spooked. The owner loves it."

His thighs pressed against hers rhythmically, which forced her to move to the slow beat of the seductive music. "Let's not spoil it so soon," he implored. "Let's at least end the song. It was for you, you know." The sincerity in his eyes, accented by the arch of his brows and tilt of his head, created enough guilt for her to stay with him.

"What are you looking for?" he blurted a minute later. She realized she had been scanning the crowd.

"I was looking for someone."

"Oh, and who might that be?"

She smiled mischievously. "Someone I was discussing the Underground with. I think maybe he was one of them."

"Oh, that's impossible."

"Why?"

"Because they know they're not welcome here."

Caffrey was taken aback. "How do *you* know that? If you know that, then...."

"Let's just say, I *know*. Trust me."

She countered with one raised eyebrow.

"And why a sudden interest in the Underground?" he asked.

Words spilled out of her. "I like the fact that they're asking questions. After the Zgeyyans invaded, the Vhurruh showed up out of nowhere to become our saviors. They're smart, and they're talented, but who's to say they should be trusted implicitly? We only have *their* word it was the Zgeyyans who pillaged our population, *their* word that they defeated them, *their* word we are now protected. What safeguards are in the Alliance? I mean, how do we know if...."

"And here I thought you *liked* the Vhurruh." Evan laughed.

"I do. I do. I just...."

"I even heard," he interrupted again, "you wanted to talk with one. I can probably arrange that, you know."

Caffrey opened her mouth and closed it. Though it was likely he could arrange such a visit, she was not going to flatter him like one of his giggling groupies. "That would be... wonderful," she commented with stiff politeness. "Perhaps I'll get the chance to ask one of them why the *liftings* they claim to have eradicated are still happening."

"Caffrey, people disappear all the time. Police files are full of them. It's only natural that everyone assumes it's the Zgeyyans sneaking back in. That was such a shock to our world. The Underground takes advantage of that to bolster all their conspiracy theories."

"No, Evan. My Brian disappeared a year ago, *after* the Vhurruh supposedly tracked the Zgeyyans to Earth and forced them to retreat."

"Whoa. Wait a minute. *Your* Brian?"

"My boyfr— well, he...my fiancé."

"You have a fiancé?"

"No...I mean, I did. He went missing a year ago. Four guys don't just disappear in the North Georgia Mountains, Evan."

"No. With *you* waiting at home, I don't suppose that's true."

"If the Vhurruh have such sophisticated weapons that they can keep the Zgeyyans at bay, even destroy them, then why is it still happening? If they're not doing it, then who?"

"Hey, hey, calm down." He spread a long-fingered palm gingerly over her cheek and stroked the soft skin with his thumb. "Was that right before you came on board at Property Resources? No wonder you had such a sad look about you all the time. I am so sorry."

Caffrey swallowed, moved by his concern. "It's not just me, Evan. Something's not right. People can feel it."

"Then it's important to put their fears at rest."

"No, it's important to *listen*, to give a voice to their fears. The Underground's a watchdog group, right? Even if it's led by fanatics, it has the ear of the people. Everyone's opinion should be considered, everyone's fears addressed. Politicians like you need to let us *know* you care, that you feel what we feel. That you're listening. Don't you think?"

He smiled slowly. "You know, you are smart and sincere, and you believe in the people the way politicians *should*. I love the way you surprise me, the way your little brain is always analyzing everything."

"Little?" Caffrey paused mid-step.

"Oh, I don't mean it that way. Just that you're a small person. I mean short. I mean...there's no way out of this, is there?"

"No." She smiled.

His eyes traveled down her body. "Okay, how about a *gorgeous* small person...with a very big heart, and... such beautiful hair," he added, sliding fingers through her mane of red hair.

Caffrey felt her skin heating. She swallowed. "Evan, you've been in politics for several years. Why won't the government help? Everybody's denying it, and...."

"Caffrey." He stopped her with a firm voice. "*Everybody* denies *everything*. It's all about liability. And it's all about power." He softened his tone. "Sometimes what matters is who's in charge, who you can influence, and whether you're in a position to do some good in the world. You—you're the kind of person who would benefit from a position of power. You genuinely care about people. You should be in politics, not behind that desk."

Caffrey stopping dancing.

"I mean it." He coaxed her into swaying again to the soulful tune. "And, speaking of influence, I'll look into the incident of your...friends, if you want me to. I have some connections. I'll call in a favor or two."

"You will?"

"Of course. For you, anything." He raised her hand and deposited a quick kiss.

"If...if you know anyone who knows someone connected to the Underground, will you let me know that, too?"

Evan lowered her hand. "I will, if that's what you want. What's this all about?"

"Evan, something hap...." Her voice faltered. She coughed and tried desperately to swallow. "Earlier today I...." She choked and coughed harder.

"Are you okay?"

She nodded and chose a different response. "Thanks. I really appreciate you looking into that."

He frowned and squinted at the evasion. "Now, will you promise to enjoy yourself tonight?"

"No, I have to find...." Caffrey took a staggered breath as the sensation occurred again. At first, she was frightened, but a calm sensation began to wash over her. "Okay, I will try."

His smile was hesitant, his eyes sad. Caffrey felt an odd stab in her heart. How long would she let her fear of intimacy rule her life? Here was someone who appeared to genuinely care about her, to whom she was attracted, yet she resisted. He was a state senator and he was rich. What was wrong with her?

Evan's eyes closed and his forehead touched the side of hers. She leaned into him and pushed her fears aside. The soulful ballad enveloped them as they swayed together.

The warmth of his cheek rubbing against hers caused her heart to pound. The room of dancers disappeared. Evan's arms tightened. His lips slid toward hers.

4

YOU MUST LIVE

"Oh, sorry," mumbled a man after bumping into Evan. Embarrassed, the man whirled away with his date. Caffrey glanced shyly at Evan.

"Where were we?" he asked, drawing her close.

"You know, if Kim sees us, I won't be able to work with her for a week."

"You promised to enjoy yourself." The song was about to end and his eyes became serious. "Listen to me, Caffrey. I want to tell you something. This world is going to be different. And I want you to be part of it, with me."

She inhaled in surprise. "What do you mean?"

"Certain levels of power are changing. They'll be revealed soon. And...will you have dinner with me tomorrow night? There's more I'd like to share. I want to talk to you alone. We can keep it a secret from Kim if you like."

Caffrey gazed into his green eyes and decided it was time to shed her fears. "I will. On both counts."

His broad, handsome smile captivated her for a moment.

Caffrey flinched and grabbed his shoulders as a loud crash erupted from the other side cf the room, accompanied by falling bodies, screams, and several pop-like shots.

Evan pushed her through the scattering crowd, despite her protest, snatched Kimberly by the arm, which surprised and delighted her, and ushered them out an emergency door before the rumble spilled over into the center dance floor. Falling onto each other into the dark parking garage, Evan claimed knowledge of the impending fight considering the dispute over drug money and territory.

As though he had merely told them what time it was, he quickly suggested another club, not far away, where they could continue the evening.

"No. Not me," Caffrey firmly declined.

"Oh, come on," Kimberly urged. "Let's find out where Frank and his friends and going. Please?"

Frank's attentions must have meant something after all, Caffrey mused.

Evan looked at Caffrey. "Well, we could…."

"No." Caffrey shook her head. "I'll call a cab if you guys want to go somewhere else."

"No." Evan's eyes were fixed on her. "I'll take you home."

She tilted her head back onto Evan's arm and enjoyed the cool spring breeze on her face as they rode back to Kimberly's apartment. The storm clouds had moved on, and the air smelled clean.

Kimberly often kept up a ridiculous but harmless monologue when situations between people around her were tense. She did so until they stopped in front of her apartment, ending with how dangerous apartment living was and how dark the stairwells were, which left Evan no excuse not to walk her to her door.

As they exited the car, Evan's phone rang. He brightened after listening for a few seconds.

"Hey, Frank's going over to the Gold & Velvet. What do you say, ladies?"

"Oh, my gosh, let's go, let's go, let's go!" pleaded Kimberly.

Evan's eyes were hopeful, but Caffrey gave a quick shake of her head. "No, I've got to talk to someone about…." She swallowed, hard.

"Is it what you wanted to talk to me about?" asked Kimberly.

Caffrey hesitated, torn by a desire to explain her dilemma, but beginning to worry she might not be able to. "Yes. But I…I don't have much time."

Evan squeezed her shoulder, his hand lingering. "Caffrey, you look serious. What's this about? Let me help you."

Caffrey opened her mouth to speak, but no words formed. He was not the right person to tell. Why that was true, she did not know.

"Um, you know what? I'm just going to go home. I'll talk to you guys in the morning." She pulled out her keys.

Kimberly stepped between them. "Evan, let's still go. Pleeeeease?"

With a quick "You guys have fun," Caffrey dashed over to her navy blue sedan. Besieged by guilt over Evan's parting glance of regret and betrayal, she sped off toward home and Maiba's. Her closest friend at the apartment complex, Maiba was an ancient but endearing African immigrant who lived down the hall from Caffrey and was the wisest person Caffrey had ever met.

Stumbling through accents and language barriers, Caffrey often listened for hours to Maiba's tales of village life, fleeing a troubled nation, and the haunting memories of her entire family being murdered in a tribal war at the hands of a dictator. They discussed everything from men to Vhurruh, all the while eating popcorn and sipping plum wine. Maiba's advice, though often bizarre and mystical, always proved on target. Maiba would know what to do.

Caffrey wondered why she hadn't thought of her before. Speeding down the highway, she had to fight an overwhelming urge to turn around and search city streets for people sympathetic to the Underground. Maiba would be better. People were always confiding in her. She might even *know* an Underground member.

Anticipation churned and cramped Caffrey's stomach forty minutes later as she steered down the drive lined with pink and white blossoming trees, gold tulips, and emerald-green grass. Such beauty was the first thing she had noticed about Atlanta in general when she had moved there with her friend Renée. Even the smallest ice cream stand or gas station had flowers and trees nicely manicured and blooming. Her apartment complex was a place of beauty from the side and front windows.

A fleeting moment of relief upon spotting the wooden Avendale Estates sign fell like a lead hammer in Caffrey's gut as she drove into a wall of flashing blue lights. Six vehicles waited in line in front of her. People were exiting their cars, unwilling to wait for an explanation. Four uniformed officers addressed the small crowd, their brass SAAF badges reflecting in the many headlights.

Leaning out the window, Caffrey tried to overhear the conversations. She caught snippets of "accident" and "gas leak," then heard a SAAF officer ask two young men and a girl with shoulder-length red hair, "Are you residents or visitors?"

The men replied they were visitors. The girl raised her hand and replied that she was a resident. Caffrey caught her breath at the speed with which two of the SAAF officers shuffled her off to the right, behind a black unmarked van where Caffrey could not see her.

The two young men began to protest. A tall officer with a mannequin-like face said, "The area's been quarantined. Residents are being moved for now. Visitors are asked to leave. Move along." He could have been a robot, she noted, except for the human beads of sweat across his brow.

One of the young men threw up his hands in frustration and turned back to his car, muttering expletives.

Caffrey remembered the apartment parking permit dangling from her rear view mirror. She snatched it off and pressed it between her seat and the console. Two more cars were approaching from behind. Soon she would be boxed in. Putting her car in reverse, she felt unnerved by the fact that no one was rushing. There were no bodies anywhere. No mounds lying on the grass with sheets over them—no crying injured being attended to. No smoke. No damage. Only several calm groups of officials, some in suits and ties, and a few men in camouflage fatigues, several of whom were moving toward the black van. One official spoke to a confused paramedic, who closed both doors of an empty ambulance and prepared to leave.

When an officer began making his way up the line of cars, Caffrey made a U-turn in the opposite direction. Fortunately, one of the approaching cars took her queue and decided to do the same, which Caffrey hoped would deflect any interest in her, or at least give them someone else to go after.

Once she cleared the bend in the long drive, she squealed tires and sped away from the place she'd called home for nearly two years. As she drove, the hair on her arms stood on end. Her chest ached from cold fury and fear. She dismissed the idea that any part of the incident could have been because of her as soon as the thought crept in. But the possibility continued to taunt her like a restless ghost.

"Get a grip, Caff," she commanded out loud to herself in the stillness of the car. "It's just a bomb scare or something."

She pulled out her phone and spoke, "Call Maiba." The line went straight to voicemail. Her heart sank. Every person and place she knew flashed before her in a vain attempt to decide where to go, who to tell. She gave the command to call Kimberly. It, too, went to voicemail. "Kim, I need to talk to you right away, even if you're at the club. It's urgent. Call me."

Caffrey dropped the phone into a slot in her console. A familiar green exit sign for Interstate 285, known to Atlantans as The Perimeter, loomed above her, and she turned west. It felt good to be anonymous on the monstrous ten-lane highway that surrounded Atlanta like an asphalt moat. It gave her time to think. Renée was in Mississippi, living with her sister. She had crumbled when Alden and Brian disappeared together. In hindsight, Caffrey decided she should have moved to Mississippi as well.

Jim. Caffrey grabbed her phone again but hesitated after the voice prompt. Surely, his wife would be suspicious of a female coworker calling this late. Even worse, Jim was a known friend. So was Kimberly. Anyone from work would be checked. Caffrey licked her lips in thought. It needed to be someone not currently connected to her.

Lots of people and lights sounded appealing, and she took the next exit, not caring where it led. Past stores and neighborhoods she drove, curling her fingers around the steering wheel until suspended at a traffic light. Glancing at each car beside her, she felt isolated as the occupants to her left engaged in laughter, immersed in some private joke.

A car pulled up behind her, and she inhaled with a throaty sound of horror. The shiny reflective blue and white roof lights were unmistakable. The tinting was too dark to discern any expression or uniform color of the lone officer. Caffrey forced herself to breathe and gripped the steering wheel until her knuckles turned white.

A circle of green flashed above her, and she nervously hit the gas pedal too hard, recovered, and forced herself to concentrate on the road ahead. *Drive. Just drive.* Her heart banged so hard in her chest it hurt. Lights and buildings passed by, and still the patrol car stayed close behind. Several side streets beckoned, but she could not muster the nerve to try any of them, afraid of where they led or how she would feel if he followed.

Without warning, blue lights flashed brightly in all her mirrors, followed by a piercing siren that made her jump in her seat. Unable to keep her hands from shaking, she pulled into the right lane, looking for a spot near the curb.

To her utter amazement, the officer sped past, made a U-turn, and disappeared in the opposite direction. Caffrey's shoulders dropped, and she gasped for air. Forcing her feet and hands to guide the car, she drove on for several minutes to be certain no one else followed, even taking unknown streets to be sure. Eager to calm her pounding heart, she stopped in front of a gaudily lit restaurant and parked. She let her head fall onto her hands, against the gray steering wheel.

She should have stayed with Evan. Maybe Kimberly had his cell number.

Glancing around, Caffrey realized she was not familiar with this part of town. She watched people walking in both directions, involved in their lives and conversations. A thought that had surfaced earlier reawakened. Rummaging in the backseat, she was overjoyed to find her brushed-leather jacket hiding under the navy-blue hoodie she always kept in the car. Still shaking, she stepped out into the chilly night.

Across the street stood a church. Caffrey froze. Anger rose into her throat. The ornate steeple rose into the night with buildings and stars to outline it. Below, flickering lights cast a golden halo around two of the stained-glass windows. Someone was there on a Thursday night? The sign in front included the word Saint. She had never been to a Catholic church. Would a priest be able to help her? Would she be able to tell him about the disc without her throat closing up as it did with Kimberly and Evan?

Caffrey took a step forward to cross the street. Speeding traffic raced toward her and she took a step back. She gazed across the street at the stained glass. The familiar sensation of anger rose again. For over a year, she had not set foot in a church.

"You let them take Brian," she whispered aloud, raising her eyes to the stars. *It should have happened to criminals, to selfish people who did not care who they hurt. Not to people like me. Like him.*

She turned away and ventured down the sidewalk to her right. Stores along the old street displayed eclectic goods, liquor and tattoos, and appeared as though they'd known a thousand owners and been redecorated a thousand times. Two were barricaded with wood, and all of them had iron bars guarding their windows.

Never had she allowed herself to walk down such a street alone at night before, but an unquenchable desire kept her moving. Every face and silhouette caught her scrutiny, and before long she realized the opposite was also true. Animal-like in their hungry stares, eyes watched from corners, alleyways, and any dark recesses the structure of buildings allowed.

This is Monte's world, she thought. Most of the men she passed did not appear safe enough to risk getting close to, and some were in groups. Several made her feel as though she wore no clothing and needed no name. The spring evening grew colder, and she drew her jacket close.

Two scantily clad women hovering near a street lamp watched her walk past, and spouted blatant offers in her direction before re-engaging in loud, bawdy voices about someone they both seemed to be angry with. Caffrey stopped and swallowed. It was now or never.

"Excuse me."

The bleached blonde, whose gaunt, splotchy face and stringy hair appeared much older than her pale, exposed legs. She sported a winning smile and look of anticipation.

"Hey, baby girl, what you need tonight?"

"I've got to find someone," Caffrey clarified. "Someone in the Underground."

"Ha!" chortled the blonde, though the girl with raven braids glanced guardedly around to see if anyone had heard. "What makes you think any o'them crazy people hang here, sweetie?"

"I... I don't know. I need to talk to someone in... that group, and...." Caffrey exhaled in frustration. "I have *no* idea what I'm doing. I'm sorry." She turned to walk away, then turned back. "Is there anybody you can think of who's ever *mentioned* one of them?"

"Hmmm. What's it worth to you, honey?" The blonde asked, with a seductive tilt of her head. Caffrey was speechless. It had never occurred to her that what she needed might have to be bought. A meager $38.43 pulled from her jacket pockets would buy precious little. Only then did she realize she had left her purse in the car.

She never left her purse. Where was her brain? A pat against her jacket pocket revealed she had left her phone as well. Panic threatened to strangle her. She breathed faster.

"Look, I...I don't have much money. But, I'll give you what I have." She held out the cash. "This could be very important...to...to...a lot of people. All I need is for you to direct me to someone who *might* know. I can get more money for you later. *Please*, just point me in the right direction."

"Honey, later don't do nothin' fo' me."

But the copper-skinned girl raised her arched brows to the blonde and silently flipped out a hand. Caffrey emptied the money into it, including the pennies, as the two girls exchanged glances.

"Girl," the braided woman offered in a sarcastic voice. "You must be legit'. Otherwise, you'd know to bring mo' money than that. But now, I expect mo' money later. You come by and see me again." She wagged a finger over her shoulder and cracked a bulbous wad of green gum. "Come on."

Caffrey followed obediently. As they turned down a darkened alley, Caffrey stopped. The rank odor of mildew and urine assaulted her. "What's down here?"

The blonde spoke. "Ya' don't think they be hangin' out on the street, do ya?" Her quick chuckle held a touch of disdain. "They got their thang goin' down, but hey, whateva'."

The raven-haired girl turned to reassure Caffrey with a side smile and added a crack of her gum. "A guy here talks 'bout 'em all the time. Name's Tony."

Certain her heart would push through her throat, Caffrey placed one, then another brown boot onto the gritty, wet pavement. The girls' flippant chatter was what reassured her as the three traveled down another cracked, forgotten walkway littered with weeds and trash. Finally they rounded a dark corner and stopped at an old wooden door at the back of what appeared to be an abandoned building. The copper-skinned girl knocked on the door. A thin, rough-looking man with unkempt black, oily hair opened the door a few inches. He regarded her with greedy eyes and widened the opening. "Hey, B.J., wassup?"

"Deon?" The dark-haired girl dropped her smile.

"You need som'in from me, baby? You know I got ev'rythang." He chuckled wickedly. "Or can git it."

"Where's Tony?" she demanded in a worried tone.

"Hey, f'get about him, all right? He don't live here no more." Changing to a sly smile and a sexually aggressive pose, he added, "I'm runnin' things now."

The smell of old liquor and stale cigarettes caused Caffrey to lift a hand to her nose involuntarily.

"You gotcha a new baby?"

The dark-haired girl jerked her head toward Caffrey. "She's looking for somebody Tony knows."

"You need a manager, baby?" He looked Caffrey's body up and down.

Everyone flinched as a sharp *plat-plat* of gunshots rang out. Yelling voices and running footsteps echoed from several directions. The man's eyes went wide, and he slammed the door shut. The two women took off without hesitation the way they had come. The blonde tossed, "Come on, girl," in Caffrey's direction.

Caffrey followed but froze as a group of hooded and blue jean clad men ran past in a small patch of trees. One slipped in the mud and tumbled onto the cracked concrete. He spied her as he pushed up.

A second figure fell directly over him. "What'd you do 'im for?" hissed the young man on top as he stumbled to his feet and pushed the other. "What's wrong wit' you, man!"

"Shut up!" the other hissed. He cursed and shoved a fist into his partner's shoulder, then gestured toward Caffrey. The other followed his gaze. Caffrey backed up several steps.

With the coldest look she had ever seen, the first young man raised a handgun toward her and shot twice.

Gray light, heat, and searing pain like a small-scale atomic explosion coursed through Caffrey's body before she hit the pavement. She squirmed to get away from the pain. Angry voices and pounding feet faded into the night.

Pain throbbed unmercifully in her abdomen as warm blood soaked her clothes.

Garbled sounds echoed in the airless alley. She forced her eyes to open and realized the strange sounds were coming from her.

Please come, please come, she found herself repeating in her mind. She could not remember who was supposed to come, but would they please hurry?

A warm presence surrounded her, but her blurred eyes could not discern anyone in the darkness. "Help," she tried to call out. Her mouth felt as though it had turned to stone and become part of the pavement.

Letting her mouth stay open, she struggled to breathe and think. All she could think of was pain and the sensation of her life force fading as blood gushed onto the mud. She wanted to stop the flow, to pull it back into her.

Faces of family, friends, and colleagues flashed before her.

Fight! a voice ordered. *Fight! Live!*

Tears ran down her face of their own volition, and she tried in vain to call out. A growl came from her own throat, and she coughed out blood.

You must live! called the strange voice again.

Caffrey closed her eyes and steeled her mind to ignore everything but the effort to move. A strange fullness gripped her head and she found herself turning to view the buildings surrounding her as if memorizing them. The fullness retracted and her head dropped.

Determined to make it out to the street, she pushed up with both elbows. Grayness whirled like a fog, and she collapsed. She felt lighter, unconcerned with physical reality. The horrific stinging and aching began to disappear.

Reveling in a sensation of floating, rising away from the pain, away from the alley, she phased from her troubled existence into something weightless, unencumbered and free. Something kept insisting it be remembered, like a child tugging at her sleeve.

Stay, came the voice again, colored with worry and panic. *You must survive. You must live!*

Instead of rising further, Caffrey focused on the strange voice. It radiated such intense passion, she could not resist it. Enveloped by the presence, she felt their hearts merge and beat as one, a shadowed, warm thump-thump in unison, a connection that coaxed her soul back toward her body.

Caffrey began to fall and cried out, fully aware of her pain-wracked torso again.

With all the will she could muster, she dragged an arm though the rubble of paper and leaves around her. Her fingers touched a piece of dirty, rumpled cardboard.

Write, said the voice.

Caffrey grabbed at anything long and thin. Twice she caught hold of objects that turned out to be sticks. Calling on her last ounce of strength, she stuck one finger in the mud and blood beside her and began to write six words on the cardboard. Her hand shook with determination as she dipped her finger again and again.

Something creaked. To her horror, the dark, shadowed wooden door near her began to open. She lowered her aching head to the gravel. It did not matter who it was. She had to rest...just for a moment.

5

UNDERGROUND

Caffrey slipped toward consciousness, aware that she was retching while petite but firm hands held her head and wiped her face with a cool, damp cloth. Shadowy curls of blonde hair framed a kind, feminine face, beyond which loomed a darker figure in the shadows with eyes black and restless. Caffrey tried to focus on the dark figure, but dizziness and weakness carried her back to a fitful sleep.

The pungent odor of medicines and alcohol, which Caffrey hated, invaded her drug-induced slumber once more. The dark figure was still there, only closer this time. Through blurred eyes she watched thick arms fold against a black leather jacket. She stiffened, remembering the thin man and the dark, smelly room she had last glimpsed.

"Well, Princess, what's your body worth?" the dark figure spoke, his voice a deep echo from a bottomless well.

"Get out of here, Mace," gently ordered the blonde. "She isn't going anywhere. You can talk to her later." The slender woman turned to Caffrey, her manner softening. "Can you talk?"

Caffrey moved her lips but stopped as her stomach churned again, which drew unbelievable pain through her abdomen. She moaned and retched, then cried out in pain.

The dark man cursed. "Is all she gonna do is throw up? I've seen worse than this."

"Mace!" The young woman whirled toward him. "Her stomach's full of blood, all right?" Her voice was high-pitched and melodious but with the air of someone used to being obeyed. Still, Caffrey was surprised when the restless, glowering figure retreated, though not before he gave Caffrey a distinct glare of hate. In that moment she decided he was quite ugly and felt better for having decided so.

She closed her eyes and whirled through nonsensical events, running from something one moment and searching for something the next. All the while, an insistent, low, humming voice kept urging her on. *You must survive.*

She woke and realized it was a dream. Medicinal smells assaulted her, and she stiffened.

Not all of it was a dream.

Knife-like pain burned across her midsection, and she winced. She breathed in short breaths. Her body felt heavy, merged with the bed around her.

Blonde hair came into view again, clearer this time, framing a young, intelligent face.

"How do you feel?" asked rosy lips against pale, velvety skin.

"Fine," Caffrey mumbled. Her jaw felt as though it had been transplanted.

"How do you *really* feel?" asked the woman.

Caffrey was not used to telling people how she *really* felt. "Pretty bad," she decided to say. A sharp throb in her left hand caused her to raise it into view, which revealed a firmly taped IV. She hated IVs in her hand.

The woman chuckled lightly. "Well, that's more like it. It'll take you a while to heal completely. You lost a *lot* of blood. But, hey, we'll have you up and about in next to no time. I'm very good at treating bullet wounds." The woman turned away to tidy up a counter.

Caffrey blinked several times and wondered why the woman offered no much-needed explanations. Obviously, Caffrey had been medically treated. But the room resembled someone's garage.

Experimentally, Caffrey turned her head. The area was small, yet every inch of wall space was covered with metal shelving, packed to the edges with boxes of food, cans, water jugs, and—guns.

Caffrey eyed the stack with wonder. At least twenty long guns of various kinds lay atop two crates of military-type equipment. All sizes of red and green ammunition boxes, which Caffrey recognized from time spent in her grandfather's basement, decorated the adjoining shelves beside plastic bins of medicines, bandages, ropes, and neatly folded clothing. Maybe they were disaster preppers, like her uncle. Although, according to her uncle, disaster preppers were not keen to reveal their supplies to anyone.

"Where am I?" asked Caffrey.

"You are...safe." Lifting a hand radio, the woman pressed a button and nonchalantly spoke Mace's name into it, then set it down on the counter. Caffrey stiffened and felt betrayed.

Silently a thick, submarine-like door at the end of the room swung open and admitted the stern, dark man, anticipation in every muscle of his body. He was not as ugly as Caffrey had first thought, which disappointed her. The absence of his angry scowl made the difference. Though standing as tall as Evan, Mace was the opposite in many ways, from his russet skin and shiny ebony hair to his wrestler-like frame and muscular arms. Most notable was his intense, challenging gaze, unconcerned with nuance or charm, aimed only to command.

The blonde woman shot him a warning glare before turning her full attention to Caffrey. "My name is Gina." She smiled with reassurance. "What's yours?"

Caffrey glanced from one face to the other. "Caffrey."

"Kaff-ree?" Gina clarified the pronunciation. "Like with a 'K'?"

"*Caffrey*, with a 'C'." Caffrey chanced a wary glance at the raven-haired Mace, whose dark eyes did not move.

"What's your last name?" Gina queried, with a curious tilt of her head.

"Hanson."

"Caffrey, why are you trying to find the Underground?"

Caffrey caught her breath and sighed. "I was hoping you were them."

"Well, we might know where to find them." Gina shuffled her feet.

"You do? You *must* get me to them. How...." She winced in pain as her stomach muscles tightened. She stopped to breathe in shallow gasps. Whatever pain medication they had given her was wearing off. "How long have I been here?"

"Mmm, 'bout a day and a half, almost two. You were nearly dead."

Caffrey recalled the dark alley and pushed the horrible memory away. "What's today?"

"Saturday. It's late in the afternoon."

Caffrey feverishly considered possibilities. Would the disc have moved into her intestines? Could the bullets have shot it out of her? Did whomever operated on her already find it? "Please, you *must* get me to someone in the Underground as quickly as possible."

"Why?"

"I...I don't think I can tell you."

Mace took a step closer. "You'll have to. We don't give you to the Underground until we know what we're giving." His voice was the deepest she had ever heard, almost a guttural growl.

Caffrey felt the hair on the back of her neck rise as she examined his stern, wolf-like eyes. The high set of his cheekbones, square jaw, and dark brows hinted at Native American ancestry. She let her silent glare serve as a pitiful insult, since she was too weak to do much else.

"Well, I can't give *you* anything until I know I'm with the *Underground*." Her chin shook slightly with the effort to be courageous. She should have cared more about the foreboding figure in front of her, but the pain and hazy events of the past few days were beginning to alter her attitude. Expecting a sharp comment from him, she watched him glance down at the floor and patiently take another step toward her.

"If you had anything worth the Underground's time," he hinted his opinion of that possibility, "you'd know where to find them, or they'd know where to find *you*."

Caffrey took a deep breath. "If I knew where to find *them*, I wouldn't...." She winced as another pain stabbed into her side, "I wouldn't have gotten lost, or gotten shot, and I wouldn't be *here*." She paused to take several smaller breaths. "And I wouldn't be talking with *you*." She sighed. "Definitely not *you*."

Gina stole a quick glance toward Mace, her eyes dancing with amusement instead of concern.

"Your little note said 'body,'" Mace continued, undaunted. "I've been over every inch of your little body, Princess, and you've got nothing to offer me."

Caffrey could not hide her shock, but she steeled her expression when he smiled with perfect, white teeth.

"Maybe that's because *my* body's evolved beyond *Neanderthal*," she replied curtly, surprising herself. She could feel her cheeks growing hot. Frustrated that she was too much of a lady to spew something vulgar at him, she averted her attention to Gina, hoping to encourage conversation with her. Instead, she caught Gina throwing Mace another guarded but amused expression. Mace glared at Gina with disapproval, as if she were somehow not cooperating with some prearranged agenda.

Catching the subtle exchange, Caffrey puzzled at the relationship between the two. Considering her vulnerability, she did not want to anger either of them. But, something in Mace's proud, arrogant demeanor seemed to bring out a rebellious fire in her soul that usually remained safely in control. The desire to kick him with her closest foot or assault him with four-letter descriptions of himself nearly overwhelmed her.

"We thought," Mace began as he shifted his stance, "perhaps your earrings were the item, but all we see is that they're made of *khram*. A Vhurruh metal. And you know what that makes us think?"

Opening her mouth for a tart comment, Caffrey changed her mind. "What earrings? Show me."

Mace and Gina exchanged looks. Mace reached into a jacket pocket and dangled green stones hanging from curled, silver wires in front of her. Caffrey grimaced and placed a shaky hand to her head. "Ugh, I've got such a headache." This time, the glance the two exchanged drained them both of color.

"Where did you get them?" Mace commanded.

"I don't think they're mine."

"*Where did you get them?* Try to remember."

"I can't."

"Try harder!"

"I can't!" Caffrey slapped both hands against her throbbing head. Mace backed up against the counter. When Caffrey opened her eyes, he was worriedly scrubbing his chin with a stocky hand. Gina cautiously rested her weight against the counter, stared at the floor, then seriously at Mace.

"Look," Caffrey implored, willing the pounding in her brain to subside, "I don't know what's wrong. I hit my head in the alley. You've just got to get me to the Underground. *Please.*"

"No way, toots. You've been messed with. You're dead meat as far as I'm concerned." Mace pulled a handgun from the inside of his jacket.

"Mace!" Gina admonished, placing her body in front of Caffrey.

"There's no telling what they've programmed, Gina. She could be a *link.*"

"It could be *Nekkai.* Or it could even be military."

"It's *not* military." Mace shifted his disdainful gaze to Caffrey. "It's Vhurruh. I can smell it."

"But Mace, I think it's a Blue one. I'm certain of it."

"You *felt* it, didn't you?" he accused.

"Yes," Gina affirmed with a guilty lift of her chin. "But he's a *Blue!* I'm sure. And he's a drone."

"Oh yeah? Which side? Some of the Blues are Swiss cheese now. We can't take that chance. You *know* that."

They both stared at each other, defiant.

"She's sincere, as far as she knows," Gina persisted. "I can read that much easily. But *Nekkai's* involved. I meditated for half an hour on it. I'm willing to take the chance."

"I don't *take* chances. And you can't read past the programming. All you're gonna get is what she believes on the surface. I trust in myself, not a slug. How long do you think it's gonna take to find the trigger? By that time she could know too much."

"She doesn't know where she is. Look at her!" Gina gestured with both hands toward Caffrey. "She lost most of her blood. What's she gonna to do? Beat us all up and take off with some information? Very *limited* information, I might add, since we might abandon this site?"

"She could be programmed to endure *anything.*" Mace pointed a thick finger toward Caffrey. "Anything. Pump her full of drugs, and she can leap buildings, crash into the pavement, and get up and run away. Besides, we're gonna waste her anyway." He folded his arms.

Gina slapped one palm to the counter and looked up as if for divine patience.

Taking advantage of the long pause, Caffrey finally spoke. "L-Look, if you guys are going to kill me, at least take my *body* to the Underground."

Mace looked straight at her, his expression one of irritation. "Your body *is* with the Underground."

Gina turned to him, eyes widening in alarm.

Caffrey examined both faces. When neither spoke, Caffrey shook her head.

"No way."

"He's telling the truth, Caffrey." Gina glared at Mace with disapproval.

"I don't believe you."

"*You*," said Mace, testily, "don't have any choice."

"Oh, yes I do. Show me Thashan Kumar, the We-The-Humans guy. Or...or Yune—what's her name—of Earth-Sentinels, and I'll believe you. I've seen them both on TV."

Mace snorted and turned a half circle. "Yeah, we just happen to have them in a back room. You actually think I'd allow all those leaders in one place?"

Gina picked up the radio. "What do you think?" she spoke into it. Mace stood taller as her index finger released a button and ground his jaw noticeably as though she were an erring child about to get the punishment of her life.

"Gina, once she knows, then *he* knows. You could undermine everything."

"I'll come down," said a metallic voice from the radio. Mace threw a hand into the air in disbelief, and rolled his eyes.

Caffrey eyed the two of them, incredulous. They ignored her until the metal door opened to admit a tall, handsome figure, younger and more vibrant than his video of weeks before.

"You're not dead." Caffrey's jaw fell open. "Oh, thank God." She let her head drop back to the pillow.

Vince Mansfield's manner was warm and confident as he strode up to her cot and laid a hand on the side. He was dressed in stained, navy-blue coveralls and a jacket that partially hid a white patch reading "Sure-Stay Plumbing." His sandy-brown hair appeared darker than it had in the video, but his azure blue eyes were brighter, and they twinkled with excitement.

"Well, mystery lady, it's nice to meet you." He flashed a dimpled smile that warmed Caffrey to her toes.

Without hesitation, she laid her IV'd hand on his arm. "Inside me is a disc...of...some kind. If it's still there—or, if I haven't...well, I assume it's still there. I don't know what it is. I hope it hasn't dissolved or something." She closed her eyes for a moment at the horrific thought but continued quickly lest anyone stop her. Gina and Mace had moved closer.

"A man gave it to me before he died. A policeman shot him— well, not a policeman, a SAAF. There was a car accident. I put it in my mouth because I had nowhere else to put it. I didn't have any pockets. When he got shot, I...I swallowed it. I fell down. I've been carrying it around ever since, looking for...w·well, somebody, *anybody* in the Underground."

Vince's mouth fell slowly open. His eyes were deep pools of blue, registering complete belief, to her utter amazement. "When was this?"

"Two days ago. Well...Thursday afternoon." Caffrey knitted her brows together. "I think."

"Where?"

"Peachtree Street, in Midtown. Where I work."

"What building?"

"Uh, Peachtree Towers," she said in a hurry, trying to keep up with him.

"What company?"

"Property Resources."

"And this accident happened in front of you?"

"W...no. Yes." She shook her head. "I was in my office. I can see out the front windows. I'm on the first floor."

"And a man just *gave* it to you?"

"Yes. No. He was...well, he was between the cars... crawling."

"Describe him."

"Well, he had brown skin and black hair, with, like, some gray, and wore a white lab coat...." Caffrey halted as recognition dawned in Vincent's eyes.

"A SAAF shot him?" Vince's lips pursed in anger.

"Yes, right in front of me. It was horrible. But, he gave me the disc right before—I mean before the SAAF guy came."

"How big is it?"

"Well, it's...." She curled her thumb and index finger together. "Like this. Like a quarter. It hurt going down."

"Where could it be?" he asked Gina curtly. "You didn't see it?" He glanced up and down Caffrey's body as though she had not just given him the most incredible story of her life. Instantly the three seemed to become as one.

"Could be lodged in the intestines, maybe the colon, assuming it's intact." Gina replied. "If it were higher, she'd have thrown it up.

One bullet went through here, grazed her liver, stomach, and cracked a rib before exiting. The other was two inches below that."

Mace glowered. "I thought Greg took her to get a scan."

"Greg tried to get her into imaging, but they were backed up and she became too unstable. We had to work hard to hold onto her and pump her full of blood. Then all hell broke loose with a bunch of gang shootings and knifings. We had exit wounds. We didn't have to dig for bullets. So we just checked organs and sewed to stem the bleeding. Then SAAFs came in, and we had to get her out of there. I can tell you it's not in her stomach. But...."

"We've got to get a scan. I've got to know what that is. If it's really there. Could we damage it? Or trigger it? Mace," Vince snapped militarily, "make ten-minute security checks with everybody. If this has a tracking device, we're in big trouble."

"If this had a tracking device...." Mace leaned toward Vince with confidence. "We'd be dead already."

Vince smiled sideways. "Let's mobilize for the hospital."

"You got it," replied Mace with a zip of his jacket.

"No!" Gina stopped him. "We've got some *overs* there now. Clarese told me this morning. SAAFs are still showing up. She said they were asking questions about any red-haired girls. Or, someone coming in to have something removed from their body." She turned to Caffrey. "And here we thought that was so strange."

Vince looked at both of them. "Make it the clinic."

"We'll use their ultrasound." Gina tilted her head. "Could the clinic use a refurbished water heater?"

Vince clapped his hands. "I love you, you know that? You always think of these things."

"Mmm-hmm," she replied, and cocked one perfectly-arched blonde eyebrow.

"Uh, folks, let's not forget the programming," Mace admonished.

"We'll deal with that later." Vince heaved an excited sigh. "Keep her out. Eyes and ears covered. Maybe I'll get in touch with Barbara for a look-see. No sign of concern?" He gestured with open hands.

Gina's eyes became unfocused as she perused Caffrey's sheet-covered body. She moved a palm across the air slightly above the sheet and breathed steadily. "Lots of trauma and fear. Searching. Something's hidden. Hidden. I keep sensing it. But this is good. I'm sure of it. Somehow *Nekkai*'s involved." She leaned toward Caffrey. "Caffrey, are you a link?"

"A what?"

"A link. Vhurruh-linked."

Caffrey frowned. "What does that mean?"

Gina turned to Vince. "She has no conscious awareness. There's no connection open, or I'd sense it. If he's there, he's hiding, which convinces me even more that he's *Nekkai*."

Vince turned to Mace, who was frowning. "Get Jimmy, and we'll go to Pop's for the water heater. Make sure it's big enough. She's pretty small, though. We'll take her in the van. Don't need two trips. Oh, we'll need Sharia. Darn, that'll mean...Gina, use the code. I've got two extra uniforms. And if we have to operate, we'll have all that there."

All three began moving in separate directions.

"H...hey," Caffrey interrupted meekly. The three whirled toward her as though she were a mannequin that spoke. "What are you going to do?"

Vince strode over and took both of her hands in his. "Caffrey, surely you must realize that we are limited in what we can tell you. Otherwise, we would not still exist. And we *must* exist, for the sake of...our world, our life, our planet. Do you remember the earrings?"

Caffrey flinched and grimaced as a spike of pain jabbed behind her eye. She managed to nod.

"Well, the...circumstances surrounding your having them—and the way you react to them—means you've probably been programmed by a Vhurruh. We don't know what that programming is, or who *he* is. We're going to have to talk about that later. Okay?"

Caffrey scowled in disbelief but found herself nodding.

"Have you always been this devoted to the Underground?" Vince flashed a friendly grin.

"No. Before a few days ago, I didn't even know what I thought about you...crazy people."

"Good. I'd have been worried if you said otherwise. You've risked a lot. Trust us a little longer. Please?"

Caffrey looked into his shining blue eyes and knew she would trust him forever. He squeezed her hands and left.

Gina inserted a needle into Caffrey's IV before she could protest. The room faded. Blurred faces and tense voices bounced in and out of Caffrey's awareness as she was hoisted and banged about. Then all was silent.

6

COUNTRY AIR

Caffrey awoke disoriented as she glanced around a beautiful bedroom decorated in old-fashioned country patterns of peach, yellow, and blue. A calico cat, perched on a worn blue overstuffed chair, returned her stare with a look of "I was here first."

"Well." Caffrey tried to address the cat but found her mouth stiff and strange tasting. She cleared her sore throat and tried again. "And who might you be?"

The cat pointed both ears forward, flabbergasted that she was alive and capable of speech.

A light twitter of birds, along with the sweet smell of honeysuckle and hay, drifted through the open window on the right. Breezes rustled the peach curtains softly. Caffrey smiled and reveled in the freedom, for the moment, from responsibilities and schedules. It jogged a similar memory of waking on a brisk early morning at a church summer camp years before as a young teenager, curled in her sleeping bag, thinking to herself before anyone else awoke.

The unmistakable moan of cows interrupted her nostalgic musings, and she became curious as to where she was. Searching her recent memory triggered a kaleidoscope of visions that assaulted her brain: dark streets, supply rooms, clinical smells, muffled voices, something being rubbed on her stomach....

A jingle of the cat's collar interrupted her recall. Caffrey tried to sit up and moaned as every movement brought pain and stiffness. Her head felt full of water. She recognized the sensation of anesthesia and pain medication wearing off.

Slow steps outside the door turned both hers and the cat's heads. After a light tapping, the door opened to admit an elderly woman who looked, Caffrey thought, like everyone's grandmother should: silver-white curls of downy hair, a round-cheeked smile, and a flowered apron.

"Well, how are ya, darlin'?" the woman said in a cheerful voice.

Abandoning its chair, the cat meowed and flaunted exaggerated rubs on the woman's legs.

Caffrey attempted a smile. "I think I'm okay."

"Well, you keep a thinkin' that, and you will be. Thought maybe you could handle a bit of lunch. Just liquids for now, then we'll see how ya' do."

Caffrey's stomach growled at the suggestion. "That sounds great." How long had it been since she had eaten? "Um, what day is it?"

"Sunday! Ah, there's nothing like a warm, lazy Sunday in the spring after plantin'. 'Specially before the real heat sets in. S'pposed to be a warm spring so we got an early jump on it. And me and Hiram didn't go to church this mornin' see'ins how you needed lookin' after."

The old woman's arms jiggled with the weight of a yellow-flowered tray laden with various bowls and mugs containing chicken broth, orange gelatin, vanilla tapioca, and hot tea. She carefully placed it on a table beside Caffrey that pivoted.

Caffrey groaned as she tried to sit up. Her left hand throbbed horribly where the IV remained. Red rashes were growing around the adhesives.

"You can call me 'Grams.'" The woman popped a thermometer into Caffrey's mouth. "Everyone does. I understand you are 'Victoria?'" Her wide-eyed, high-browed look revealed her doubts about the name.

Caffrey's eyes also widened. *Victoria?*

The thermometer beeped, and Grams snatched it out of Caffrey's mouth. While reading it, she pulled an envelope from her apron pocket.

"Gina asked me to give you this. She tells me you're recovering from an operation and have no one to take care of you, no family here. You were asleep when they brought you in last night. Gina stayed through the night. Bradley carried you all the way up these stairs. My goodness, he is strong. 'Course, you're a little bitty thing."

Caffrey knitted her brows at the unfamiliar name.

"Oh, you prob'ly know him as Mace, like Gina calls him."

Caffrey felt her entire body freeze. *That man* had her in his arms?

Grams continued in a slow, Southern drawl. "I love company, especially the young folks. They remind me how to feel young." Again, the warm, cheeky smile. "Gina asked if you could stay here, and I said that was just fine with me. I always like to help folks out when I can. 'Specially friends of *hers.*"

Grams lifted her gray brows and pressed her wrinkled lips, secretive. "And no matter what happens, that is all I need to know, dear. I trust Gina. She's a good girl. Sound okay to you?" Grams smiled with reassurance. Her chubby cheeks were smooth and white as snow, like Gina's.

Crazed butterflies danced inside Caffrey's stomach as she nodded.

Grams chuckled and patted Caffrey's foot. "No fever. I can tell when someone has a fever anyhow. I kinda have a sixth sense about it. That little machine there will give you more doses of morphine, every four hours, in your IV. Great pain medicine, that. Now this pill here...." She held up a tiny sample pack. "Will help with nausea. Very important. That orange bottle is an antibiotic you're supposed to finish, three times a day. I reckon your stomach's been through a lot, so if you can't keep nothin' down, we'll put everything in your IV. Gina left me with loads of instructions, but I know how to nurse someone just fine. Anyhow, Gina gets it from me. Can I get you anything else, dear?"

Nothing and everything raced through Caffrey's mind. "No. I'm...okay."

"Well, good." Grams plodded over to the door, rubbing her back all the way. "Whoooah, these steps are a-gittin' longer every day. I'll be back shortly, hon. Custard 'll be a scratchin' at the door, I'm sure. Don't want to be left out, and don't want to be left in. All right with you if I leave it open a tad?"

"Sure," Caffrey replied, pleased to feel an open connection with the rest of the place, wherever it was.

"All-righty, then." Grams disappeared down the stairs, taking slow, carefully-placed steps.

Anxiety filled Caffrey's chest as she tore open the envelope. A small plastic card fell out. She recognized her driver's license. Upon closer examination, her jaw dropped at the name of Victoria Williamson, 5114 Fairfield Drive, Peachtree City, Georgia. Strangely, she felt resentful at the alias beside her picture, then rectified her thinking as she realized what the Underground was doing.

Plain old Caffrey Hanson, receptionist, late of Alpharetta, Georgia, now had a secret identity. She made a face, rolled her eyes, and felt a quiver of fear run through her abdomen.

A small white piece of paper was in the envelope. She unfolded it.

Be back to see you soon. Rest and heal. Do not contact anyone or go out of the house. Your life is in danger. Gina.

7

PRESENCE

The next morning, Grams coaxed Caffrey into a short walk about the room, dragging her IV stand with her. Stopping to lean against the breezy window for support, Caffrey was startled to discover the massive round form of Stone Mountain looming in the distance. She blinked at the brilliance of the white tower perched at the top.

A rush of memory overwhelmed her, and she unconsciously placed a hand to her heart. She had not been back to the mountain park since Brian had disappeared. It was bittersweet to remember playing cards with her friends in the hot sun and eating fried chicken, potato salad, and coleslaw on the great green lawn that spread out before the grandiose carvings of Robert E. Lee, Jefferson Davis, and Stonewall Jackson. When it became dark, and the laser light show flashed for an hour, they had sung "Georgia" by Ray Charles, which was played at the end before the fireworks display.

A great lump formed in Caffrey's throat, and she pulled back from the window, tired. She was not far from Atlanta at all, maybe an hour from her apartment. How in the world Grams still had *cows* in Stone Mountain, she didn't know, but she was *not* in a distant rural area as she had assumed, which would explain the constant hum of traffic, probably from Highway 78.

Grams left to tend to chores, and Caffrey melded into the heavily quilted bed, alarmed at her weakness. Questions began taunting her. What about her apartment, all her belongings, her job. Maiba?

The room, she discovered, had no telephone or television. *Rest and heal,* Gina had written.

Well, you made sure I couldn't do anything else, didn't you? Caffrey fumed at the total absence of electronics.

She dreamed of the voice she had heard in the alley. As she opened her eyes, the dream enveloped her in a warm sense of presence. Amazed she could still hold onto the dream, the presence probed her emotions. She was alive. She was in no danger. Satisfied, it disappeared, as if a door in her head slammed shut. Caffrey sat up, alarmed. Was she going crazy?

A comical tapping on the door revealed a wiry, weather-beaten old man carrying a tray of bowls.

"Well, there she is! A-hidin' up here in the attic when there's chores to be done." He winked and grinned. After depositing the tray, he did a slight jig and held out a wrinkled hand. "Gramps is my name. Ask me again, and I'll tell you the same."

Caffrey laughed and shook his hand, then pressed her stomach to keep it from hurting. While she ate, Gramps carried on his end of the conversation with a consistent stream of jokes, none of which were very good, or funny, but his obvious joy at telling them made Caffrey laugh. At one point, she feared she would lose her supper.

"Hi-*ram!*" Called Grams from the bottom of the stairs.

"Oh, she's done found me. Well, it was nice ta meet ya, youngin'." He shook her hand again. "Best keep the Missus happy. 'Cause if mama ain't happy, ain't nooobody happy." He chuckled merrily. "Young men nowadays just don't git that part, do they?"

"Uh, no, they definitely don't," Caffrey agreed. She pressed the morphine button the minute he left.

As she waited for the drug to ease her aching body, she sensed a fullness in the room, a distortion, like underwater pressure. It felt like *someone*. She glanced about the room to determine if the presence had a body to go with it. The space was empty. A ghost? *Of course, it's the morphine.*

She snorted and closed her eyes. The pressure altered in her head, like someone else's thoughts shifting. She opened her eyes and began to shake. The only person she had ever communicated with in her head was God. This was not God.

With calm bravado, she closed her eyelids and reached for the source. It felt young, energetic, proud. It felt male.

Who are you? she demanded, fearful of the answer. Instantly the presence withdrew with the same clipped sensation of a lid slamming shut. Caffrey pulled the quilt over her head, and slept with a Bible she had discovered on the side table.

"Wake up, dear," said Grams. On the tray beside her was a grilled cheese sandwich and a bowl of homemade vegetable soup. "I think it's time we removed your IV."

"Oh, my gosh, yes." Caffrey was almost giddy with relief. "Is Gina coming here soon?" She groaned for having sat up too quickly. "It's been three days and I was just wondering...."

"I don't know, dear. I hope so. We don't git to see her much nowadays. How're you feelin'?"

"A lot better," Caffrey answered with sincerity. "Hospitals should be like this."

"Ain't it the truth. You know, we lived on a farm out in Covington years ago. Then we moved to the city when Hiram got wind of job there. The city was different then, a' course. It wasn't built up like it is now.

"On hot days, why, Momma'd pack us a lunch, and the whole family'd go out to the spring in Atlanta, at the Water Works. And it was so good and cold and fresh. You can't imagine how good that water tasted."

"There was a spring in Atlanta?"

Grams smiled wistfully. "Ooo, yes. We just had us a time. And everyone would be out there a-doin' the same. Hiram says he thinks it's still there, but I don't reckon there's a nice green lawn for folks to picnic on now.

"Well, Hiram did real good at his job, but, we missed the country so much we moved back to a farm again." She smiled fondly at Caffrey. "Everything got built up around us, but this is where we'll stay. Cleanest air around, or was, even with the manure about. Although..." She scrunched her shoulders. "I even like the smell of that."

"Hey, Victoria. How've you been?"

Caffrey sat up with a start and blinked to focus. "What?"

"Victoria? Didn't you get the new license?"

"Oh."

"You okay?" Gina spied Caffrey's hand pressed to her stomach.

"I got up too fast. I keep doing it."

"Oh, sorry. Here, I'll turn on the side lamp. Other than that, how are you?"

"Pretty good."

"Well, we've gone from 'pretty bad' to 'pretty good.' Not bad. I told you I was good." Half-grinning for the boast, Gina deposited a small bundle of clothing onto the bed.

"Where have you guys been?" Caffrey blurted.

"So! Missed us, eh?"

"Well, not *all* of you." Caffrey grimaced as she readjusted her position.

Gina smirked, but with an air of unquestionable devotion to her group. "Mace is...the way he is. And for good reason."

"Whatever it is, *it ain't good enough*."

"Well, let me put it this way. If you're someplace where there's shooting going on, and he's with you, *you'll* be the one who walks away. And he's not *usually* difficult. Just lately he...well, anyway." She sat down on the bed and looked about the room with longing. "So, how do you like Gram and Gramps? Aren't they sweet?" She scrunched her shoulders in the same child-like way Grams had done.

"Yes, they are wonderful. Except for no radio, no phone, no computer, no e-mail, no cable, no satellite TV. No game apps in sight. No apps of *any kind* in sight. Nothing to touch except Farming Today, Cottage Gardens, and Quilt Time. I'm *seriously* communication-deprived. My brain is melting."

Gina released a sly smile and became interested in the print on the bed.

"So, aside from the torture of knowing absolutely nothing, your grandparents are wonderful. I wish they were mine."

"Well, you can't have them. Although, I guess that's not true. They seem to belong to everybody, no matter what I do." For a moment, a sad expression came over Gina. In an instant it was gone. "Only a few *friends* have had to visit here, even Mace once. Now, let's have a look at those incisions."

Caffrey stiffened as Gina reached toward her. Gina glared with a nurse–like air of command.

"I need to check your incisions. I *did* sew you up, you know."

"Okay. But I want some decent explanations this time."

Gina eyed her evasively. "I'll give you what I can. How's that?"

"Not good enough."

With quick, clinical expertise, Gina removed the gauze wrapping from around Caffrey's ribs and examined her abdominal incisions.

"Ow!" Caffrey fumed. "Why do doctors and nurses always press on everything that hurts? I could *tell* them it hurts."

"Pain is a messenger," Gina stated. "I need to know where the message is." She meticulously queried Caffrey about symptoms, and instructed her to let the stitches dissolve on their own. "Your color looks better, too," she mumbled to herself as she looked over Caffrey's face.

"Do you know who the guys were who shot me?" Caffrey asked, anxious to settle questions that had taunted her for several days.

Gina took a deep breath. "We don't know which one shot you, but we know the gang. There were several shootings in town. The emergency room was a nightmare." She rolled her eyes. "We were contacted by...well, a number of people in a chain. Seems you visited The Brim."

Caffrey's jaw dropped. "I *knew* that guy knew something!"

"Guy?"

"Come on, the *waiter*. Did he tell you about me?"

"I can't confirm or deny a specific person. Let's just say, word got to us. The guy who actually found you—and Mace knows most of this, since we were already looking for you...."

"Whoah...what do you mean, already looking for me? How could you possibly know who I was?"

"Um...that's classified."

Caffrey blinked several times. "Excuse me?"

"Certain information is going to be classified for a while. You worked in a classified atmosphere. Well, it was becoming classified, so I'm sure you understand the term. I will tell you what I can, but certain answers I'll have to leave out for a while. Next question."

Caffrey stared, dumbfounded. The air had stifled between them, and Caffrey did not like the feel of it. Wasn't *she* the one who had risked her life here? Didn't she deserve to know *everything?*

She folded her arms. "So who found me?"

"The guy who found you saw your note about getting your body to the Underground and, like most people on the street, saw an opportunity for money. So, he started calling people. Mace ended up paying almost a thousand dollars by the time he finally got to you. He threatened a few people when he found out you were almost dead, especially since they were trying to get more money out of him."

Gina paused to examine Caffrey's astonished gaze, seeming to note every change in expression or eye movement. "How'd you end up near Five Points?"

"Is that where I was? No wonder people talk about it the way they do."

"Actually, you were a little southwest of it, but...you didn't *know* that's where you were?"

"No, I...Hey, it's a long story. Remember, I was looking for *you* people. I couldn't go to my apartment. SAAFs were crawling all over the place. So I was...it seems so stupid now. I didn't know what I was doing. I just kept going."

Gina nodded to encourage her.

"I was afraid to go to anybody I knew. I thought if I asked some people on the street, I'd be able to find you guys. Some hookers were helping me, I think. But they took me to a guy who was the wrong guy, and...well, everything got crazy. There was shooting, and people running everywhere, and...I think maybe I was shot because I overheard the guy talk about killing someone. I think he got scared because I saw his face."

"Sounds like you're not used to dealing with street people and gangs."

"*Definitely* not. I'll pass on the next trip, okay?"

"Well, I understand their world now. Sometimes it's about being down on your luck, or about being raised by wrecked parents and finding a gang that's the closest thing you know to family. Or, needing a place to hide. Drugs. Depression. People running away from their past, from their future. Sometimes it's even about trying hard *not* to be normal." She leaned back on both arms. "You get used to it."

"I don't know if I care to get used to it."

"You might have to."

Caffrey let out a *humph* of complaint. "So. You operated on me?"

"Yep. Twice."

"In *that* little room?"

"Nope. We started somewhere else. You *recovered* in that little room."

"I knew I remembered a hospital. Which hospital?"

Gina hesitated. "That's classified."

Caffrey exhaled loudly in frustration.

"It's not important, anyway. Next question."

"Fine. Did I hear you saying you didn't have to take out bullets?"

"Correct. Both bullets went through. Better off that way, although you can lose more blood. But, you don't have to go searching or cut into other tissue to get it, as long as you know what organs might be damaged. Now, buckshot—whooo, that's nasty!"

"The disc!" Caffrey slapped the bed. "I can't believe I forgot about...what was the disc thing?"

"Uhhhhh, we're not sure yet. We have an idea."

"What?" Caffrey felt an icy chill roll over her skin. "You mean you don't *know* what it is?"

"Mace and Vince, and...some other people...are looking into it." Concern was etched on Gina's face.

Caffrey stared at Gina and shook her head. "No. No. After all this, you have to know what that is. I mean...the guy...." Caffrey 's throat tightened. The realization of losing everything—nearly her life—for a tiny, foreign object that no one knew anything about squeezed a tight fist of despair into her chest.

"Did the guy tell you *anything* about it?" Gina prodded.

"No!" Caffrey shouted. "He just...shoved it at me. I remember *him*. He was, like, desperate. Scared. He was bleeding and everything. And he said, 'Get this to the Underground.' When I touched it I felt that it was...*something*...I don't know, important. It didn't look like...well, it looked like something high-tech, you know. The fact that it was all that mattered to him. I mean...he didn't even *care* about his own life.

"Then when I saw the SAAF, I knew something was *wrong*. Anybody I have ever seen in uniform—well, y' know, policemen or especially SAAF officers on TV—always have that air of...." She puffed her shoulders. "Stalwart, serious, mega-trained. But that SAAF looked *weird*. I certainly didn't intend on swallowing the stupid thing. Nearly choked to death. I was afraid I'd throw it up right in front of the SAAF."

"Yeah, that did present a few problems. But, you know, it was probably the safest way to carry it."

With a lead feeling in her chest, Caffrey noticed suspicion flicker in Gina's blue eyes. "Hey, I did *not* know what that was. You've got to believe me. I never saw that man before, and wish I never *had.*"

"I can believe that, Ca...Victoria...."

"And where'd you come up with *Victoria*?" Caffrey interrupted. "Like, who's named that anymore."

"There's a reason, okay? But, most importantly, you *do* realize some programming has taken place here?"

"That's crap. I would have *some* memory, some inkling of something bizarre, and...I'm not buying it. In fact, I find it *totally* insulting." Fear crept up her spine. The faceless presence in her mind *could* have been an illusion caused by the morphine.

"All right, look." Gina sat up. "Let's think about the earrings for a minute. I mean, close your eyes, and *think* about them."

Caffrey did not have to close her eyes. The low throb in her forehead preceded the need.

"You're getting a headache, aren't you?" Gina asked.

Caffrey swallowed.

"You see?"

"But that could just be *coincidence*." Icy tingles of fear and mindfulness swept over body and made her shiver.

"Caffrey, *coincidence* is a word people use when they don't get the bigger picture."

Caffrey forced herself to breathe normally. "You forgot my new name."

"No, I used it on purpose. But I do forget, believe me." Gina repositioned herself on the bed. "Mace gets on to me all the time. 'Remember your cover! Remember everybody's cover.'" Gina frowned and whirled her eyes.

Caffrey felt relieved to see her complain. "Gina. I have a really dull life. So we had access to some classified information at work—so what? I was not around anybody who would have the slightest idea how to 'mind-program' somebody. And if by some chance in a million I *was*, I would remember...*something*."

"You would have been programmed *not* to remember it until a special moment." Gina's voice was soft and sympathetic.

Caffrey snorted with disgust.

"Don't worry about this now. You'll drive yourself crazy. Just remember, there are good guys on our side who could have programmed you. Listen, we're having a meeting tomorrow night. I want you to come and tell us as much as you can. We need to hear *everything*."

Caffrey opened her mouth to decline, but getting out of the house would be a nice change. "Okay. But, you know, I've *got* to get back to work. I'm going to lose my job. They don't know anything. And I need to...well, I don't know about my apartment."

"Your apartment complex has been in the news, Caffrey. Well, it was only mentioned a few times before the story disappeared. The official word is that there was a major gas leak that night—four people died, and many were hospitalized."

"Oh, no. But...do they know who died? Who might be still alive? I've got somebody I need to know about."

"It's under FBI and SAAF investigation. And a few other acronyms I could name. Nobody can touch it. There's a bunch of stories floating around on the Internet, but, don't worry, *we'll* find out."

"Don't worry?"

"I mean...Mace will find out for us. Our people are going to make sure the story doesn't go away as quickly as they want it to."

Caffrey placed a hand to her chest. "I hope so. I've got to know about Maiba."

"Who's Maiba?"

"A good friend of mine."

"What's her whole name?"

"Uh, let's see. Maiba Savimbi, I think. I'm not positive on the spelling. She's from Africa. Been here a couple years."

"I'll let Mace know. See what he can dig up."

Caffrey pursed her lips. "He gets around, doesn't he?"

"He's got his ways."

"Probably investigating me."

Gina smirked. "By now, Mace probably knows all there is to know about you from the day you were born."

Caffrey snorted.

"Look," Gina began, "when we get together tomorrow we'll talk out everything, okay?"

"Is *he* going be there?"

Gina hesitated, then stated, "Yes. He *needs* to be there. He's really very good at what he does."

"How nice," Caffrey remarked acidly.

Gina smirked and rolled her eyes. "He's got a good side, really. He can actually be a lot of fun."

Caffrey tilted her head with sarcastic disbelief.

Gina chuckled. "Well, what can I say? He's a part of us, and we need him. It's just that lately...." She let the statement drop. "So, let's go see the farm."

Caffrey enjoyed the tour and found the chickens hilariously entertaining. However, after talking to the cows, throwing crusts of bread and biscuits to the ducks at the small pond, and insisting on seeing Grams' spring garden, her entire body ached, and she grew light-headed. Wearily, she rested on the living room couch and listened to Gina and Grams chattering in the kitchen.

"Well, you gonna sleep there all day, youngin'!" boomed a voice that woke her with a start. Gramps wore a mischievous grin and rocked on his heels.

"Gramps!" yelled Gina from the kitchen. "Don't scare her like that."

"Tee-hee," he chuckled, ignoring Gina.

Caffrey smiled and sat up with painful movements. She found the old man's attitude pleasantly infectious. He offered a gallant arm, as though at attention, so she curled both hands around it and let him lead her to the dinner table. Wonderful scents overwhelmed her and she breathed deep with anticipation.

On a cloth of old linen and lace sat flowered china bowls of steaming white rice, brown gravy with chunks of meat, a crusty beef roast on a large antique platter in the center, and several bowls of homegrown vegetables, including green beans, butter peas and sweet potatoes dusted with brown sugar and cinnamon. On a side table sat a basket of golden cornbread next to a freshly baked pecan pie cooling on several old towels.

"Maybe I'll stay another day," said Caffrey.

"Not gonna happen," Gina whispered in a low voice.

8

INTERROGATION

Gina undid Caffrey's blindfold. Agitated with fear and insult, Caffrey blinked at total darkness. The tiny beam from Gina's sweeping flashlight revealed walls of curling, flowered wallpaper and a faded lime-green and orange print sofa beside a matching chair. Two tawny, laminated end tables, surely left over from the 1950's, sat on either side. In a small alcove to the left stood a rickety-looking wooden table surrounded by mismatched kitchen chairs. A shrill chorus of crickets and tree frogs vibrated the walls of the abandoned house as though trying to overtake it.

"Something's not right," Gina whispered, which sent chills through Caffrey's chest. Gina leaned toward a window and allowed one eye to view the sliver of night between the frame and the ragged curtain hanging to one side of dusty, crooked blinds.

"Come on." She grabbed Caffrey's sleeve and pushed her down to the floor inside another room.

Caffrey's elbow touched a spiderweb. She squeaked and recoiled.

"Shhh!" Gina hissed.

A tiny, metallic *clack* broke the stillness. As the waning moon slipped curious fingers through the discolored blinds, Caffrey could see Gina holding a black handgun at her shoulder. More familiar with rifles than handguns, Caffrey surmised that the barely audible click had been Gina taking the safety off.

After a few torturous minutes during which Caffrey's stomach wounds turned to ice and her knees went numb, the unmistakable sound of a car on the graveled road they had traveled grew steadily louder. Gina aimed the small gun with steady hands toward the door. Caffrey could see the scant moonlight reflected in Gina's wide, unblinking eyes.

Two car doors shut softly, as though those approaching sought to muffle the sound. Caffrey stopped breathing. Steps crunched toward them. Caffrey flinched as knuckles rapped lightly on the door— tap-tap... tap-tap-tap... tap... tap-tap... and it slowly creaked open.

"Red sky," came Vince's clear voice into the musty room.

"White sand." Gina dropped her arms and let all the air out of her lungs. Caffrey leaned against the cabinet beside her and willed herself to breathe. Flashlights clicked on.

"Geez, honey," Gina raised her voice. "That looks like a SAAF car!"

"Sorry, babe," Vince apologized. "It's been a rough night. It's actually an old county police car with a rack on top painted black and gold."

"Someone's hot on the Princess's trail." Mace's voice was gruff. He shined his flashlight rudely on Caffrey's face and pointed into the rest of the room she was crouched in. Caffrey followed the light as it illuminated an old kitchen with an ancient sink and stove, and pale green countertops. Another door on the far side came into view. Clouds of cobwebs danced in the disturbed air.

"Did you clear this place?" Mace asked Gina.

"No. It's empty."

Mace cursed and stomped past Caffrey to a louvered door. Leaning against the wall beside the door frame, he turned the knob and shoved open the door. Lightning-quick, he pointed the flashlight around the edge, then leapt into the small room aiming a handgun at any would-be assassins.

Gina helped Caffrey up as Mace returned.

"Why didn't you clear this?" he demanded.

"I couldn't feel anyone here."

"You trust that too much."

"I've learned to. And so have *you*, dude!"

"Living room and bathroom's clear," offered Vince as he rounded the corner. He unbuttoned his jacket. "SAAF are checking white vans everywhere. Someone recognized Caffrey's picture from the hospital Friday morning—God knows how, I mean, we had her face and hair covered—and remembered us leaving in a white van. Our guess is someone started checking hospitals waving a picture around and got lucky. Security tapes would show the rest. We're going to have to keep the plumbing labels on for a while and definitely change the paint. Might have to junk the van." He placed his hands on his hips. "Come on, let's sit down."

Wordlessly, they gathered around a worn wooden table. Caffrey stole measured glances at everyone, concerned by the tense, weary faces. She felt lost. She was with them, but not part of them.

Painful cramps raced through her back as she sat on a hard wooden chair. Her legs felt less sturdy than they had that morning.

Gina wiped the table with an old cloth from the kitchen, which made everyone cough. The smell of mildew was strong. Vince lit a rusted oil lantern. Caffrey watched them both so she would not have to look at Mace, whom she found glaring at her when he was not monitoring the windows. She could almost feel anger and suspicion radiating from him.

"Okay," Vince began. "Caffrey, we're going to need you to tell us everything you can, every detail, every moment of what's been going on with you."

They waited and watched her. Caffrey cleared her throat. For a brief moment she was tempted not to tell them anything. The temptation dissolved when she looked at Vince.

"Where do you want me to start? With the accident?"

"Is that where you think you should start?" Vince asked, as if it were a therapy session.

"Yes. Before that, I had a *normal* life."

"I doubt that," countered Mace.

Caffrey glared darkly at him. "And just how would *you* know?"

"Oh, honey, I know everything there is to know about *you*."

Caffrey rolled her eyes in disgust. "And I sure *ain't* your honey." She watched his unblinking eyes squint slightly. "And if you really know all about me, then you know I had a pretty dull life."

"Oh really. Seems people close to you have turned up missing *before*."

Heat rushed through Caffrey's face. "That was...how could you *possibly* think I had anything to do with that?"

"Didn't you?"

Caffrey steeled her jaw to force back brimming tears. "You're an idiot!"

"Okay. Okay. Let's not get off in the wrong direction here." Vince motioned a hand toward each of them. "Let's focus now. Caffrey, please, go ahead. We're *listening.*" He added a sharp glance in Mace's direction.

Caffrey thought hard about the door behind her and realized she had no idea where she was.

"I'm not saying anything." She folded her arms. One glance at Vince and her resolve crumbled. Why did he defuse her? Instead, she jerked a thumb in Mace's direction. "He's already decided I'm guilty of...something! I'm not even sure what."

"Caffrey." Vince's voice was gentle and imploring as he placed his hands softly on the table. "*I* really need to know. Please?"

Caffrey could not look away from him. After a long, deep breath, she relayed the events of the previous week, starting with the accident. She had to swallow hard to keep from crying when she spoke of the dying man, and again when she arrived at her apartment to find the rescue equipment and SAAF officers. From the corner of her eye she could tell that Mace, sitting stiff and proud as ever, barely moved a muscle through the entire rendition. Ending with waking up in what she could only refer to as "the ammunition cellar," she thought that would be the end, until Vince and Gina took turns questioning every part of the story.

Mace blurted a question, and Caffrey whirled. "Excuse me. I'm not talking to you."

"Caffrey," Vince pleaded. "Mace might think of a question we missed."

"I don't care. He's a pig."

Mace rolled his black eyes before reaffixing them on her. Caffrey was glad for the meager human reaction. His accusations had triggered all of the horror, fear, and sorrow from the night Brian had disappeared. She hoped no one could see her arms shaking. She hadn't called anyone a "pig" since the fourth grade.

"Caffrey, right now I *need* him," stated Vince. "Please, just answer the questions. That's all I ask."

Why did her mouth start moving in response to Vince? She had never reacted that way to anyone. Mace followed with a question about the SAAF officer. Caffrey noticed his voice was less intimidating.

After she answered him, Mace continued with questions, fast and to the point, with military precision. His memory of events astounded Caffrey. If she changed her description in any way, his questions came faster and more persistent.

Sensing his desire to find some discrepancy, she became determined not to err in anything. In her first telling, she had carefully left out the obese man. But, when Mace asked her to name quickly every visitor to the office, Caffrey blurted, "The sumo guy," without thinking.

Steely eyes flashed, and he fired questions about the man's clothes, hair, demeanor, anything to force Caffrey to disclose details. Realizing it was useless and that somehow he already knew, Caffrey finally gave in and admitted the man touched her face. The entire group became alert. Mace carefully came back from different angles to her interaction with the obese man, which had them all rubbing chins and running fingers through hair.

Vince stood and began to pace. "Well, he couldn't have been a hypnotist. He would've had to use something—unless he's a previous arrangement, and the whole *thing's* a program."

"Maybe she was programmed before to accept an instant trance," offered Mace with a worried frown. "Had to be somewhere else. The detector registered nothing in the building."

"Maybe he's programmed as well," suggested Vince, continuing to pace. "And she accepted instructions."

"Well, that would mean she had to be involved before and doesn't know it," Gina countered. "No, no." She shook her head. "The whole thing's too bizarre to be a complete plan. Charlie couldn't have just wrecked right *there*. It's too much. And, they'd have us already."

Mace leaned forward and clasped his hands. "I don't know. They could have planned a wreck there, if they knew what route he would take. Plant *her* there." He motioned toward Caffrey with a finger. "Pretty girl. Innocent-looking. Just *happens* to work at secure real estate law office that handles *lifted* property owners."

Caffrey glared at his insinuation, but with a sinking feeling, realized he had voiced a truth she had ignored about her job. No longer a real estate law firm handling difficult cases and abandonment, it had become a clearing house for property of the poor souls who had been snatched away by secretive, hostile aliens. What if Brian had owned property? Would his be up for grabs? Caffrey felt sick and pressed a hand to her heart.

"Program her to accept a job. Send her to search for the Underground," Mace continued. "Then, they get inside. Maybe they're waiting to get the whole bunch—not leave any leaders to start the whole the resistance up again."

"They'd have to go after every division," Gina argued. "Besides Mace, she was half-dead in an alley. I mean, *really* half-dead. She flatlined while we were trying to pump her full of blood."

"What?" Caffrey asked, incredulous.

"Sorry, didn't tell you," Gina said, and turned back to Mace. "You talked to everybody at Five Points. You had all the witnesses at Peachtree Street polled. Their stories jived, except for Charlie giving Caffrey the disc. No one saw that, although two people said they saw the SAAF examining Caffrey's clothes when they got back to their car. They would have to have—the angle of Charlie, the disc, the SAAF men, the witnesses, Caffrey, the big guy, Five Points, everything. That would be an incredible plan!"

"Not too much to dump the whole Underground at once," Mace countered.

Gina sighed heavily. "There are other voices out there."

"But *we're* the loudest."

"What about from the big guy on?" Vince halted his pacing. "What if from that point on is the program?"

"No," said Mace. "The people in the office check out. They would *all* have to be programmed, too. Not that I'm not considering that."

"All right, wait a minute," Caffrey interjected, tired of being discussed as though she were not in the room. "I worked there, okay? I mean, you people act as if these events are some kind of a dream. And we're not talking about missing time or anything. I can tell you every detail of every day—well, practically, if I cared to remember it."

"Your *life* could be a dream," said Mace, raising his chin with a disconcerting curiosity that made her more uneasy than angry. "It all depends on how big this plan is."

Caffrey rolled her eyes and focused on the peeling wallpaper instead of anyone in particular.

"Nope, he touched her." Vince sat in the rickety chair and rested his arms on the table. "The program would have to be that he was human, but in reality was a Vhurruh. There's no getting around that. She's had a visual reprogram to leave out memory of the Vhurruh."

"Except that if it was on the premises, the detector would *register* the Vhurruh. It's good for 48 hours," argued Mace. "They had to take her somewhere else."

"What *detector* are you talking about?" asked Caffrey, irritated.

"We'll explain that one later," answered Vince. Caffrey exhaled with renewed disgust.

"SAAFs didn't come back looking for her until six," Mace continued. "They wouldn't have bothered if a Vhurruh got to her. And, two people in that office *saw* the big guy. Kimberly saw him touching her."

Gina rubbed both hands against her cheeks and sighed. "Everybody in the office would have to be programmed, and that's too much. The Vhurruh must have been somewhere else, unless she's preprogrammed. This is going around in circles."

In the lull that followed Caffrey glanced at each puzzled face. "You guys talked to Kimberly?"

"Of course we talked to Kimberly—and everybody else." Mace looked almost insulted. Caffrey mocked him with an icy sneer. She wanted to ask how Kimberly was reacting to her absence but would not dare give him the satisfaction of an emotional question.

Vince squirmed in his chair. "Who *is* this guy? A human with telepathic ability? Can't be a hybrid. That's for sure. No way of mixing that DNA!"

"Their DNA's been mapped. No possibility of a natural hybrid," Gina stated. "Well, any time soon. Who knows what the future holds."

Vince rubbed his chin. "Try a regression?"

"No way. Not with that programming. He's still hiding. He hasn't even revealed himself to the other links."

Vince exhaled and raised his eyes to Caffrey. "Caffrey, please describe the feeling you had when the big man touched you."

Caffrey averted her gaze to prevent her mouth from answering for her. Heat blossomed in her cheeks. She did not wish to share the strange euphoric sensation. It was a fuzzy memory at best. As seconds ticked by, she glanced at Vince and found it impossible to resist the pleading, handsome blue eyes, which was beginning to frighten her.

"Okay. I remember this slight buzz in my head. I don't know how to describe it. Like a flash of electricity or something. The whole scene is hazy. Although, I do remember for a split second feeling...." Caffrey halted. "I cleared my head and asked him what he said. That's all."

"What was that feeling you were about to describe?" Gina's eyes were fixed on Caffrey's.

Caffrey's legs quivered. She shifted position but felt more uncomfortable.

"It wasn't a big deal, okay? He probably shocked me walking across the carpet. We do that to each other all the time there." She had no problem resisting Gina or Mace, but the moment she glanced at Vince, her mouth began to move. "It was...I don't know, oddly pleasant." She lowered her eyes, embarrassed.

"How pleasant?" Vince leaned forward.

"I don't know...." Caffrey replied, keeping her eyes averted.

"Caffrey," Vince implored. "This is *very* important. *Please,* try to describe it to me."

Caffrey growled in frustration and hit the table with a fist. "I don't remember, *okay!*"

For a moment there was silence.

"Okay." Vince's voice was soft. "I'm going to give you a couple words. Blissful. Warm. Soul-blending. Connection. Etheric. Loving. Sensual. Do those fit?"

"Okay, fine!" Caffrey fumed, furious that she could not resist his suggestions. "It was like being transported to a warm beach with a hot guy and a cold drink in your hand. I mean, seriously, what do you want me to say? It was just a good *feeling,* nothing more!"

"Beach?" asked Vince good-naturedly, suppressing a smile.

"Gee, what a guy," Mace countered.

"I'm sure *you* wouldn't know," Caffrey remarked.

"Try me," he jeered in a low voice.

"In *your* dreams." Caffrey turned her attention to Gina. To her surprise, Gina shot Mace an icy look that suggested he back off, which gave Caffrey some measure of satisfaction.

Vince, too, was glaring sideways at Mace.

"That is a Blue drone, guys," Vince stated with authority.

Gina nodded. "Sounds like classic Vhurruh programming. A jolt to the nervous system, the whole joining thing, euphoria, and then instill the programming into that trust. It's classic, except...he's human."

"That's not what it's about!" Vince shouted, sweeping the air with both hands.

Gina and Mace stared at him. So did Caffrey.

"O-kaaay," said Gina slowly, as if in apology.

Vince took a calming breath as he avoided everyone's eyes. He propped his elbows, clasped his hands, and lowered his head onto them.

Caffrey watched them all, trying to understand the unspoken conflict. She read only regret from Gina and Mace, almost pity.

"It's a joining of the souls." Vince steadied his voice, lowering his arms. "There's a sensation of...of...ecstasy is the only word that fits. A one-ness on a level you've never experienced. Something that...."

"*Not* when it's forced," Gina reminded him softly.

Vince looked down at the table, his face stiff. "The Gray faction drones force it. It's brutal, and it's an assault. This was not forced." His gaze shifted to Caffrey. "She described pleasure, not fear or trauma."

Mace cleared his throat. Caffrey glanced at him, shocked to find him staring at the table. Gina was focused on her folded hands. Vince crossed his arms as if in rebellion. She watched them, baffled.

"Kimberly said he was there for five minutes," Gina spoke into the silence. She looked to Caffrey for confirmation.

Caffrey shrugged and rubbed her arms and cramping midsection. Everything ached. Suddenly, warm pressure filled her brain. She reached for the sensation, unafraid this time.

It was *him*. She wouldn't have said *him* before, but he felt more solid, instead of a spirit-like essence. Though she was unnerved that he chose that moment to connect, he was a welcome presence in a tense room of interrogators.

Like microscopic fingers on nerve endings, he delicately searched her thoughts and emotions so fast Caffrey was both amazed and unsettled. He was pleased that she was not frightened by him.

With a wordless thought, he questioned who her antagonists were. Caffrey automatically visualized faces without thinking. He was immensely relieved to understand who she was with. Realizing he yearned to defend her and put her at ease, Caffrey almost smiled. It was like having a secret protector.

To her dismay, he withdrew, but he sent her a sweet sensation, as though he had kissed her cheek with affection. She extended all her senses in a desperate attempt to hold onto him, but was not fast enough, or familiar enough, with the phenomenon. She truly regretted the quiet collapse of the obscure connection.

"....a pretty long time. But you don't remember that?" Vince was asking her.

"What?" Caffrey blinked.

"The big guy. You don't remember him being there for several minutes?"

"Uh. No. He was only there for a second." Caffrey brushed hair out of her eyes. "Kim said he was there longer."

She realized Gina was staring at her with a strained expression as if she had sensed the communication. Caffrey avoided her scrutiny. That woman knew too much.

"You trust her?" Vince continued.

"What? Who?" asked Caffrey.

"Kim-ber-ly," Vince sounded the word as if she were a fidgeting child.

All three of them looked at her now.

"Yes," Caffrey quipped. "No." she amended.

"Um...which is it?" Vince's expression was comical.

"It's not a big deal, okay?" Caffrey snapped at him. "Kim's been known to exaggerate, a little. It's...nothing."

Vince's brows raised in disagreement. Caffrey heaved a sigh and rolled her shoulders.

Mace sat back in his chair. "I don't like this. I gotta find out who this guy is." He turned to Gina. "You can't sense anything else about this guy?"

Gina shook her head, her eyes fixed on Caffrey. "It feels Vhurruh, but there's a faint human element I can't pinpoint. Maybe a Gray trained a human to pass on a mind program."

"If I hadn't checked out her office," Mace examined Caffrey as though she were an equation, "I'd swear the whole incident was a program."

She shifted on the hard wooden chair and tried to find a position where her stomach and back would not protest. Nausea began to wash over her as the pain medication dissipated.

"He's *got* to be the program, unless something's missing." Vince rubbed both hands over his tired face. "Which is, of course, quite possible."

Mace drummed lightly with his fingers on the table. "Let's not worry about it now. I'm gonna find out who he is. He came about an hour later, right?"

In the silence, Caffrey realized he had addressed her. "Yes." She propped her elbows and lowered her head into her hands. "Maybe more, I'm not sure. I don't care."

"All right, let's go back to the earrings. When you were at work," Mace continued.

Caffrey's head began to pound, and she rubbed at her temples. "Look, I have really had it with this. I told you. The first time I saw them was at Kim's. I put the sweater on, and she said my earrings were cool. I looked closer, and my head began to hurt. That's *all*."

"And that didn't strike you as odd that your head began to hurt just then?" Mace asked. "Like it's hurting right now."

"No!" Caffrey yelled, angry that he was correct. "I had Evan in the next room. He always gives me a freakin' headache."

"Okay. Then you *looked* at them again, right?"

"No. I completely forgot about the stupid earrings." The throbbing increased to a fierce pounding at the back of her skull.

"You mean to tell me that you had a completely strange pair of earrings on and you didn't take a second....?"

"No!" She held her head with both hands. "Leave me the hell alone! I had a lot of things on my mind that night. I had to find you idiots...people, I mean. No, for you I'll find another word."

"Tired, Caff?" Gina offered.

"Yes," Caffrey snapped. "And I don't feel well. I'm tired of this. And I don't owe you people anything else."

"Oh, I think you do." Mace's voice was low and threatening.

"Oh, I don't *think* so." Caffrey leaned forward. "My life is totally ruined here. I've gotten shot. I wake up in some...*basement*. I've probably lost my job. I may have lost a very good friend. I can't even *find out* about my apartment since nobody'll let me near a phone or anything with a battery. You *idiots* don't even know what the disc *is*. I have no idea what direction to go in...and...and I'm tired of *you*."

"Is 'at right." Mace sat forward. "Well, for your information, sweets, since you got involved, all hell has broken loose. We've had heat on us before, but this is one hot fire. There is much more here than you know. And, believe me, I'm going to find out what it is...and who you are."

"Well, fine. You *do* that." Caffrey pointed a thumb at her chest. "But, you can do it without me."

"Where you gonna go?" Mace opened his arms to the air.

"Hey, I have friends. Unlike *you,* I'm sure. You've got the disc, *and* the stupid earrings. I am done with this. Okay? I want out."

"Caffrey." Vince raised both palms in caution. "You walk out of our protection now—assuming we would let you—and no one will ever see you again. You have no idea what you are dealing with."

Caffrey swallowed. "Maybe I'd be better off."

"Besides the fact that I'd shoot your ass if you tried it," added Mace.

"Mace." Vince threw him a warning glance. "Maybe we should call it a night." Vince leaned back in his chair, which made it creak, and stretched his arms behind him.

Mace raised both black eyebrows as though to question the move, and Vince gave him a barely perceptible shake of his head.

"Wait a minute." Caffrey slammed her hand onto the table. "How about some of my questions?"

Mace looked amused. "For instance?" He crossed his arms. Everyone turned expectantly to Caffrey.

"Okay. How 'bout, does anyone know about my car?" She also crossed her arms. "Are you guys *that* good?"

Mace answered quickly. "Local police impounded your car. SAAFs came and took it. No questions allowed."

"How do *you* know that?"

An unfriendly smile spread across his face.

Caffrey rolled her eyes. "Okay. What about my apartment? Does anyone know what happened there?"

"Lifted," answered Mace bluntly.

"What do you mean?"

"Yep. You didn't know it was lifted?"

"But...it was a gas leak. Gina said...."

"That was the cover story. We found out about the lift this morning."

Caffrey's throat constricted. "Is...everyone gone? *Really* gone?"

"Let's just say, '*Everyone's accounted for,*'" Vince interjected. "That's the official word, of course. But yes, Caffrey, except for a couple guys they allowed the press to question briefly, everyone from that building—your building—is gone."

"But...but Maiba! What about...wait a minute! You don't know that for sure." A knife was stabbing into her heart. Her knees began to shake. *Not again. Not someone she loved.* "Somebody else could have been out that night—like me."

"Only *your* building was taken," stated Vince, in a tone of patient compassion. "SAAF officers aren't always told who the target is. We did find out some were told to look for a Caucasian girl with red hair."

Caffrey closed her eyes in pain. A sob caught in her throat. "Oh, God, that poor girl."

"What girl?"

"I saw them pull a red-haired girl aside and take her behind a black van. I turned around and got out of there."

After a moment of silence, Vince said, "Then you were seconds away from being taken. They obviously know they didn't get the right girl. Because the witch hunt for you is still out of the ordinary, in my opinion. Somebody wants you, or what you *had,* assuming you're not a plant."

Caffrey turned to stare at Vince, dumbfounded. She had not realized he, too, was suspicious of her. "I've got to warn my family," she said out loud. Her breath became rough and staggered at the thought of her parents being upset.

"It's a little too late for that, Princess," said Mace, but with the first touch of sympathy from him. "Any relations of yours have got their phones tapped, living rooms bugged, satellite surveillance, everything. If they haven't been taken."

"Oh, no." Caffrey covered her face with both hands.

"You don't know that, Mace." Gina whirled on him. "Don't give her more than she can handle."

"You *know* they're being watched."

"Yes, but...."

"I have...I have to go." Caffrey stood and looked around the strange room as though it were not there. Dizziness made the walls appear to move.

"Caffrey, I'm sorry," said Vince in a patronly way. "Any call, any email, would be traced, and you'd be picked up within a half-hour. Absolute silence is the only way, unless we decide to start a rumor about you."

Caffrey legs turned to mush, and she sat down to keep her knees from buckling. She didn't care whether she looked weak to Mace or not. The pain of possibly losing her family was unbearable.

"Not a bad idea," said Mace.

Caffrey looked up, confused.

"We'd have to give the hounds something to go after," Vince said. "Fake your death. Have you spotted in another city and let the press get word out—then we take you out. Something along those lines. Things would be crazy, but your parents would know you're alive. As far as we know, they don't actually think you're dead. They received an e-mail from you."

"But...I didn't send one," Caffrey murmured.

"We know. Someone used your e-mail address and sent it. SAAF often fake communications to hold off family members knowing of someone's disappearance."

Caffrey's stomach constricted and threatened to disgorge dinner.

A shrill chime pierced the dusty air and caused everyone to jump. Vince yanked a phone from his belt. He and Mace peered closely at it.

"Sharia," said Vince. "Eight-eight-six-six-five. Somebody's after her, but she's hiding."

Mace cursed vehemently. "That means they've traced the clinic. Somebody leaked."

"I can't *believe* they found the clinic!" Vince pressed his eyes shut and clenched his fists in exasperation.

Mace dialed furiously into a cell phone, with Vince showing him the phone display. Mace glanced at everyone in the room. "Everybody better get ready to run if this is a setup and not Sharia."

"Hey, mailman there?" Mace paused to listen. "Uh-huh. Good. Will these people use bug spray if there's a raid? Mmm, hmm. Give me a 'C' number.... All right. Hang tight, kid. See you as the blackbird flies."

Mace whirled on Caffrey as he closed the phone. "Somebody wants you *real* bad, babe. Know who it is?"

"No!" Caffrey yelled, her lip quivering. "And if I did, I wouldn't tell you!"

"Is 'at right? Gina, we gotta keep her movin'. The Grams know nothing, right?"

"Right."

"Okay," said Mace, resolute. "If they've traced the clinic, might as well assume they'll trace you and then the Grams."

"No!" Caffrey and Gina exclaimed together.

"Don't tell me I have to *move* them." Gina was vividly dismayed. "I'm under a fake name at the clinic. I work through a temp agency. They can't get me."

"Think it through," ordered Mace. "If they want her bad enough to trace clinics at random, or however they did it, they can find you. At the very least, you know you can't use the agency again, or the alias. Send the Grams on vacation. I mean it."

Gina moaned and pulled out a phone. "Hi, um, Grams? You have to bug out. Now. Okay. I love you, too."

Vince raised his hands. "What about taking Caffrey in and out of a different city—get her viewed somewhere?"

"I'd never get her out," said Mace. "Too much heat. She'd be covered by satellite surveillance in seconds and scooped up in a scout ship. I'd have to have a complete underground network. And they'd have to be fast."

Vince steeled his jaw. "I am *not* giving up every keep I've got in this city. Let's use a look-alike if we have to. Let's call everybody we've got. I'm puttin' some heat on. I want these hounds looking in lots of wrong places. And, Mace, I think she needs to be moved to Tower or Remote. Get her out of Atlanta."

"Not tonight, unless it's after Sharia. Not Remote, anyway. She's too hot. I won't risk it. Gina could take her to Tower. But that's one-on-one."

Vince locked eyes with Mace for a moment, then with mixed emotions gazed endearingly at Gina. "All right. She's had every opportunity. In the ammunition room. Even at Grams."

"Doesn't matter if that's not the program," said Mace cautiously.

"Wait a minute." Gina pointed an arm in Caffrey's direction. "Not in her condition. She's white as a sheet. We'd have to hike to Tower. What if there are road blocks? I'm only one person. Isn't there somewhere else?"

"She'll make it," said Mace. "Hell, she's had three days to rest."

"No, Mace," Gina replied through gritted teeth. "She's had two surgeries. I am not taking her up mountains on foot."

"You will, if it's all we've got."

The two glared at each other.

"What about Caveman?" Gina suggested. "It's twenty minutes from here."

"No. It's too small, and I can't take a chance that she'll lead them there. The stuff's got to stay separate from her, so we don't lose both. Besides, there're no supplies and there's no back door."

The three rebels glared at each other. Mace broke the silence. "We've got to get Sharia."

"What about Conrad's?" Gina blurted.

Mace and Vince exchanged glances.

"Go for it," said Mace. "We'll find you."

9

CONRAD'S

Through the fingers of her right hand, Caffrey watched endless faces go by and wondered if anyone would actually recognize her. A secret, tiny part of her sported an irrational desire to see it happen. Her arm ached from being braced up so long on the old car door to spread her hand over her face, but it was Gina's compromise for not cocooning her on the floor of the backseat. Caffrey's red hair, being too obvious to chance, had been swiftly braided and tucked up under an overlarge Atlanta Braves cap. She was wearing sunglasses in the dead of night. Though Caffrey had protested the disguise, she noticed the eyes of everyone walking *were* on every passing car.

Caffrey recognized East Ponce de Leon Avenue, but not the area they were approaching. Old, plantation-style homes of ornate designs, many with balconies and columns, whisked by. Several appeared to be converted to apartments, with college-aged people hanging out on porches and sidewalks. Quickly the scene changed to rows of shops, swarmed with groups of late-night gatherers and partiers.

"This is *Little* Five Points." Gina finally spoke, as if reading her mind. "Not to be confused with 'Five Points,' which I'm sure you remember. You ever come here?"

For half an hour, their shared paranoia had made each somber and tense, so Caffrey was glad for the sudden conversation. "No, I never got down here. Always meant to, though."

"This is Conrad's place. He loves it. He loves the noise, the people, the crazy shops—all of it. He brought me here a few years back. We had fun, just me and him out on the town. He's the one person who would go explore interesting places with me. There's a cool little restaurant down a few streets that way, called The Sour Biscuit. The biscuits are to *die for*. Homemade. And their cheese grits—oh! *Heaven*."

"Somehow, I cannot picture you eating cheese grits," Caffrey stated, her voice flat.

"Why? Haven't you ever had them?"

"No." Caffrey shrugged. "I guess I picture you going for the healthiest thing on the menu."

"Hey, I had a salad with it."

"You had a salad—and *cheese grits?*"

"Sure. A carb, a protein, and greens. They have a 'mixed greens' salad there, and I'm not kidding you, it is *just* what it says. Looks like somebody pulled weeds out of Gram's garden—along with half the garden. Of course, before that, the only kind of salad I had ever eaten was iceberg lettuce, so it was a shock to me. Conrad laughed at me and said, 'Now you're officially a grownup. Eating a *real* salad.'"

Gina shook her head and smiled at the memory. "I especially liked the wood floor. It's got that cool hollow sound like my parents' cabin. If we ever get the chance, I promise I'll take you to that restaurant."

"Thanks," Caffrey murmured in the dark, glad Gina could not observe her ungrateful expression.

"Haven't seen Conrad in about eight months, but I know he'll let us stay the night. We'll be safe there, unless you're spotted or something, which hopefully we've taken care of. But, at this rate, I don't know."

Caffrey placed her hand back over her face so she could look out the window. She felt guilty for being the focus of Gina's fears, then felt angry at Gina for making her feel that way.

They turned down a side road, passed several groups of town houses, and stopped at a stately brick entrance with brass lamps. At the keypad Gina punched in a code. The gate slowly slid to the right. She glanced with quick, practiced eyes around the security-brightened lot as she parked and turned off the car. She raised the hood of her jacket over her hair. "Okay, let's go. Keep your head down."

Inside a glass door, Gina pressed a button next to a list of condo numbers. In response, a male voice, distorted by the speaker box, cheerfully asked who was calling.

"Conrad?" Gina kept her voice low. "'Member me, it's Gina-mina!"

"Gina Chormanski? Secret agent girl?"

"Shhhhhh, Conrad!"

"Just kidding! But, you're on a mission, right?" A loud buzzer startled Caffrey, but Gina was ready for it and pushed quickly through the door as though it were on fire.

Atop the third flight of stairs, Caffrey leaned on the railing in front of number 304 for support. Every muscle in her body protested the arduous climb. She laid hands on her incisions gingerly.

The door flew open as Gina began to knock, and a tall, vivacious blond man pulled her into his arms. "Hey, girl, how are you? You look good!" He squeezed her tight.

Gina laughed. "I'm great, I'm great. How are *you*?"

"Oh, can't complain—maybe."

Gina waited until Conrad had locked the door before introducing Caffrey as Victoria. Conrad offered her a handshake and a side wink. Caffrey liked him immediately. His face was kind, confident, and full of mischief. With a dare in his eyes, he began badgering Gina with one question after another in what appeared to be an old game of asking so many questions that she could not keep up with him.

Gina blurted one or two-word answers in attempt to outsmart him. Half the time she cheated by saying, "Classified."

Caffrey took off her cap, which was giving her a headache, and began to undo the braids.

A tall, thin man with jet-black hair shuffled into the room. He brightened when he spotted Gina.

"Tinman!" Gina exclaimed, and crossed the room to embrace him. "You keepin' this guy straight?"

"Ha! That's a good one." The man replied with a shy smile.

"Victoria, this is Tim Inman. *Tinman* to me, 'cause I can't say his name."

"Nice to meet you." Caffrey offered her hand.

Tim's smile evaporated as he shook Caffrey's hand. Then he pointed. "You're that girl."

Caffrey froze.

Gina's face fell. "What?"

Conrad examined Caffrey, then shifted to Gina, his mouth slightly agape. "Always in the hot seat, aren't you? You haven't changed a bit."

"Conny!" Gina warned.

"We just saw it on the news." Tim explained.

"Tim never forgets a face." Conrad added.

"Her car was found abandoned down near Five Points a few days ago."

Caffrey's eyes filled with tears. "Oh, no...my parents are going to freak."

"Mind if we sit down?" asked Gina in an exhausted voice.

"Sure." Conrad raised his brows at Tim, who was looking alarmed.

Gina plopped into a loveseat and let her head fall back against the cushion. Caffrey sat as well, but carefully.

"Did they give any other details?" asked Gina.

"Uh, let's see..." Conrad began. "Her purse was found at a restaurant in Five Points. Something about petty cash missing where she worked. They said it looked like she did it, but they don't know why. Like, maybe she was on the run."

"Oh, my gosh!" Caffrey's throat tightened, and she fought back tears of indignation. "That is *so* not true. It's a lie!"

Conrad raised a hand. "Hey, it's okay. Besides, if you're with Gina-mina, I know you're trying to save the planet."

Gina added a slight snort.

"Oh, and there was this guy, too," Conrad added. "You know, that tall guy that's done so much for the city and all. I think he's a mayor or senator. Evan-something...Parkek?"

"Evan Parchek," Tim clarified.

"Yeah, he was interviewed about the gas main break in Alpharetta where a fire broke out. He was saying what a tragedy it was and how he was allocating money to help out the tenants. Several people died, and they had to seal off the area for a while. Something about noxious chemicals and stuff. They were thinking this missing girl died there at first, but then they went on to speculate about the...well, her car being found and all."

"Oh, no." Caffrey moaned.

"And I remember her name started with, like, Kat or Kallie-something," Conrad continued as though on remote control.

"Okay, okay—wait a minute." Gina stood and held up her hands. She advanced slowly toward the glass doors of their balcony, then turned back. "Okay." She slapped her palms together. "Conrad, Tim, this is my friend, Victoria. She and I are going on a hiking trip. We're old friends from..." she waved a hand. "From way back. We were out late tonight, having some fun, riding around Little Five Points, and since we were near your place, I decided to...stop by and say hello. It's pretty wild that Victoria *looks* like that girl on TV. What a strange coincidence. I sure hope they find her, and that she's okay. At any rate, in case anyone happens to ask about us, seeing how we're fixin' to go up to the Blue Ridge Mountains in North Carolina and it's always nice to let someone know you're planning that sort of trip, this way I wanted to be sure *I told you everything myself.* That way, *that's...the...story... you'll...know.* Right?"

Conrad held her gaze for a moment, then darted his eyes comically from Caffrey to Gina. "Absolutely." He added several nods. Tim grew pale. His brown eyes bulged as he glanced from Gina to Conrad.

"Okay," added Conrad, his voice high and whimsical. "And, uh, since you're, uh, *in the area*, do y'all need a place to spend the night?"

Tim flinched.

"Wow, that would be great!" Gina clapped her hands. "I really appreciate that. Don't you, Victoria?"

Caffrey gave the barest nod and blinked back tears. Her life was falling apart. Her parents and brother would be so upset. If she could just manage one phone call....

Conrad rocked on his heels, sporting a mischievous expression. "Would you guys like something to drink?"

"Actually, I would love a caffeine-free soda, or something cold." Gina flopped back onto the vine-patterned loveseat and brushed a hand across her forehead.

"How 'bout you, uh... Victoria?" asked Conrad. "Soft drink...water...hot tea?

"Um...." Caffrey's voice shook. "Hot tea...if it's no trouble." She eyed the cell phone on Conrad's belt.

While Tim and Conrad busied themselves preparing beverages, Gina whispered to Caffrey. "Touch the phone and you die."

Caffrey glared at her. There were disadvantages to traveling with a psychic on a mission.

"So, how's everything *else*?" called Conrad from the kitchen.

"Oh, okay. I guess," said Gina. "The Grams are doing good."

"Aw, man, I miss them. They were great. Do they still sell stuff at that county fair?"

"They're debatin' it for this year. But, I guarantee you, they'll go. It's too much of a tradition. Gramps says he likes to see all the silly young folk and what they're wearin'."

"Ha! Sounds like him. Okay, one caffeine-free soda and one hot tea coming up. You'll have to let that tea steep for a minute."

Tim nearly dropped the hot teacup he was handing to Caffrey when Conrad's cell phone rang. Conrad pulled the phone from his pocket, puzzled at the display, but offered a cheery hello. His face quickly lost its smile. Wide-eyed with alarm, he placed the phone against his chest. "Some guy says he's 'the wolf,' and wants to talk to the blonde."

Gina leapt from the couch.

Tim stepped back into the kitchen and began biting his nails.

"Hello?" Gina spoke with mock cheerfulness. She licked her lips in concentration. "No, but I heard. Understood. Conny, do you mind if I take this in the bedroom?"

"Uh, sure. It's right back here."

Caffrey spilled tea into the saucer while hastily placing it on a side table. She vaulted from her chair, determined that whoever it was, she was not going to be left out of the loop, nor left alone with two strangers not knowing what to say.

Gina stiffened and frowned as Caffrey sat on the burgundy-quilted bed beside her. Caffrey crossed both arms in silent challenge. Gina's face grew serious as the deep tones of Mace's voice carried through the phone. Caffrey leaned closer.

"...was broadcast tonight. Candyland is closed for renovations. Inventory will have to be written off and new management found. Plumbing and medical supplies don't seem to be where the money is, either. We need to rethink our investments here. May use some of the same help, though. Good people. Got one of 'em with us. Traffic was difficult, but we're clear. Let's take some time off to regroup and plan some strategy. We could meet for, say, a late breakfast in the morning. Log Cabin syrup is still my favorite."

Gina's eyes darted back and forth in concentration. "Okay, a late breakfast sounds good. Uh...long trips could mean...stops along the way...."

"Be prepared for anything. Even a flat tire where you might have to walk. Use line two if you need me. Head South-Cat. Need to cut it short. Don't want air time to cost us. See you when the hotcakes hit the griddle. Do you copy?"

"Yes, that's a copy." Gina closed the connection and let her hand drop.

"What is it?" asked Caffrey.

"The...location where we had you, is gone. Which is pretty scary, because it's right down the road. We had you in a candy and crystal shop here in Little Five Points. It was my idea—the shop. Had a bomb shelter left over from the forties. Man, that means they've got all my supplies." She let her head drop back for a moment, sighed heavily, then grimaced and straightened her shoulders. "Mace and Vince had to sneak one of our people out of her apartment. Mace was talking in code and he makes it difficult. I hope they're not being followed. He must be worried, since he's having us travel separately."

Fatigue washed over Caffrey. She was tired of running, tired of hiding, tired of being upset. The Underground had the disc now. If she knew nothing of Gina, Vince, and Mace's whereabouts, could she go back to her old life, her job?

Gina stood. "Okay, the store's gone, the clinic's gone, and the plumbing shop's gone. We've had this happen before. Right at the beginning, when we voiced our concerns a little too loudly. They don't have *us*. We're *still* in the lead. Mace wants us to meet up in...well, I won't say for now. We'll meet them tomorrow morning if everything goes okay. Man, I hope they don't have roadblocks set up. I need more people."

"Why South? What's there?"

"He said South-Cat. It's code for going the opposite—like catty-corner. I probably shouldn't tell you that, but...oh, they know about the broadcast. Mace said to tell you to hang tight. The petty cash story is a lure to get you to come out of hiding, to clear your name. And don't worry about your parents."

Caffrey was torn between surprise that Mace would say anything to encourage her and shock that such an outrageous plot would be created for her.

"Gina?"

"Yes."

"Do you know why I never got drunk, or took drugs?"

Gina sat on the bed. "No."

"Partly because of my religious upbringing." She looked away. "But also because I heard some girls in school talking about how people were telling them what they did the night before. They were dancing and stripping at a party. And they had no memory of it. They were mortified."

"And?"

"I decided right there that would never be me. I am never going to have someone tell me what I did, and me have no memory of it. And now, here I am, plopped right in the middle of it. People telling me I did things I don't remember."

She raised her eyes to Gina's. "I want out. Now."

Gina grabbed Caffrey's shoulders. "Caffrey, listen to me closely. Your life has been changed. Forever. There is no going back. There is only going forward. Embrace it. Own it. And champion it."

"And what about my parents? My Mom's probably crying...." Caffrey halted as a lump caught in her throat.

"Do you want your parents in harm's way?"

"No. Of course not."

"Then let this play out. As long as they react like normal parents would, horrified and crying, they are safe."

When they entered the living room, Gina smiled with gratitude. "Wow, Conny. I owe you one." The sofa and loveseat were neatly covered with sheets and topped with blankets and pillows, ready for their weary heads. Tim stood slightly behind Conrad, biting what was left of his fingernails.

"Don't mention it." Conrad smiled sideways in return. "I'll think of something to make you pay me back."

"Ha!"

"One thing's for sure."

"What?"

"If I ever get into trouble…" Conrad pointed at her. "I'm lookin' you up."

Gina grinned wide and pointed at him. "If you can find me."

10

LOG CABIN SYRUP

Waiting in the car while Gina shopped for supplies at the REI outdoor store was an irritant to Caffrey, since she had heard so much about the store from other people and had always wanted to go there. Here she was, and she couldn't do anything but sit dejectedly with one hand over her face, sunglasses covering her eyes, and hair tightly braided under the blue Atlanta Braves cap, giving her a headache. Which gave her too much time to think and worry. She could not visualize her parents, or she'd get weepy.

Resting her chin on her propped forearm, she watched the traffic whiz by on Interstate 85. She noted every shadowed place along the road, in bushes, under exit bridges, where a person could hide if they needed to. She rubbed her head, alarmed at her fugitive mode of thinking.

To her surprise, Gina opened the car door after only seventeen minutes in the store.

"How can anybody buy something that fast?" Caffrey asked.

Gina shrugged. "I know what we need, and I'm in a hurry."

As they pulled onto the highway, Caffrey nearly made herself carsick examining new backpacks, sleeping bags, water sterilization equipment, plastic bottles, soaps, lotions, and lastly, ready-to-eat food pouches—which were the most fun.

"Chocolate pudding?" Caffrey held up a silver pouch. "Can we have that now?"

"No."

"How do you guys pay for all of this?"

"That's classified."

"Of course it is."

The two-hour trip to the mountains was strained, with both women tense from worry, especially after the heart-stopping moment when a policeman turned on his lights and siren two cars behind, only to zoom past when everyone pulled over. Caffrey's chest and stomach ached for the remainder of the trip.

As the North Georgia Mountains came into view, calm and neon green with spring leaves, Gina breathed a sigh of relief and mentioned they might not need the equipment after all, since she had prepared for abandoning the car.

Caffrey responded simply with, "Humph." She had made several attempts to glean information out of Gina as they traveled, hoping to understand more about the Underground, but Gina's answers had been short and evasive, reminding Caffrey that she was still suspect.

Focusing on the rustic scenery, Caffrey decided if someone didn't answer more of her questions, she was going to find her own way out.

They reached the small town of Dillard, nestled on the edge of a mountain range. Gina turned up an elusive drive marked only with a small, weathered sign that read "New Reflections Conference Center."

The road quickly turned into a myriad of twists and turns, winding always upward, with every curve producing a sign advertising "Billy's Trout Farm." Rabbits and squirrels scurried blindly in front of the car and caused Gina to hit the brakes several times. At one point, a deer loped lazily back into the woods as if the car was a mere inconvenience. Caffrey found herself smiling at the wildlife's antics, but also at the yellow and blue wildflowers peeking through the lush green forest at every turn.

Finally, Gina parked in front of a plain wooden building. Caffrey stepped out, inhaled the heady richness of forest air, and was overwhelmed by the giddiness of the familiar "camper" feeling. Cabins were spaced at various points up the mountain. Loud and large insects dominated the misty haze, their creaks and burrs reverberating against the sides of every building. A large weaver spider claimed a three-foot area from the overhang of the building to the window on the right, while several neon green and yellow moths clung firmly to the walls, waiting for the moon.

Inside the lodge, the rustic lobby was decorated with pictures of previous campers and events. Dominating the center room was a large round fireplace recessed into the floor, inlaid with wide gray stones and surrounded by wooden benches topped with faded maroon cushions. Caffrey peered over her sunglasses at antique pictures and an old map while Gina spoke with the desk clerk.

Gina emerged jingling a green-tagged key. As they returned to the old station wagon, Gina briefly explained that the cabin was rented year-round, and if anyone asked, her name was Heather Waters from South Carolina.

"Got that? I'm Heather, you're Victoria," schooled Gina. Caffrey groaned.

Gina drove the old car up a slope that snaked at a dangerous vertical tilt until it finally leveled out in front of a spacious log cabin. Smoke curled lazily from a mammoth chimney while six wooden rockers sat waiting to be warmed on a wide wooden porch that was decorated at the edges with several pots of hardy pansies. A dark blue SUV sat parked to the right of the porch.

"It's them. Thank God!" Gina exclaimed in a hushed but excited voice.

"How do you know?"

Gina pointed at the front door. An oval wreath of vines surrounding a diamond of wildflowers hung from the door. Caffrey gasped.

She noticed Gina's hand rest cautiously under the flap of her purse as she rapped on the door in the sequence from the night before. Before she could finish, the door flew open, and a long arm reached out and yanked her inside. Caffrey froze, terrified, until she could hear Gina laughing merrily. She leaned forward to find Gina and Vince embracing. Caffrey let her shoulders drop and rolled her eyes.

Vince rounded the door, still holding onto Gina. "Come on in, girl!"

Caffrey stepped inside and noticed Mace seated in a cushioned armchair to the right, next to the fireplace. He was dressed in a red and blue plaid shirt, and blue jeans. His black eyes surveyed her every movement as though he possessed x-ray vision and could see her bones. She found herself unwilling to cross the room. Vince seemed to realize her dilemma. He reluctantly broke apart from Gina.

"Come in, don't be shy. Have a seat."

A rustic wooden door to the left of the fireplace opened and admitted a slim, bronze-skinned girl with a kind, intelligent face and childlike, almond eyes. Her mahogany hair hung almost to her waist, with several thin accent braids on each side highlighted with gold and red tones. At the sight of Gina, she brightened into a smile, which lit up her entire heart-shaped face.

Gina eagerly embraced her. "Sharia! How are you, girl?"

"I'm doin' fine," the girl replied in a sweet voice, tinged with regret.

"It's a bummer about the clinic, isn't it?" Gina read her tone correctly.

"Yeah. I've been there for almost two years, now. But, you know, I was ready for a change. Probably have to go out of state, though, since my face is known. Mace insists on a new name. Says I might have to go into one of the keeps."

"Wouldn't take a whole lot to find you," he barked from across the room.

The two women smirked at each other. "He's always right, you know," Gina teased.

"Whoa, don't give him *always.*" Sharia whirled and squinted wickedly at Mace. "He'll be outta control."

Mace smiled wide. Caffrey froze, shocked that he was capable of a genuine smile. She looked at Sharia and wondered if there was something between them.

Sharia frowned and crinkled her nose. "I hate fictitious names. The hard part is parents and friends and stuff. You either have to tell 'em or be evasive all the time. And then, they *really* start wondering what's going on in your life." She turned to acknowledge Caffrey. "So, you're the girl who's gotten things all fired up?"

"Sharia, this is Caffrey, though for code it will be Victoria," offered Gina.

"Nice to meet you." Caffrey added a timid smile and stepped forward to shake Sharia's hand. "I'm not so sure this is about *me.* I think I just ended up in the wrong place at the wrong time."

"Humph," came a low, male voice from across the room. Caffrey frowned in Mace's direction.

"Well, a lot's happened, kiddo." Vince addressed Caffrey. "There's a couple more people coming over, but...you want to see the cabin first?"

"Sure," Caffrey replied with relief. "I've been sitting for a long time."

Sharia remained in the living room with Mace, sharing flirtatious insults, while Vince and Gina showed off the various rooms and interrupted each other constantly. Caffrey enjoyed seeing a more animated side to them. The cozy living room contained several chairs and a sofa; it also had two cushioned window seats along the front wall. A large Native American designed rug lay in the center and modestly covered a rustic but well-preserved wooden floor.

Two doors on both sides of the fireplace led to a large sleeping room, arranged with six sets of bunk beds. Several had clothing and gear sitting on them. Caffrey spied a bulging black backpack and knew instantly it had to be Mace's. Additional roll-out beds were tucked away beneath each bunk so that eighteen people, though a little cramped, could be accommodated if the need arose. Caffrey envisioned the entire room full of people and smiled at the thought of the camaraderie and fun, thinking how her old friends would have enjoyed it.

A folding wall hung from the ceiling to the floor like a stiff, heavy curtain, "to give the girls and the guys privacy," Gina explained, though it was pushed back to allow space. The huge fireplace had a thick iron-mesh opening into the back, so that one fire could heat two rooms if a double-sided flew was opened.

The kitchen was a long, rectangular room opposite the living room, with a cooking area at one end and a long table surrounded by benches at the other. When Gina and Vince realized Caffrey was interested in the self-reliant preparations, they became even more enthused about showing her how they cooked, how the well water was piped, and how they worked the oil lamps.

"If a storm comes through and electricity goes out, we're just sittin' pretty, doin' our thing," stated Gina with pride. " 'Course, we *have* electricity, but try not to use it much, except for cooking."

"This is great," said Caffrey wistfully. "I took a disaster preparedness course with the Red Cross and was collecting safety supplies in my apartment before...." Caffrey's face fell at mention of items she no longer possessed.

Movement caught Caffrey's eye, and she realized Mace was leaning against the doorframe, arms folded, his head cocked to one side in silent observation. Surprised at his curiosity, she pretended to ignore him and threw Gina a look to continue with tidbits about the kitchen.

Suddenly, Mace stiffened and disappeared. Gina and Vince lurched to follow him. Caffrey realized she could hear a vehicle on the graveled road outside. *Ears like wolves*, she thought to herself.

Mace was plastered against the wall by the window, with one eye peering past the edge of the curtains. He did not appear overly concerned, but he watched with practiced caution. Gina, however, stood by the door with her eyes closed.

"It's Patrick," Mace and Gina confirmed at the same time. Vince threw his head back and laughed. Mace offered Gina a look of disgust. Gina opened her eyes to grin at him.

"I don't know what the heck you need me for," Mace said dejectedly.

"To keep us alive, dear," said Gina.

Mace snorted.

"Besides, ability isn't failsafe. I'm often wrong, you know."

"Remember that." Mace pointed a finger.

Rapping resounded on the door in the same sequence from the night before. Sharia threw it open and blurted, "Daniel Boone!"

"Get outta here," said a tall, dark-haired man with a chiding smile. He wore blue jeans and brown hiking boots. Caffrey stared at him, spellbound. Muscles showed through the ribbed black tank top underneath an unbuttoned, forest-green cotton shirt. His presence radiated masculinity, but of a time gone by, when men rode horses, carried rifles and canteens, and knew the land. His dark, wavy hair was long and partly pulled back in a ponytail, the remainder of which cascaded onto his shoulders in perfect round locks any woman would envy. Caffrey guessed him to be close to forty. Though his hair was not receded far, his face held many lines, and there was a slight puffiness under his eyes that probably never left.

Spotting Vince, a grin spread across the man's face. "Yo, dead man walking."

Vince returned the grin and clasped the man's hand. Everyone followed, clamoring to shake hands with the man and give hearty hugs. It felt like a family reunion to Caffrey. She straightened as the newcomer peered across the room at her. The man did not take his eyes from hers or even blink as they were introduced.

Instead of being alarmed, Caffrey found his open soul refreshing. It was as though he had seen much in his life and had no time for evasive games.

"So you're the *fire*, huh? Red hair and all?" He cast a high-browed look at Mace.

Gina giggled beside him.

Mace gestured with a cutting motion. "Don't even start with that. You don't even know if she meant me."

"Heck yeah, she did, and you know it," said Patrick, looking back at Caffrey.

Assuming he meant all the events that had taken place, Caffrey mumbled, "I guess I ended up in the middle of a...big thing."

"You might say that." Patrick nodded. "Worldwide."

Unable to think of a suitable reply, Caffrey gave a flat smile and averted her eyes.

"Well," said Vince, "have a seat, man. We're waiting on Ron and Barbara. They were coming for the conference anyway. Kevin's coming later, too. We decided to keep it small for now. Jimmy might be here in the morning, and Joe Meyers. Somebody at Jimmy's company's gotten suspicious, and he's worried about having to give up his job. I'm keeping my trusted units aware of my status but not my location. Some of our followers still need to think I'm dead for a while."

The statement sobered everyone as they gathered around the crackling fire.

"Conference?" Caffrey whispered to Gina.

"There's a quilting and craft conference up here this weekend, but it's a cover for a psychic conference, and us."

"Oh." Caffrey envisioned people sitting in a circle with eyes closed chanting, "Om."

"Why's Kevin coming?" Patrick blurted, not quite masking his disapproval.

Vince took a deep breath. "Well, he's been trying to get in touch with us. Says he's got something important. And he knows Telenex. He still keeps in contact with people there. According to other links, Kevin's Vhurruh is still 'asleep,' which means he's been poisoned and they've got him in stasis. Wish I could've gotten more people. But so many are at risk now, I want to keep them undercover. I've got a link coming tomorrow night—LaTanna. She was one of the early *Nekkai* links. Her father is also a U.S. senator. And…we needed a place to rest and regroup."

Caffrey turned to Vince. "What is *Nekkai?*" As Vince opened his mouth to speak, Caffrey added, "And don't tell me it's classified, or I swear I'm walking out of here."

"The hell you are," Mace blurted.

"Caffrey," Vince answered, "we told you some things would have to remain classified. But, *Nekkai* is not one of them. It is a movement on Hurratt to unify hives and share knowledge. It was started years ago by a queen who received a vision that joining together telepathically was the only way to defeat the Zgeyyans. From there, older queens worked together to draft agreements of cooperation to avoid wars and expand knowledge. Most of the Blue Vhurruh are loyal to *Nekkai*. Some of the Grays are not. Well, they may have been at one time, but a handful went rogue."

"I've read everything I could about the Vhurruh. Why did I never hear the term?"

"Because there was a coup, and the term was suppressed by the Gray *Tarreken*. They started limiting what humans were told."

"*Tarreken?*"

"Commanders."

"Oh."

Crackles from the fireplace filled the silence.

"Well," said Patrick in a teasing tone, "did we invite Flies With Raven?"

"*No.*" Mace offered Patrick a scathing glare. Everyone in the room snickered knowingly. Caffrey sighed with quiet irritation at being left the outsider.

"That woman's always after me." Mace rubbed his brow. "I got enough problems."

"Oh, Mace, you know she loooves you," mocked Gina. A caustic glower was Mace's response. The others chuckled all the more. Caffrey snuggled into one of the worn, cushioned chairs, and glanced at Vince, hoping to catch his eye and prompt him to explain. His blue eyes landed on her, then quickly danced away.

"Leah told me about the quilting and craft cover this time." Patrick looked amused.

"All the good psychics are disappearing," said Gina. "It's obvious what's going on. The Vhurruh are suppressing anyone with ability. A lot of psychics knew something was coming, knew it was extraterrestrial, even a few years ago."

Patrick nodded. "Yeah, I saw that news piece about a crackdown on psychic scammers."

"Unfortunately," said Gina, "there are plenty of *them*, too. It was Barbara's idea to hide the conference as a quilting seminar. People are really bringing quilts and stuff. Some are legit' so the staff won't know the difference."

Patrick shook his head. "You know, Leah's gotten pretty good."

"Really?" Gina brightened. "I didn't know she had developed. I mean, I always considered her intuitive, but...."

"Yeah. I guess I didn't believe it at first." Patrick looked guilty and scratched the back of his neck. "You know, her grandmother was Choctaw. My first wife was always thinking she had some 'gift,' but she was neurotic. So, I guess Leah was pretty hesitant to admit she could sense things. I began to notice that she always knew when someone was almost to the house. She'd be standin' there at the sink and say, 'Oh, they're almost here.' Seconds later they'd pull up at the house. I was lookin' for a book the other day. Couldn't find it anywhere. I walked in on her standin' in the den with her eyes closed and her hands up in front of her. Then she walked over to the sofa, reached under the corner, and pulled out that book."

"Wow, she's a finder!" exclaimed Gina.

"Well, I realized I'd been kinda hard on her, and now I've seen so many weird things, nothin' surprises me anymore."

"I'll go along with that," added Mace. "If you told me you saw a little green man hiding in the corner, I'd have to go look."

"Ain't it the dang truth," Patrick exclaimed.

"So, Patrick," Vince said, changing the subject, "how is the new place? Might need a new safe house."

Everyone listened as Patrick talked of his cabin-building efforts, an eco-friendly business venture shared with two cousins. She noticed him hesitate several times as he began sentences and wondered if he was being careful not to reveal details concerning the Underground. Perhaps Patrick's cabins were more than they seemed. Clearly, she was not "safe" enough to know. She thought about going outside to get away from the distrust.

Only twenty minutes later, Ron and Barbara Pratin arrived. Caffrey felt at ease with Ron the moment she shook his hand. She guessed him to be in his fifties; he was a bit stout, only a few inches taller than Caffrey, and had graying light brown hair and a kind, nonjudgmental face. He seemed amiable with everyone except Mace, who appeared to make him nervous.

Barbara was completely his opposite. She had coal black hair and dark chocolate eyes, a formidable stance, and a commanding tone of voice. Caffrey was certain if there were past lives, this woman had been a ship's captain in one of them. Heavier and taller than her husband, Barbara had a way of standing to her full height with both feet firmly planted, tilting her chin up and looking down as if to say, "Don't lie to me. I'll know it immediately." Caffrey flinched when Barbara shook her hand as hard as a man and peered down in a scrutinizing, though not unfriendly way.

"So...this is the girl who wrote, *Get my body to the Underground.*"

Caffrey shivered as her brain recalled that fateful moment in the alley. She half-frowned and looked at the carpet. Barbara continued to hold her hand and wait for a reply. Caffrey cleared her throat. "Heard about that, huh?"

"Oh, honey," said Barbara in a matronly way, "that's the best story I've heard in some time. It was a very brave thing to do." She peered into Caffrey's eyes as though seeing right through her.

Caffrey tugged to retrieve her hand, but to no avail.

"I have a feeling...." Barbara's focused beyond Caffrey's head. "That we're going to hear a lot more from you."

Caffrey stared at her, wide-eyed.

"Oh, yes," Barbara continued. "Big things are going to happen. You're hot, honey."

"What do you see?" Gina stepped closer.

The woman abruptly let go of Caffrey's hand and turned to Gina. "Her intentions are pure. She's gonna be involved big-time. But, opposing forces are definitely gathering. She is surrounded by so many hidden agendas, like a giant tug of war, like spokes on a wheel. She'll have to fight all of them. Something tells me we will, too. I gotta see this girl's chart."

"That's kind of what I felt, but I'm just never sure." Gina bit her lip.

"You've got to quit doubting yourself." Barbara wagged a finger.

"Please," whined Mace, "I can't keep her safe *now.*" Everyone in the room laughed.

Vince placed both hands on Caffrey's shoulders, which startled her since she hadn't seen him move. "Caffrey, we need to meet—unfortunately, without you present. I hope you don't mind. And I hope you understand." Caffrey's smile dropped as he spoke. "Would you mind walking with Patrick for a while outside? I'd certainly appreciate it. Patrick, I'll clue you in later, if that's all right."

Patrick nodded.

Tendrils of fear crept around Caffrey's heart. What decisions might transpire in her absence? Would they decide she was too much of a risk to their operation and...do something with her? Allow Mace to shoot her and dump her somewhere? No, she forced sensibility into her brain. They wouldn't get rid of her as long as she held information they might need.

She managed to suppress the urge to stomp out the door and keep on walking, though she felt certain if she did, Mace would find her with little effort, and would not be smiling when he did. With a smirk to herself, she thought it would certainly be worth her while to force him to do it.

Patrick smiled. "Come on, girl, let me show you this mountain. It's a nice, sunny mornin'."

"You got a piece on you?" asked Mace.

"No," Patrick replied. "The only 'piece' I own is three feet long and has to be muzzle-loaded. Got my bow in the trunk, though. Barb? Gina? The mountain safe?"

Barbara squinted toward the window. Gina closed her eyes. Caffrey watched them in wonder, amazed that the practice could be so commonplace among them. She felt privileged in an odd way to experience such people, regardless of what else happened.

"Yes, for now." Gina wore a worried frown. "But...something...."

"Whoo, what energy!" said Barbara. "It's mostly around *her*." She shook her head. "Definitely Vhurruh energy, my guess. I'd swear she has a link."

"I knew it," blurted Mace.

"Yes," Gina agreed, "but I can't figure it all out. He feels like *Nekkai*, but no attempt to contact us, or any of our known links. And he hides from her."

Anger and fear danced inside Caffrey's chest. Was the strange entity that touched her mind something more etheric than an alien? An angel? A demon?

Suddenly, Barbara surveyed the room. "The future energy's heavy on this mountain."

"What does *that* mean?" Vince was skeptical.

"Don't know," said Barbara. "Just...heavy. Stormy. Something's coming."

"Do we need to leave?"

"Mmm, not right now."

Vince heaved a sigh. "That was reassuring, Barb. Okay, Patrick? Caff? If you would, please?"

Caffrey stepped outside. The clean, heady smells of the forest were like a drink of purest water to her senses. She rubbed her arms against the slight chill in the air, even though the sun stretched long, warm rays through the canopy of leaves and branches. Patrick pointed out the beautiful views and interesting facts about the mountaintop and valley below, but mostly he talked with pleasure of his home and business in Tennessee, which eased her nerves.

"I'd love to have you come visit sometime. My wife would love the company."

"Wow, I'd love to." Caffrey was surprised by the invitation. "If I can ever get away from *here*, of course, and...what's happening. I love mountains."

"Well, we've definitely got those! 'Specially on the eastern side."

"I'm surprised you think me *safe*," Caffrey added with sarcasm.

"I sort of have my own way of assessing people. You're honest. Your face says what you see is what you get. That's a pretty rare thing."

Caffrey smiled, thinking he was exactly the same way. "Thanks."

"You're welcome."

After a few minutes they turned back toward the cabin in silence. A sweet-scented breeze rustled through the new leaves and blossoms. Birds chirped fiercely in mating and nesting fever, fussing at them as they passed.

"You know," said Caffrey, "everybody in this group seems to have some kind of ability. Barbara and Gina are *really* psychic, aren't they?"

"Well," said Patrick after a moment's thought, "I suppose that's true of many of us in a way. Mostly because we've experienced something rare, or...paranormal I guess you could say. Which is kind of what brought all of us together, before the Zgeyyans and the Vhurruh came. Ya know, even though people *know* there are aliens, officially now, it doesn't mean they're ready to deal with other... *things* out there. Usually, anyone who has alien contact begins to have psychic abilities. We all have it, they say. It's just a matter of triggering it. But, personally, I think telepathic contact with aliens, like, makes your mind wake up and use other abilities. My wife says psychics can be fooled easily if they 'don't have it turned on.'"

Caffrey smiled. Patrick continued, "A lot of people coming to this conference are people who were just ordinary 'ol people, until contact. Not the official 'Contact,' ya know, but personal contact. The kind the government still doesn't want you and me to believe in. Your life's changed forever, I can tell you that."

Caffrey wondered at his own personal story, and hoped he would offer more of it. But, with knitted brows, he seemed to withdraw from the subject.

As they approached the cabin, Caffrey stared its now unfriendly appearance. Patrick turned back when he realized she wasn't moving.

"Sure is a nice place, isn't it?"

"It *was*." She sighed.

"Oh, don't worry about it."

"I'm just wondering what they're deciding, in there. I mean...suddenly, I don't feel safe."

"Hey, they're trying to decide what's best for the Underground. For the planet, really. I mean, they can't let you know everything until they know what's going on with you. Wouldn't *you* think them pretty stupid if they did?" He rested his hands on his hips and watched her in silence for a moment. "Then again, you're one of the few people that know Vince is alive. That's something to protect."

Caffrey frowned and chose not to reply.

Patrick chivalrously offered an arm, then grinned.

ll

THE GRASS IS ALWAYS GREENER

Caffrey took Patrick's arm and they reentered the cabin together. Several voices stopped at once, all with an air of concern and heated debate.

Vince stood. "Have a seat."

"I'll stand, thanks." Caffrey folded her arms and avoided his scrutiny by examining the others. Several faces looked surprised; others looked guilty. Patrick stepped over to the nearest chair and leaned against it as if by not sitting, he was supporting her.

"As you wish." Vince took a deep breath. "We've had a lot to discuss, Caffrey. Especially since for the moment we're not running. But, we've got to find a way to protect you—and ourselves—until we can find out what you know, not to mention the items you carried. I want to send you to a site we call 'Remote.' It's well protected. There are a lot of people there, and supplies. We've got radar shielding and technology to make it difficult to find.

"Mace will take you there tomorrow. We have a lot of important things to do, and we—Gina and I, and these others—we need to be other places to do them. So, we *can't* be there with you. I know you've been through a lot. My main goal is to keep you safe, and the *rest* of my people safe. I think you can be a real asset to us, but we have to be certain about the remainder of the programming. That's where we stand right now." He paused to let his statements sink in. "Do you understand? Will you help us?"

Caffrey fought the indignation that had swelled within her the whole time he spoke and silently cursed him for being so persuasive. The impulse to say yes was overwhelming, but Caffrey fought it, even pressing her lips together. She had to gain control of that weird compulsion.

Vince waited.

Caffrey exhaled and kept her focus on the rug. "I understand why you're deciding what you're deciding, but I'm not going there."

Nervous silence hung in the room. She raised her chin and noticed everyone glancing from her to Vince, waiting for a response.

"Why not?"

"Because I'm getting further and further away from everything I know." What she could not explain was that she was *supposed* to be with them, with *him*, that to go anywhere else would simply be the wrong direction. "I don't want to go off to some...*Remote* place where I don't know anybody. I've done everything you asked. I believe in what you're trying to do. I really do. But, I mean, how long is this supposed to go on? If I'm going to be in this, I want to be worth something. I want to be part of something, to contribute. I'm not doing anything but being shipped all over the place, like some...secret document that nobody can read but they don't want the enemy to get it."

"Caffrey." Vince spoke with an edge. "I *am* sorry about that. But, we have to be very careful now. A Vhurruh, as far as we know, has placed something inside your head, and we...*I*...can't take any chances on what that something is, or who *he* is."

"Then, I'll find someone who can." Caffrey felt her chin trembling. She jerked a finger toward her head. "There is someone, somewhere, who knows how to help with this...*if* it exists—and I'm not so sure it *does*—but I'll find them. I mean, people are *paid* to do this, y'know? I've seen a therapist before. When my fiancé disappeared. I'll go to her."

"Caffrey, we've tried that before." Concern was etched across Gina's face. "You'll just experience pain, or whatever suggestion the Vhurruh gave you to protect the program."

Caffrey swallowed hard. "Well...so what? It's worth a try, isn't it? We haven't even—*you* haven't even tried yet. I mean, what if I want more than anything else to...to pull this information, or whatever, out of my head? Doesn't...wouldn't that determination *mean* something? I'm not just giving in to this." She shook her head. *Or all of you*, she thought.

"I sympathize with you." Gina's voice was gentle. "And, as a rule, *this* group doesn't normally give in to anything, either. I guess it's worth a try." Gina glanced around for possible objections.

"Wait a minute." Mace stood and waved a hand. "I don't want her screwed up."

Everyone stared at him, including Caffrey.

"Mace," said Gina, puzzled. "I don't think that's going to happen here. We've got experienced people. And besides, this isn't a *full* programming. It was only a few minutes."

Mace shook his head and pointed at Gina. "*You* don't know that. How *full* does programming have to be? We don't even know who did it."

Gina eyed him for a moment, considering his objections.

Patrick spoke in a slow, confident, southern drawl. "Well, I think it should be Caffrey's decision. It's *her* head."

Vince exhaled slowly, then challenged the group with his eyes. "It's been done before, people, and not with good results. Except two cases I know of."

No one else spoke. Concern and dissension were palpable in the room.

Vince's face looked heavy with the weight of the decision. "Well, she's no good to us without the trigger, realistically. Perhaps she has the right to *try*." He rubbed the back of his neck as though questioning his own decision.

"No." Mace insisted, with a firm step toward him. "You're gonna fry her brain. You *know* that."

"All right, *what* do you mean?" Caffrey demanded.

Mace seemed unwilling to answer her directly, but suddenly changed his mind. "There've been a few people that aren't exactly in the picture anymore, because someone attempted to override their programming."

Gina raised a hand as if to stop his disclosure. "Let *me* explain this. Caffrey, when programming was done in the past—human, I mean—it was done using hypnotizing, shock treatments, drugs, pain, whatever. But, if a person's will was strong enough to *want* to get past it, to get at the...suppressed memories, or get to the programs—assuming they even *knew* they were there—then a qualified person could regress them and give the suggestion that the pain, or whatever the block was, could no longer work. Tell them to rise above it. See the events from up high where the emotion can't touch them. But, Vhurruh programming *deeply affects* the psyche, making their control so connected that people can believe they are being destroyed, betrayed, even become psychotic at the effort to 'undo' it. And...they become strangely devoted to the Vhurruh that programmed them."

Vince turned to Caffrey with sad eyes. "I can assure you that's true."

"Plus," Gina added, "SAAFs appear out of nowhere whenever someone's programming is tampered with. The Vhurruh, if he's a rogue, taps into the link, gets a sense of the location, and then you have to run."

Barbara and Vince nodded in agreement.

"And, there's another danger," said Gina with a nervous swallow.

"What else?" asked Caffrey, disgusted.

"Opening your closets."

"Excuse me?"

"When people are regressed, it often triggers buried memories from childhood. Memories of trauma, and...memories of sexual or emotional abuse."

"Well, I don't have any of that."

"Caffrey, millions of people are walking around oblivious to traumatic memories locked away in closets of their brain where they are kept safe. The human brain does amazing things so we can function. If we trigger your program, any suppressed memories you have could come bursting out when you least expect it, in a flashback."

"And, it ain't pretty," said Barbara with a pained expression. "A flashback will bring you to your knees."

Caffrey tried to keep her breathing steady, wondering what horrors Barbara had experienced. "Well, that's great. So, this leaves me nowhere."

Vince pursed his lips in thought. "I wouldn't exactly say nowhere. Your determination will make a difference. You're not an *over*, certainly, even though you may have a link."

"Over?"

He brushed a hand in the air. "Someone who's been corrupted. Programmed to the point that the will's been completely submerged, or 'taken over.' They may not remember their true selves, even with help. It's our term."

"Oh. Well, thanks that I'm not in *that* category."

Vince nodded in acknowledgement. "No, not in this case. And I intend to make sure it doesn't *become* the case. As far as we can judge, your contact was short. SAAFs haven't been able to find you, obviously, and my plan is to place you at Remote, possibly at Tower first, just to make sure you're not followed. I need you where they can't get you—and where they can't get *us*. That's why I want you to go. You're a part of us now."

Caffrey shuffled her feet and stared at the floor. "I...I don't know...." She exhaled as anger billowed inside her like a churning storm. "Vince, if I were *really* a part of you, I wouldn't have been on the other side of that door."

Vince's face darkened in frustration. "Caffrey, we risk our lives every day for the *survival* of our world. Being careful is more than just a priority. It's *us!* I will *not* jeopardize the entire Underground for one person."

Caffrey felt her face redden. Tears stung her eyes. "So, what help can I be to you there? It would be a prison to me. I wanted to be here, with you. Make a difference somehow. I'm damaged goods now—or, *dangerous* goods." She looked at Mace to emphasize the point. His eyes met hers with a softer quality, but did not flinch.

"I...I need to think about this," she continued. "I am *not* going to be told what to do. I'm tired of running, and...." Her throat tightened with emotion. She swallowed hard to mask it, knowing somehow that everyone here *would* tell her what to do. "I need to find my own way. I can't go back to where I came from. I can't be a part of you guys." She flapped her hands at her sides, at a loss for words.

There was silence as positions shifted. Vince took a deep breath and smiled ruefully. "I wouldn't be too quick to join us. The grass is always greener on the other side of the mountain."

Caffrey stiffened and felt nauseated. A great weight gathered in her throat. The room blurred, and her mouth moved of its own power, in an odd accent. *"But once on the otherr side, you still have annotherr side to drrream about."*

All color drained from Vince's face. His jaw fell slack. Caffrey saw this, his vivid blue eyes, and waited, not entirely sure why. Chiffon images of a tall obese man floated like a ghost before her, glassy black eyes with yellow rings locked on hers. Pressure filled her head. And there he was, a presence like etheric water spilling into her skull—into her soul.

In a graveled, almost imperceptible whisper, Vince spoke as he took several steps toward her. "So, if you stayed on this side and made it better...."

"You would always beee on the greennnest side," Caffrey completed, vaguely aware of everyone getting to their feet. The room began to spin, and she bent over. "Oh, I'm gonna be sick."

"No...here!" Vince's arms were around her. She felt another firm grip on an arm, and wasn't sure if it was Mace or Patrick. "Let's get her into a chair," commanded Vince.

"No, take her to the bathroom," said someone else.

"No, here!" Patrick insisted, pulling over the high-backed chair.

"I got a bucket," offered Sharia.

Caffrey realized as she opened her eyes that Sharia was holding an old, stained trashcan. She felt more squeamish after looking at it and turned away.

Questions flew back and forth, but Caffrey ignored them.

"Oh, God...." she whimpered a formless prayer. Memories and visions flooded through her and she had no ability to stop them. Thoughts weaving from horrible to exhilarating, her mind expanded so that the room, the forest, the sky, and the universe became part of one instantaneous reality in which there were no borders. Her head felt hollow, weightless, indistinct. She realized she was panting. Her face was wet. Tears were dripping into the trashcan.

Movement buzzed around her. Everyone gave orders to each other and tried to question her. But, she could only cover her face with her hands and swallow back threatening nausea. She did not want to vomit in front of these people. She breathed with her mouth partly open. Tears continued to fall through her fingers, from where she did not know.

"Caffrey," commanded Gina. "Here's a cold towel. Come on. Come on."

Caffrey reluctantly removed a hand from her face as Gina pushed the chilled wet cloth determinedly against Caffrey's cheek. It felt wonderful.

With shaky hands Caffrey wiped the tears away and worked her facial muscles hard to gain control of her emotions. Gina kept telling her to take slow, deep breaths. She did so, holding the wet kitchen towel against her face to hide from the many intense eyes focused on her. The Vhurruh's mind withdrew suddenly, satisfied that she was safe, leaving a lonely void. She bent over the trashcan. She waited, but the wave of nausea passed.

"Okay, okay, everything's fine," Gina soothed, lightly patting Caffrey's arm. Barbara murmured something calming, her voice soft.

Sharia was mumbling in an excited whisper, "Oh my god, oh my god, oh my god," until Barbara shushed her.

Voices blurted questions, but Caffrey held up a hand to silence them. Words, pictures, and concepts were flashing by at a frightening speed. She wanted to halt the sickening visions, the onslaught of so much information. Nausea rose every time she tried to block the images. There was no fighting it. Caffrey wiped her face again. She straightened up, but placed a hand to her stomach to quell the roiling.

"She's been with *Herrengae*," Vince was whispering, awestruck. "She's been *with* him. It was his favorite human saying."

Peripherally, Caffrey realized he had pulled away and was doing some sort of dance, but she did not dare watch his movements.

"Whoa," Patrick exclaimed.

"Was it exact?" Mace's tone was cautious.

"Yes! Well, sometimes we changed a couple words, but basically that was it. We thought it to each other most of the time, of course. But, originally it was spoken. Which is odd because Caffrey just repeated it like *Herrengae* would have tried to speak English."

"Oh, wow." Sharia could barely contain her excitement. "Then he must be okay."

"*Nobody else* knew about it." Vince heaved excited breaths. "I think."

"Caffrey, take a sip of this." Gina pressed a chilled can of ginger ale into Caffrey's hand.

"I told you we hadn't heard the last out of this girl." Barbara sounded smug. "Not by a long shot."

Caffrey sipped the bubbling soda. Her chest quivered as the frosty liquid traveled down into her body, bringing back the unpleasant memory of the disc sliding painfully down her throat. Her hand began to shake, and she lowered the can to her thigh and closed her eyes. Broad hands spread across her knees, and she popped her eyes open, surprised to see Mace kneeling there.

Black and fierce, his eyes were focused on her every facial movement. He squeezed her knees gently in reassurance, but Caffrey sensed it was also a command.

"Okay, Princess, take it slow and easy. Just tell us what you know."

Caffrey bristled at the use of his nickname for her. And, who was he to speak with encouragement, or dare to touch her after scaring her every time she turned around?

A strange hope glistened in his eyes, which distracted her anger. Without his gruff, menacing demeanor, there was no way to keep him safely tucked away on her list of most hated people...though she was certain it would not take much effort to reaffirm his place on top of that list.

A tighter squeeze on her knees made her flinch. She took a deep breath. "The...big man told me something. He thanked me for helping. He...he was real sweet." She swallowed hard. "The earrings are to be placed front to front, interlocking opposing facets in the crystals. Held in a narrow beam of sunlight, they display an image. A message. I'm not sure what it is. *Unfiltered sunlight will activate. Himenta will not produce the image.* I mean—it won't work with a...a...."

"Laser," Vince answered.

Caffrey nodded and continued, trying to translate thoughts into words. *"If rogue Tarreken obtain crystals and trigger display, image will fracture and self-distort. Parameters must be met. Darkness. Single beam of Earth's sunlight filtered through the atmosphere. Cloudless. No interference. Within circle of khram."* Caffrey's arms shook. She paused to take another sip of ginger ale.

"You mean, aim sunlight inside the rings of metal onto the crystals?" Vince knelt on one knee beside Mace. The others shushed him.

"Yes." She swallowed, hesitant to continue.

Mace cursed in a low voice, though with grudging respect. Caffrey decided to focus on Vince instead of the face before her.

She cleared her throat and tried to translate the message running through her brain. "*The seeker gathered what was needed. The disc contains reports. Must be transferred. Rogue contamination is expanding. Tarreken are compromised. Must reintegrate. Hahmurent working to brood a queen-mother. Surranenn being forced to comply. M'hye's are attacked. They die to keep the secret.*"

"Caffrey," Vince interjected when she paused. "*Hahmurent* means queenless drones. Are you telling me the drones are without a queen?"

Searching to understand the meaning behind the alien words, she nodded. "Some. A Gray queen died. Um...*Mrennah?* The new Captain, *Vrenenjurr,* has prevailed somehow over links belonging to the other two queens. I hear their names. *Ghissella* and *Vinrrahi.*"

"Is somebody getting this down?"

Barbara and Sharia scrambled for paper and pen. Gina tapped the keyboard of her phone.

"Caffrey, repeat that," demanded Vince.

"All right." Suddenly, she wasn't sure what to repeat. "You want the message?"

"I want everything."

Caffrey repeated the phrases, then added. "I'm...seeing pictures, visions, to explain some of it."

"Okay," Vince prompted. "Describe them."

Caffrey rubbed her temples. "*Tarreken are compromised. Vrenenjurr* has used his psychic abilities to overpower the other leaders."

Vince nodded. "We know about that. Go on."

"The Gray queen, *Mrennah,* died a couple weeks ago. No one controls her drones now."

"So that's why," Vince whispered, nodding.

"It looks like she was sick for...a while," Caffrey continued. "So, this *Vrenenjurr* was free to do what he wanted. Anybody who resisted him has been put in these big black boxes with glass on the front...some kind of stasis thing. *M'hye's are attacked.*" She scrunched her face. "He uses a machine—*teknaht*—and puts his hands on their heads, and tries to attack everybody's link to their queen. They scream."

"Good Lord," Gina whispered, horrified.

"And...after he gained control of the Grays on the first ship, he did the same with the Blues on the second mother ship. Most were linked to the Blue queen, *Vinrrahi.*" Caffrey watched the visions in disgust. "It was a huge power struggle. Like a war. It's still going on. He killed the *Mazak.* Um... *Rhemerett.*"

"The Captain. On the Blue ship," said Vince.

"It's like... everybody's just standing there... watching." Caffrey viewed the surreal scene, bewildered and horrified. "I think guards fought each other. The others seem to be accepting that the drones and guards are allowed to fight. And nobody's supposed to get in the way. Weird. They obey whoever wins."

"It's their way," said Vince with a tight voice.

"Yes...I think *Rhemerett's* guards gave in once he was down."

"Guards usually fight intruders and protect the queen. There's neither there."

With a furrowed brow, Caffrey puzzled over the feelings projected into the image. "But it wasn't supposed to be this way."

"Yes," Vince agreed. "The three queens were supposed to maintain control over their drones and the mission. With *Vrenenjurr* loose, everything changed."

"Yes, and he's, like, Captain of both ships now, controlling everybody. Although, I'm getting a sense of secrets within secrets, like secret religious societies with sub-links or something that help guide and protect the Blues, and some Grays, and lots of other confusing things. The word *Nemeygenyah* comes to mind."

Vince nodded vigorously. "*Herrengae* was part of that."

Caffrey took a measured, steady breath. "*Hahmurent working to brood a queen-mother.* I'm seeing that the workers, *surranenn*, know a secret formula...um, special glands and plants used to turn an egg into a queen."

"Yes."

"*Vrenenjurr* is trying to force the workers to turn one of their own, an adult, so it will be able to produce eggs."

Gina gasped. "Seriously?"

Caffrey nodded, unfocused. "If *Vrenenjurr* cannot accomplish this, his plan is to use the *lifting* technology in the two mother ships to go back to Hurratt and steal a queen from a remote location."

"Whoa!" Vince exclaimed, nearly falling backward. "That is huge."

Patrick looked dumbfounded. "Are they nuts? That would cause a civil war, right? Their whole planet would be involved."

Caffrey continued deciphering the images. The effort made her motion-sick. "The others know the hives will come after him. They all will be considered enemies, traitors. Hurratt only has one more working mother ship, and it wasn't quite ready for space flight. So, *Vrenenjurr* holds all the power. They sent all the telepathically strongest on this mission, to chase down the Zgeyyans."

"I wonder why the other links we know haven't heard this thing about a new queen?" asked Barbara.

Caffrey shook her head. "This feels recent. Whether *Vrenenjurr* can create a queen or he steals a queen, he wants a colony—here. On Earth."

"There you go," said Mace. "I knew that was coming."

"And I got a flicker of something." Caffrey mulled over the sensation. "There's some kind of rule they fear. Once a cave is occupied, the reigning hive is not deposed if it has a queen and she has mated. It's like a new thing, not an old rule. If they establish a hive on Earth, the others won't remove him."

"Are you freakin' kidding me?" Mace exclaimed.

Patrick made an exasperated sound. "That's like saying, 'if a criminal steals your daughter, but he manages to get her into a new house, well, sorry, he gets to keep her.'"

"Wow, that's pretty ridiculous," said Ron. "I don't care if they *are* aliens and have their own society."

Vince spoke to the others. "Some of this is what *Herrengae* suspected, before I lost contact with him."

Mace's hands gripped Caffrey's knees again. "What about the liftings? Who's been taking the people?"

Caffrey took a deep breath and concentrated, though the answer was not clear. Instead, a vision of a strange planet came into view. *"New planet is successfully contained. Human population con‐taminated with indigenous species. Some observed to assess dangers, possibly being harvested."*

"*What?*" Vince asked in disbelief. "What do you mean, harvested?"

Caffrey covered her face with her hands. "Oh, I can't look at this."

"Princess, we need this." Mace's tone bordered on desperation. "I don't care if it's ugly."

Gina shushed him and rubbed Caffrey's shoulder. "It's okay. It's okay. Just take your time. Remember, he wanted to pass on this information. Take a drink, and try to tell us."

Caffrey obeyed and sipped the ginger ale noisily. Then she purposefully shifted position, dislodging Mace's hands. Gina was right. She had to find the strength to verbalize the horrific pictures in her mind, or the loss of her normal life was for nothing.

"Some of the humans escaped the buildings the *Zgeyyans's* built, and are now contaminated. *Vrenenjurr* kept some humans pure to be…harvested for food." She grimaced. "He has no proof, but he was told this."

Low curses and exclamations resounded around her. Ron made the sign of a cross on his chest and mumbled something that sounded Latin. Sharia seemed to be frozen except for swallowing hard to hold back tears. Several questions flew at Caffrey from the group, though it was Mace's black eyes growing menacingly darker and his jaw grinding that held her attention.

Caffrey watched righteous anger possess him, not knowing why, but she was fascinated with the scared and excited way it made her feel. She shifted her gaze, straight ahead at no one in particular, anywhere but at him, surprised that she could think of anything else but the secret message she had carried for days unaware.

"*A tone sequence....*" she continued with slow, steady breaths. "*Opens the disc.* I hear it. Except I...I'm not supposed to remember what's in it yet. *Only when it opens.*"

"Oh, boy." Barbara sounded concerned.

Mace cursed outright.

"I don't like the sound of that," Vince murmured. Ron crossed himself again, and stepped part way behind Vince.

"*August 24th they will arrive. Searching for pure hearts, clear minds.*"

Caffrey sensed that the statement was more complex than it sounded, but when she pushed her mind to understand, she felt a warning to leave it alone. Clarity would come later.

"Are you talking about the *Blues?*" Gina's face was white with excitement. "Who is coming? The Blues, looking for pure hearts?"

"No, no." Caffrey shook her head. "*Varraay and Wennatt have agreed.* I mean, the Blue and Gray hives are united on Hurratt. Other races are still joining *Nekkai*. Oh! That's what *Nekkai* is." She smiled at the vision of Vhurruh in brilliant mantle colors, stripes and spots—greens, blues, grays, browns and golds—coming toward each other on a vast round plateau. Their many eye antennae moved like excited reeds in the wind.

The vision shifted to a large, shallow pool of water. She dropped the smile. "*The pale one has been born.* It's some creature there. Ew. Looks like an octopus. It holds some religious significance. I think they're normally a reddish color. Um, the others don't want...they don't want combat with them—the Gray drones here that went rogue. They want them to...reintegrate." She paused, open-mouthed. "They're really incredible. Such caring...and consideration." Reluctantly, she glanced at the widened eyes around her. "I think that's kind of it."

"Are you sure?" Barbara and Vince chimed.

"Yes, I think so. Except for all these blurred images. And then, feelings...thoughts of his. I'm still getting stuff." She rubbed her head.

"And what does he feel?" Gina prompted.

"Well, it's...he's upset about what's happened. This was supposed a mission of honor, and everything's gone crazy. *Nekkai* is conflicted. They want to undo the damage but are limited by agreements. Like, hive treaties of non-interference."

"*Non-interference?*" Mace glared at her in disbelief. "Oh, that's just great!"

Caffrey glowered at him, caught between the aura of the Vhurruh's thought patterns and memories, and his sharp words bringing her back to humanity. "Look, he volunteered to help. He is really sorry about what happened. He's risking a lot."

"Yeah, well, *he's* all heart, isn't he?" Mace's eyes narrowed.

"Hey, *you* weren't there!" Caffrey fumed. How dare he make light of the incredible being she had been privileged to experience. Suddenly, Caffrey realized that she could read all of Mace's emotions with little effort. She focused on him in fascination. Fierce emotions flashed through him so fast she could barely keep up with them—suspicion of the message, hope for the truth of it, concern for the group, excitement at the experience, frustration that it was beyond his control, and deep revulsion and anger at the possible danger to a female, someone with ebony hair and cocoa-brown eyes....

"Oh, and I suppose you know exactly where *you were?*"

Caffrey saw clearly how he wanted to goad her into searching every aspect of the message, every minute detail of the encounter, so that there would be no question of the truth, no assumptions read into it. Nothing left concealed. His carefully placed words were *meant* to anger her. She decided not to disappoint him.

"Of course I do!" She jumped to her feet. "I was in my office. I know *exactly* what happened. *I remember!*"

A sputter of curses startled her, and everyone else, as Mace was on his feet, his fists clenched. "What a bunch of...! You know what you were *told* to know! If even *half* of that's true, they're idiots. You don't convince the enemy of a *better way* when he's having you for dinner—you blow his twisted brains out!" He whirled in frustration. Bodies moved back as one to avoid his flailing limbs. Free of them, he continued cursing in strings of four letter words, the ferocity of which raised Caffrey's eyebrows.

"*Mace!*" Vince threw out an arm as though to will him to calm down. "You don't know if she was one of them. She could still be alive. Think it through. I know some of what Caffrey's saying. Vhurruh are capable of great feeling—*and* sense of purpose. They worked so hard to civilize their planet and unite the hives. *Nekkai* is looking at the bigger picture. I can believe they want a reunion instead of war."

Mace glared fiercely at Vince and pressed both fists against his hips. "A reunion? A *reunion,* when we're being eaten alive? I don't think so." His jaw ground in a visible effort to control his temper.

"Let's also think about the ramifications of buying into this. This could be a *really* good trap."

"Okay, okay, I know what you're saying." Vince pressed the air with his palms. "I see that. But the rogues that took over here—the Grays—are desperate and fractured without their queen. They're obsessed with power right now. If they have to, they'll threaten *our* planet, and us, to hold onto that power."

Caffrey stood, energized. "Don't you see?" she implored, more to the others than Mace. "They care about us, but they care about the rogue Grays. They don't want to just kill them, they want to do this the *right* way."

Mace took two strides toward her, his eyes full of disdain. "Excuse me? The *right* way? The right way would be to get them *off* my planet!"

"But they did good things here!" Caffrey argued. "They fought the Zgeyyans, helped with peace treaties, got laws passes we would have *never* accomplished, and shared technology to defend ourselves...."

"Yeah, it looks that way, doesn't it? Do you know who mans the space station and the new moon station, sweetie?"

"Mace," cautioned Vince, leaning toward him. Vince's concern for her, worry over Mace's actions, respect for his tactics, and disapproval of his assault on her, hit Caffrey all at once. Did people actually feel all this at the same time? What an exhausting jumble of energy.

Caffrey took a step back, almost falling into her chair at the barrage of emotions from Vince and Mace. The information she was now privy to was confusing, multi-layered. Mace was fearful of her accepting Vhurruh propaganda without question, but more afraid that she was being controlled by a Vhurruh.

Caffrey pressed a hand to her head to stifle the onslaught. "Well, astronauts from different countries...and...and the Vhurruh have a couple scout ships docked there." She was certain whatever answer she gave him was going to be the wrong one.

"No." he countered. "A cruiser from the Gray mother ship is docked there, and all of the astronauts have been allowed on it for special *visits* by the drone Captain, *Vrenenjurr*. All programmed. Do you know who holds the command in every branch of our military now?"

She crossed her arms and shifted her stance. "Well, no...."

"*Only* a superior officer who's been up to a mother ship, or to the new moon station, or the space station, or to a Vhurruh embassy. Are you putting this together?" His patronization flickered to regret as he looked into her eyes. She realized he deeply regretted having to berate her, though at the same he was determined to do so for her own good. "I'd like to believe in everything you were told, Princess, but I'm afraid it's bull they've fed you. To set us up."

"*Mace*," Vince implored, "we have to consider *everything* they told her. There's a message in this."

Mace whirled on Vince. "There's an *agenda* in this. The perfect trap. Nice Vhurruh to the rescue. Come to help the Underground free the world. Give us an *exact* date. Except that we know Vhurruh are territorial, run by queens and drones that don't like to share. They're just smarter about it than we are. They don't have to bomb anything. They won't have to fire a single shot." He glanced back at Caffrey, besieged by intense anger and heart-wrenching fear for her, for the dark-haired girl, and for his comrades.

Caffrey swallowed. She had assumed he challenged Vince for reasons of mere posturing, but she now felt the tremendous respect and love he held for Vince, and his regret at angering him further. She also sensed devotion so strong that he would give his life for Vince. It was too much information. Caffrey's brain began to throb.

Barbara sighed heavily and tilted back her head. "Let's take it down a couple notches, shall we?" Caffrey felt Barbara's irritation at Mace's outburst and lack of control. Yet, Barbara admired and envied his bravery and physical prowess, even his authority in the Underground. Above that, she also felt genuine concern for his welfare and belief in his abilities and his success. She loved him like a brother. "Mace, buddy, you need some air."

"I don't need any freakin' air."

"Yes," said Ron, backing her up with a nod of his head, though he swallowed nervously. "Yes, you do."

"Good idea. Come on," ordered Vince, but still with a comrade's respect. Mace made no effort to comply. The two of them eyed each other. Everyone watched the altercation with anxiety, not wishing the two to challenge each other. Though, strangely enough, Caffrey noted it was also with deep sympathy. They were all concerned about Mace. They knew something.

Caffrey glanced at Sharia and felt her connection to him as a comrade and brother, something about their blood....

Caffrey reached with her mind to understand more, then actually *felt* Sharia and Mace's blood connection—*Cherokee*. The strange ethereal sensation extended, and Caffrey realized she could feel Sharia's blood connection to Asian and African ancestry as well. Caffrey was stunned by the intuition and wondered how such a thing was possible, why it was happening.

Mace caught her attention as he ran fingers through his dark, thick hair, obsessed with thoughts of the black-haired female. Caffrey pushed with her newfound abilities.

Sister. The sensation came into focus. Caffrey marveled at the subtle connection, how it could be read like a language of knowing, *hearing* without words. He had a sister. She had been taken.

Vince spoke, his voice firm but calm. "Mace, I don't need you out of control here. We need to go over this information and work with it."

Mace glared at Vince, then at Caffrey as though she were the devil in disguise. Instantly, Caffrey felt guilty, but she corrected herself, letting her temper rise. She was not to blame. He was responsible for his own feelings.

Patrick moved casually in front of Mace with an easy swagger. "Come on, man. We'll come back to this in a minute. We'll sort it out and pick it apart to your heart's content." He laid a hand on Mace's shoulder.

Without looking back, his face stiff with anger, Mace reached for the door, threw it open—and stopped. A small woman with leathery skin stood there, peering up at him with piercing, brown eyes, as though she had been waiting for him.

12

THEY HOLD SECRETS TOGETHER

Mace exhaled in frustration and glowered at the woman, who stood no taller than his chest. The morning sun shone on her silver hair, which hung in two long braids to frame a brown, deeply wrinkled, no-nonsense face. She wore old blue jeans under a tasseled skirt, a heavy brown and tan shirt, and a leather vest adorned with several necklaces, small objects and pouches.

"Well, move it, soldier," she demanded. "I didn't come up here to stand on your doorstep all day."

"Yeah, well, how long have you *been* standing on my doorstep?"

"Long enough." She laid the back of her hand against his stomach roughly in a gesture of pushing him out of the way, which he tolerated because she did little to move him.

"Now I am definitely leaving," said Mace to no one in particular. He shut the front door firmly behind him and left Patrick inside staring at the door. Patrick turned to the group, perturbed.

Without acknowledging anyone else, the woman padded across the room in moccasin-clad feet and stopped in front of Caffrey. She leaned forward and scrutinized Caffrey's face.

"So. You come."

Caffrey leaned backward. The dark, piercing eyes danced with child-like energy, yet with the intensity of ancient, hidden wisdom. Suddenly, the woman broke out in a wrinkled grin. "He's a pain, isn't he? Good ol' wolf to have around, though." She pointed a crooked finger up at Caffrey. "Especially on a cold night."

Caffrey moved back several inches, felt the chair against the back of her legs, and fell into the cushion. It was a good, safe place to be.

Abruptly, the woman whirled toward Gina and Barbara and threw a teasing glance at Sharia. "Hello, sisters. How *are* you?"

Clearly honored to see her, each of them hugged her warmly with an unspoken spirit of respect. Though short, the woman cast an overwhelming sense of presence, a heavy field of invisible electricity, warm as the thick fur of animals. While exploring the strange energy, Caffrey realized her ability to feel everyone's emotions was dissipating, becoming fuzzy.

Oh no, wait, she implored.

The Native American woman spied Ron and called him shy brother, which endeared and humbled him. Barbara looked on with pride but also with the barest touch of jealousy, Caffrey noted.

Without warning or greeting, the woman pointed a brown, gnarled finger at Vince.

"Hold council with your chiefs. Hawk has good eyes, but he will lose his sight. Weasel will smoke your enemy, but she will crave his power for her own desires. Wolf guards your pack, but he is afraid of fire. Make him *respect* fire. A she-wolf is in the fire, and a young he-lynx is her friend. They hold *secrets* together."

Leaving Vince wide-eyed and perplexed, the woman smiled coyishly up at Patrick. "We need more white men like you, dear." She boldly patted his firm stomach. Patrick stood with his mouth slightly agape, a tinge of color in his suntanned cheeks.

Expecting her to disappear as magically as she had arrived, the group seemed to flinch as one when she turned suddenly and pointed the same brown finger at Gina and Barbara.

"See you girls at *next* conference. Six new moons from now. Much to hear and learn. But, hold it like the lynx. Run into Mother Earth. She is your womb. Go inside her and be safe. But *do not* sleep!" With that warning, she headed out the door. Sharia sent quick, comical glances to the others. As one, they rushed to the open door like children.

Unable to resist their whispering excitement, Caffrey joined them. Too many bodies were at the door, all taller than her. The ancient woman's voice carried in sharp, admonishing tones as she berated Mace.

"The lynx laughs at you and your heart of stone. If you tend the fire, it will keep you warm. If you do not, it will go cold and another will claim the embers, make it blaze while you watch. Listen to your heart while it still beats and keep your eyes sharp, old wolf."

In frustration Caffrey resorted to pulling back the beige window curtain. Mace stood with both hands on his hips, glaring back at the group in disgust. Then his eyes noticed her at the window's edge. Instantly, she let go of the curtain.

"Oh! I have to look those up," Sharia exclaimed, running for the bunk room. She returned with a green, hardbound book. "Let's see…weasel, lynx, wolf…." Barbara and Gina leaned close as Sharia flipped the pages, her tongue held between her teeth in anticipation.

Feeling a twinge of residual nausea, Caffrey decided to ignore everyone and head for the kitchen. Gina appeared behind her.

"Caffrey?"

"Food." Caffrey brazenly began opening cabinets. At her back, Caffrey could feel Gina's desire to ask her additional questions concerning the messages, so she was surprised when Gina yelled, "lunch!" to the crew in the living room.

Sharia read aloud from her book of animal medicine signs and focused on the meanings for weasel and lynx as the group settled down to a simple lunch of turkey and tuna sandwiches, carrots, celery, and corn chips.

The air crackled with excitement, as though the diners had springs under them and were anxious to launch into a new barrage of questions. Caffrey could not swallow her sandwich fast enough and drank two bottles of water, under the watchful eye of Gina. She caught Gina throwing glances to Vince, which she had no idea how to interpret now that her short-lived intuition was waning.

Mace returned in the midst of the meal, still tense. Vince motioned for him to have a seat at the long wooden table, making it easy for him to rejoin the group where the men had separated themselves by conversation from the women, though Ron and Barbara still sat next to each other.

"Did you know," said Vince, swallowing a mouthful of tuna sandwich, "Joe Meyers swears he saw her turn into a blackbird and fly off?"

"Get outta here," said Patrick as the others guffawed. "He's crazy."

"No, no. I'm serious. He *swears* it."

Patrick turned toward Mace. "Did *you* see that Indian turn into a bird?"

"Nope," answered Mace, busy fixing a sandwich. "But in less than twenty seconds, I couldn't see or hear her in the woods. I wish *I* was that good."

"Ha!" Patrick laughed again.

"This was about six months ago." Vince continued with his story. "Joe *swore* to me he was not kidding. Got mad when I doubted him. Says he was resting out on a picnic bench up at Lake Rabun. Movement caught his eye through the trees, and he saw her. Then he says she just turned into a bird and flew off."

"I don't know." Patrick shook his head.

"Well, what can I say?" Vince shrugged. "I've always thought the guy pretty credible."

"Well, 'course now, in all fairness, I've seen some unbelievable things in my lifetime." Patrick wrinkled his brow. "So, I guess I shouldn't judge him. I've seen ghosts twice, saw a Bigfoot at the edge of the woods, and saw a Zgeyyan in a cornfield a couple years ago. Looked like a praying mantis on steroids. Mace, sounds like a tactic we could use, don't it?"

"Yeah, maybe she can fly around and give me some useable intel," Mace jested dryly, "*and* take over guard duty." All the men chuckled, the previous discord easily mended.

Sharia attempted to interject another excerpt from her book, raising her voice to be heard. "Uh, by the way, Mace, in case you didn't hear, lynx is the secret-keeper." She munched on a corn chip and held up the green book. "'The powerful medicine of the lynx indicates secrets abound, in yourself, or in others.' And, in case you're interested, it also says...."

"Did I *say* I was interested?" he interrupted.

"Nooo, but you probably need to hear it, sourpuss."

Several people at the table smiled at the exchange.

"'If lynx has crossed your path,'" Sharia continued reading aloud, "'he may lead you to hidden treasures or important mysteries. Mother Earth may be sending omens your way. It is time to listen. Perhaps your secrets....'"

"All right, that's it," Mace declared, reaching for the book.

"No, no, no!" Sharia squealed. She twisted from his reach and laughed wickedly. "This is good stuff!"

"Who gave you that thing, anyway?" Mace groped for her over the table, but she ran around Vince and grabbed his shirt.

"I did!" declared Barbara, and she placed her body squarely in front of Mace. Instead of challenging her, Mace reached out and tickled her sides. She screamed and buckled. He darted around her with the grace of a cat.

Sharia screeched in mock terror, and ran for the living room, nearly tearing Vince's sleeve in the process. She nimbly danced around several living-room chairs. Mace easily judged her direction and leaped over them, causing her to squeal all the louder. Everyone in the kitchen moved to see the display, except Patrick, who took advantage of the missing bodies and swung both long legs comfortably across the bench while stuffing the last bite of a sandwich in his mouth.

Mace captured Sharia on one of the sofas, but not before she threw the book across the room. Vince caught the flying book before it hit his face.

"Hide it, bury it!" Sharia screamed louder as Mace began tickling her in frustration.

"Bad 'ol wolf! Bad! Bad!" She slapped his head with a pillow while everyone laughed. Caffrey was grateful for a bit of levity, but found she could not smile or enjoy it. No one, especially Mace, treated her this way: like family, like part of the inner circle. Plus, disturbing thoughts and images continued to flutter like anxious moths escaping a dark closet. She returned to the table for another bottle of water. Patrick was dumping the remains of two bags of chips onto his plate.

"You wouldn't believe he's five older than me, would you?" Vince asked Caffrey, giving her a start by appearing next to her. She widened eyes at Vince in genuine shock, trying to decide how old he was. She guessed he might be more than 25, perhaps 28.

"Yeah, he's an old fart!" taunted Patrick.

"Hey, watch how you talk about age," Barbara protested, leaning toward Vince. "I'm fifty-eight, and I got a lot of livin' to do, buddy."

Vince merely laughed. "I don't think of you as old."

"Don't use that word in front of me." Barbara wagged a finger. "I don't do that word. If I'm 99, you can use that word, okay?"

Patrick snorted. "If *I'm* 99, I'll use that word on myself."

Vince chuckled. "Mace exercises constantly. Tries to make me, too."

"Tries to make *everybody* exercise." Barbara frowned her opinion of that tactic. "Just watch him wake us up at 6 AM and call for a morning march."

"Hey, I've been keeping up." Vince feigned insult. "Okay, I don't do as much as I should."

"I think you look pretty good." Gina slid hands up his chest and tilted her chin up at him.

He crunched on a chip and mumbled. "'Hank 'oo."

"Oh, you are so romantic with your mouth full."

"Mmmm." Vince kissed her with a salty mouth.

"Get a room, ya'll!" Patrick frowned and waved an arm from the table. "Oh, wait, we're all in the *same* dang room." He cowered as Gina swatted at him with a dish towel.

Vince gestured with open hands. "All right, this group is getting totally out of control."

Gina snapped the towel with better aim as Patrick jumped over the wooden table. Caffrey grabbed her bottle of water before it could spill over.

"Everybody in this group's crazy anyway," Barbara stated firmly. "That's a requirement."

"Only crazy things are happening." Ron offered an amiable smile and rocked slightly on his heels. "By the way, I didn't get to hear about Sharia."

"*That's* a good one." Vince's face became serious and comical at the same time.

Sharia was still assaulting Mace with the tasseled pillow while he deftly tickled her sides. "I've...never...been...so scared in my life!"

Mace retreated and stood, panting.

"There were two SAAFs at my door!" Sharia distanced herself from Mace's reach. "And a vanload out in the parking lot. 'Course, I didn't know about *them* until Mace told me. But, I was over at T.J.'s apartment right across the walkway. We have this open balcony walkway area. Anyway, it's two guys. They play video games and invite me over."

"Sure, sure," Patrick called out.

"Hey!" She threw the pillow at the doorway, causing everyone to duck. "I was so nervous when I texted. The guys were deciding what story to give. One of 'em even ran and hid my drink. We tried to see my apartment door through the peephole on their door."

"So what happened?" prompted Patrick as he sauntered over to the doorway.

"We delivered a pizza," interrupted Mace with a self-satisfied grin.

"This guy shows up with a pizza at like, ten thirty," Sharia continued, excited, and pushed disheveled locks of hair out of her face. "And he puts his face up by the peephole with a note sticking out of his mouth, saying, *'The wolf is here.'* And it's a good thing 'cause we weren't opening that door."

Patrick offered Mace an approving nod.

"Friend of mine," Mace explained. "Gave his jacket and hat to her. She walked right out and took his car. He later came out with the other two guys: different shirt. They left in one of their cars. Very smooth."

"Yeah," added Vince. "It worked out great, because the guy had long dark hair, and we had him put it in a ponytail, then had her do the same. I didn't think we'd get away with it at first, because she looked kind of little in his jacket and hat."

"Oh, funny! I was scared out of my mind." Sharia rolled her eyes. "He says, 'Walk like a pizza guy in a hurry.' I almost tripped on the curb!"

"Plus, this carload of girls showed up," said Vince. "Four of 'em got out. I mean, SAAFs are still *guys*. They couldn't help looking at the girls. We got *very* lucky."

Sharia sighed. "All my stuff's gone."

"I told you not to collect personal things that you couldn't leave," Mace chastised her.

"I know, I know. I tried."

"Hey, how 'bout some help here," Gina called from the kitchen.

"KP duty!" Vince called out. The group yelled, "KP!" as though shouting the command had become a tradition. When the kitchen was clean, Caffrey noticed Mace raise his brows at Vince in an unspoken question.

Vince loudly cleared his throat. "Well, I think it's time to go over a few items, everybody. Caffrey, I want to ask some more questions about what you've told us, if you don't mind. Why don't we all gather in the living room for a while?"

Caffrey shot a nervous glance toward Mace and back to Vince. Vince, too, threw a silent question at Mace, who had settled into the old chair near the dwindling fire, one elbow propped with a hand resting under his jaw, as if to convey a tolerant pose of listening. Caffrey tried to read him, but the clarity had evaporated to wisps of emotions. She grunted in frustration and reached with her mind to try and get it back. Focusing made the connection clearer but she would not be allowed time to explore it.

"Okay, Caffrey." Vince rubbed his hands together. "First of all, how did you get *Herrengae*'s code? What do you remember?"

Caffrey cleared her throat and swallowed. "The...uh, well...*guy*...I don't know, he's a...well, the sumo guy that came into the office gave it to me. I can remember now getting the instruction that I would not remember anything until the phrase was spoken by you."

"What if someone else had triggered this?" Patrick frowned. "I mean, it's an old saying."

Vince and Caffrey both said, "No" at the same time.

Vince looked at Caffrey. "They had to know *Herrengae*'s response, didn't they?"

She nodded.

"But how'd he get it from *Herrengae*?" Patrick asked.

Everyone turned to Caffrey. "I think...he's, like, *Herrengae*'s nephew?" Caffrey nervously rubbed her palms on her knees.

"Excuse me?" Vince looked skeptical.

"He's...his nephew. I think that's how you'd translate it."

"Caffrey, the guy was *human*. Are you remembering something else?"

"I'm telling you, he *said* he was *Herrengae*'s nephew. Only, he didn't actually use the word 'nephew.' It was conveyed like 'offspring of drone brother' or something. I *felt* his connection to *Herrengae*. Like a blood connection." After the brief silence that followed, with meaningful side glances passing between members, Caffrey added, "Uh, there's more."

Vince raised his brows.

"I don't know how to say this, but...." Caffrey took a deep breath. She scrunched her shoulders in preparation. "I don't think *Herrengae*'s completely... alive."

"What?" Vince exclaimed in alarm.

"Well, it was... it's like... he went into a coma, and... they put him in one of those stasis pods. But they don't know if it's working because they're made for Zgeyyans, and they don't fit right, and...."

"How? What...when?" Fear paled Vince's skin.

"I have a sense that he was attacked slowly. Like being poisoned. He said, *Herrengae's no longer with us—we do not hear him.* He's very sad, and angry. He volunteered to complete *Herrengae's* mission. *Herrengae* gave him the memory of your saying while he was still able to. I was to obey your orders if I found you."

Caffrey gasped, her jaw falling open. "That's it! That's why I keep finding it hard to say, 'No' to you." She swallowed, embarrassed, wishing she had not said that out loud.

Vince blinked as if dazed. Anger, confusion, and sorrow colored his face all at once. Inadvertently, he placed a hand on his chest and rubbed.

Caffrey's heart constricted to see him in pain. She licked her lips and glanced from the floor to him and back. Why did she have to be the bearer of such terrible news?

"I'm really sorry. I...I wish I understood more."

Gina placed a comforting hand on Vince's shoulder. Vince's eyes moved toward Barbara.

"I said he was ill, Vince." Barbara's voice was soft. "I didn't sense a soul separation then."

"But, if it's true...well, I haven't heard him in weeks." Vince spoke in a rough voice to no one in particular, and stared at the orange and brown Native American rug covering the center of the living room. "It's as if he's been slowly disappearing. I couldn't reach him. Couldn't feel him." Vince heaved a worried sigh. "Maybe if he's in stasis, like the others, he can be revived later."

Silence hung heavy in the room as no one dared suggest an alternative.

"I hope so." Barbara broke the stillness. "Caffrey, you said you *sensed* he was poisoned. What did you feel that conveyed that to you?"

Caffrey realized Barbara would at least understand *feeling* information, so she carefully revisited the memory. "Well, he was...sending information to me very fast, more pictures than words." Several heads turned to each other in the room. "It is so weird remembering this. It's in a different language. I think he was trying to convey that the faction silenced *Herrengae* through illness because his mind was too strong and they couldn't control him. All of his feelings came to me in a rush, so it's...hard to verbalize. He did say words, but, what he felt with those words, I think... *I* felt."

"Hmmm." Barbara wrinkled her brows, and eyes narrowed. She turned to Gina. "Something's missing here. Are we talking about the big guy in the lobby?"

Gina looked to Caffrey for the answer.

"Yes." Caffrey swallowed.

"This is nuts," Vince grumbled, visibly upset. "Caffrey, there's *got* to be something still hidden. This guy was a *human* messenger. Somewhere in your story, there's a *Vhurruh.*"

"He *is*...he.... Look, it doesn't make *any* more sense to me than it does to you," Caffrey sputtered. "I feel both. I don't know *how* he can be a Vhurruh. I saw him. He was a man. That's what I know. Huge. Sickly. Could hardly walk."

She shook her head. "You want it all? Okay, *fine*. He's a Blue. A young drone. He was given some special consideration because of his telepathic abilities, which for some reason he is extremely proud of." She looked around the room at the confused expressions. "Just dump me out on the road somewhere. I'm sure somebody in a white jacket will pick me up eventually and take me away."

"Oh, my god." Patrick stood. "Oh, my god, y'all."

Barbara suddenly put her hands to her mouth, awareness dawning in her face.

"What?" asked Vince, annoyed.

"Aren't you getting this?" said Patrick. "We're talking about a *huge*, *obese* man with the build of a sumo wrestler, who could barely walk, and moved as if he'd had a stroke. She says the Vhurruh felt *young*."

"Yeah...?" Vince urged.

"That was a Vhurruh in there."

13

SPECIAL DRONE

A hush fell over the group. Barbara turned away, stepped several paces with a hand to her brow, then turned back to the group. "This is it—I can feel it."

"No way," Vince insisted, defiant.

Barbara opened her arms. "Young. *Young. Teenager* young!"

"Of course." Gina's face became ghostly white. "Of course! It would disguise the detectors. It would only be human pheromones the machine would register."

Mace cursed with a ripe, four-letter word, then stood and turned to the simmering embers of the fire to contain himself, one hand resting on the mantle.

"Oh, my gosh." Barbara sat on the sofa and rocked.

"But, how big is a teenaged Vhurruh?" Ron asked.

Vince shook his head. "They're all too big."

"Wait a minute, Vince," Gina said, "you told me *Herrengae* gave you a visual of the Vhurruh on the Blue mother ship, because you wanted as much intel as possible. You described *several* sizes of Blues."

"Yeah, but adult drones are, like, 18 to 20 feet long. Those guys are *huge*—two tons. Workers are maybe, 8 to 10 feet? It would *have* to be a worker, but they aren't as telepathically strong or aggressive. Plus, *Herrengae* said older adults were chosen for this mission, in their late 30s or early 40s in case space travel made them sterile. That was the big side effect they were afraid of. So it couldn't be...." He froze, a blank stare on his face. "Oh, no. There *was* a small drone. He had the gold mane on his back and the bright blue colors, which made him stand out from the workers. He was so small, it caught my eye. Just for a second *Herrengae* flashed that picture, and I heard him say, 'My brother's. *Special drone. Chosen.*'"

Vince continued to stare, his eyes unfocused. "I think he meant 'my brother's offspring.' The small drone was chosen because of his advanced talent. *Herrengae* might have told me more because he felt my curiosity at the small drone, but I interrupted him with other questions."

Patrick cocked his head to one side. "So, how did he work the arms and legs? I mean, their back legs have fins on 'em, so how did the rascal *do* it? And he would have to ditch the bones. He could only wear the skin, right? So, maybe it was a fake frame. Fake skin."

"Their fingers are webbed, but they're longer than ours." Gina breathed heavy with excitement, her face ghostly pale. "They probably had to cut the claws. And their elbows are partially double jointed. They can stand on those back legs when they want. He could *do it*, well, for a short period of time, anyway, if he had a scout ship nearby."

"But, if it *was* real human skin...." Ron was unable to finish his sentence.

"One human down," said Mace dryly. He turned to Caffrey. "So maybe you *were* programmed by a slug. The one part I couldn't figure out."

Gina frowned. "You know, Vhurruh medicine is *not* superior to ours. Could they have found a way to reseal a human skin? They would have to remove it from a body, and then seal it somehow, keep it pliable and oxygenated, keep the cells fed. Unless it was treated like softened leather or something. And what about the face? All their facial muscles would have to move the face. And the jaw...did he use the jaw, or discard it?"

"I think I'm going to be sick." Sharia pressed a hand to her stomach.

"Just think of it," said Gina, still enthralled, "arms, legs, moving in a walk, not to mention the human head without a skull. Vhurruh have skulls but they're kind of triangular, so he would have to, like, push it up in there. Hmmm, maybe they kept the front of the human skull. Wonder about the eyes. Now, how did he move the eyeballs? I bet he stuck his own eyeballs in the sockets."

"Oh, I'm really going to be sick," said Sharia. She headed for the bunkroom, her shoulders hunched.

"You can't be sick," Gina admonished. "You work in a *clinic!*"

"I'm in billing," Sharia said without looking back.

Barbara followed Sharia, looking worried. "I'm going to check on her."

Caffrey was relieved finally to understand what had happened, but picturing her Vhurruh getting into a human skin made her queasy as well. She wrapped her arms around her stomach. It was a reality she did not want to know. He had touched her with a dead human's hand. She shivered. Had he done something wonderful, or horrible?

"If this is true, it's fantastic." Vince shook his head in amazement. "Think of the effort. And all to get that report to us after Charlie went down."

Mace let out a sound of air from his lips and rubbed his face with a nervous hand.

"All right." Vince pursed his lips. "What?"

Mace squared his jaw and faced the group. "If this is exactly as she says, it's crazy, but great. And, it explains how he avoided the pheromone detectors. But if this is a setup to suck us in, we're sitting ducks here." He gestured with both hands. "If the crystals give locations and dates, we could be *right* where they need us to be. Blast the area, and resistance leaders are gone."

"I'm not the only leader, Mace."

"Yes you are, Vince." Mace pointed a finger. "You're the one that matters. You started this movement. Every division looks to you for leadership, and inspiration. You *can't* go down, no matter what."

Vince pressed his lips tight as if considering arguing the point.

Mace heaved a cautious sigh. "On the other hand, if this information is legit, we've got the edge we've needed all along. And, it would explain why they're hot for her. If that disc contains a report on the faction's plans, and evidence, then they would spare no effort to recover it. She's dead meat when they find her, and so are we."

"Well," said Gina soberly, "the fact that SAAFs went looking for Caffrey later shows they figured Charlie must have passed the disc on to her somehow. All the people involved in the accident were tired of being harassed by SAAF and having their clothing and cars searched by the time we got to them, even though we posed as local reporters."

Vince balanced his forearms on his knees. "If she wasn't initially involved—if she was clean, when she went missing they put two and two together...."

"And lifted a whole apartment complex to get her." Mace glanced at Caffrey. She avoided his piercing gaze. It had a different quality now that made her uncomfortable. Plus, the thought of all those people being abducted because they lived in her building made her sick with guilt.

"They'll do anything to stop that report from being sent to Hurratt," said Vince. "Wait a minute. 'On August 24th, they will arrive.' If Vhurruh are *coming*, then they got the third ship working. Even so...what difference does this report make? It sounds like *Nekkai* already knows. Why else would they come?"

Caffrey shook her head and shrugged. A dark cloud, indistinct, a barrier, hovered in her mind. She wasn't supposed to touch it. Not yet.

Ron cleared his throat. "The Vhurruh on the ships are linked to their queens even though they're billions of miles away on Hurratt. Right? Can the others send a telepathic message that far?"

"Yes!" Vince pointed at Ron and made him jump. "*Herrengae* said he could link minds with the others and communicate with his queen on Hurratt, especially if they were allowed to use the *teknaht*. They probably conveyed the seriousness of their situation while they still could. However, if they're watched as closely as I think they are now, a group gathered together would be noticed. Still, why did Charlie try to get the disc to us? So we'd know?"

Ron considered the question. "If we aired this kind of information all over the media, it would certainly be a thorn in their side."

"Would it?" asked Mace. "Or would they just chalk it up to fanaticism and claim it was a conspiracy theory?"

Vince nodded. "They understand how the press works now. They would create a fake report to make us look as though we made up the information. They may not want the publicity, but, they don't believe *we're* a great military presence to thwart their plans. They don't know how big we've grown. So, if the report only contains faction plans and names, they wouldn't be after Caffrey, not like this."

"I agree," said Mace. "They act like she's got the Hope Diamond—no, make that the launch code to a silo."

"Yeah, but a launch code could be changed. It *has* to be something they want to keep secret, something important enough to search the entire city for."

"Well, what are we waitin' for?" Patrick gestured a palm in the air. "Let's find out what's *in* the dang thing."

"It's not here," said Mace quietly. "It's at Caveman."

"Well, let's go get the thing opened." Patrick took a step forward as though ready to launch out the door.

"We need her to do it." Mace's eyes included Caffrey.

"And this is a problem?" Patrick countered with a baleful glare, anxious to take action.

Vince exhaled roughly. "Take her there?"

"I could give you the tune," Caffrey offered with a quick shrug. Everyone was silent. "And I could draw you the picture I see of how to get the crystals to work."

"Don't you want to go?" asked Mace, distrustful.

"Okay, *fine*." Caffrey lifted her arms in exasperation. "I'll go!"

"I don't really *want* her to go." Vince stood and frowned. "I don't want everything in one place. If there's a tracking device or alarm, and we trigger it, I'd rather Caffrey be somewhere else."

"I don't know, y'all," Patrick objected. "It'd be a big waste of time if someone else tried it and it didn't work. This sounds like a one-shot deal. Caffrey should open it. I don't want to drive three hours for nothing."

"Um...." Ron raised his hand, then retracted it. "Why don't we let her give us the tune, and the instructions? That way, when we get down there, we'll have the choice. You can always bring her in if you need to."

"Good idea." Vince nodded his approval. Ron shyly averted his eyes at the compliment.

Mace glanced at each face. "All right, let's do this."

Half an hour later, Caffrey could not help laughing at Patrick and Mace's attempts to hum back the tune in high-pitched notes. Gina tried but could not stay on key. Sharia and Barbara repeated the tune pitch-perfect.

Mace pointed at Sharia and Barbara. "All right, if we decide not to use Caffrey, it's going to be either of you. I should probably tell you, the entrance to Caveman is so small I can barely fit through it."

"What a minute." Barbara held up a hand. "*You* can barely fit through this hole?"

"Yep," said Mace.

"Well, honey, you ain't lookin' at Twiggy, here."

"Who's Twiggy?" asked Sharia.

"You're too young to know." Barbara waved a hand. "She was the first skinny super model. And I *ain't* her."

"I'll make you fit." Mace grinned mischievously.

"Uh-huh, and just how do you plan to do that?"

"I've always been known to push people beyond their perceived limitations." Mace's eyes twinkled. "Wear some rough clothes."

"You know, I just realized something." Gina frowned. "Flies With Raven's said she would see us at the *next* conference. Why not the one tomorrow?"

"Hmmm." Barbara looked concerned.

"Oh, come on, ya'll," Patrick chided. "It was mistake."

"Unh-unh." Barbara shook her head. "That shaman doesn't get anything wrong."

"I don't know," Gina turned to Barbara, "what do you feel?

Barbara relaxed her facial muscles, her eyes became unfocused. Gina bit her lip, waiting.

Barbara took a deep breath. "I feel threatening energy but it's unsteady and mushy—I don't think we're supposed to know yet."

"Now, what kind of crock is that?" Mace complained.

"Hey, bud, the spirit world operates on a very delicate balance, with certain things guarded from the top. If God doesn't want me to know, I ain't supposed to know. And at the rate things are going, I'm the last of a dying breed. So, don't press your luck." Barbara eyed him strangely and knitted her brows together. "We have a visitor."

Mace sat up, though not with great alarm. "Know who it is?" he tested her.

Barbara closed her eyes. "Can't really see him. He's not alone."

Mace dropped his smile. "Well, he's *supposed* to be." He ran to the edge of the curtains. "Vince, get that disguise on!"

"You think so? It's just Kev—"

"Absolutely. Now. Gina, help him get it on straight."

The room fell silent as Vince and Gina left.

Mace's eyes widened as he noticed Caffrey. He pointed to the back room. "Caffr—"

Too late, Patrick had opened the door and was greeting a taupe-haired man and his young, shapely companion. Mace glared at Patrick with both fists on his hips.

Mace produced a fake smile and welcomed the guests, but gave names for each person that Caffrey had not heard before. He introduced her as "Victoria" and passed a sharp look to everyone in the room to do the same. To Caffrey's surprise, Barbara, Ron, and Sharia became charming and attentive, as if they had been waiting for these two people to arrive all day.

Kevin, which Caffrey felt was his real name, was clearly bothered by introductions in code names and seemed to realize that his companion was not going to be accepted. He was dressed haphazardly in faded blue jeans and a wrinkled white dress shirt, both of which stretched tightly across his chubby frame and short legs. His timid smile was directed at Caffrey in a round, meaty face, warm and sincere, with laugh lines happily enhancing his gray eyes. He extended his hand with gracious courtesy, though his female companion, Nadine, was coldly polite and merely nodded.

Extreme jealousy hit Caffrey with a nerve-tingling blast, and she blinked in confusion, more from the reason why than from the fact that it was from Nadine. Caffrey guessed her to be in her early twenties, and though not stunning, she was certainly lovely, with long locks of gold-tinted, dark-brown hair softly curled below her shoulders. Her shapely silhouette was garbed in tight blue jeans and a yellow, lace-patterned blouse that revealed the outlines of everything under it.

Caffrey attempted to project kindness and acceptance in hopes of unruffling Nadine's feathers, but it was soon obvious nothing would change the girl's demeanor. Somewhat to her relief, Caffrey felt the heated sting aimed at Sharia as well. She finally understood that this was the type of woman who did not care for competition in the same room. She smiled, realizing she had *read* the emotion, and her new sixth sense had not completely dissipated after all.

"Hey, I'm sorry," Kevin apologized to Mace. "I didn't have a chance to tell you about Nadine. But...."

Mace nodded, his dark eyes masked. "I told you this was a classified meeting."

"I know, I know." Kevin waved it off. "But...."

"Well, more guests! Excellent." Vince crossed the room in long strides wearing a black beard and wig, and a pair of glasses. Gina was close behind, to Caffrey's shock, wearing a short, black wig, bright red lipstick and lots of eyeliner. How Gina had stuffed all her blonde hair under the wig, Caffrey did not know. Amazingly, Gina had managed to color her eyebrows black as well in the few seconds she and Vince were gone. The combination truly altered Gina's appearance. Except for her voice, Caffrey would not have known her.

"I'm Dan Matthews." Vince reached out a hand toward Nadine. "And this is my friend, Heather Waters. Kevin, it's good to see you. And who's our lovely guest here?"

"Uh, uh...." Kevin stumbled over his response, recognizing this was Vince and Gina, but unnerved by the disguises and false names. He licked his lips. "This is Nadine Salazar."

Nadine shook the hand Vince offered and scanned the room. "I heard a rumor that Vince Mansfield was really alive and could even show up at this meeting."

Kevin flicked sheepish eyes toward Mace. The piercing, threatening gaze that met him left no doubt what Mace was thinking. Caffrey was not surprised when Kevin swallowed nervously and returned his attention to Nadine.

Vince's expression became intense and sincere. "No. We're hearing lots of rumors, and of course we want them to be true. But, if he's alive somewhere, I hope he's hiding. I'm his cousin, by the way, on his mother's side. I've been hiding out myself for months now, but...the group needs leadership, and I believe in Vince's mission."

"And we do, too," Kevin added passionately. "Don't we Nadine?"

"Of course." Her smile was warm as she held Vince's eyes.

"And we've got lots of reasons to feel strongly about this...uh, Dan," said Kevin. "I've been working with her, and you guys just wouldn't believe what's been going on. She worked as a secretary at

McCauley Air Base. They gave her a disability discharge for *migraines*. Can you believe that? I mean, how often does *that* happen? Jackie Henderson and I regressed her and she remembers, oh...man, you would *not* believe it. Cool technology coming through—with no paperwork or anything. Vhurruh scout ships in and out, and cruisers sometimes. Lots of visits by government officials. Other spacecrafts...everything hush-hush...."

"Well!" Vince clapped his hands together. "Sounds like a story we need to hear. Nadine, we've been discussing plans today—just some future endeavors. But, we'd really like to hear your story."

"No kidding, this is big," Kevin spoke quickly, sensing the cover in Vince's voice. "She remembers—under regression, that is—discussions about top officials, Vhurruh visits, you name it. You know that plane that crashed several months ago?"

Vince nodded politely.

"She heard several guys talking about the missile fired at it by mistake. You know, the report that got shushed real fast, then they gave some lame mechanical excuse?"

As he spoke, Caffrey caught Nadine's hard stare and knew that she had been recognized. She wondered if she should find a subtle way to let Mace know. She surprised herself by wanting to let him know *anything*.

"Yes." Vince nodded with tolerance. "We heard about that. Lots of stories flying around. Wonder who was on board?"

"Well, let me tell you...." Kevin emphatically told his tale to an interested but covertly alert group. He talked for an hour straight.

Mace hovered in the background, periodically sending glances to Patrick and Vince. Clearly, he was growing more concerned about the presence of Nadine. Caffrey was immensely relieved to have him concerned about someone else. At one point, Mace caught Caffrey's eye, glanced down at Kevin and back to her with a minimal shake of his head. Caffrey understood not to reveal anything about herself or to converse with him. She nodded compliance. She felt elated to be part of the inner circle but uncomfortable taking orders from Mace.

Vince asked Nadine several questions, which she happily answered. "I didn't even realize all this was here, part of my life, until Kevin started pointing out different inconsistencies in my situation, and the strange dreams I've had. Now I'm kind of, you know, angry. I want to know what happened. I mean, I'm going on with my life, but still...." she left off with that and shrugged without emotion. Kevin chimed in to tell the group more about her, pleased with his prize.

Gina offered them both bottled water. Kevin chatted on about several more questionable stories and conspiracy theories. After

Mace quietly answered two cell calls, Kevin blurted. "Oh, hey, I need y'all's new numbers."

Mace shook his head. "We'll have new phones by tomorrow. We'll call you."

"Oh," Kevin responded, disappointed.

"You'll have to continue using the quilting website for now," Vince instructed. "We'll change it over to something else in a couple weeks. Things are a little hot right now. So, are you planning on staying for the conference tomorrow?"

"Oh, uh…. We've got a cabin down by the lodge." Kevin smiled in mild embarrassment at the admission, but Caffrey felt sure Vince was relieved.

"We're *all* staying this weekend for the *whole* conference." Mace spoke up, loud enough for everyone to hear. Then he glanced at his watch. "You'll have to come by and visit us again tomorrow. We've got a meeting in another cabin tonight."

"Oh, really? Anybody I know?"

"I don't think you've met them yet. But, for now, this one's going to be classified. I'm sure that…Dan can fill you in tomorrow."

"Oh." Kevin seemed dismayed. "Well, we haven't had dinner yet, so I guess we'll go on down to the lodge. Will your meeting be long?"

"It may last until well after midnight. All depends on how much planning we need to do. We won't be back to this cabin until 0100 or later."

"Yeah," answered Gina, keenly backing Mace up and stretching. "It's going to be a rough night for us. Lots of things have been going on. I'll have to fill you in tomorrow. If I'm not too groggy. Don't forget, first class starts at nine."

"Oh, we'll *be* there!" Kevin said with excitement, then turned to Nadine for confirmation, who smiled sweetly in return. Vince rose and moved toward the door. Reluctantly, Kevin followed.

Nadine stood and turned to Vince with a winning smile that did not match her eyes. "By the way, Dan, I think what you've done is really great. I think it takes a lot of nerve to speak up about these issues. I'm glad the group has you. It was so nice meeting you." She held out an inviting hand.

"Well, thank you," Vince responded with a genuine smile. He shook her hand, which she held a moment longer than necessary. Instantly, Kevin placed a possessive arm about her shoulders and waved a cheery goodbye to everyone.

"Take care," said Nadine to Vince.

Vince smiled. "You, too."

"Oh, nice meeting you all." She added a wave as she exited. Her eyes landed a moment on Caffrey. Mace watched them drive away from the edge of the curtains.

"Well," murmured Vince to no one in particular.

"*I'm so glad the group has you*," Gina teased in a girlish voice, her arms folded across her chest, eyes sparking.

"What did he think he was doing?" Barbara let her arms flop to her sides.

"Being an idiot," answered Mace from the window.

Vince ignored Gina's scathing glower. "Feelings? Impressions?" He glanced at Barbara and eyed Gina sideways.

"Way too much being hidden there," Barbara replied. "It's not good. The stupid little dweeb, bringing her here."

Gina remained in place, her arms still crossed. "She's hiding something, all right. She may not even know it. Why didn't Kevin have us check her out? He knows the drill."

"Well, he's been alone a long time," Vince said to temper their emotions. "He and his wife had just separated when she was lifted two years ago, but it was still very hard on him, and...."

"Yeah, well, I *still* don't like him," added Barbara pointedly, "and he's still a dweeb."

"It was a dangerous thing for him to do," Patrick agreed. "You don't jeopardize the Underground. He could have arranged a separate meeting or something."

"Absolutely," said Mace. "If I had seen them get out of the car, I wouldn't have let them in the door." His eyes landed reproachfully on Patrick. "We would have talked outside. Caffrey's a hot face. Not to mention risking Vince."

"Well, he's been a valuable and reliable source of information," offered Vince in Kevin's defense. "Remember, he worked at Telenex when everything went down, and he had a link."

"Yeah, well, his link went down two months ago," said Mace.

Vince's chin lifted. Gina lost her jealous glare and regarded Mace with disapproval.

"Sorry, man," said Mace, his lips pressed together with regret. The room was quiet for a moment.

"Well," said Patrick, continuing the discussion, "anyway, I don't believe half the crap Kevin's told me. All he talks about is these people he knows, and how SAAFs are after him and Telenex is stealing his inventions. Has anyone seen *any* of it?"

"Not me." Barbara crossed her arms.

"Well, I think he has a...need to impress," said Vince.

"You've got way too much heart," Mace accused.

Vince gestured with opened arms. "I care about people."

"You need to care about your hide right now. She's an *over,* if I ever saw one."

"I agree," said Barbara, tight-lipped. "Her emotions aren't genuine. I feel 'military' all over her. Probably SAAF. And she's supposed to be out."

Vince exhaled forcefully. "What else can happen?"

After a hurried dinner of low-fat hotdogs, grilled by Ron, raw carrots and celery, and more chips, Patrick complained that he was going to go shoot a deer if that was what they were eating the whole weekend. Mace suggested an early evening and, with military bluntness, ordered each person's belongings organized and compact, ready to grab at a moment's notice.

Caffrey zipped herself into the forest green sleeping bag and snuggled into a fetal position, waiting for body heat to gather around her. She smiled, thinking grudgingly that she had never been with such an exciting group of people in her entire life. What would her life be like, if the accident had never happened? She would probably have spent this night talking and laughing with Maiba, who would have reminded her that she was too young to be wasting her evening on an old woman. And Caffrey would have argued that Maiba was more interesting than most of the men she met. Maiba would have waved the comment aside, and smiled with her lips together to hide several missing teeth, which she had lost trying to defend herself. Thoughts of Maiba made Caffrey's heart hurt. Wearily, she closed her eyes and felt the weight of the entire day close in on her.

14

RUN INTO MOTHER EARTH

"You are being watched," came a liquid voice from a strange, shadowy dream in which Caffrey was running down endless corridors, frustrated because her feet kept sticking to the floor. The voice woke her into the sleepy grayness between dreams and reality, and she blinked away her blurred vision.

Unfamiliar walls and ceiling beams loomed above. After a moment, she remembered she was in the Underground log cabin. Snores from two different people, occasional sputters from hot coals in the dying fire, and endless chirping from thousands of forest crickets and tree frogs outside permeated the darkness around her.

"You are being watched," came the voice again, firm, powerful, and masculine. It filled her head, as though it were part of her own brain and skull, but from a point not belonging to either. Instinctively her mind reached for the source. As she touched the connection, it quickly shut, like a window falling down in front of her. She sat up and scanned the dark room, confused.

Not knowing quite what to do, she tried to remember which bunk contained Gina. She tugged at the zipper of her sleeping bag and shivered in the night chill.

On tiptoe, she crossed the wooden floor to the nearest window. She peered through a break in the faded, blue-checked curtains, not wishing to move it, lest any observers be looking in. Unsure of what to expect, she looked to her right and focused on the dark, graveled roadway. The SUV and part of the black sedan were all she could see, aside from surrounding mountain forest. The only movement was a soft rocking of nearby trees, their crooked arms waving, sinister and cold. Above and beyond the tree line, a cloudless midnight sky rose to a great purple-black expanse, awash with a breathtaking display of crystalline stars but nothing else.

A soft rustling of clothing caused her to turn. She stumbled backward into the window as Mace's looming form appeared nearly against her in the dark. Indeed, he looked wolf-like with starlight glistening in his wary black eyes. His hairy, sun-browned skin almost blended with the ebony T-shirt and boxers he wore.

It occurred to Caffrey that she was wearing nothing but a dark-green T-shirt and underwear, though she had donned socks before getting into bed to keep her feet from freezing. Even in the sleeping bag, she was certain they would get cold, and they did.

"Problem sleeping?" Mace asked with obvious suspicion. Both hands rested on his hips in a parental fashion.

"I...heard someone."

"Heard someone?" His watchful nature came alert.

"Someone," Caffrey realized how ridiculous she was going to sound, "in my head...said I was being watched." She held her breath and waited for Mace's sure response of ridicule.

Mace raised both eyebrows, his coal-like eyes never leaving hers, and tilted his chin up in scrutiny. "And, what else did this *voice* say?"

Caffrey inhaled nervously. "Well...nothing. He kind of closed up. I mean, he cut off the contact."

"He?"

"Yeah. I think it was the Vhurruh. It felt like him. He sounded real concerned, kind of upset. Look, I know this sounds crazy...."

"Okay. Again." Mace raised a hand to silence her protest. "What *exactly* did he say?"

Caffrey swallowed, and looked into the piercing, wolf eyes. "He just said, *'You are being watched.'* Twice. He said it twice."

"Did he say who was watching?"

"No." Caffrey shook her head. "He seemed like he was trying to warn me. Like he wanted me to...*move.*"

Mace glanced above her head and out the window, his eyes shifting back and forth in thought, as though he could survey the entire mountain top through the walls. Suddenly, he turned.

"Everybody up," he commanded in a low voice.

Toward the first bunk, he reached out and shook the sleeping mound. As Sharia stirred, he quickly put a broad hand over her mouth and laid a finger to his own lips, signaling quiet. Sharia's eyes opened wide. "Everybody up. *Now,*" Mace whispered to her. She threw off her sleeping bag.

Mace moved like a shadow to each bunk, although Vince was already walking across the room; he was obviously a light sleeper as well. Ron was sitting up. As each person awoke to Mace's tone of voice, they came instantly alive and began tugging on clothing.

After standing frozen and ignored in the corner, Caffrey ran past everyone to her own bunk, and grabbed the gray jogging pants she had worn that day. She moved fast, afraid to be the last one ready.

"The camouflage!" came Mace's whisper at her ear. She jumped and watched him disappear amidst moving bodies. Caffrey dropped the gray pants and fumbled in the darkness for the, stiff, multi-pocketed camouflage pants Gina had purchased for her at the outdoor store.

Flushed, worried, but ready for action, the group gathered around Mace in the center of the room at the edge of the dual fireplace. Mace knelt on one knee, and everyone followed. Caffrey was still awkwardly fastening one of the buttons on the front of her britches, wondering why in the world it possessed buttons instead of a zipper. She stooped to join the others, wishing for light to see what she was doing. Mace grabbed her firmly by the arm and pulled her to his side before she could fasten the last button.

"All right," he spoke, in full command. "Princess here says she just got a message that she is being watched." All eyes turned incredulously to Caffrey amidst heavy breathing and shivers. "We don't know why she's being warned, or if it's even legit, but I'm not waitin' around to find out." He turned to Caffrey and searched her eyes in the dim light of expiring coals. Caffrey was amazed at the strength of purpose and complete lack of fear she read there. "Still think it was the Vhurruh?" he asked.

"It seemed like him," Caffrey replied meekly, doubt beginning to unnerve her. She had caused a whole room of people to react to something she didn't understand herself, something that seemed less real with each passing moment.

"All right." Mace included each face in the circle. "We've got three possibilities. Either she was dreaming...."

"Nope," came a swift reply from Barbara. "Something's up. I can feel it. It's all over."

"I can, too," said Ron. Obviously surprised, he rubbed a hand over his chest. "I've been awake for the past hour."

"All right," said Mace, "scratch that one. This could be a ploy to make us run and reveal ourselves in the night. We don't know whether they absolutely *know* which cabin she's in. The message could be to rouse her, wherever she is." He looked at Barbara for comment.

"Don't know." Her eyes were tense. "Can't feel that."

Mace raised his brows at Gina.

"I'm too nervous," she replied. "I'd have to concentrate."

"So *concentrate*. All right. Third possibility is that that damn Vhurruh is really on her side and is trying to warn her." He peered at Caffrey, looking disturbed. "God help us," he said, more to himself than the others. Resolutely, he looked to Vince.

Vince panned the group. "All right, thoughts? Caffrey, do you feel open contact with him right now?"

"No." Caffrey shook her head. "He cut the contact."

"And you're sure you weren't dreaming?"

"I'm positive." That was the only thing she was certain of.

Vince turned to lock knowing eyes with Gina and Mace. "Just like *Herrengae*." His voice was wistful. "He'd send me a quick message, then lock up tight. Only in the beginning did we ever get to talk."

"Do we know *who* exactly is watching?" asked Patrick in a skeptical tone.

Mace glanced at Caffrey for an answer. She shrugged, wide-eyed.

"Okay. I don't want *any* electronic equipment on. No phones, no computers. Anything that uses a battery, turn it off. Do you all have your Faraday casings with you?"

All heads nodded except Caffrey's. *Faraday casings? What the....*

"Patrick, Barbara, Ron, you've got cars out there registered in your names. Think about it now. If *whoever* is already here, going back down that road is not an option." He pointed backward with his thumb. "Your names'll be known from now on. We *have* to leave 'em."

"Oh, no." Ron was dismayed.

"But, where we gonna go?" asked Patrick. "In the woods?"

"Shhhh." Mace held up a hand. "I don't want to say out loud."

"What about Leah? If I leave my car, then somebody might go hassle *her*. She's not on the registration, but it's our address. I've got to warn her."

"Patrick," said Vince, his tone was firm but sympathetic, "what if you leave and you're stopped at the bottom of the hill by SAAFs who decide to pick your brain? We'll find another way."

Patrick exhaled sharply and looked down at the floor. "Are we sure about this? I'm between a rock and hard place, here. I'm not afraid of SAAFs, but I don't want L—"

"Don't say her name." Mace raised a hand. "Our first priority when we're in the clear is to contact your wife," assured Mace, with sincerity. "Is she at home?"

"Oh, wait a minute." Patrick brightened. "She said she might leave tonight to go to...." Mace's hand stopped him again. "Well, uh, all right. If she did, she won't be at the house when they check it. Man, I hope she left."

"She did." Barbara stared blankly ahead as though seeing into another room. "We've been close many times. I've got her." She turned.

Patrick gazed with disbelief into her eyes.

"I'm telling you, she did. I feel her away. She's not at the house."

Patrick reached over and gently squeezed Barbara's knee in gratitude. The gesture moved Barbara deeply, and she averted her eyes to the floor.

Mace brightened and turned his attention to Gina. "Did you ever tell her about the red...."

"Yes, I think I did. But I thought you wanted the phones off."

"I do. I'm taking a chance. He's right. They'll go straight for her. Patrick, open your phone."

Patrick looked puzzled but took his phone out of a dark gray box and turned it on.

Gina smiled sideways. "I thought you didn't take chances."

Mace took Patrick's phone and began tapping the screen. "Yeah, well, shoot me," he said while continuing to touch the glass.

Gina's smile widened and she exchanged glances with the other women, including Caffrey who gave a quick smile, thrilled to be included in the exchange.

Mace lowered his voice to a barely audible whisper and leaned toward Patrick. "Type her email address right there."

Patrick complied.

Mace turned the screen back toward him and continued tapping. "I've just ordered a pair of red socks for her. She should get a confirmation in about one minute."

Patrick scrunched his face in confusion.

Gina whispered. "I joked with the women a while back that we should warn each other of imminent danger by ordering red socks from an online site. We laughed at the time but realized a confirmation email only takes a minute. The owner of the site is an old friend, so I worked out a code with her to accept bogus account information if someone orders only red socks."

Patrick shot an appreciative glance at Mace and Gina. "Thanks, y'all."

Mace nodded. "They *will* go after her. But first, they'll pursue *us* as much as possible, if we're not blown off this mountain. Ron? Barbara?"

Ron reached over and took Barbara's hand. "Up until now, we've just been on the edge. We knew this could happen. It's time."

Barbara smiled at him. "I guess a little action at my age is a good thing. I have no children. Ron has a grown son in California, but he knows nothing of our connection with you guys."

"And you've all heard too much today." Mace took a deep breath, resolute.

"It's getting stronger," Barbara warned.

"What is?" asked Mace.

"Whatever is out there. I can feel it closer. The energy's getting heavy."

"Okay, I want all gear in backpacks if it's not already there. Take all personal effects—leave *nothing* than can I.D. you. Take your sleeping bag if you want, but nothing else bulky. Nothing heavy. Everything you carry is going to get a lot heavier. Gina, Sharia, bring some food packs. Make sure everyone's got water bottles. If you don't have the roughest, darkest clothes you've got on your body now, get 'em on. No time for privacy. Only take what you can carry. Stay low to the floor." Mace gestured with an arm toward the kitchen beyond the wall. "And meet me *there*. It's 2:44. I expect all hands at 2:45. Go!"

Like nervous buffalo in the night, great shadowy mounds galloped into movement in stooped positions. Caffrey was certain she'd never moved so fast or been so frightened in all of her life, and yet she was exhilarated in a way she'd never felt before. Her heart pounded painfully in her chest. Getting her belongings together was easy, since Mace had pestered everyone into organization and readiness four hours before. Though she had been resentful at the time, now she understood why.

After lacing her boots, she tried to roll her sleeping bag as tightly as possible, but knife-like pains shot through her abdomen at each surgery point, and, of all things, her fingernails kept getting in the way. One of them snapped back, and she gasped. Everyone in the room stopped dead still. She grimaced, whispered "sorry" and went back to rolling the protesting bag with greater fervor.

Gina appeared beside her and murmured, "Forget it. Save your stomach."

Caffrey stood, puzzled over what do next. Gina handed the pack to Patrick, who carried only a small duffle bag.

One by one, dark bodies moved across the floor and through the living room, which now seemed menacing with its two wide windows covered by thin beige curtains. The kitchen quickly became crowded. To Caffrey's amazement, Mace was halfway under the kitchen sink, with only his hips and camouflaged legs showing. Vince hovered over him with a flashlight.

"No snakes," came Mace's muffled voice.

"Did he say 'snakes?'" asked Sharia in a shrill whisper.

"All right," Mace said to Vince as he re-emerged with something odd strapped to his head. "Gimme your pack. I'm gonna get everybody d—wait, better not say in case our voices are being picked up. You take point. I'll take the rear. Go!"

Vince leaned sideways and planted a kiss on Gina's lips, which left her starry-eyed for a second. Then he twisted sideways and wormed his long legs into the cabinet until it swallowed his chest, arms, and hands. Caffrey realized that the curious objects on Vince's and Mace's heads were small lights like one she had seen her dentist wear, except these were not turned on. Mace passed Vince's backpack into the cupboard, and it disappeared.

Gina began her descent the moment Mace moved out of the way. Ron leaned toward Barbara, and Caffrey could hear the smack of two kisses. Everyone else looked down or away, being single or without their mate.

"Ron." Mace indicated he was next.

Ron rotated as he had seen the others do. Mace leaned toward him and strapped a thin flashlight to his wrist. "No light till you're in."

"Okay," Ron whispered with a shaky voice. He breathed heavily as he squirmed to accommodate his larger midsection, seemingly determined to move as fast as the others.

"There you go. You've got it." The patience in Mace's voice surprised Caffrey.

"I can find the bottom!" Ron sputtered in panic, and Caffrey could hear Barbara's sharp intake of breath.

Mace grasped Ron's arms tightly and moved further into the cabinet. "Yes, there is. Find the bricks with your feet. They're there."

"Okay, okay," came Ron's panting reply. Caffrey found herself breathing faster. Mace slid his grasp to Ron's remaining visible hand in a loose gesture of reassurance, then let go, watching as Ron slowly disappeared.

Mace exhaled and looked up at Barbara.

She took a deep breath. "Honey, this better be bigger than it looks."

"It is. In places."

"I knew you were going to say that. I'm gonna regret not sticking with my *Sweatin' With the Sixties* tapes."

Mace grinned wide, but the expression was replaced with one of serious concentration as he worked to direct every part of Barbara's body downward, shushed her fears, and coached her with encouragement. Caffrey watched in amazement. She had not thought such consideration possible from him. Insult and impatience, yes, but not courtesy and concern. Faint light flickered at the edges of the cabinet, enough for her to make out old brick flooring under the water pipes near Mace's hands.

Sharia was next, moving her slender body agilely. She grasped Mace's hand for reassurance while working to find footholds. Before her shoulders lowered, she smiled up at him in an unspoken affirmation of comradeship and devotion. Caffrey felt an odd sensation in her chest and rolled her eyes at herself in disgust. She was not going to be part of his fan club, ever. Anticipating Mace's call for her, she was surprised when he called for Patrick, who hesitated as though to question putting himself in front of Caffrey.

"Caffrey's in back with me," Mace stated resolutely. Caffrey caught her breath.

"All right." Patrick deferred to Mace's strategy with a shrug of his shoulders, then dipped his feet into the rough circular hole, dimly lit by dancing rays of light from moving flashlights. Caffrey watched Patrick slowly disappear as the others had done, unnerved by the fact that Mace would be right behind her when she was uncertain of his intentions.

Not waiting for his command, she turned to put her feet into the dark abyss, determined not to let him see fear in her. Squirming uncomfortably, having forgotten to ask Gina for more pain pills, she gripped the crumbling bricks and gritted her teeth when her abdomen shivered as though rubbery icicles had formed in it.

"Here." Mace clenched her right wrist with firm hands to tape a thin, royal blue flashlight to her sleeve.

"Thanks," she mumbled, not knowing what else to say.

"Don't mention it," he responded with an odd tone. She glanced up quickly for interpretation of the tone, but his eyes met hers in the dark and revealed nothing.

Poker face, Caffrey thought to herself.

The new camouflage pants were stiff and uncomfortable, but they served as adequate protection while Caffrey pressed her thighs over the rough bricks and groped for footholds. Stones sticking out in random places seemed to be the meager supports. None was any wider than her shoe, and each jutted out only five inches. Her limbs began to shake. She understood Ron's fear. She had expected holes in the wall, or real steps. When she pressed her left foot onto a brick, it partly dislodged, and she slipped. She cried out at the burning sensation in her stomach. Mace's arm was instantly around her shoulders. "You're okay. Just breathe. Feel for another foothold."

Caffrey grimaced. "I think I ripped some stitches open."

"You'll be fine." His deep voice echoed as if the brick shaft extended for miles. "Shift your weight. One foot, one arm at a time."

Caffrey focused on his commands. Her arms continued to shake, but she was determined not to need his help again. Lights flickered from an A-shaped tunnel that curved away from the house in a northern direction. Relief washed over Caffrey as she carefully stepped onto the last protruding brick and dropped to the muddy bottom, exclaiming from the jolt.

Cold, damp air rose around her as she stood in what appeared to be ancient, round walls of a partially bricked, nearly dry well. Water seeped from several places but did not accumulate at the bottom. Hearing a scraping sound above, Caffrey caught sight of Mace's backpack coming toward her. Without thinking, she reached out to cushion its fall. She cried out and dropped the pack instantly, curling her arms around her throbbing torso. In shock, she leaned against the wall, then moved sideways as Mace's boots came swiftly down the footholds. He dropped easily to the floor.

After quickly donning the pack, he turned on her wrist flashlight. The sudden light outlined his strong jaw, high cheekbones, and rugged black brows, which gave a squared-off effect to his intense face. Clearly, not a face to be messed with. Not when he was focused on protecting his people. Mace placed a concerned, firm hand on her shoulder, as though she were one of the others. He noted her arms curled protectively.

"You okay?"

"I tried to catch your pack." She swallowed against the pain.

"Don't do that," he admonished lightheartedly. "Let's go."

Caffrey frowned and, with careful movements, crawled into the damp tunnel.

Suddenly, Patrick's flashlight blinded her.

"Sorry!" he whispered. "Just checkin' on you guys." He turned and continued shuffling away in the crooked passage.

Caffrey moved fast to keep up with Patrick, embarrassed that her backside was toward Mace, as Patrick's was in front of her.

The heady scents of earth, wet stone and indecipherable smells overwhelmed her nostrils. She wrinkled her nose to deflect the strange, musty odors. The tunnel was three and a half feet tall in places, not enough to walk stooped over, with craggy stalactites and roots attacking her head.

It wasn't long before Caffrey's knees ached from crawling on the cold, uneven stone and dirt floor. She stopped to twist the legs of her camouflage pants so that one of the many thick pockets would be over each kneecap. She hurried, lest she lose sight of Patrick's boots and blue jeans ahead.

The jagged walls and ceiling, mostly of dull red clay and patches of silver granite, slanted ever downward. Fuzzy, moss-like plants and spidery roots surrounded every damp place. Occasionally Caffrey saw tiny, quick movements, but she determined to ignore them as long as they scurried out of her way and did not touch her. She heard a short squeal from Sharia up ahead and the words, "Is that a snake?"

"That's just a lizard," came Patrick's chiding voice.

"Eeuuuww!" was Sharia's shrill response. "Get it."

"What do you want me to do, eat it?"

"Just get rid of it!"

"Hey, it's his home."

"Come on, Patrick. I hate snakes."

"It's not a snake."

Caffrey chuckled, but the smile was quickly replaced by a frown as they trudged onward. Certain her aching knees would never be the same, she heard Patrick's boots scrape onto rocks and she gratefully stepped out into a tall, narrow V-shaped cave with a stream running along the bottom. The relief of open space was overwhelming.

Everyone walked in an awkward left-right swaying motion to keep from getting their shoes wet. Caffrey concentrated on maintaining her balance but couldn't help looking around in wonder. A marvel of shiny, wet sculptures hung amidst swirls of earthy colors, alien in appearance. Some were craggy and rough, others glassy-smooth, carved from a millennia of rushing and dripping water.

Patrick moved farther away, and she scrambled over the uneven rocks to keep up, which caused her to slip several times. Mace was right behind her, effortlessly stepping over the terrain as though it were his own backyard. Caffrey panted heavily with the effort of climbing and sliding, then finally paused to hold her sides, hoping to quell the stabs of pain.

"You all right?" asked Mace. Caffrey was happy to see him at least breathing heavier. She nodded, opting not to speak.

Patrick began to get smaller ahead, so she pushed herself to catch up. Without warning, the cave ended, and she nearly collided with Patrick as he crouched sideways to navigate a half-moon-shaped crevice surrounded by jagged edges.

"Oh, no," said Caffrey. She wondered how Vince had managed to get around the sharp outcroppings with his broad shoulders.

Mace stood beside her as they watched Patrick carefully work his way through, as he had the original opening in the cupboard, which seemed a world away now. An emphatic 'ouch!' resounded past the opening, and Mace stooped over to whisper.

"Hey, keep it down up there, will you?"

A choice four-letter word was Patrick's expressive reply, and Mace and Caffrey both laughed. As Caffrey reached for the opening, a jagged outcropping crumbled beneath her hand, and one of the points pierced her palm. She exclaimed and balled her fist.

"Let me see." Mace reached for her hand.

Caffrey flinched from his touch.

"Excuse *me*," he retorted in a low voice, keeping his eyes on her hand. "We need to bind that."

"It's okay," she offered, apologetically. She *was* truly sorry. His touch had sparked like raw electricity, taking her by surprise.

Mace dropped his backpack, pulled out a plastic bag of bandages, and surprised her by squeezing her hand to make the blood flow.

"Ow!" Caffrey jerked back her hand, but he was prepared for it and held firm while slapping an antiseptic-laden bandage around it. "This will keep it from getting infected and keep you from leaving a blood trail. Although, I have a feeling we'll all be leaving one before this is over."

"Thanks," Caffrey mumbled, and aimed her flash-lighted wrist into the tunnel ahead. The width barely accommodated Patrick's shoulders as he squirmed along on his stomach. The tunnel was collapsing and swallowing him. For the first time, claustrophobia grabbed at Caffrey's chest with a cold fist of panic. She backed up into Mace.

"I can't do that."

"Yes, you can. Just breathe, and take it step by step," Mace ordered. He gripped her shoulders. "Just concentrate on Patrick's feet. Focus on his feet. We're all together. Okay? Patrick, you, me. It's no different than if we were in a tight hallway."

"Yes, it is," Caffrey protested. Swallowing hard, she bent into the opening but froze. "My stomach won't make it."

"Caffrey." Mace spoke low next to her ear and squeezed her shoulders again, his broad hands lingering. Somewhere in Caffrey's brain, it registered that he had used her real name. His hands felt warm.

"If they've followed us, they'll be moving fast. We have to go as fast as we can. Think about the light ahead. We can rest when we get to the end. Just think about that. Rest and light are ahead. The end is up there. And I'm right behind you. You are not alone. I've been in this cave twice. It opens up to a big cave where you'll have all the room you want. Come on. Let's go."

Caffrey nodded, anxious to reward his attempt at encouragement. She knew retreat was not an option. But, the tunnel ahead was a mouth waiting to consume her. Acute concern hit in the center of her head. This time, she recognized the Vhurruh's touch. His croon of encouragement was warm as a drink of cocoa on a winter's night pouring down inside her. Fear leaked through the encouragement. He was afraid for her. That sharpened her resolve.

Gritting her teeth, she thrust herself as fast as she could into the opening. She was aware of her body scraping on all sides against the rocks, but she did not care. She only knew that if she stopped moving, hundreds feet of rock and clay would surely squash her. And, if the Vhurruh was afraid, she should be afraid.

Arm over arm, hips and knees swaying from side to side, she crept ever onward. All too quickly it became brutal for her stomach muscles as well as her elbows and knees, each movement bringing a grimace of pain, causing her to stop at times to rest and breath.

Suddenly, her face was at Patrick's feet.

"We're backed up," he whispered over his shoulder in a tired voice.

Caffrey dropped her head onto the ankle of his hiking boot, relieved for the moment to rest. The Vhurruh had retreated, as always leaving a blank, lonely space in her brain. Opening her eyes to the slick stone wall close to her face was a mistake, and her throat began to constrict. She reached out instinctively to grab Patrick's legs. He twisted to look back at her.

"Ya'll still alive and kicking?" he jested, not mentioning her desperate hold on his calf.

Her heavy breathing stirred up dust around her face. "I just need to get out of here."

"Yep. Me, too."

"It's all right. We're doin' good," came Mace's deep, confident voice behind her. She felt a reassuring hand squeeze her right leg. Oddly, it felt good and strong, and she concentrated on it. Part of her was still wary of him. She had seen his dark side first, and it was vividly etched in her memory.

After a moment, she risked a look back at him and found him lying with his chin on his hands. Caffrey froze, spellbound at the darkness behind him, blacker than any blackness she had ever seen. It was as though nothing existed beyond him, and everything started from the point at which he lay. Visions from horror movies flashed through her mind with gruesome clarity. She was amazed her brain could recall so many film clips of horrible creatures coming at people from dark tunnels. Tremendously grateful she was not the last person in line, she felt sorry for his having to be.

Scraping and movement, accented by moans, echoed down the shaft. With relief and regret, Caffrey heaved herself forward, every muscle protesting. A thrill passed through her when the passage widened enough to crawl on hands and knees, except for clusters of star-like white crystals reaching from the ceiling like sprouting coral ready to snag her hair. The thrill of additional space was short-lived, as the passage seemed to go on unevenly for hours, even with periodic short stops from the crew ahead.

Caffrey wondered how Ron and Barbara were faring. Thoughts of their pain and physical exhaustion depressed her. Pictures of thousands of tons of rock bearing down on her dominated her mind. She wondered if they could be only yards from the surface, then decided against asking for fear the answer would be hundreds of yards. She countered by visualizing the group skipping along a grassy field, smiling and laughing like children. The visualization was silly but made a small difference, so she forced her mind to hold the picture.

Sweat poured from her body and soaked the heavy camouflage shirt, making her skin hot though the damp, musty air was cool. Shuffling of bodies, heavy breathing, and groaning became the only sounds. Every muscle she possessed ached and screamed with continued movement. The hazardous passage turned and twisted mercilessly.

Several more times they halted and bunched together like a train. Each time, she laid her head down on the sides of Patrick's feet. Behind her, Mace stretched his arms across her lower legs as they bonded together in mutual misery.

Finally, Patrick's foot scooped out from under her, and he was standing. With renewed vigor Caffrey squirmed forward, grasped several rocky ledges with raw, bloodied hands, and happily pulled herself out. Exhausted, she struggled to stand, but thought better of it and sank onto the damp floor of a cavern. Deep breathing and coughing was everywhere.

Beside her, Mace wiped sweat from his brow and diligently surveyed everyone with keen, practiced eyes. "Better?" he asked Caffrey.

Caffrey nodded slowly. "Just don't... ask me... to ever... move again."

"Can't make that promise." He sat on a sandy ledge, stretched all four limbs, and looked around the house-sized cave. Fat, wet stalactites hung from the ceiling, some merged with multi-hued orange, green and blue stalagmites beneath them. Caffrey watched where Patrick's flashlight went since she was too tired to lift her own.

A gurgling stream of water wound along the floor, only inches deep in places. Strangely, Caffrey could hear a louder rush of water nearby, seemingly in the walls around her.

The V-shaped floor slanted ever downward, to Caffrey's dismay, and Vince was already laboring toward another dark tunnel. Shadows and flashes cast from the small head and wrist lights were dizzying as they bounced around the room.

Caffrey stole a glance at Mace, whose watchful eyes were on the horrible passage from whence they had come. The malicious tunnel looked smaller and more menacing than before, like a mouth that was closing. Staring at the ink-black, bottomless maw, another monster scene from some obscure movie flashed into Caffrey's tired brain. She turned away. Patrick offered her a friendly smile, and she returned it with one of her own, grateful for the camaraderie.

"I am never going into a cave for rest of my natural life," Caffrey managed to vow.

Patrick and Mace both guffawed, and someone passed back an "Amen." Caffrey was sure it was Barbara.

"Actually, this wouldn't be so bad if we weren't in a hurry," said Sharia, still catching her breath. "It's really kind of pretty in here."

"Yeah, if you're a rat," Caffrey answered testily.

Patrick stood. "Well, now, if we weren't in a hurry, I'd really like to explore it." His flashlight landed on several more sculptures.

"Except that we *are* in a hurry." Mace heaved up his backpack. "Let's roll." Caffrey found herself wondering what was in his black backpack, visualizing an endless cache of weapons and other deadly devices. It was certainly heavy enough. That she knew.

Every person in succession wearily followed the body in front, stepping over boulders and rounding stalagmites, always with both ankles bent in different directions. At one turn, Caffrey's left foot slipped, and she grabbed at the cave walls. To her horror, the place she grabbed was furry and moving. She screamed as it became a brown bat which flew off into the tunnel ahead, squealing in protest the whole way. Exclamations resounded around her, and Mace laughed. Caffrey slapped her hand repeatedly against her clothing to slough off the furry touch and shot Mace a scathing glare.

Mace came up beside her. "Man, I think that scared *me*."

"Whelp, that's it," Caffrey said. "It's all over for me. You've ruined it now."

"What?"

"I thought you were fearless. Now, nothing will be the same." She waved a weary arm for sarcastic emphasis.

He chuckled. "Yeah, well... don't grab any more hairy rocks, hear?"

She glared sideways but offered him a token smile. To her surprise, he grinned an easy, carefree grin. She turned back to the task ahead, smiling.

Her smile dropped as she stooped before the next tunnel entrance, which was not as narrow as the previous but sloped downward for a few yards. Patrick looked as if he was stepping out into another cavern. Caffrey brightened and reached forward.

A wave of cold pressure ran over her, making her shiver. Instinctively, she put a hand out to avoid falling sideways against slick rocks. She shook her head. It crossed her mind that she was fainting, but when Mace stumbled beside her and rubbed the side of his face, she knew whatever the phenomenon was, it was affecting both of them.

"Oh, no." He looked into her eyes. "Gas?" He questioned. "No! Move, Caffrey! Keep your body moving—don't stop!"

The desperation in his voice pumped adrenaline into her veins, and she dove into the narrow passage.

"Go! Go!" he urged from behind, and pushed against her legs. She tumbled several feet down and landed in pale sand. She groaned as Mace fell across her legs. Cold sleepiness took over, and she fell in an attempt to stand. Her whole body was suddenly too heavy, and she scrambled as though under water.

"No!" Mace exclaimed through gritted teeth. He grabbed Caffrey fiercely by the shirtsleeves and pulled her with all his might across the sand before collapsing beside her.

Caffrey became aware of being dragged across rough stones and of labored breathing and panting all around her. Someone was slapping her face, and she focused with all her strength to see who the assailant was. Barbara loomed above her—at least, it seemed like Barbara. The odd face above was covered with dirt and smears of blood. Wild, disheveled black hair poked out in all directions and was stuck in places to the blood on her face.

"I can't wake him up!" Sharia cried in desperation. Barbara moved away from Caffrey, revealing Mace lying beside her, completely unconscious. It was strange to see him so vulnerable, with scratches, dirt, and sweat all over his relaxed face. He looked younger without the usual stern expression, though the high cheekbones and dark eyebrows still emanated an aura of strength and determination.

Barbara began slapping him, hard. "Bradley Mason, wake up! Come on! Out of it!"

Mace turned his face side to side and groaned. Though he barely opened his eyes, his arm shot out and grabbed Barbara's.

"Ho!" Vince threw a firm hand across Mace's chest to deflect him. "Just wake up buddy. It's us."

"Don't use my real name, Barb," Mace admonished in a slurred voice. He let his head and arms drop back to the muddy, smelly floor of the massive cavern.

Caffrey struggled to sit up in the squishy muck, confused at the sight around her. In the dim flashes of many wild flashlights, great shadowy columns of stalactites hung in wavelike patterns over most of the ceiling, as though a stormy sea had frozen in place. Flutters of uncountable, tiny, black creatures with beady, shiny eyes moved like boiling oil between crevices. Birdlike squeaks reverberated with a deafening roar.

"Well, I think we can pretty much confirm how they do the lifts," said Vince, panting heavily. "I don't know what form of energy they use, but, around a certain trajectory, through tons of rock and everything...." He again took several breaths. "They emit something that puts everybody to sleep. The few who have lived to tell about it...always said they only remembered being disoriented and blacking out, nothing else. Now we know why."

Mace rolled onto his stomach and groaned. "What the crap did you dump me in?"

"Crap," answered Barbara and Vince together, laughing.

"Oh, jeez, I forgot about the bat cave." Mace growled with disgust and sat up. "How'd we get out of that?"

"I *ran* out of it!" said Vince, with a breathless chuckle. "I kept trying to move, and suddenly I was out of it, like walking out of a shadow into sunlight. The only problem was when I ran back to grab Gina, I was back in it. It's like a circular beam of energy. You're either in it or not. Fortunately, it moved away and kept shifting back and forth, like they were trying to cover too big an area. We had to work hard, then wait a few minutes and go back for somebody else. You guys were the hardest. You were the farthest back. We had to tie a rope to each other. Good thing Gina bought some."

"Whew!" Barbara brushed back a wild lock of muddy hair. "That was tough. I can die now."

"I seriously considered leaving you," said Vince lightheartedly, his chest still heaving.

"Oh, thanks." Mace wiped a spot of dirt from his face only to put more on it.

"But, without you two, I decided the group would be kind of dull."

Mace snorted and threw a chunk of black goo at Vince. Vince dodged it, but not before a piece caught in his sandy hair.

"Uugh!" Barbara exclaimed. "Stop it! It's going to take ten showers to get this smell off. And there's bugs everywhere!"

Sharia squealed. "Ew! Ew! They're on my legs!" She jumped up and slapped at her blue jeans.

Caffrey watched one of the strange beetles crawl over her boot. She gasped and scrambled for a boulder, only to find it, too, was covered in bat dung and beetles. "Gross! This is so gross!" She noticed Sharia going for an indention in a curved wall that did not appear to contain bat dung, and joined her.

Vince pushed against a wet stalagmite and wearily pulled himself up. "We gotta keep movin'. They're sure to go down the well now, if they haven't already. Unless... maybe they're just flashing this thing all over the mountains. I wonder if they knew we were in these caves and decided to hit us with the beam, or whether it's something that can travel through tunnels? I don't see how. I wish I understood this technology.

"I mean...some of these walls are solid granite. I hear our guys at Remote have been working on something like this. Wonder if they stole it from the Vhurruh—who stole it from the Zgeyyans, of course." He smiled, then knitted his brows together. "The beam's still on, I think, so maybe they haven't gone down in. Otherwise, they'd put whoever they sent down to sleep. Unless, of course, they've got some immunity or something."

"Well, that'd be just our luck." Mace struggled to his feet. "How in the world are you supposed to save a planet with this going on?"

Barbara laughed tiredly behind him. "Sorry, bud, even Superman had kryptonite."

Mace smirked. "Let's go. Are we sure which tunnel is right?"

"Gina says she's certain it's that one." Vince pointed to one of four dark fissures in the cavern wall. "The bats are using that one and that one. One comes out to the falls, which we don't want. Although a stinging shower sounds nice. I think the one there on the far left comes out onto Black Rock Mountain. I've only been in here twice, but I'm pretty sure that's it. They'll probably have satellites focused on these mountains, or even scout ships out. Hey! I just remembered, it's a state park. There'll be campers everywhere. It would give us cover, even if they're using satellites. They wouldn't know us from the campers. Even if they spot us emerging from the cave, it could be after the fact, while they're reviewing video. Make sure everybody knows not to look up."

Gina and Ron emerged from the dark tunnel Vince had suggested. Their wrist lights flashed like fireflies on the cave floor from tired, dangling arms.

"Looks good to me," said Gina, her voice weary. Blonde hair hung in strings, gray and limp around her face.

"Humph," remarked Sharia. "That is, if anything can look good in here."

"Now, don't go on with that," Patrick admonished. "You were just telling me how 'pretty' it was in here."

"*That* was hours ago—no, that was *days* ago. No, that was my last life ago." Sharia knocked a blob of bat dung off her elbow.

"I'm with *her*," added Caffrey, in a low whisper.

"Caffrey, you doin' okay?" asked Gina, her face a tired knot of concern.

Caffrey breathed with effort and shrugged. "I'm pretty shaky—and everything hurts—and I think I've probably busted every stitch you gave me. But, I don't reckon it matters since somebody's going to tell me I have to move."

"Yep," said Mace, drowsy but determined.

Onward, in single file, the group plodded, revitalized by the thought of *exit*. When the moment came, it was bittersweet.

Caffrey and Barbara groaned at the vertical fifteen-foot wall. With help from comrades and rope, they scaled it one by one. Caffrey had to be hoisted up the treacherous wall, her battered abdominal muscles having completely given out. Outside the hole, lying flat on a perilous ledge over a twenty-foot fissure, Vince and Ron held her still, lest she roll over the edge. After resting for a moment against the rock, they gently lowered her to Patrick and Gina below.

Lying still in the grass, Caffrey was certain the air and clover never smelled so sweet, nor had the pre-dawn, purple-gold sky looked more beautiful. Birds had already begun their morning jubilee, and some chose to squawk at the invading humans. Cool breezes blew whirls of forest debris across the mountain base, heralding a gathering storm.

Last in line, Mace struggled down ledges within the fissure, trying to salvage the rope as he went. As his boots hit the grass, everyone heard the low rumble of a helicopter. Bodies flew into the nearest grove of trees.

While they held their breath, the vibration died down, and they all began to uncurl from their tight positions. Mace drew out a small pair of field glasses from his pack to view the terrain. "All right, Vince. Where would *you* expect your quarry to go?"

Vince took a swallow from a bottle of water being passed around. "Well, giving them the benefit of a doubt...I would first send people down the cave. Did you close up the cabinet and well cover?"

"Yep."

"Good. Next, I'd pull all my resources to scour surrounding areas. I'd assume my target would stay with the thickest trees for cover. Try to find transportation. I would also consider that they would split up—go in many directions to confuse me. If SAAF's knew enough to find us at the cabin...come to think of it, how did they find us?"

"Two possibilities, maybe three. Either a leak from Tweetie and Kevin, which has my vote, or the Vhurruh's double-dealing. Or, Marjorie and Dr. Lucas from the clinic I.D.'d us. Which also means they would have used the truth drug, since I'm real sure those two are loyal. The only reason they would have checked the cabin would be they checked out Gina, found her parents' own it, and sent a team to check it out. Which means they're leaving no stone unturned."

"It was sold to a fictitious name," Gina spoke up.

"Doesn't matter. Your family was connected." Mace shook his head. "I would have found it."

"I can't imagine them injecting truth serum all over the place. Something's missing here," said Vince.

"Vince, they've probably got people all over the city concentrating on nothing but this. Look what they sent after Charlie for the report in the disc. And remember, they've taken over top officers in every division of military and law enforcement. State and Federal."

"My contacts say that many of those officers are smart enough to see what's happening." Vince's brow was furrowed with worry. "Some are still trying to take action."

"And where are they gonna go? Underground, just like us. How long do you think they'd be able to play along? FBI, CIA, NSA, DIA—name an acronym. It won't matter if an agency goes dark. They've all got access to everything. They've all got facial recognition software. If they have to, slap a witness in front of a computer, and they'll pick out the face."

Mace peered at Caffrey, then back to Vince. "I considered her link might be double-dealing. But, he warned her to run before they got there. So, I'm ruling him out, for now. The important thing is whether they've made Gina, and that's been one connection they didn't have through all of this. Whether they have me or not won't matter as much, except for my security business, which will affect my income."

Vince took a deep breath and blew it out. "So, whatever we do, we've got to go somewhere that Gina knows nothing about."

"Nor can the others. Judging our enemy's current performance, they'll check every person connected, every relative. Unless, of course, Tweetie leaked on us, which would have brought them right to us with a simple phone call. Look at the timing. One o'clock, exactly when I told her we might get out of a meeting at another cabin. She probably had to wait until Kevin was asleep. I know him. He's a night owl, always up until after midnight."

Caffrey elbowed Gina next to her. "I think she recognized me."

"Nadine?" Gina asked.

"Yeah."

"What was that?" Mace perked up.

Gina frowned darkly. "Caffrey says Nadine recognized her."

Mace glanced at Caffrey, incredulous. "Great. When were you going to tell me that?"

Caffrey opened her mouth to retort, but Patrick crawled up behind them. "Let's go," he urged.

Caffrey could not imagine moving.

"So," Vince prodded, "back to the original question...."

Mace stared out at the distant hills, focused on nothing in particular. "I know where we're goin'. I know just the place. Someone I haven't seen in ten years."

15

FOREVER CHANGED

Eight battered, muddy, and smelly fugitives crouched low at the wooded edge of a two-lane highway, ready to run on Mace's signal. Caffrey's entire body screamed for rest, but there was time for none. Every rebel knew that at any moment they could be discovered. Any far-off hum or rumble resembling a scout ship or helicopter caused every footstep to pause. Anxiety was high; nerves and muscles were stretched to the limit. Caffrey's legs were going numb from remaining crouched amongst bushes that gouged her flesh. She was certain every insect in the forest was crawling on her body.

Sharia stepped out onto the road and stuck out her thumb at the right moment for the third passing truck. The sound of air brakes sent eight hearts racing. Sharia blocked the side mirror with her body as she delayed the driver by inquiring over directions scribbled on a scrap of paper and claiming her phone was dead. Mace's arm dropped, and the group leaped as one from the trees to the back of the truck. Quicker than Caffrey would have thought possible, Mace had the door open. Everyone scrambled to fit between tightly packed pallets loaded with tall boxes wrapped in plastic. Vince and Mace tied their belts together to hold the door closed, as it would not shut completely from the inside. With a huge rumble, the truck began to move.

An hour later the truck began to slow, and Caffrey panicked as she discovered one of her legs was asleep. The other was tingling.

The huge tractor-trailer leaned to one side, and a box slid against Caffrey. She cried out and pushed against it with all her might. Exclamations of alarm erupted all through the truck, so she was not the only one scrambling against the shifting pallets. An arm appeared beside her. It was Patrick pulling himself between two pallets. With a great heave, he pushed one of the boxes a few inches away, enough for Caffrey to free one leg. Together they pulled out the other leg, which had fallen asleep during the ride.

Trumpeting its air brakes, the truck mercifully came to a stop. Mace and Vince quickly opened the trailer door while the sounds were masked by the incredibly loud motors of trucks on either side. Brilliant sunlight blinded everyone. White, puffy clouds decorated an expansive sapphire-blue sky. Such beauty seemed unnatural in the midst of their panicked scramble.

With biting pain shooting through one leg from the blood recirculating, Caffrey held onto Patrick to hurry past rows of tractor-trailers. Vince, again wearing his disguise, instructed the band to talk low, smile and joke as though they were a group of friends off on a hike, passing through the truck stop.

Mace left the group to follow discreetly behind Sharia and the trucker as they entered a restaurant. Heading across a park-like area, Caffrey's leg burned like fire as the blood flow reawakened hampered nerve endings. Tears began to stream down her face uncontrollably. Unresponsive to her commands, her entire body shook and became weaker with each step. Fearful of falling forward, she stopped on the asphalt and held onto Patrick's shirt, forcing him to stop. But, it was too late; she felt herself sinking beside him. Immediately, Gina and Barbara took hold of her arms.

"Caffrey," Gina hissed with alarm. "Stay with us!"

Vince burst out laughing, and hoisted Caffrey up into his arms.

"Laugh everybody," Vince ordered sharply. He hefted Caffrey to one side and her head lolled against his shoulder. She could feel him kissing her face playfully.

Following his lead, Gina teased both of them, and Barbara acted as though she was laughing with Patrick.

Vince kept up the menagerie and swung Caffrey in a circle, which made her stomach roil. Once inside a grove of trees, Vince lowered Caffrey gingerly to the ground.

"You all right, sweetie? Stay conscious, okay?"

"It's too soon after two surgeries," answered Gina for her. "I'm amazed she's lasted this far. Caffrey, I am so sorry. I know you're hurting."

Caffrey attempted to open her eyes, but the sincerity of Gina's words caused tears to fall again. Cool air hit her stomach, and she realized Gina had loosened buttons on her camo shirt and was touching her incisions. Embarrassed, Caffrey pushed her hands away.

"Caffrey, I've got to check these incisions...oh, my god, her entire abdomen is purple."

Barbara gasped. "Are those stitches tearing away from her skin?"

"Just let me rest," Caffrey entreated, pushing at Gina again.

"She needs something to *eat*," declared Ron.

"We can't move her for a while." Gina shook her head in frustration and regret, and rebuttoned Caffrey's shirt. "Vince, I need butterfly strips to tightened these incisions back up."

"Hey, there's a park with camping facilities two miles from here," said Ron as he scanned a GPS device.

Vince hissed. "Ron, what are you doing?"

"It's just a GPS, not a phone."

"Is it registered?

"Nope."

"Purchased by you?"

"Cash. Yard sale."

"All right. Rest and food, people." Vince began ordering everyone into tasks.

There were *mmmm's* all around as water was heated and food packs passed along. Barbara coaxed Caffrey into sipping reconstituted chicken soup. Her stern commands kept Caffrey sipping.

Laughing and talking loudly to announce their presence, Sharia and Mace reappeared. Sharia talked excitedly about the nice truck driver with his family pictures decorating the dashboard and the stories he had told of his travels. Every female in the group fussed jealously at her opportunity to use a real restroom at the truck stop.

Patrick was overwhelmed with relief when Mace informed him Sharia had borrowed a cell phone to contact Underground members who, in turn, verified that Leah had understood the confirmation and was staying with a loyal friend who would protect her identity.

Vince pulled Mace aside to whisper something, and Caffrey watched Mace's eyes dart toward her in alarm. She heard the words "internal bleeding." Mace quickly masked his expression, then sidestepped so that Vince's body blocked Caffrey's view of him. She wondered at that, since he had never concerned himself with concealing his expressions before.

"Hey, what else you got in here?" asked Sharia as she began pulling out all the food packs from Gina's backpack and reading the labels out loud.

Caffrey rolled onto the cool grass and rested, listening to the laughter and joking over the food choices Gina made, with admonishing jests from Mace as he spied the double-chocolate pudding and lasagna packets.

"Hey, if you're stuck with ready-to-eat rations, go for the best," Gina countered the chiding voices.

"Man, why didn't you give me lasagna at the cabin?" Patrick complained.

As the sun shone warm and bright close to the noon hour the following day, the hot, sweaty, and exhausted group tramped up a dirt road. They stopped in front of a tall wooden gateway. Creaking on two links of chain, an old, carved sign read, "Forever Changed Ranch."

Beyond a small, brilliant blue lake and several vegetable gardens, the spire of a white chapel rose. Footpaths snaked away from it like ribbons toward cabins scattered across rolling hills. Two dogs barked fiercely to announce the visitors.

A rugged, stalwart man stepped out of a weathered, yellow, double-wide trailer, the only building near the gateway. Standing on the small deck, with both feet planted in much the same way Barbara did, the man rested both hands on his hips and silently surveyed the group. His face appeared a cross between a Shar-pei and a gnarled oak tree, deeply tanned and deeply wrinkled. His expression held caution and curiosity, until he focused on Mace advancing toward him.

"Well, I'll be danged," he called out. "The Marine's still alive."

"Hello, John." Mace smiled and offered his hand as he bridged the gap between them.

The man smiled with thick, wide teeth that looked able to crack walnuts. "What in the world brings you way out here?"

Mace paused. "Nothing of *this* world."

The man observed him with squinted, wary brown eyes, then took in the rest of the group in his evaluation. "Somethin' tells me we'd better go inside and have us a seat."

The women sighed in unison as he offered directions to the restroom. Finally, everyone gathered in the kitchen, where a three-inch thick, roughly hewn wooden table took up most of the space. Smiling with pride from exclamations over the table, the man hefted a large plastic pitcher from the refrigerator and began serving glasses of iced tea.

The chairs lacked cushions for which Caffrey was grateful, for she would have felt too dirty to sit on them. She was so tired she feared her head would nod and the rest of her would follow. The cold tea revived her. The trailer was neat and tidy, the living room sparsely furnished with an old sofa, recliner, television, and two side tables that looked to be handmade.

"This is John Mathiason." Mace introduced their host. Everyone greeted him without giving their names, and glanced silently at Mace for direction.

John sipped his tea and observed his guests. His gaze lingered on Vince, who had removed his beard and wide-brimmed fishing hat. Noticing Caffrey, John blinked and squinted.

"I think I'm getting the picture here. Explains why no one offered up any names. I do watch TV, you know." John and Mace eyed each other for a moment. "What do you want?"

"I need a place to stay, John," said Mace quietly.

John panned the group. "You and all the relations here?"

"Yep."

"Got a little heat on you, I reckon."

Mace paused before commenting. "You might say that. Not the kind that belongs on this planet, though."

"Uh-huh." John leaned back and linked his fingers together in his lap. "Can't say as I've got any love for the unearthly." He pursed sun-browned lips. "Didn't you notice who was the first to go when it all started up again?"

Mace merely raised his brows in question, though knowledge of the answer twinkled in his eye.

"Prisons and jails," John spat, with veiled vehemence. "Some ain't got nobody in 'em. The air conditioning, or the water, suddenly messes up, and everybody has to get *transferred*. Except they're never found. You heard about Rabun County Jail, I assume?"

"No, I didn't," Mace answered honestly.

"Two days back. Yep, one of mine had a friend there. Had one week left of a ten month sentence. He was a new believer and was turning his life around, was gonna make a new start. He's gone. They're all gone. Cells are empty. This time, coupl'a guards went in the lift. Figure *that* one out."

"Sounds like a pretty choosy lift."

"Real choosy," John agreed. "Zgeyyans didn't care who they took, but they stuck to isolated areas. Now that Vhurruh are at the helm, lifts are precise, calculated. Disposable people."

Mace nodded in silent understanding.

John leaned forward and planted massive elbows onto the table. "So. How's Marie?" He asked the question as if they had not been talking about missing people and aliens.

Mace cleared his throat. "Lifted." His eyes shifted to the glass of tea in front of him.

John's face paled and seemed to draw inward. "I'm real sorry."

"Yep." Mace's voice was gruff.

"I always wanted to look her up again."

Mace turned his glass with his fingertips. "If you had, you wouldn't be here."

John's eyes softened at the bitterness in Mace's voice. He swallowed several times. "I expect to be gone any day now, actually."

Mace glanced up.

"Look at what I do here." John nodded toward the camp. "I bring God's word to ex-cons who need a miracle, a second chance in life. Someone to help set 'em straight, get some education. Give 'em a job and a reason to do good in the world. We're disposable people, Mace."

Mace stared at him with growing concern.

John averted his eyes to his own glass of tea. "Poor Marie." He leaned back in his chair and clasped his hands behind his head. "Such a beautiful girl. She'd have dated me, if you hadn't turned her against me, you know."

Mace snorted at John's audacity. "Hey, that wasn't my doing."

"Yeah, it was, too. You told her I was nothin' but trouble."

Caffrey glanced at the two, amazed they could so quickly change from grief to friendly banter.

"You *were* nothin' but trouble," Mace accused. "That's why I was *with* you."

John chuckled wickedly. His face became strained again. "Did she marry?"

"Yeah." Mace examined the table. Caffrey could see his jaw clenching. "Had a daughter. They all went in the lift." He took a drink from his glass of tea, subtly ending the subject.

Caffrey watched him stifle his emotions with expert skill, and empathized with his need to mask his emotions, to remain in control. The empathy was quickly abandoned as she realized he knew she had lost Brian and close friends, and he had mocked it three days before at the old house. *Was it only three days ago?*

With a heavy sigh, John swept the group with his eyes, this time slowly. "Tell you what, you remember the old mansion at the edge of the mountain? Ol' Dorothy's been alone there for some time since Robert died."

"She's been alive all this time?"

"Yep. Good old woman. Helped out at the camp a lot last year. Even taught Sunday School. Took several bad falls this past winter. Been at a nursing home for a month or so. I hope she pulls through. She's an inspiration to my people. New guys come in, looking tough. She pats 'em on the arm and grins like they're a teddy bear. Doesn't faze her a bit. She's been suffering with pneumonia. It's lookin' kinda bad."

"I'm sorry to hear that."

John's eyes misted for a moment, and he tore into another sentence quickly. "She always had guests stay there who were interested in contributing to the ranch. She believed anybody could be rehabilitated. If you're willin' to work on it, it's yours for a few days. Everybody knows I find work for people who need it, so you'll be the work crew, if you know what I mean. There's a garage with tools behind the house. An' I got some tools out back here, too. Not much in the fridge up there. I cleaned it out for her."

"We'll take it."

"Two things." John sat forward, his eyes firm. "One, my people are ex-cons, as you know. They don't need the wrong kind of publicity. They're in the process of changing their lives. Though, like I said, at the way things have been goin', I expect us all to be lifted any day now. But, keep yourself clean—no outside exposure while you're here. No drugs. No alcohol. Two, everyone's required to attend church on Sunday." He tapped a finger expressively onto the table. "'Less you're sick, a'course."

Mace sat back in his chair. "That last one could be a bit of a problem. First of all, uh, my *family*...needs to worship alone. For our sakes, and...*everyone else's*." He paused long enough to let the words and his veiled eyes speak for themselves.

A knowing but stubborn glare was John's response. "Everybody needs God in their life, Mace."

"I'm sure they do."

"You could use him yerself, you know."

"Right now, you're absolutely right." Mace nodded.

"I'll see to it that request is put through."

Mace nodded again, a warm smile teasing at the corner of his mouth. "I appreciate that."

Nestled deep amidst tall oaks and taller pines, the old white and blue house spoke of happier, wealthier days. Six white pillars accented a wide porch and curved steps, which led to double golden oak front doors, ornately carved and inlayed with tinted glass in tulip patterns. The navy-blue shutters on the wide windows were not mere decorations, but sported hinges and latches.

In delight and relief, the weary group entered the beautiful, quiet house. Once inside, they were loath to move, afraid to touch anything, for the entrance opened into an expansive, beautiful foyer. The round room was outlined in red-cushioned Victorian chairs that sat on a richly embroidered red, black and gold rug as if waiting patiently for a party to begin. From the lofty cathedral ceiling, a crystalline chandelier glistened in silence, several cobwebs belying its tidy appearance.

Beyond it, a mahogany balcony ran the length of the room, accessed by richly carved staircases on either end. To the right was the dining room and kitchen, revealing an etched glass back door and a small patio, the edges of which stopped at the forest, rising tall and massive as if trying to take back the space on which the house lay.

Mace surveyed the ceiling. "Well, it's isolated, and they can't trace us here for now. They don't know about me, I think, and I'm the only link to John—from years back, at that."

"Okay, everybody," Vince addressed the group. "Let's get organized. How many bedrooms have we got, and bathrooms? Have we got food? I want to know what electronics are here—telephone, cable, Internet, whatever. See if there's a satellite dish or a cable link."

Everyone groaned.

"I'll check for cable and Internet," volunteered Ron in a tired voice, moving very slowly toward what appeared to be a den. Gina and Barbara opted for the kitchen to survey food, while Sharia headed for the upstairs rooms, grumbling to no one in particular why she should go up stairs after walking *thousands* of miles.

Patrick dared the basement and wine cellar without hesitation, throwing over his shoulder, "I ain't obeyin' that alcohol rule. Just so y'all know."

Mace chose to inspect the entire perimeter of the house, taking in every view and vantage point. Vince joined Ron to assess what electronics were available, and instructed all to reconvene in ten minutes, which they eagerly did, anxious to do nothing but rest.

Caffrey collapsed onto the floor in the sitting area, afraid of ruining any furniture. All the jobs were taken, and she didn't care whether there was food, whether a spy satellite had her clearly in view, or whether SAAFs were coming up the graveled driveway. She lay down with her hands folded under her head and ignored anyone who attempted to move her.

Two hours later, Barbara and Gina did coax her to stand, the mention of hot bath being the only catalyst for movement. Not even the mention of dinner or bed had persuaded her. Once in the tub, she complained loudly over the weird smell.

"It's a Burow's solution," Gina explained. "It'll reduce the pain and take the swelling down."

"I don't care, it stinks," Caffrey wined like a child. Despite the strange medicinal aroma, she remained in the pleasantly silky water until it turned cold, falling asleep and waking up sputtering and spitting. Gina yelled orders at her like a soldier until she succumbed to having her cuts tended and incisions re-taped while she fought to collapse into a bed. She finally succeeded, while terse remarks from Gina evaporated into oblivion.

16

COMPROMISES

From a patio rocker that Caffrey had to clear of leaves before sitting in, she watched a scraggly raven land in a nearby pink dogwood tree and thought about the old Cherokee woman. How wonderful it would be to fly away, the sky being an open, endless highway of possibilities. Instead she was forced to hole up in someone else's house, hiding her face from the world.

At least this tiny section of the cobblestone patio had a slatted awning, allowing thin beams of amber sunlight to speckle Caffrey's face and arms, which felt delicious, while disguising her face from unearthly eyes. Earlier that morning, she had started to dust side tables in the round foyer but was caught by Gina and order to rest.

Today was a quiet, beautiful Sunday. At least her abdomen was changing from red and purple to green and yellow, which Gina said was good.

Caffrey hardly felt it was an improvement. She was disturbed by her body's condition and thoughtfully planned out morning and evening stretches and yoga to rebuild her strength and stamina. She was tired of being the sick one in the group. She wanted to be fit like she was before all of this.

The black raven squawked as Mace rounded the corner of the building during his surveillance of the surrounding mountains, which he did often. He glared at the scraggly bird.

"You don't ever relax, do you?" Caffrey said obligingly.

Only the slight jerk of one shoulder and the rise of one brow over his ever-alert eyes gave any indication he was surprised by her presence.

"You're alive, aren't you?"

"Yeeehhhss." She drew out the word musically. "I guess that's true."

Abruptly, Mace turned away and scrutinized the rise of the mountain. Caffrey felt dismissed. She watched him a moment longer to see if he would acknowledge her presence. It was the second time that day she had gone out of her way to engage him in conversation, but he remained cold and distant. As he wordlessly continued his trek around the house, she retreated through the back door, determined not to be nice to him again.

"What's wrong?" Gina asked as Caffrey stomped into the kitchen.

"*Mace.*" Caffrey scowled.

"What'd he do?"

"Nothing, I guess. He's...I guess it's just as well."

"Why do you say that?" Gina dipped a tea bag into a flowered china cup. The steam from the teacup wafted around her face.

"No reason."

Gina dumped powdered cream into her cup and eyed Caffrey. "Want some?"

"Sure. Think I'll toast me a couple slices of that brown bread from the freezer. Did you know that hot tea and toast'll cure anything?"

"Uh...no, I never quite got to that part in med school," Gina teased.

Caffrey smiled. "My grandmother was English. We always had hot tea growing up. My mother said there was a time when she would go to other people's houses, and they would say, "*hot* tea?" like she was crazy. One time, my parents were fighting and my brother and I kind of got caught in the crossfire. He was upset, and I made him some toast and tea. We sat in a room by ourselves and ate in silence, but we both felt a lot better."

Caffrey breathed deeply and sighed. "Funny, I'd forgotten about that until now. Strange, the things you forget until something triggers it." They both looked at each other and burst out laughing.

"Okay, that wasn't on purpose," Caffrey remarked. "But seriously, it cures everything."

"Well." Gina pulled out a cup and teabag for Caffrey. "Now, I have a new reason for drinking it." As she poured the hot water, Mace entered from the patio, his habit of scrutiny taking in their every movement.

Caffrey concentrated on the teacup in front of her. Mace silently walked through the kitchen and disappeared beyond the foyer.

"He's such a jerk," whispered Caffrey with disdain.

"*Caffrey,*" Gina admonished.

"And don't give me another speech about how he keeps us all alive."

"Okay, I won't. But I must say, there's some interesting tension between the two of you."

"Yeah, it's called *hate.*"

"Mmm, hmm." Gina watched her over the tea cup's steamy edge.

"Look, don't even go there. Sharia told me about the cute little prophecy from Flies With Raven. You guys are really reading a lot into that. It could mean a zillion things."

"Mmm, hmm."

"I hate it when you do that."

"Let's see if I remember it correctly." Gina gazed thoughtfully at the ceiling. *"Look for the hair of fire and the heart of fire, for both will have to be hidden. Your wolf guards the pack, but he must watch for fire. Ignore fire, and warmth will be lost. Let fire escape, and the forest will burn down."*

Caffrey glared at her through the steam rising out of her cup. "I'm warning you."

"Hey, y'all need to come see this!" called Ron from the den. Feet pounded from many directions as Ron keyed up the volume on the television.

In front of the Vhurruh embassy in Washington, D.C., with SAAF and police officers moving about behind him, a journalist conveyed in melodramatic splendor the report of a bomb in a backpack discovered near the embassy. A separate film clip flashed to the left of the screen, showing a yellow-jacketed bomb crew leaving with small, odd pieces of dismantled machinery. Exclamations resounded around the sofa as the reporter announced the Underground claimed responsibility for the unsuccessful bomb. A Gray Vhurruh in a steamy quarandome filled the screen, stressing in purring English to a journalist that they wished no ill will toward the obviously mislead group and offered to meet with them at the embassy to address their concerns.

Vince bellowed, "Just great! I cannot *believe* they're going to keep setting us up like this! Wonder who claimed us? I can't believe things are this corrupt. Is there no structure left?"

Patrick shook his head. "So, Vince, you wanna take a little ride up to Washington and have a barbeque at the embassy with the nice Vhurruh?"

"We'd all be barbequed brains by the time we came out. I'm calling Holly," Vince fumed. "They are not getting away with this."

"Vince," Mace warned. "You know they're watchin' her just to see if you or anybody else contacts her. They have to know by now that wasn't your DNA in the fire."

"We'll just have to get around them, won't we?" Vince smiled and rubbed his hands together.

"I'm right behind you," said Mace with a wicked grin.

"Are you guys nuts?" Barbara chided.

"A little ring around the rosy," said Vince. "We'll get a note hand-delivered to Holly downtown. Maybe to one of her associates.

Reporters will do anything for a story. The message will change hands enough times that it'll take them a while to trace it. And, a quick call to her admin will be too short to trace to a burner phone's location. Plus, her assistant's phone rings off the hook—we'll be gone by the time they figure out which one it was. As a bonus, I'll get some of my web guys to arrange a pop-up message."

Vince, Patrick, and Mace disappeared in an old Cadillac they discovered garaged behind the house, all three of them wearing heavy disguises. Caffrey couldn't help breaking out into a cheek-stretching grin when she realized the fat gray-haired man with the fishing pole was Mace. Now she knew more of what his backpack contained.

Disguises.

The remaining group gathered in the den to worry and wait. It was there that Caffrey learned the incredible personal tales of the small band of rebels with whom she had spent the past four harrowing days. From alien close encounters to angelic visions, each spoke nonchalantly of what to Caffrey was the fluid edge of reality. She listened quietly, spellbound, realizing for the first time that her tale was not so extraordinary compared to their astonishing stories.

After a search of the cupboards, they prepared a supper of canned vegetables, rice, chicken wings found in the freezer, and biscuits. Barbara made the biscuits from scratch and Sharia made a BBQ sauce for the wings from canned tomatoes, BBQ sauce, and other ingredients pulled from cabinets, claiming her grandmother's recipe was "the best ever."

Caffrey felt a stab of longing for her family far away as the group gathered around the shiny, cherry wood dining table, much larger than her mother's but similar in its antique, curvy shape. Silently, she plotted several ways to get a message to them, perhaps through her uncle, or a neighbor. Her parents would be smart enough to continue acting upset. Perhaps Vince would listen to reason. She doubted Mace would.

In the middle of the meal, the secret knock resounded, and Gina leapt from her chair. Instantly Caffrey knew Vince, Patrick, and Mace were upset. Though she could not see them in the other room, their disturbed emotions hit her like heat at the center of her body. She examined her chest and arms in wonder, expecting her eyes somehow to confirm what she was feeling. Only Barbara caught the motion.

"Something wrong, hon?"

"They're all...upset."

Vince began raging in the next room.

"You're getting sensitive." Barbara hinted approval.

"But, how?"

"Contact with aliens. Does it every time. Of course, I hear talking with ghosts does it, too." She chuckled. "Ron can't handle ghosts, though. He says if ghosts shows up in our house, he's pulling out a cross and kicking their butts out. But, they don't scare me. They're just people hangin' around for a visit."

Vince entered the dining room, still venting his frustrations, and threw his jacket into a chair. "I work my tail off to be a voice for these people, to gain some measure of respect for this whole movement, and they go and screw me! You know this was Rex. You *know* it was!" He gestured an accusing finger toward Mace for emphasis.

"Probably," said Mace, with a resigned nod. "But, it could have also been Hawk. He's pretty trigger-happy, and he's got a big following in the Midwest."

"Well, is somebody going to tell us what's going on?" Barbara asked.

"You're a psychic—figure it out," Vince spat tartly.

Barbara moved to rise from her chair and exit.

"I'm sorry, Barb." Vince rubbed the side of his face. "I'm just angry. I can't *believe* they did this to me." He plopped into a chair.

Barbara stiffly reseated herself and stared down at her plate, not quite ready to forgive him.

Vince sighed. "Leading sucks. No matter how much you try to help people, sell your soul for them, they screw you anyway."

"Vince, take command," Mace ordered with a touch of irritation. "Let MAP know they're out for good, or until they can be trusted. Make sure they're cut off from all intel."

Vince glared at him and panned the rest of his waiting listeners. "MAP planted the bomb 'To bring attention to the danger of the Vhurruh influence,' and I quote. We don't know under whose direction, but we've narrowed it down to them."

"I told you Hawk was trouble," said Barbara. "He's carrying a lot of anger and he's into power. The energy was all over him. Hey. Didn't Flies With Raven say something about Hawk losing his sight? She meant *him!* She saw it coming."

Vince rolled his eyes. "Well, she could have been a *little* more specific, instead of sounding like she was talking about mangy animals." He stared at the table. "Months of work to show that we are intelligent citizens working toward liberation of our government and military from an alien faction with their own happy little agendas just went straight to the dirt."

Gina attempted a diversion with the suggestion that he eat something. Ron silently passed Patrick and Mace the remaining wings and biscuits.

"What's MAP?" Caffrey asked Ron in a low voice.

Vince turned in his chair before Ron could answer. "It's a bunch of gun-loving, backwoods militia nuts that call themselves *Militia of the American People*. They're pyros using any excuse to blow up something in the guise of 'just cause'—without having to consult anyone. Diversity and teamwork didn't make it into their little rule book. They're like an alien-hating KKK, and they're making *us* look like one in the process."

Gina cleared her throat. "Did you get the word out that it's *not* us, that we knew nothing about this?"

"Of course I did!" Vince yelled. He grabbed a cold biscuit, slapped it on a plate, then dropped his head and exhaled to gain control of his emotions. He looked up at Gina quietly, and their eyes locked with mutual apology and forgiveness. A slight smile curved Vince's lips in appreciation of her presence and patience. He took a slow, deep breath. "And I also got the word out to a few divisions that bombs will not be sanctioned by us. We are not terrorists. Not now, not ever."

"Hey, Vince!" called Ron from the den. "They're saying now the Underground is denying responsibility. Holly Dunn's on!"

Vince vaulted from the chair, which crashed to the floor.

Holly Dunn, a slim, dark-haired girl with an olive complexion and Asian eyes spoke from a newsroom. "This was *not* an act of terrorism by the Underground," Holly reiterated, "but apparently the act of a separatist militia group. My sources claim the Underground, specifically AllianceWatch, stands by its original promise never to knowingly cause harm to any human or alien in the effort to proclaim its message, except in defense of their lives." Other journalists launched into her with a barrage of questions, practically drooling over the juicy tidbit, thrilled that their station had the information before others did.

After a few questions, the main newscaster abruptly changed to a story about flooding in a Midwestern town.

"And that's all we're going to get," said Patrick. "For now."

Appearing somewhat vindicated, Vince, Mace, and Patrick began to peck at the leftovers from dinner while Gina heated up more food and Sharia badgered them into answering her questions.

Vince announced a trip to Stone Mountain was planned for the next day, since it was spring break and the mountain would be full of families enjoying the warm weather and various attractions to occupy energy-filled children.

"You good to go?" Mace asked Caffrey in a stern military tone.

"I'll do my part." Caffrey stared at Mace as if it were a challenge. She was tired of his grumpy moods. The others watched them, surprised at the additional chill in the air.

"Think you can make it up the mountain?" Mace asked, not quite masking his opinion of that possibility.

Gina cleared her throat with unquestionable reproach.

"You do *your* part, and I'll do *mine*," Caffrey replied acidly.

"Do we have a problem here?" Vince was clearly annoyed at the conflict.

"Wouldn't want to put her out of her way," Mace said.

"Oh, please don't," Caffrey retorted, "but, I'm sure you will." She exited the room without looking back. Behind her, she heard Patrick's southern drawl. "Why don't you just bite her face off and get it over with?"

Thankful for Patrick's affront, she paused mid-stride in the round foyer as heavenly piano and organ music wafted through the front windows. Such beauty was a sharp contrast to the energy in the previous room and the past few days of her life. She pushed open the ornate front doors and sat in one of the rockers to allow the smooth, soulful hymn to relax her tense shoulders.

"They sound pretty good." Barbara joined Caffrey in one of the chairs.

"It's beautiful," Caffrey commented wistfully, wondering if Barbara had come out to keep an eye on her. "I love old hymns like that." She continued to rock and listen. "Sure wish I could go over there." *Anyplace but here.*

"Yeah, well, you *cain't*," Barbara stated with a hint of regret.

The hymn ended, and a new one began, with a faster tempo. The crisp chinking of tambourines accented the joyful voices in harmony.

"Hey, I know this one," Barbara exclaimed. "*This world is not my home, I'm just a passin' through....*"

Caffrey smiled and began to clap with the beat.

"Are we having church?" Patrick teased at the doorway.

"Amen," Caffrey replied. "It's better than what's back in there." She nodded toward the front doors.

A shrill *'meow'* resounded from edge of the porch.

"Awww, you want to sing too?" Caffrey remarked to a small calico head peeping up over the edge.

"There's the little rascal!" Gina exclaimed, skirting around Patrick. "Think I'll get it for Sharia. She was so tickled with it this morning. Mace didn't want her bringing it into the house."

"Is *that* what he was fussing at her for?" Caffrey bristled. "Geez!"

Gina hoisted the tiny kitten into the air and stroked its multi-colored head. "Oooo, you little sweetie." The kitten mewed louder. "I think he didn't want Sharia getting attached to it."

"Sounds like the ol' boy's a little leery of attachments," said Barbara, with a side glance to Gina.

"Yeah, well, we've *all* had a bumpy road there," growled Caffrey. "*We* don't stop caring just because we got burnt." The moment the words escaped, her conscience smote her. For the past year, she had evaded and maneuvered around men, rejected dates, even avoided getting too close to girlfriends. Instead of reaching out, she had reached inside herself, gone into hibernation, waiting for the next spring to brave the world again.

"I don't know what's gotten into him." Gina shook her head with a guilty expression, as though she were speaking treason. "He *is* being sensible, but...."

"Oh!" Sharia squealed and jumped through the open door Patrick was still holding.

"Anybody else?" said Patrick with a good-natured frown.

Sharia grasped the amiable kitten and curled him into her shoulder. "Let's take him upstairs."

Patrick threw up his hands. "I know nothing...I see nothing...."

The women giggled mutinously and tiptoed up the stairs all the way to the master bedroom on the right. Sprawled on the floor, they played with the kitten and enjoyed the all-female companionship for nearly an hour before a knock on the door interrupted them.

Being old and warped, the door creaked open. Mace stood in the entryway, hands on hips, looking formidable and disapproving. He was wearing blue jeans and a sleeveless white T-shirt, which accented his tan skin. The muscles of his chest and arms bulged as if he had been lifting weights. Caffrey's eyes roamed over him of their own accord, then she caught herself. She had stayed furious at him all day and did not want to feel anything *but* anger.

Mace opened his mouth to speak, but then he spotted the kitten. "*What* is that thing doing in here?"

Sharia grabbed the furry body and shoved it behind her back. A startled "meow" rang in the air. Caffrey could see muscles working in Mace's jaw as Sharia gave him a mocking, toothy grin.

With quick precision, his eyes circled the room and landed on Caffrey, before diverting back to Sharia. "I told you to get that thing out of here."

Every smile in the room dropped.

"*Hey,* Mace," said Gina with a warning edge to her voice. "It's *just* a kitten."

"That's not the point. I gave *you*...." He pointed a finger at Sharia. "A direct order. And if it stays here, you'll become attached to it. No sense in becoming attached to anything in this damn war." He stomped briskly toward Sharia.

Caffrey reached over Sharia, which caused Sharia to fall sideways, and grabbed the kitten. She tossed it quickly to Gina, who cringed as four sets of tiny claws dug into her clothing. Caffrey jumped to her feet and stood in Mace's path, which forced him to halt inches from her face.

Barbara was scrambling to her feet. "Mace, what the heck is wrong with you?"

Staring defiantly into Mace's eyes, Caffrey wondered what possessed her to do what she did. His deadly glare became a challenge from which she did not look away. Mace squinted, focused beyond Caffrey, to Sharia, then shifted his attention menacingly on Caffrey.

"Bradley!" Barbara scolded. "If we're not supposed to care about anything in this war, then why are we fighting it?"

Mace ignored Barbara's question, but his lips pressed together at the use of his real name. Instead of the fear Caffrey should have been feeling, a rush of elation raced through her body, something dark, earthy and untamed. The hair on her arms rose. Her heart pumped faster. "He can't help it, he's just given *over,*" she spoke, shocked at her own audacity.

Mace gripped her throat with an icy hand and nearly lifted her off her feet. Everyone seemed to move as one. Arms were pulling at Mace. Gina, Barbara, and Sharia were screaming at him. Unable to breathe and having no other defense against his vice-like grip, Caffrey kneed him fully in the groin.

Mace buckled with a grunt. Caffrey wrenched from his grip and bolted out the door. She ran the length of the balcony and vaulted down the stairs two at a time, wincing in pain. Her heart pounded wildly as she cleared the last two steps with a stomach-jarring leap. Frightened by her own actions, but more from his, she intended to get as far away as possible. A stab of guilt attacked her conscience for insulting him. She quickly suppressed it and decided the altercation was his fault.

How he managed to recover so fast she never knew, but she heard his body hit the hallway paneling above her and his feet stamp across the balcony. Gina and Barbara were still yelling at him in fury. Caffrey ran across the foyer and turned the lock on the ornate front doors. Movement caught her eye. Patrick and Vince were staring at her from the dining room doorway, disbelief and confusion on their faces.

"Hey, what's going on?" Vince demanded, but Caffrey kept running.

Icy-hot flashes seared through her abdomen as she hurled herself down the porch steps and around the back of the house. Even with the unbearable pain, it felt good to run, farther and farther away from her prison—the building as well as the people.

Beyond the free-standing garage, up the hill, and into the evergreens she ran. As the trees enveloped her, the last week of her life seemed to fade, along with the voices that had consumed it.

Blindly, she tore past layers of thick fir trees with only glimmers from a paling purple and orange sunset to guide her. Under sharp branches and between trees she wove like a panther in the ever-growing darkness. Finally, her stomach forced her to stop. She crouched low and tried to catch her breath, hugging her sides with both arms.

Gina and Vince's voices carried on the chill wind, calling for Mace, and for her. She smiled as Gina loudly cursed Mace's name.

Deciding it was time to move again, Caffrey wove carefully through prickly trees and thick brush, ever upward. Near the top of the small mountain, Caffrey muffled her ragged breath with the front of her T-shirt, and bent low to rest and listen. All around her, the wind blew at the forest in great gasps, foretelling the arrival of an unpredictable mountain thunderstorm. Leaves and branches rustled together in high-pitched, crispy sounds, which could easily disguise careful, practiced footsteps.

Caffrey surveyed every branch and tree around her but could detect no sign of Mace. With a hint of golden remaining on the horizon, shadows grew long. Faint wisps of disturbed voices carried from the direction of the house, and then ceased.

Spying a thick group of bushes to her left, Caffrey crawled carefully, but two mourning doves shrieked in protest and flapped noisily into the dark sky. Caffrey cursed under her breath and moved to an alternate concealed spot where she had a partial view of the lighted church far below. Mace would head for the direction of the birds...if he was still in pursuit.

She hoped he was not. Shaking with cold, she snuggled under an umbrella of branches that encircled a giant spruce. For the first time in days, she was free. It was a bittersweet freedom. She *had* grown attached to the group. Yet, here, there was no one to tell her what she should or should not do, no one to glare with suspicion, no one halting a conversation when she walked into a room.

She smiled. If Mace were not pursuing her, she might stay out for a while and revel in liberty until the cold forced her back in. Which would not be long, she realized, and vigorously rubbed her chilly arms. The army-green T-shirt was little protection, although the gray jogging pants were warm enough.

Night descended like a damp, cold blanket around her. Moon beams blinked through the canopy of branches but disappeared as rumbling, dark clouds rushed in. Caffrey wished vainly for better night vision, especially with only a smudge of light from the church and cabins further out.

Something tickled the side of her face, and she sloughed off what was surely a spider's web. As she batted her hair and clothes, fearful she may have taken the spider with her, she snorted to herself. How crazy she had been fuming at Mace's ridiculous temper. Who'd he think he was, anyway? A mere kitten in the grand scheme of things was no reason for him to bully everyone. *Cold-hearted animal*, she thought angrily, and pondered why looking at her always made him so stiff and irritated.

Movement caught her eye, and she scrambled toward the wide trunk of the spruce, but she was not fast enough. Mace fell on her, knocking her hard against the forest floor. Caffrey squirmed to get free of him and gasped at the tearing pain in her abdomen.

"You little witch!" Mace sputtered.

"Stop it, Mace. Leave me alone!"

"No way, Sweets, not after that. If you weren't a woman...."

Caffrey twisted under his firm muscles with all her might, but she had to stop when sparkles decorated her eyelids from the incredible pain. "Well, I *am* a woman." She gritted her teeth.

"Unfortunately."

Nearly popping her hip socket, Caffrey raised one knee to push against him, but she halted. Not only did the attempt feel as though her stitches were tearing open, but with incredible agility Mace pinned her flailing arms and held her legs with his. His right knee dug into her thigh, making her cry out. He backed off instantly, but not enough to free her.

"I wish your butt was in the military," he growled, panting. "The next time I give an order, I *expect*..."

"This *isn't* the military!" she yelled. "Don't you get it? We're a *group*, not a... *unit!* And if you give stupid orders, nobody's going to follow them."

"That's *not* the point. The structure of command must be maintained. No team functions without it."

"No, *you* can't function without it. It gives you an excuse not to feel."

He stopped moving. He was staring at her as if in shock. Caffrey became acutely aware of his heavy body molded against hers, of his male scent, his stern face so close. Unnerved by the unruly sensations racing through her torso, she jerked an arm and twisted to break free. He wrested the arm firmly against the jutting roots of the spruce.

With his arm poised in front of her face, Caffrey lifted her head, and with more nerve than she'd ever had in her life, aimed her teeth at his wrist.

Mace pulled her arms further apart as her teeth scraped his skin, which made them both slide nearly three feet down the steep slope, into the umbrella-like branches of the tree.

"Try that again, and I'll break your pretty little face open."

"Go ahead, *big guy*," she challenged sarcastically. "That's all you've *wanted* all along, isn't it? Shoot me? Get rid of me? You don't have a gun now, so what are you going to do, strangle me?" She considered that, in fact, he might be tempted to strangle her, and most likely had several weapons hidden on him. She stared into his wild eyes, waiting.

Mace's facial muscles shook in an attempt to control whatever raged within his soul. Caffrey feared for a moment he would strike her, and strangely wanted to know if he was capable, thinking it better to know now. Besides, if he did, maybe the group would let her go somewhere else, somewhere away from him.

"Want to tell me now how the SAAFs keep finding us, Princess?"

She glared at him in astonishment. "I don't know any more than you do."

"The rest of them might believe that, but *I'm* not that stupid."

"Oh, trust me, you *are* stupid." Warm furry energy enveloped her, and it took Caffrey a moment to realize the Vhurruh had tapped in, alarmed at her alarm.

"The X-rays say you don't have bugs in you," said Mace. "But they can't see into your brain, now, can they?"

Caffrey's eyes widened. Could he sense the Vhurruh? She could feel the Vhurruh probing desperately to assess whether she was in danger. Caffrey reached for the Vhurruh's mind, and the cold reality of her own suspicions flooded over her. Up until that moment, she had not faced the fear that she could be coerced unaware, that some untouchable part of her brain could be telling the Vhurruh exactly what he needed to track the group.

No, the Vhurruh spoke clearly into her head. *I would never betray you. I warned you earlier.*

How do I know? Caffrey thought back to him. *Am I controlled by you?*

We do not control queens. I gave you what was needed. Nothing more. You are the messenger now. I will protect you when I can. Have I asked you anything that compromises you?

No, Caffrey answered with uncertainty. *But...you told me to get the disc to the Underground.*

You carried it within you. I could not retrieve it without damaging you. We are watched. You were our best hope. In case we did not survive. When you were wounded and in...I must go now.

No! Caffrey implored. But his warmth had retreated, leaving a sense of alarm behind.

Mace was watching Caffrey's eyes curiously as clouds shifted to allow bright moonlight through the branches.

"I am absolutely certain," Caffrey said with conviction, "that I am doing nothing to aid the SAAFs, or the faction, and neither is the Vhurruh."

Mace waited to respond. "Maybe you really believe that. But, the truth is, you wouldn't know, even if you were."

"Yes, I would."

"No, you wouldn't."

"Yes, I *would*," she insisted.

"*No*, you wouldn't."

"How do you know?"

"Trust me, I know."

"Have you ever been linked?"

"Not gonna happen."

"Then you don't know what you think you know."

"I've *seen* an over, you haven't."

"Sharia told me about them. The vacant look in their eyes, how you can always tell because they suddenly have no personality. They start acting like unemotional soldiers under orders. Do *I* look like that? Hmmm, wonder who does?"

The muscles in his face twitched. Their eyes remained fixed on each other. Wind blew a lock of Caffrey's red hair across her face, which brushed Mace's cheek as well. Mace's jaw relaxed, and the quality of his gaze altered. The muscles around his ebony eyes softened. He glanced over Caffrey's entire face as if searching for something.

"I told you Nadine recognized me." Caffrey was suddenly uncomfortable in a different way.

"Yeah, after we were out of the caves. Timing a little off?"

"Well, you pissed me off that night. You're such an ass. I didn't *want* to tell you anything."

"Something as important as *that?*"

"Yes! And...stuff was going on and...everybody was talking at once. And...you piss me off anyway!"

His eyes squinted. "Why?" he asked in a deceptively mild voice, as though to see what she would say.

"Because you're mean. You're just...*mean.*"

"You'd better get mean, too, Princess, if you want to survive."

"I'm not a mean person. And I'm not going to become one because of *you.* I could have hurt you just now if I wanted to."

"Oh, big talker, aren't we? If you could have, you should have. Don't ever let your enemy have an edge. If I had already trained you, I'd kick your butt for letting me get this far."

Waving pine boughs caused milky glimmers of moonlight to flash intermittently across one side of their tense faces. Caffrey decided to stay focused on Mace and not blink. Mace seemed intent on not looking away from her either, as though it were a test of will.

"Why didn't you just let me die in that alley?" Caffrey whispered, surprising them both.

Mace's eyes widened and his lips parted. Uncertainty and fear replaced his rigid anger. His bottom lip quivered once, or had Caffrey imagined it. Not the response she was expecting. Not from him. He should have jumped at the chance to propose it would have been a better alternative. She waited, still expecting him to do so.

Watching his black brows knit together in puzzlement, she became aware of his chest rising and falling against hers. He was breathing heavy from emotion, not from the effort to hold her still. She had stopped struggling and remained non-combative.

With the shock of her question fading, his fierce eyes softened to contemplation, curiosity. His scrutiny caused her blood to pump faster. She broke eye contact to deflect the crackling energy and took in his hard, rough features in greater detail: the frown wrinkles at the corners of his eyes, the heavy lids and long, straight, black lashes. His strong, square jaw and copper skin were scarred in several places. One scar shined near his right eye as if a knife blade had just missed it.

Silently, he, too, surveyed her face, not even bothering to feign anger. Something different had passed between them. Though both relaxed the strain on arms and legs, neither spoke. Minutes passed, and the tempestuous wind blew leaves around them.

Suddenly Mace leaned down and placed his lips on hers. A slight sound of surprise escaped Caffrey. For a split second, she considered fighting him, but the thought evaporated as the warmth of his full lips on hers caused an explosion in her body. Desire, so long suppressed, overwhelmed her like waves of summer heat. The taste of him was delicious and utterly masculine. She kissed him willingly in return.

Impassioned by her response, Mace pressed his mouth hungrily, as though possessed. Their bodies seemed to melt together. Slowly, his right hand released her arm, and his fingers slid into her hair.

"Brad?" Vince called out, his voice only yards away in the darkness.

Mace froze with his lips over Caffrey's, then pulled reluctantly away. He blinked several times and gazed at her as though awakening in a strange room. Lifting himself effortlessly, he disappeared between the boughs of the spruce, leaving the spikey branches rustling wildly in the moonlight.

Caffrey stared at the space where he had been. Above, the moon disappeared as dark clouds reclaimed it.

"Caffrey?" Vince called out, worried.

Caffrey could hear Vince's careful footsteps getting closer. She took a long, deep breath, and slowly let it out. A groan escaped her as she rolled under the pine boughs, and stood. Cold set into her limbs and made her shiver as she brushed leaves and sticks off her rumpled clothes. Light flashed in her direction, and she shaded her eyes.

"Are you okay?" Vince asked. Concern wrinkled Vince's brow as he scanned her face and arms with the flashlight. He looked strangely at her hair.

"I'm fine," Caffrey replied, but she avoided his eyes. She began to descend through the trees.

"Ho! Wait a minute. What happened?"

"I don't know what happened."

"What do you mean? Where's Mace? I thought I saw him."

She looked at Vince then.

"You look like you're in a daze. Did he find you?"

"Yes." Again, Caffrey moved toward the house.

Vince held her still with one arm. She glared back at him. Instantly, he looked hurt.

"You're bleeding." He shined the flashlight on her wrist. Caffrey watched as blood beaded from a jagged scratch which had pieces of wood still stuck on it. There was a puncture mark further down, also dabbed with a tiny smear of blood.

"Caffrey," Vince demanded roughly, "did Mace hurt you?"

Caffrey looked blankly at his chest, since it was eye-level, as though it would somehow give her the answer.

"Gina said you guys had a fight," Vince urged. "Mace got...a little crazy."

Caffrey nodded. "Yeah...he's a little crazy. Can I go now?"

Vince dropped his arms and breathed a sigh of frustration. "I hate leading."

Caffrey thought of several responses, one of them an apology, but she turned and continued silently downward through the trees. Vince followed a few paces behind, shining the light ahead for both of them.

Caffrey was embarrassed to find everyone gathered at the front of the house, worry and curiosity on their faces.

"Mace come back here?" Vince asked the group.

"Nope." Barbara watched Caffrey intently.

Vince cursed, and scanned the woods with his flashlight. Caffrey continued past everyone and into the house. Gina jumped in front of her halfway up the stairs, her arms folded. "What happened?"

"It's okay," Caffrey lied, and tried to pass her on the stairs.

"*Caffrey*, I *know* something happened. I can feel it."

"I need to lie down. Where're the bandages?"

Gina sighed. "Let's go upstairs."

As Caffrey ascended the stairs, a warm, feathery touch of worry stroked her mind. With ethereal fingertips, the Vhurruh touched the edges of her soul and seemed to shiver with anger. Curious, Caffrey reached for him lest he escape. A mixture of displeasure and jealousy hit her. Of course; he was a drone. He might be young, but he was insulted and angry at Mace's behavior.

It's okay now, she said. *Thank you for caring.* She threw him a sensation of endearment, like a kiss blown across the room. He experienced the equivalent of a smile. She did not know if Vhurruh could physically smile, but she felt his happiness as he drew back into the dimension from whence he came.

In the master bathroom, Gina tended Caffrey's small wounds in silence. Caffrey seethed under the icy spring water as Gina forced her arms into the sink, after which the cold water began to feel good. Caffrey flinched as Gina sponged an antiseptic, a different kind of cold.

"Well, as long as you're okay, I guess I won't try to *pull* it out of you." She placed both hands on her hips, and her expression changed to tolerant sarcasm. "So, *are* you going to tell me how you got these cuts, or do I have to steal your shirt and meditate all night to get the scoop?"

Caffrey chuckled in spite of her reclusive mood. "I tripped."

"Nice try. I *am* a psychic, after all."

"Ha! You're probably just guessing."

Gina pursed her lips.

"Okay, so we had a little tousle." Caffrey stole a quick glance to find Gina's eyebrows rising in protest. "But...he didn't kill me. That's good—isn't it?"

Gina was not pleased with her humor. "Did he...hit you, or anything? Seriously?"

Caffrey hesitated a moment. "No, he didn't *hit* me. He hurt me, but he didn't hit me. I'm sure I would have hit back or screamed if he had. It would have been a quick contest, though. His arms are hard as rocks." Caffrey rolled her shoulder to stretch the sore muscles. "Of course, I kind of hurt him in the room, I guess." She snorted. "I tried to bite him, too."

Gina sucked in an angry, deep breath and blew it out.

"He's a leader, Caffrey. He doesn't have the right to lose control. I don't know what's going on, but something's got to give. He's been crazy these last few days." She shook her head. "Just like before when...." Gina halted.

"When?"

"When he and.... Never mind. His behavior is unacceptable. He's been under emotional stress before, but he's never cracked."

Caffrey stared at the floor. Many thoughts explored and weighed themselves in her tired brain, none of which made sense. She noticed white gauze wrapped in several places on her arms. "Hey," she protested.

"You leave these just like they are. I want to make sure these wounds don't get infected, and I want to make sure Mr. Wolf can't miss them."

"Mr. Wolf?"

"Take these off, and I'll give you demerits for disobeying the doctor." Before Caffrey could stop her, Gina grabbed her arm and pressed a large, square bandage across a tiny scrape.

"I think I *am* in the military," Caffrey protested.

Gina crossed her arms and arched one eyebrow. "No, the military would have put you both in the brig and rationed the bandages. You know you have leaves in your hair?"

"Oh, my gosh." Caffrey patted her hair and touched several leaves and pine needles.

"Here, let me." Gina pulled out the debris piece by piece. A small, woolly black spider ran across Gina's hand and plopped to the floor. Both women screamed, and danced across the tile before they conquered their fear at the same time and nearly killed each other trying to kill the spider.

Once it was reduced to black mush on the floor, they collapsed in laughter.

Mace turned the handle on the double doors and frowned. Vince knew better than to leave any door unlocked, even if he knew Mace was still out. He halted at sight of Vince and Gina sitting on two of the red chairs in the foyer, both with arms folded and faces set, waiting for him.

"Let's go in the den," Vince ordered. Mace locked the front doors and followed them, his stomach churning.

"Sit." Vince motioned toward one of the overstuffed chairs.

Mace sat. This was not going to be good. Vince rarely took that tone.

"Want to tell me what that was about?" asked Vince.

Mace sighed. "We had a disagreement."

"I had to bandage a couple of cuts on her arm," said Gina in a deceptively mild voice. "She said she tripped. You going to try that story, too?"

Mace inhaled and exhaled slowly. So, she didn't come in raving about his mad temper. He had been fighting his temper his whole life, but the loss of his parents, and then his sister, had accelerated the problem. Sometimes, his fierce temper was his ally, giving him strength when he needed it. This was not one of those times. He did not know she had cuts. Must have happened when he pinned her and they slid. He had just wanted to hold her still, to get answers.

Suspicions and questions had been tormenting him for days. Unexplainable thoughts and feelings had kept him awake each night. Nothing had been the same since he found her in that cursed alley. Covered in blood and yet, so beautiful.

He still remembered the strange electric feeling that had zipped through him. With faint hope he had pressed two fingers into her neck, detected a weak, slow pulse. He had brushed mud-soaked red hair out of her pallid face. What he felt in that moment still haunted him. He pushed the memory aside.

"I don't have any answers for you," he stated firmly. "I over-reacted. It won't happen again."

"Oh, you're not getting off that easy," said Gina, her leg vibrating up and down with irritation. "We've seen you like this before."

Mace stared at her, confused, then comprehension dawned. "That was different."

"Oh, that was different, all right. This is *worse*."

Anger rose hot in his chest, and Mace breathed through it while he considered several responses. Was this any of their business? He knew what Vince would say. He'd heard him say to others: "If it affects the team, then it *is* my business." Mace pondered his feelings. They whirled inside him like an uncontrollable tornado. This was not the time for crazed feelings and fruitless hopes. He needed to think straight. He did not need this distraction.

"I told you," he looked hard at Vince, "it won't happen again."

"Maybe it was supposed to happen," Gina stated, watching him keenly.

"Don't even start with that," he responded, raising a hand. She *knew* how he felt about those stupid prophecies. Flies With Raven had been throwing them at him for three years.

"There's a fine line between love and hate," Gina continued, "and you and Caffrey are walking that line. You both just haven't figured it out, yet."

Mace glared at her. "I don't need this right now."

"Need what?" asked Gina, her expression darkening. "You mean her?"

"I mean, this...whole situation. This distraction."

"Oh, that's what this is. This is a distraction?"

He was surprised to find a smile toying at her lips. He had thought she was angry.

"Do you have feelings for her?" Vince asked.

"No!" Mace exclaimed, surprising himself.

Both Vince and Gina's eyebrows rose. It was a lie and they all knew it.

"Look...." Mace began, trying to find a way to deflect them. "Whatever this is, it's my problem. I don't...I'm not sure what she feels, but we need to keep our distance right now. We've got a lot of heat on us, and we're tired. We have work to do, and I need to think straight."

After a thoughtful moment, Vince said, "Agreed. But she didn't *lose* it tonight. You did."

Mace held his gaze. He knew Vince was angry, but also knew he couldn't stay that way for long.

"She's not a soldier, Mace," Vince added. "Whether willing or unwilling, she's just a messenger. You need to think of her as a civilian: a civilian who is part of *us*. Whatever is going on between you two is your business—*until* you make it *my* business." Vince exhaled and placed both hands on his hips. "I need back the protector, advisor, and friend that you've always been. Can I have back that sensible person?" Vince's face softened and his mouth twitched. "Even if he's a pain in the ass?"

Mace gave him a side smile. "Absolutely."

17

CAVEMAN

Butterflies danced in Caffrey's stomach, which made the drive to Stone Mountain seem longer than three hours. Conflicting emotions vied for her attention but she could not decide where they belonged or how to categorize them. She tried to focus on how wonderful it would feel to finally get the disc open and discover its contents, but memories of the night before, on a moonlit mountain, took precedence. Mace's kiss had awakened something in her. Now it would not quietly go back to sleep.

In the beginning, he had been her enemy, her antagonist at every turn. At the cabin, after her memories had been triggered, he began to change. During the escape through the caves, he had become a comrade, a leader. Then, at the mansion, he had reverted to being cold, distant, suspicious. What had changed him? She had seen the distrust in his eyes when they exited the cave, after she disclosed that Nadine might have recognized her. What was his first question when he caught up with her on the mountain behind the mansion? "Want to tell me now how the SAAFs keep finding us, Princess?"

Maybe you were starting to trust me, after all, Mr. Angry Face. She let out a slow sigh. She had not meant to deceive him. She was angry that he was angry. Would it have made any difference if she had confided in him? Would he have chosen for the group to leave immediately? Perhaps. Would they have had time to drive to another location? She would never know.

Caffrey sighed again and watched the countryside go by. It had been an awkward and uncomfortable morning. In relative silence, the women around her had stuffed backpacks and tactfully evaded any reference to the previous evening. Barbara had hummed obscure tunes while Gina made small talk. Sharia stole curious glances at Caffrey as if waiting for an opening to pose questions, but Caffrey avoided her curious gaze.

When the women had arrived at the breakfast table, Caffrey expected a special look, maybe even a tentative smile from Mace. But, his eyes slid from Caffrey as fast as they landed. Whatever bridge she thought they had built, somehow crumbled.

Mace's statements were short and clipped as he reviewed strategies and issued instructions to everyone at the table. Heavy lines under his eyes made him appear to not have slept. Caffrey had continued to glance at him, hoping for some acknowledgement that the kiss they had shared meant something more than an obscure flare of passion. But when he mentioned her name, it was in third person as to where she would be or which group she would be with.

As everyone left the mansion, gear in tow, Gina stopped Caffrey at the ornate wooden doors and leaned close to whisper.

"Vince and I had...words...with Mace last night. He promised to keep his emotions under control. Concerning you, that is. He has assured us there will not be a problem in the future."

Caffrey's heart dropped. What did that mean? If Mace had not kissed her, she would have translated his response to Gina as a promise of civility. But, he *had* kissed her, and the flame he ignited was being doused with cold water. Caffrey had watched for an opportunity to talk to Mace privately as they gathered outside the mansion, but did not get the chance because Underground members Cameron, Hank and Eileen joined the group in order to provide vehicles for the mission.

Caffrey judged Cameron to be in his early twenties and of Hispanic heritage. Handsome and jovially even-tempered, he was passionate in his devotion to the cause of the Underground. Barbara whispered to Caffrey that his favorite cousin had disappeared ten months earlier.

Hank was clearly much older, had part of his shirttail hanging out, and was long overdue for a haircut. He was quick to smile sideways with a two-day-old whiskered cheek that bulged from a wad of chewing tobacco. Winks were thrown Cameron's way with every barb Hank threw at the younger man, including references to Cameron as the "college boy." Though different from each other in appearance and age they obviously enjoyed each other's company, and constantly joked and insulted one another, which afforded the group welcomed entertainment.

Eileen was vivacious and sharp-witted, laughed easily, and held everyone's attention with her model-thin figure, long raven hair and beautiful, full-lipped smile. She spoke with an oddly sensual military voice and stance. She hugged Mace boldly, pressing her entire body against him, then slyly glimpsed Caffrey and Sharia under long black lashes to assess their reactions. Caffrey watched

Mace's arm hesitate before releasing her. Fortunately for Caffrey, Eileen and Mace rode in Hank's Hummer.

Though Caffrey's emotions were in a whirl, she was fairly comfortable riding in Cameron's SUV with Ron, Barbara, and Sharia. While Cameron drove, they chatted about religious experiences, extra-terrestrial contact, and Native American medicine, which Caffrey realized she would dearly miss if she was stationed somewhere without them. She decided Vince was going to have a fight on his hands if he tried to send her somewhere else.

When they finally reached Stone Mountain, Caffrey's heart fluttered and constricted at sight of the great carving on the north side of the mountain. Old memories rushed in with pain and pleasure: scenes of basking on the lake's beach, riding horses along the wooded trail, and picnicking with the girls while their die-hard fishermen repeatedly cast unsuccessful lures for bass. Caffrey swallowed hard. Focusing on what she was about to do lifted her spirits, which helped to push the memories aside.

The cable car tower adorning the pinnacle of the mountain shone white in the sun against a perfect blue sky, calm and ageless as the mountain. Lines at the main entrance were already 15 cars deep at 9:30 a.m. Mace and Vince were thrilled that the mountain was crowded, a definite advantage.

Wearing a thick, gray beard, weathered jacket, and baseball clap, Mace took point toward the granite trail and led the group around anyone in uniform, keeping in the thickest crowds of families or upbeat teenagers. Eileen was ordered to coach Caffrey's face away from the view of security guards or curious public. Eileen was all-business and carried out her assignment as though she were being graded, with keen, razor-sharp eyes that equaled Mace's. Caffrey wondered if they had been in some type of training together.

As though starting pleasant conversation, Eileen would smile and rattle off data and commands almost too fast for Caffrey to keep up with. "Two police officers in vehicle at three o'clock, driving north slowly through the cars—keep turned to me, smile, think of something to laugh about—what was the last funny movie you saw? Group of males at one o'clock. They've turned around twice—walk slower. Link your arm with Patrick's so they'll assume you're together and lose interest." All the while she smiled. Several times she chuckled as though she and Caffrey were recalling some humorous event.

Determined to show Eileen she could perform as well, Caffrey learned to create idle banter at a moment's notice and produce a smile while asking Eileen if the danger had passed. Gina, Barbara, and Sharia were well-versed in the practice and appeared part of different, jovial family groups.

Caffrey's brilliant red hair was again tightly braided to her skull, but this time a brown wig was added, which was hot, and itched. A rattan summer hat placed on top made it hotter. Thick black sunglasses served to obscure her eyes. Sharia had outfitted her in the drabbest of colors, with a large, baggy T-shirt and a hoodie hanging loose to hide her figure.

No chances were taken with Vince, either. He sported a cap, sunglasses, and a light-brown mustache and wig. Gina had stuffed his shirt with clothing to make him appear pot-bellied. Even Patrick, Barbara, and Ron were dressed in leisure tourist clothing. Ron had been given a hat, mustache and beard, supplied by Cameron, who loved disguises whether they were needed or not.

With continuous groans, the group labored up the kindest side of the breast-shaped mountain. Eileen quickly berated everyone for their slow progress and insisted that if they were well-exercised and fit, it would be a "cinch." She glanced to Mace for approval. Caffrey was secretly pleased when he mumbled, "We go as fast as she can go." Eileen glared back at Caffrey with something akin to pity. Caffrey made a face at Eileen's back once she turned around, which made Sharia giggle.

Several times during the climb, Eileen skipped ahead and attempted to engage Mace in conversation at the lead. Watching them carefully, Caffrey noticed his responses were short and vague. Eileen quickly countered with jokes to woo other members, adding recollections of past humorous adventures.

Caffrey frowned and wondered why the girl couldn't leave Mace alone to do his job. It further irritated her to find that each male in the group grinned like a schoolboy every time Eileen addressed him, and nearly tripped on the slick rocks.

Every step of the wide path had to be traversed with slanted footsteps. Most of the stone slabs and boulders were worn smooth from decades of climbs by millions of determined hands and feet. Caffrey was glad for the treaded hiking boots Gina had purchased for her but regretted the newness of them as they chafed her ankles.

Halfway up the mountain, Mace glanced back at Caffrey and called a rest. Patrick exclaimed with delight as he read out loud names and dates carved into the granite, his favorite being an adventurous couple in 1852. A group of gray-haired men, their wrinkled faces shining, passed by at a faster pace than the Underground members had traveled, clearly enjoying the exercise and adventure. Caffrey's jaw fell open in shock. Patrick laughed at her and commented how that was going to be him at seventy, by

God. Caffrey chuckled, more as a panting effect than an actual laugh; she cut it short, knowing she would need to save her breath for the remainder of the arduous climb.

"Let's go." Mace motioned the group forward. After a short distance, he stopped near tall, split sections of rock that created sheer walls on either side of the trail. Six handsome and fit young men slipped off a flat boulder on which they were sunning themselves and meandered toward Mace. Their eyes darted toward Sharia and Caffrey. Sharia threw Caffrey a look of approval, and Caffrey raised her brows to agree. While Mace whispered greetings and instructions, the young men gave him their attention. They focused on Sharia and Caffrey the moment he was done. Eileen sauntered toward them and positioned her long-legged body right in front of the two girls.

"Oh, nice." Sharia bristled with indignation, but before she could complain further, Mace nodded a "follow" motion to Caffrey, Vince, Gina, and Patrick. Surprised she was being included, Caffrey followed them into the tight crevice. Mace whispered sharp, low instructions to the six young men, and they obediently created a barrier of bodies that blocked all view of the angled path.

Forty feet in, the path became a hazardous, twisted climb through bushes and trees, beyond which the rounded mountain appeared to drop off. Each traveler slipped several times on loose rocks or dirt and had to grab for any shrub or spindly pine sapling available while small stones fell away beneath them.

Mace raised a hand, squatted, then pointed a hand to an unseen opening. One by one they slithered into a brush-covered, black crevice under a treacherous outcropping of rock. The narrow opening slanted forward and dropped into a triangular, small cave, nearly ten feet in height.

"And I said I'd never go into another cave." Caffrey's tart comment drew a snicker from Patrick. She brushed off her clothes, adding to the cloud of dust growing from everyone's movements.

"I'll have to let Alan know I let four more people know about this," said Mace. He shed his backpack. "He'll kill me."

"Humph." Caffrey raised both brows.

Mace turned to her. "What?"

"I'm just amazed you would confess to someone having such a capability."

He snorted and retrieved a pouch from behind several rocks on a natural shelf.

She heard a soft chuckle behind her. "Good one," whispered Patrick.

Caffrey tried to suppress a smile while the group duct-taped pieces of cardboard from Mace's pack. Hands held the cardboard in place while jackets and shirts were used to block any light escaping into the narrow entrance. Vince forced a knife point into the center, which allowed a single golden ray of sun into the darkness. Mace and Caffrey stood on either side of the narrow beam as Mace arranged the dangling crystals front to front for the display.

"Is this right?" he asked.

Caffrey met his shadowed eyes across the beam of light, and her heart beat faster.

"Yes. But..." She placed her palm into the beam of light and raised it until the circle of light was only a centimeter wide, which placed her hand nearly against Patrick's shoulder. "It has to fall inside the circle of metal holding the crystal, right here." She reached out for the earrings, but Mace remained frozen, a flicker of distrust in his eyes.

"Seriously, Mace? Do you want this done right or not?"

"I'll hold them."

Caffrey glared at his grip on the stones enclosed by thin wires. "Your fingers are too fat."

"Could we get this done?" said Vince, an edge in his voice.

Mace stepped closer to Caffrey. "All right. Together."

Caffrey frowned and pushed his beefy fingers out of the way one by one until only their thumbs and forefingers held the stones in place. She had no intention of letting him screw this up. She wanted free from the headaches.

With careful grace, she moved their hands and the crystals slowly into the light, and held her breath. For a moment nothing happened; then a tiny starburst flashed within the stones, and a colossal, neon-blue Vhurruh materialized in the cave. Everyone gasped.

"Don't move," Mace ordered to keep their hands still.

A mane of brilliant gold surrounded the Vhurruh's head like a lion, while his tortoise-like mantle, striped in white, yellow, and blue, moved like a living, oval cape. The four eye antennae were a simple bronze color, which matched the branch-like gills on his tail. His forearms, ample belly, and side fins shined the same sky blue as Vince's eyes.

Caffrey felt tears burn at the alien's beauty. The image flickered, and she doubled her efforts to keep her hands from shaking.

"*Wuvena* Vinnncent." The Blue Vhurruh expended great effort to mouth the human words slowly. His floor-length, sky-blue whiskers quivered. "I fear soon not to hearrr you. I am detected. My commmunicationnns have at lassst betrayed mmeee. Mmuch beinng donnne to correct Vhurrruh mission, and preserve your sovereignty. Informationnn gathered. Transsssmissions will soonn sennd to Hurratt. If *zizza nnnetae* falls into Unndderground hannnds, pleeease try sennd. Must transfer in *mahyen nde-dehye,* the small unit. I dare nnnot say mmore. Do nnot loose hearrrt. I miss grreatly mind talk with youuu. This mmouth talk...cummmbersomme."

The noble alien breathed with difficulty. His bronze eye antennae curled slightly inward, a known sign of affection. "I bid you farewell, trrue frrriennd. To mme you arre *rinuut and zinzamey*—friend and brother in your language. May yourr hivve prosperrr and your queenn produce mmanyy. Farrrewelll."

As abruptly as it began, the massive blue image evaporated into darkness. No one moved in the cold silence. Mace and Caffrey watched the crystal earrings, both hoping a further transmission would occur. Their eyes raised and met. A barely audible *pssst* emanated from the earrings.

"Let 'em go," Mace ordered, and they dropped the stones to the dusty, leaf-strewn floor. After a spark and a tiny puff of smoke, Mace nudged them gingerly. He scooped them up. A quick juggle in his hands proved them cool. Caffrey noted they no longer gave her a headache as they lay lifeless in his open palm.

The somber group lowered the cardboard barrier. Crescent-shaped sunlight illuminated the floor of the cave. Vince turned his back on the others and dropped his head onto his arm against the cold stone. A controlled exhale and sniff in the silence betrayed his attempts to hide his sorrow.

Gina brushed tears from her cheeks as she wrapped an arm around him.

Caffrey swallowed and felt moisture well up again in her own eyes. What would it be like to lose her secret friend, now that she had him? What if he was discovered? She could not imagine. Her mind would be so silent.

Mace squeezed Vince's shoulder. "I'm sorry, man."

Patrick lightly slapped Vince's shoulder. "Me, too."

Mace surveyed Caffrey for a moment, his dark eyes bereft of their usual suspicion. "Let's sing your song." It was a suggestion of rescue more than a command. He held out the small, silver-gray disc. Caffrey stared open-mouthed at the strange alien technology that had traveled inside her for days. So small, yet able to change her life forever, and give her new scars to remind her.

Vince straightened and joined them, his arm tightly curled around Gina.

Caffrey continued to stare at the disc in Mace's hand. What if this also held bad news? What if it revealed something horrible about her Vhurruh?

"Princess," Mace urged, his voice soft but firm. "Let's do this."

Caffrey took a deep breath, cleared her throat, and sang eight clear, treble notes in a combination "A-E-O" pattern, as she remembered it from the mind of the Vhurruh. With the barest click, the disc opened like a smooth, gray clamshell. In its center rested a shiny crystalline disc, the width of a penny. Light appeared to swirl within as though it were alive. All heads in the dim light leaned toward it.

"Oh, my god, it's the *zizza netae*," said Vince, in quiet shock.

"The what?" asked Patrick.

"The information disc. It's what he was talking about. He sent me a visual of one of these some time ago."

"What, we gotta send this?"

Mace shook his head at Vince. "We can't even *read* this."

"Nobody at Remote obtained a drive?" asked Vince, his face looking hopeful.

"No. Word is, the big product release was postponed on Saturday. No one can get one."

Patrick frowned. "Hmmph. A couple days after Caffrey got this."

"You know, you're right," said Vince. "Did they halt the entire product release all because Charlie ran off with a single disc?"

Mace's eyebrows rose. "Your enemy can't use it if your enemy can't read it. Except for a few embassies and military sites, only one manufacturer has the drive."

"Telenex," Patrick, Gina, and Vince chimed together. Caffrey remembered Charlie's bloody lab coat with Telenex emblazoned on his pocket.

Everyone was silent for a moment. A great sense of destiny hung in the dust-filled air.

"Just great," Patrick drawled in a low voice. "Why couldn't they put it on a danged flash drive?"

"We're going to have to get *in* there." Vince winced at his own contemplation.

Mace thoughtfully rubbed his chin. "There's a way into everything from the inside." He gazed at the open disc in his palm.

Caffrey stared, transfixed, at the beautiful, iridescent circle. Like a dark cloud, nausea rolled over her. She swallowed and squinted against the onslaught. Snippets of knowledge swirled in a foreboding, gray storm in her brain.

Oh no, she thought, *not again.* She averted her eyes from the disc in hopes of forestalling whatever was triggering the images.

Patrick leaned against the cave wall. "Poor 'ol Charlie. I liked him. Sure 'nough computer guru, but he was a regular guy, too. And he liked everybody, ya know."

"Lots of people liked him, too," Gina added. "Have we touched base with all his coworkers?"

All eyes turned to Mace. "Still checking. SAAFs have been busy. Two coworkers have disappeared. One was fired. All the rest have been transferred. Tameel, Darrell, Jeanie, and...who was that other girl...Alaina. All replaced by new people."

Vince wagged a finger. "Wasn't there a Carol—something...uh...?"

"Thomas," blurted Gina. "Yes, the girl he felt sorry for. Smart girl, real timid. Had this frizzy gray hair, he said. He always tried to get her to talk because she didn't make friends easy."

"Yeah," said Vince, warming to the idea. "Carol Thomas. Maybe she could be our door."

Mace narrowed his eyes. "I'll just pay her a visit."

"Mace." Patrick snorted. "Don't scare the crap out of her."

Caffrey stifled a giggle that came out as a gag in an attempt to control the rising nausea.

Mace glared at Patrick. "Hey, I can be diplomatic when I need to. It's only been a week and a half, but if Charlie didn't tell anybody what he was doing, maybe Carol came up clean." He straightened. "All right, let's regroup and figure out how to get in. This one's gonna take some planning."

The walls of the small cave seemed to be moving, closing in on Caffrey. She wrapped both arms around her stomach. There was no denying this sensation now, this pushing, whirling pressure, nausea, and scattered images. She closed her eyes.

"Princess?" Mace was standing so close she could smell his familiar masculine scent. He placed a gentle hand on her shoulder. "Hey."

"I...um, remember something."

"What?" the others chimed loudly.

Caffrey flinched. More images became clearer as she regrettably gave her mind permission. "Oh, no." Some were images she did not want to see. She opened her eyes but it made no difference. She was in three places again: in the lobby, with glassy eyes staring into hers, in the cave with Underground members, and in someone's memories of a harsh, forsaken planet of human castaways.

"This contains the *findings of the seeker. Herrengae.* He was to report back to his queen on Hurratt. When he knew he was...in trouble, he made *my* Vhurruh the seeker." She frowned in thought. "Wonder why he thought no one would suspect *him*?"

"I bet I know," Vince murmured softly. "Young drones are kept out of the loop once they become teenagers. Fertile drones see them as a threat."

Caffrey stared at the disc in Mace's hand and winced as she experienced new images. "It...it feels like Charlie's Vhurruh somehow gave this disc to Charlie. No one was allowed to send anything to Hurratt from the mother ship. So, Charlie was supposed to send it from Telenex to Hurratt using the…uh… *mahyen* machine. Anyway, it contains the whole report: who the faction members are, everything that transpired, everything that's being planned. And… I see… star maps of some kind. Like… coordinates to the new planet."

Patrick whistled softly.

"Star maps?" Vince exclaimed in a hushed voice. He flexed his hands with delight. "Oh, we have got to download this thing."

"So…is that all, Caffrey?" Patrick questioned.

"Unfortunately, no," said Caffrey, feeling sicker. She bent over and glanced around the small cave for a place to vomit.

"Do you need to sit down?" Mace asked.

Patrick was beside her now, one hand under her elbow.

"Um…." She could not form a reply to Mace's question. Scenes were still flashing across her brain like a horror show. She rubbed her chest and throat, and swallowed back the queasiness. "They've been traveling to the new planet using that *mahyen nde-dehye* thing. I mean…." she shook her head again.

"It's an interdimensional electromagnetic field generator," Vince finished for her.

Caffrey nodded appreciatively. "Thanks. I can see what it does, but I couldn't put it into English. I hear Vhurruh words. Thoughts. The new planet's close, much closer than Hurratt. Just a different kind of direction."

"Heck, we could get there in a scout ship, if we could confiscate one." Patrick whispered.

"I like the way you're thinking." Mace grinned. Then he frowned. "But, would a scout ship have a subspace drive strong enough? Might need the mother ship, or one of the cruisers. The cruisers can hold up to fifteen Vhurruh."

"You have to be able to use the thought-guidance system." Vince knitted his brows together. "*And* the subspace drive."

"We've got enough brains in the Underground for that," countered Mace. He touched Caffrey's arm. "Hey." She looked up, surprised at his gentle tone.

"Are you okay?"

She nodded, though she felt her body sway.

"Do *you* know how to use the drive?" Mace asked, hopeful.

Caffrey shook her head slowly, unsure. A blurry, muddy space was all that met her. "Not how to use the drive, but…."

"But what?" he prompted.

"Something…." Caffrey searched for details in the guarded memory, but the object of her search kept dissolving. "I have the strange feeling that I know something about... something to do with...." She frowned in concentration. "Ughh! I can't find it."

"Whoah," Patrick commented low.

Mace grumbled and pursed his lips.

Caffrey jammed a hand to her hip. "Look, I'm doing the best I can here."

"It's not that," Mace fumed. "There's no telling how much more you're programmed. You could be a gold mine—or a ticking time bomb."

"Hey," Gina admonished. "That is *so* not helping." Mace glanced at Gina and looked a touch guilty. Caffrey wondered if his expression was because of their "agreement." He took a step back, away from her.

With a sudden change, Mace brightened. "Do you know if many humans are still alive?"

"Well...." Caffrey grimaced as distorted scenes filled her with revulsion. It was as if each question asked triggered more memories. How could she tell Mace she saw hundreds of decaying and plant-covered bodies—perhaps thousands? Surely, he would worry that his sister was one of the dead. She avoided Mace's hopeful eyes for a moment, licked her lips, and searched for a safe reply.

"Princess, give it to me straight."

She met his intense gaze. Somehow he knew she was avoiding the answer. The hard lines of his face proved he was no stranger to tragedy or information difficult to endure.

After a deep breath, she let out a slow exhale. "What I see is dead bodies everywhere."

Groans erupted around her.

"But they're not normal. The picture I have in my mind is... like, vast fields, with some vine-like creatures all over the bodies. The picture is fuzzy, as if passed on through many minds. There are difficulties with what to eat, um... climate problems. The plants are...like, part of them. They *move*. On their bodies, even. But, the confusing thing is I'm also seeing so many conspiracies. So many plans. Human, not just Vhurruh."

"Give us the Vhurruh agendas first," Vince instructed. "Then the human."

"Well, what I'm seeing is that they didn't just want to chase and kill the Zgeyyans. They wanted more ships." She paused, puzzled. "I didn't know that before."

"Yes," Vince confirmed. "Downing Zgeyyan ships threw them into an age of technology overnight. *Herrengae* told me they have no factories. They learned how to fly the ships by probing the minds of a few surviving Zgeyyans. Do you know of any new directions, other than what you told us before?"

More visions came into focus, prompted by his question. Quick flashes of shared memories and thoughts materialized, in color. Caffrey scrunched her face in revulsion.

"What?" Vince prodded.

Caffrey closed her eyes and shook her head. "I don't want to see any more. I...I'm done. I'm done with this. Don't ask me anything else."

Vince grabbed her shoulders. "Caffrey, it's okay. I know what it's like to see their memories. Just take a deep breath."

"No." She shook her head more violently.

"Caffrey, look at me." Vince took hold of her chin. "I just watched what might be the last vision of my dying friend."

Caffrey swallowed as his eyes reddened. So did hers.

"I need you to tell me." Vince gave her shoulder a squeeze. "No, don't look away. I'm giving you an order."

"That's not fair."

"I know it's not, but I need every piece of information you have. I don't care what it is, or what I have to do to get it."

Caffrey clenched her jaw, but could feel the words erupting in her throat against her will. Why the Vhurruh's instructions to obey him still functioned, she did not know. She needed to talk to the Vhurruh about that.

"Humans in two buildings. Big ones. And some small ones that look like huts. Outside is moving plant life, kept out. The Zgeyyans supervised them, but...." She swallowed and pushed away the image. "It's horrible...I need to sit down."

"Okay," said Vince. "I'll sit with you." Together they sat in the dirt and leaves. Gina joined them and rested a hand on Caffrey's arm.

Caffrey took a deep breath and focused on Vince's chest to avoid his eyes. "My Vhurruh showed me if the mission leaders couldn't kill the Zgeyyans, they were supposed to send a message to Hurratt to notify the queens, and some older queens were going to travel using that...drive thing. They tracked them to, um, Veerinay? That's the planet's name. But the Vhurruh commanders couldn't down the Zgeyyan ships. They followed the escaping Zgeyyans back to Earth. That's how they found us. Then everything changed."

Vince nodded encouragement.

"You know all this?" Caffrey asked.

"I know most of it, but go ahead."

"Are you sure? Maybe I don't need to...."

"Yes," Patrick interjected. "You might know something we haven't heard."

"All right." Caffrey inhaled deep, and exhaled with resolve. "*Vrenenjurr* realizes how fragile the human mind is when he first links with a human. He knows what we can build. He can be a hero. He starts arguing with the other leaders about forcing humans to reverse engineer new ships."

"Could have just asked," Patrick mocked softly. "Our military would be drooling to build one of those ships."

"Yeah," Caffrey responded absently, lost in the blurred visions, "but our human leaders want more. They want the drive. That would change everything for us. We wouldn't need the Vhurruh. *Vrenenjurr* ignores them. He doesn't want us to be equal partners."

Vince scoffed. "Sounds like *Vrenenjurr*. All control, all the time."

"The other image I'm seeing is *Vrenenjurr* linking with military leaders. Oh my gosh, their faces, wide-eyed...then they go blank. Others fight him. They cringe in pain."

"Go on," Vince pressed when she halted.

"He wants new weapons. Nuclear bombs on his ship. I'm seeing a weird scene with many Vhurruh on a ship cheering him on as he tells them they're going after the Zgeyyans again, with human bombs. There's a single cruiser and some scout ships left guarding Earth. *Vrenenjurr* chases the Zgeyyans back to Veerinay in the two mother ships. But the Zgeyyans dodge the bombs. They move their ships so fast. *Vrenenjurr* tries the sound weapon again, this time with amplifiers. The Zgeyyans had gotten smarter. They drive them off, but they can't kill them. *Vrenenjurr* is furious. He's thrashing around and yelling."

"Epic fail," Patrick murmured. "You sorry sack of...." He pressed his lips together to stop himself.

Caffrey closed her eyes and breathed. "It's so weird to see this like a choppy, fuzzy film, and it's not in order. There's flashes of memories back and forth."

"It's okay." Vince took one of her hands in his. "Keep going."

A lump caught in Caffrey's throat at his touch, but she obeyed. "*Vrenenjurr* follows the Zgeyyans. They come right back to Earth. The scout ships left behind are no match. *Vrenenjurr* discovers they have taken more humans." Tears burned Caffrey's widened eyes. Her throat constricted. "That's it...that's when...it was a year ago, I think. That would be...that would be when they took Brian, and my friends."

Vince squeezed her hand. "I'm so sorry."

Gina rubbed her arm, her face full of pain. "We lost people then, too."

Caffrey fought to contain her emotions. *Of course, they had. They all had.* A warm tear traveled down her cheek. She focused on

Vince's face and sniffed, waiting for him to give her an order. That would help.

"What happened after that?" Vince asked. "Follow the memories."

"Back and forth they go. And each time," she shook her head, "each time more humans are taken. *Vrenenjurr* does not want word getting out about the Zgeyyan attacks on Earth. His queen is sick and dying. Well, she's dead now, so this memory is from before. If he returns to Hurratt, he will be seen as a failure. And, he's afraid he'll become *genahm*. Um, it looks like being old, and sometimes you have to leave the hive. I don't understand why."

"*Herrengae* explained some of it to me." Vince nodded. "When you're too old to mate, and your queen has been disposed by a new one, you can be cast out to live your existence banding with other elders, or tied to an aging queen who cannot reproduce."

"Wow, that's kind of...cold."

Vince raised both brows. "Hey, think about retirement communities. Not the same, but still.... And, they are kind of like our bees. New queens kill the old queens. The irony is that now the *genahm* have become teachers and philosophers for the young. They formed *Nekkai*. Without hormones dictating their lives, they can devote themselves to educating all Vhurruh societies, and sharing resources and wisdom."

"Okay," said Caffrey, wiping the tear off her cheek. "Apparently, *Vrenenjurr* didn't want any parts of that. He starts poisoning, or putting in stasis, anyone who won't go along with him. After killing *Rhemerett*, he tries to undo other links with queens. His mind is so powerful. He just overpowers everybody. All the Vhurruh are terrified of him. But, he doesn't know that *Ghissella*, a Gray queen, secretly holds onto her links to her Grays. *Vrenenjurr* knows he needs the power of a queen. Or better weapons. He tries to force the workers to create a queen. It's, like, so many different schemes going on at the same time."

"Was it realizing the timing for your fiancé, Brian, that was so horrible for you to see?" Vince asked.

Caffrey sniffed and exhaled. "Not at first. It's those horrible pictures of people...bodies everywhere. I thought of my three friends—and Brian." She shivered. "Now I know why Brian and my friends disappeared when they did. The Zgeyyans really did come back. But also, there's so many leaders wanting different things. Ours. Theirs."

She looked at Vince in disbelief. "And what's worse, I'm seeing confirmation that *Vrenenjurr* did take some of the humans that were trapped in the buildings for food. They ran out on the ship. So in a sense, he has become as horrible as the Zgeyyans. And all this time I thought...I thought...."

"I know," Vince whispered.

"I adored the Vhurruh!" blurted Caffrey. "Thought they were so wonderful."

"Yeah, news flash," Mace scoffed.

Vince and Caffrey rolled their eyes at Mace. Vince gave Caffrey a sad smile. "There's good guys and bad guys in every race, Caffrey. Ours too."

"I guess," Caffrey agreed, resigned to the reality. "But the worst part...it looks like *Vrenenjurr's* the one who released the humans into the wild to see what the plants would do. They didn't just escape. It was *him*. He needed to know if Vhurruh could live there. At least the Zgeyyans protected them. Oh my god, Vince. Plants climbing all over people. Somehow...somehow these plants incorporate themselves into whatever they consume. I'm seeing creatures that look...half-human and half-plant. Like zombies. *For real* zombies. Except, they're alive. I can't believe this is actual Vhurruh *memories*."

Patrick whispered expletives, while Mace paced the length of the cave and back, breathing heavy and clenching his fists.

Vince stared at the cave floor, then looked up. "You said there were human agendas, too."

"Oh, god, this is the worst. *Vrenenjurr's* building an army of workers to produce the equipment he wants, away from here so no one sees. He's using the lifting technology to take humans—just like the Zgeyyans did. And, they focused on prisons...because they were *told* to."

"What?" Mace stopped his pacing to stare, aghast.

Vince did not look surprised, so she continued. "They've made, like, trade agreements with all the governments on Earth. So many different leaders want the edge against other leaders. They all had secret contact with the Vhurruh. *Vrenenjurr* just plays everybody."

"My father was right all along," said Vince. "Everything he suspected." After a moment, he asked, "Did your link give you any indication of which humans were working to stop *Vrenenjurr?*"

Caffrey searched the horrid memories. She shook her head in sadness and disappointment. "Some of our leaders realized the Vhurruh were taking humans, but were willing to sacrifice us to have that edge. They just let them have us. And *Vrenenjurr* was kind of spooning out bits of technology. So, our leaders tolerated it. The Alliance was supposed to be about the Vhurruh protecting us, and both sides sharing information, but neither side is protecting us. Everybody thinks they're justified in doing whatever they have to in order to be on top. To win.

"That's pretty much it. All the deceptions. The craziness going on in the ships. It's like a civil war up there. The planet's the worst, though. The Veerinay visions are so frightening to me, I want to push them out of my mind. I'm going to have nightmares for the rest of my life."

She rubbed her face, then her temple. "These are pieces of knowledge I was supposed to hold back in case SAAFs got me before you got the disc open. The less I revealed, the more likely I would not be killed. But if you got the disc open, then you needed it all. That's how the Vhurruh reasoned it. He programmed as much as he could."

Her own statement shocked her. There was no denying it now. She had, in fact, been programmed. Locked deep within her brain were hidden messages that could only be accessed by suggested triggers—to stay there, forever, if those events never materialized. Would she have gone her whole life, oblivious?

Several horrible scenes reappeared, and she pushed them away, determined to gain control over her mind.

"How can I believe in anybody now, Vince?"

"What do you mean?"

"Everybody sucks. Everybody's in it for themselves." The reality of it made her heart ache. Her face began to burn as more tears filled her eyes.

"Caffrey," Vince placed a hand on her knee. "Remember what I told you. There're good guys, and bad guys, in everything. Sometimes the bad guys *think* they're the good guys. They think they're doing the right thing for *their* people, *their* country. They're in such high positions of power that there's no one higher to question them, to hold them accountable."

Caffrey sniffed as tears streamed down her cheeks. She did not bother to wipe them away. "So who do I believe in now?"

"Believe in us."

"Hey, Caff." Patrick squatted next to her. "I felt the same way after seeing a Zgeyyan in a neighbor's corn field. I watched it turn and run away. I got so angry hearing government officials on TV claiming it was all a hoax, we were perfectly safe. They even laughed and made fun of my neighbors who reported it. Hell, I reported it. We, who know the truth, must stick together. We must believe in each other, and not let the world tell us we didn't see what we saw."

"And know this Caff," Gina added. "I was in the medical field. We're trained to assume that every alien experience is a psychotic episode, or a mental illness. Now, sometimes it can be, and it's always wise to consider that possibility. Very wise. But for you, the only true defense is a spiritual defense—and people who believe in you."

"You have seen something horrific." Vince's face was stoic. "But you have also been given a gift. The gift of truth. Actual Vhurruh memories. Most people in the government—in the world—could not imagine such images, and would not believe in them even if you tried to tell them. We *must* be a voice for the voiceless. We must survive. We must believe in each other."

Caffrey lowered her head, lost in thought. When warmth and pressure flowed into her mind, she ignored it. She had nothing to say to the Vhurruh. She was lost.

Feather light, his mental exploration brushed over her sorrow. He did not speak. To her surprise, he opened his soul and allowed his own sorrows to pour into her like thickened, contaminated water. Loneliness, grief, fear, disappointment. The weight of gloom pressed in on her like a backpack growing too heavy to carry.

How are you alone? she asked, puzzled. *You are surrounded by...your kind, who can speak to your mind.*

I am the messenger. I am alone, he replied, his sadness palpable. *To allow a single thought to stray is to die here. Staying vigilant is exhausting. We were so excited to be part of the mission. We were the chosen. Though we failed to kill the Zgeyyans, we chased them and met you, the humans, and that lifted our spirits. Now, all is lost. There is no joy here, only fear and worry, and staying alive.*

I'm so sorry.

We must be strong. We must survive. You must survive at all cost.

Caffrey blinked in surprise, trying to determine if he had overhead Vince's edict. But he had not. That he had chosen the same words made her sit up straight.

You are the messenger now. Herrengae said the drone Vincent would protect you. Listen to him. Stay close to him. You must complete the mission.

What mission? I gave them everything.

There is more.

What more?

Only you and I have the code now. If I die, you must continue. You must survive. Do not speak of this conversation. Share it with no one. Keep it safe. I must go.

Wait! I need to know....

The etheric door closed like a book slamming on a dusty table. Caffrey dropped her shoulders. She heaved a sigh and realized the room was quiet. Everyone seemed to be lost in reflective silence.

Gina raised her head and spoke. "Caffrey, thank you. This information is, without a doubt, horrible. Especially for those of us who have had someone taken. But, we're going to hope for the best. We'll think about the ones we can save when we get there. And we *will* get there. We'll keep that in front of us and carry on. When the lists come in, we'll deal with our personal sorrows then."

"You're right," Patrick agreed, nodding.

Caffrey's thoughts returned to Brian. Could he be alive on that planet, searching for edible food, battling illnesses, fighting a predator that wraps around his body? Her heart was at war with itself. How long had she mourned Brian, accepting that he was dead? His crafty ways and determination to win might have kept him alive.

Maybe he had changed. No, *she* had changed. She had truly loved Brian, but even in the midst of wedding plans, seeds of doubt had sprouted. He had become increasingly irresponsible, expecting her to take care of issues and deadlines for him. His finances were deplorable, creditors hounded him, and his grades had fallen. She overheard his parents' phone call, complaining. But, in Brian's mind, other people were always responsible for his failings. His boss wasn't giving him enough hours; he didn't get his paycheck on time; his instructors were unfair; and on and on.

Believing him the victim, Caffrey had taken care of him, oblivious to his manipulations. She was sure he loved her and needed her forever, as he told her every day. Brian had liked her compliant nature and quiet intellect, the way she had always bolstered his big, elusive dreams. She didn't think she could be that for him anymore. She wanted more than a lover and a dreamer. She wanted an equal. Someone mature, strong, responsible.

"What else do you know about the planet?" Mace was asking her.

"What? Oh...I don't know anything more about the planet. Just...." She grimaced. "It's bad there." She stood and dusted off her clothes. Vince and Gina followed.

"Maybe if all this goes down, or if *Nekkai* comes, an Allied mission could be launched to go rescue those poor souls," suggested Patrick.

Mace exhaled and rubbed the side of his face. "My sister was taken in one of the early lifts. It's more than I can hope for that she's alive."

"It's better than nothing, people." Vince opened his arms. "We have to hang onto something, and hope is a good choice. What are we fighting for here? We're fighting for our freedom again, yes. But, let's reach farther, higher. Once the public hears about this, even if there's a cover-up, this spark will stay in anyone's heart who has had a loved one lifted."

Mace surveyed the air in front of him. "Yep. You're right about that."

Vince continued. "We settle for nothing less than defeat of the faction and a mission to the new planet to rescue our loved ones, or at least discover their fate and honor them."

"Danged right." Patrick shifted his stance. "Hey, if people in the government know this, why haven't *they* gone? I mean, secretly gone. If I knew, I'd try to negotiate getting somebody I cared about back."

Everyone turned to Caffrey. She lifted her shoulders and hands. "I don't know who knows."

Patrick squinted. "You sure you don't have anything else stashed in there?"

Caffrey crossed her arms and glared at him.

Vince gingerly took the disc from Mace, careful not to close the lid, and gazed at the glowing crystalline surface. "Well, one thing's for sure, we've definitely got something stashed in here."

"Time to head for Remote." Mace glanced at Vince for his concurrence.

"Yep. But let's keep Caff at Rev's place or the Soul House. If nobody shows up at John's ranch, then we'll know she's not giving off a signal she doesn't know about. Her link's obviously with *Nekkai*, but he could get discovered, too. Has he contacted you much, Caffrey?"

Caffrey caught her breath. She was not ready to share the secret contacts. "Not...really," she stammered. "Only a few times—like to warn me, or...or check on me if I was scared or upset."

"And you didn't speak up about this?" The sudden mistrust in Mace's eyes was fierce.

"He didn't *speak* before," Caffrey exclaimed. "I didn't know what he was."

"And so he talks all the time now?"

"No! Not...well...." Caffrey flustered over a response. "The first time I heard him, I think, was the night we escaped through the caves. After that, he didn't say much."

Mace shifted his stance. "So, when's the last time you talked to him?"

Caffrey hesitated. Mace would be furious if he knew they had just spoken. But the Vhurruh had been clear: keep their conversion about the mission safe, even though she had no clue what the "mission" was. Why wouldn't he just tell her now? Especially since she thought her part was done. She would have to trust him. She desperately needed to trust someone.

"Last night," she replied.

Mace visibly stiffened.

Caffrey opened her mouth to explain, but Vince interrupted. "Caffrey, what does he convey when he talks to you?" Everyone waited for her answer.

She shrugged. "Well...before, he kept running away. And, once he decides I'm not being killed or something bad, he disappears. He wasn't...sure last night. That's why...." She swallowed.

Mace averted his eyes.

Vince watched Mace's reaction, but refocused on Caffrey. "Does he say goodbye or anything?"

"No, he...just cuts everything off."

Vince smiled, though it was a sad smile. "That's a good sign, Caffrey. He is linked telepathically to his *rezefhen*, a Vhurruh's battalion, so to speak. They're groups of twenty to thirty. If he's having a conversation with you and his Battalion Commander's mind reaches for his, like they do all the time, the open connection with you could be detected. That's why he can't contact you much." Vince smiled with sadness and regret.

Mace pointed at her. "If he contacts you, I want to know about it."

Caffrey glared at him. It would be a cold day in hell before she told him *anything* about her Vhurruh. Besides, if he was going to pretend nothing happened the night before, then she owed him nothing.

"All right." Vince addressed the group. "No one but us knows where we're headed. We can plan out the mission to Telenex from Remote."

"Wait a minute." Caffrey held up her hands. "Is this some kind of desert place?"

"Not exactly." Vince's smile was secretive as he scrambled out of the cave.

18

REMOTE

"*This*...is *Remote*?" Caffrey scanned the vast property through the windshield as Cameron parked his SUV beside Hank's Hummer. The graveled area was wide enough to accommodate twenty cars.

Nestled between a half-circle of mountains she surveyed lovely pastures and fields of grazing ostriches, cows, and goats. A cozy yellow and white farmhouse stood to their right, with several barns and workshops on either side. A small lake glistened in the distance, bordered by groves of apple and pecan trees. As Caffrey watched, a wild deer sailed effortlessly over one of the six-foot, barbed-wire fences beside a tall windmill at the edge of the property. Atop the windmill was what appeared to be antennae and satellite dishes.

"Almost." Cameron grinned at her from the driver's seat mirror. "Except, I'm not coming in today. I have to be somewhere else."

Caffrey stepped out and breathed in the sweet, country air, unable to get enough of it.

Ron stepped out beside her. "I thought it was some barren place out in the middle of nowhere."

A handsome, cocoa-skinned man, carrying a pitchfork, came out of the large red barn on their left and called out a greeting to Eileen, Hank and Cameron.

"And here comes the devil!" yelled Eileen. The man flipped a finger at her, and the three headed toward the man, laughing.

"Let's go," Mace quipped, glancing at the others. "Nobody look up. Princess, where the hell is your Braves cap?"

Caffrey flopped the cap to her head and made a face at him as he turned away. Then she whispered to Ron with a muted snort. "Guess he thinks satellites are right on us."

Ron whispered back, "I'm sure they followed us all the way up the highway. Should we wave?"

Caffrey chuckled. The excited group crunched across the gravel toward the front porch of the farmhouse.

"Wish Patrick didn't have to leave." Caffrey said in a grumpy voice.

"Yeah." Sharia agreed. "But, I guess he'd worry himself to death if he didn't try to join Leah."

"Yeah." A thick lump had formed in Caffrey's throat when they dropped Patrick off at an Underground member's house. She felt like one of her advocates had left her.

Mace halted at the porch steps, and everyone bunched up behind him. Something small and black whizzed by Caffrey's head. She screamed and ducked. Sharia and Barbara jumped back as well. Caffrey watched it slowly circle Mace and realized it was a large, black and green dragonfly.

It hovered at Mace's shoulder, which drew his half-lidded, recalcitrant eyes sideways. "Afternoon, gentleman," he addressed the dragonfly.

"Dude, it's the Wolf! Aauuugh!" said a tiny, digital voice.

"I love these guys," Vince said. He skipped ahead of Mace and opened the screen door without knocking. Caffrey followed behind Mace as the dragonfly floated toward her again and made no sound except for a faint whir of wings.

"Fire, boys. Brought her home." Mace said to the tiny machine before guiding Caffrey into the house. A shrill whistle of approval emanated from the insect.

Caffrey opened her mouth at him, but was pushed into the living room by Sharia who was anxious to escape the stalking dragonfly. Vince began pulling off his disguise. The others followed and Caffrey took off her hat and sunglasses and tried to undo the braids.

"Here, let me help," Sharia offered, releasing them section by section in record speed.

"Well, how ya' doin', boys?" said a plump woman with curly, graying hair.

"Mama, you're a sight for sore eyes!" Vince wrapped his arms around the rotund woman and squeezed.

"Oh, you!" She slapped him playfully and blushed strawberry red. "Awww, Gina, you're as pretty as a yellow daisy." Her warm, doughy hug enveloped Gina. "And Mr. Mace." The woman pursed her lips. "Have you smiled today?"

"Haven't had a reason to, Mama." Mace groaned as she surprised him with a hug. *"Mama!"* He rolled his eyes and tried to look angry.

"Everybody needs a hug, Mace, 'specially you!" She wagged a chubby finger at him.

Mace cleared his throat. "Mama, these are some friends of mine. We're going to look around the farm, if it's okay with you."

She smiled and winked. "Sure." She led them into the kitchen and tapped some numbers into a small keypad over her oven. Caffrey gasped as two tall cupboard doors slowly opened. At first, all she could see was shelves of canned goods. But the shelves opened up to reveal a gray, metal door that appeared to have no handle. Mace walked over and looked up at a spot near the top of the door frame, and said, "Gentlemen?"

With a pronounced click, the metal door swung open.

Caffrey's shoulders fell at the sight of subterranean stone walls. "No way."

"Are you kidding me?" Sharia wailed behind her.

"Oh, come on, Mace," Barbara complained loudly. "Please tell me this leads to another house."

Vince put a comforting hand on Caffrey and Sharia's shoulders and raised his brows at Barbara. "Ladies, this cave I think you can live with."

"I'm not doin' it." Sharia crossed her arms and glowered.

"Me neither," Caffrey added.

"Let's go," Mace ordered. He glared at Sharia. "That means you."

"I'm stayin' somewhere else," Sharia insisted, doing her best to scowl at him. She tried to twist her body away from him but he caught her arm.

"No you're not. And don't make me drag you."

"I'm not doin' it, Mace."

"I will flip you over my shoulder."

"Don't you dare!" She pointed at his face.

"Thank you, Mama." Vince kissed the plump woman's check. Mama swatted at him again but missed as he jumped toward the entrance, grinning as he skipped down steps.

Ignoring Sharia's child-like wining, Mace gripped her waist and pulled her in front of him. She mumbled expletives and stiffened her legs so he was forced to keep pushing her down wooden steps.

Caffrey followed reluctantly, only because he turned every few seconds to insure she was right behind him.

"Caffrey, you're going to love it here," came Barbara's voice behind her.

Caffrey whirled. "I thought you'd never been here."

"I haven't. I'm just reading *you*."

"Well, what about you?"

"I can't read myself."

"*Now*, people," Mace called up the entrance. An angry Sharia was stomping away from him.

Caffrey held tight to the railing as she descended, wondering over Barbara's prediction. Ron and Barbara trailed close behind her, choosing their steps carefully. Mace veered into a slanted, winding tunnel. For some reason Vince was grinning as he waited for them near an archway. He motioned the group to precede him. Sharia groaned at sight of another descending staircase, one made entirely of concrete, with metal arm railings.

"Wolf!" called out a young man who stood at attention in an alcove at the bottom. Beyond him the space opened up to a two-story cave about thirty feet in diameter. He smiled and slapped a palm to his chest, then closed his fingers to form a fist. "Good to see you, sir."

Mace returned the salute, then shook the young man's hand. "Roadrunner?" he asked as if unsure of the name.

The young man nodded. "I just got back. I was out west." Roadrunner spotted Vince and saluted again. "Eagle, sir! Hot damn, it's good to see you alive! Didn't believe the rumors, of course."

Vince smiled broadly and returned his salute. "Good to see you too, Roadrunner." He reached out and shook Roadrunner's hand with enthusiasm. "Did you ever get to meet Nightengale?"

"No, sir. Have not had the pleasure."

Gina offered a hand. "A pleasure to meet you, Roadrunner."

"Glad to have you aboard, Ma'am. Heard a lot about you. Who else do we have here?" His eyes brighten as he surveyed Caffrey and Sharia.

"This is Fire." Mace pointed to Caffrey.

Caffrey turned to Mace in surprise. "What?"

"Uh, *the* Fire?" Roadrunner glanced at Caffrey's hair. "The one that...?"

"Yes." Mace cut him off.

Caffrey opened her mouth to protest, but Mace quickly addressed Barbara. "We need a code name for you and...your husband. Your friends usually choose a nickname, or you can choose a simple one or two-word name. Do not use any other real or temporary name down here. Ever. Always use code names."

"Oooh-kay." Barbara looked at Ron. "How about Capricorn? That's my sun sign."

"Got that one?" Mace asked. Roadrunner scrolled down the screen of an electronic tablet that rested on a clipboard. "Nope."

"Done." Mace nodded at Ron.

"Uh...." Ron flustered. "Engineer?"

"I think that's taken...yep," said Roadrunner.

"Um, how about Trainman?"

Roadrunner gave him a thumbs-up. Mace raised his brows inquisitively.

"What?" Ron shrugged. "I make model train sets. Then I sell them."

Mace continued to raise his brows, but he turned to Sharia.

"Dancer?" she asked hopefully.

After a pause, Roadrunner gave her a warm smile. "You're good to go." He typed her name into the tablet, then wrote notes on the clipboard. Caffrey watched his eyes flit from the clipboard to Sharia and back.

"Wonder what Patrick would have chosen?" asked Sharia.

"Hey!" Mace admonished her. "Code names only."

"*Sooorry*. Jeez!"

"There's a very good reason for this, Sh– um, *Dancer*." Vince chuckled at himself for almost slipping. "Same reason as above Remote. If you only use code names, you're not likely to reveal anyone's true identity."

"Glad to have you folks aboard." Roadrunner offered a welcoming grin. "I don't see you on the schedule, sirs," he addressed Mace and Vince. "Do you have a plan for this afternoon?"

Mace smiled. "Good man. Keeping track of us. We'll see the Caretaker first—get these folks a bed. Then we'll see the Foreman. Eagle and I will check with Com. We'll have Vows at dinner. Is it still at six-thirty?"

"Yes, sir."

"Thanks." Mace motioned the group around a corner, further down into the abyss.

Caffrey crossed her arms and walked slow.

Sharia lingered behind the others and whispered, "He's cute, huh?"

Caffrey realized Sharia mistook her reason for delaying. The two glanced back and caught Roadrunner watching. Sharia giggled.

"Ladies?" Mace queried with impatience as the others waited at a turn in the adjoining corridor.

"Hey, why didn't I get to choose my name?" Caffrey called out to him in an angry tone.

"Her fault." He jerked a thumb at Gina with a perturbed look, then continued down the stone pathway.

"Um, I referred to you as 'Fire' after Mace found you," said Gina sheepishly. "I saw your red hair and said, 'Maybe she's the fire.' You know, because of the prophecy from Flies With Raven? The name became a code in communications, even with some people here at Remote. Unfortunately, since you've been on the news, people might recognize you. But, it still helps to use code names. And…that one kind of stuck."

Caffrey stood immobile. Like everything else, her option to choose was denied. She watched the others disappear into the darkness.

"Where is she?" Mace's voice echoed along the stone walls, followed by footsteps. Caffrey remained rooted to the spot, stiff-lipped as he reappeared.

"We need to stick together." His tone was parental but softer than she expected.

"I'm not sticking with anything. Just once, I would like to make my own choice."

"That wasn't my fault."

"This time."

He held her eyes, took a deep breath, and exhaled loud enough to indicate his displeasure. Vince appeared beside him, confused.

"I want out." Caffrey looked at Vince.

"We all want out," Vince replied. "But like you, we need to hide to survive."

"Vince, I didn't hide the disc, I swallowed it. Well, I *was* hiding it, but the stupid SAAF shot. And I didn't choose to be brainwashed with visions that haunt me at night. I didn't even get to choose the clothes I'm wearing. Let alone my own name. I am so sick of being denied any choice—in anything. I'm not a freakin' zombie."

"Well, if it makes you feel any better, I didn't get to choose my name either."

Caffrey's anger deflated.

He stepped closer. "Caffrey, I'm asking you to give this place a chance. Let's live another day to fight for our freedom. No matter what, we must survive."

Caffrey's shoulders fell. She uncrossed her arms. Without looking at either of them, she shuffled forward.

Mace stopped the group at a high multi-colored cavern with three connecting tunnels. Rippled stalactites hung from the ceiling like frozen flags. A raised tunnel entrance to the left had a winding staircase that curled upward and disappeared; the others had ramps or rough steps leading in other directions. Large fans ran with a loud hum at each entrance.

"Okay, listen up." Mace turned to face them. "Remote has security cameras everywhere, so behave yourself. You'll notice cables and pipes run along the ceiling and floor. They're for electricity, water, and communications. This traffic light...." He pointed to an actual traffic light attached to the wall, which Caffrey thought looked rather huge up close. "It's a warning system. Green is 'all clear' like it is now. That is, until we decide to test you with a drill."

His eyes twinkled mischievously. "Yellow means 'all quiet'—no talking, no running water, no music. It's always yellow for deliveries or visitors at the main house. Nobody goes upstairs. Yellow blinking is greater caution. Be prepared, contain equipment or tasks, and get ready for red. Red means full alert drill. You drop what you're doing, go to your bunk if possible and grab your backpack, which should *always* be available and ready in the center of your cot every morning.

"Access to all secret entrances on the property is denied, unless you are scheduled to exit. There are four. The escape route into the forest and nearby mountains is the only exit open in a red drill. We do *not* use it for travel, so that no attention is brought to it. No tracks are there. Don't get caught in that hallway. You've no reason to be there except a red drill. Blinking red is the highest alarm. That means discovery is imminent. All hands prepare for battle and escape routes."

A thin young man with black-rimmed glasses entered through one of the tunnels, waved timidly at the group, then went back to an electronic pad he was carrying before exiting into another tunnel.

Vince whispered to Mace, "Was that Brainteaser?"

"I think so," said Mace. "The geeks all look the same to me."

"Liar." Vince chuckled, then turned to address the group. "Well, as you can see, folks, we've got great minds down here. Fresh spring water is cold and dee-lish. Fans keep the air circulated. Dehumidifiers keep your clothes dry. The food's grown upstairs. And, we generate our own electricity." He rocked on his heels and grinned with pride.

Mace cleared his throat.

"Oh, sorry, Professor. Carry on."

"All duties are assigned and rotated," said Mace, his face serious again. "You have to see the Foreman every day. One day you'll empty trash and clean latrines, next day you'll have cooking or KP duty, and so on. Everybody pulls their own weight. There's also a lot of arts and crafts made for sale at Helen, which is very close to us. Lots of people sign up for that. It generates money for supplies and food."

Caffrey had an instant flashback to her and Brian's first trip to Helen. How she had loved the beautiful Dutch-style shops, restaurants, and hotels. Splashes of color and costumes had been everywhere, along with horse-drawn carriages and families relaxing in tube rides down the shallow beginnings of the Chattahoochee River. Brian had tired of the shops and scenery quickly and wanted to go home after only an hour.

"We also contribute to chores upstairs on the farm," Mace continued. "You wear full disguise if you work upstairs, and you'd better have permission. We take care of animals, and help with planting and harvesting. These people risk a lot to have us here. They've had relatives lifted. Two military officers related to this family had to go into hiding because they knew too much. So, we do what we can to pay them back.

"Friday nights are youth meetings at the house, and special events are sometimes held on Saturdays. Mama's son is a youth minister. Yellow is on, and the kitchen and tool shed entrances are closed during the meetings. Teenagers come to visit him a lot, so yellow goes on and off.

"It's a good cover for rocketmen and geeks who have jobs during the week, and come here on weekends to work on special projects. Rocketmen are scientists. Geeks are programmers and gamers. Docs are medical personnel. Falcons are military officers who can't show their face upstairs anymore. Apples are teachers, Sharpies are artists. You get the idea. They've probably come up with new ones while I've been gone."

He moved toward one of the tunnels. "We're going to see Caretaker. She keeps track of rooms and anything personal that you need. By the way, we just came from the south corridor. This cave right here is the hub for four main tunnels—we call it Spaghetti Junction, for obvious reasons. All right, let's go."

Caffrey frowned. The last time she had driven through "Spaghetti Junction," the spiraling intersections of Highways 285 and 85, she had been headed to Stone Mountain with Brian and friends, a year ago.

She was quiet as she followed Mace, amazed at the transformation in him since they had entered Remote. He was completely at home. Others in the group changed as well. Barbara, Ron, and Sharia whispered with excitement, while Gina and Vince grew cozy. Twice they stopped to kiss, then rushed like children to catch up. It was as though the underground complex was a hiding place for their love as well.

Caffrey was certain she would never remember all the winding, interconnecting tunnels and caves. She reached out often to touch shiny surfaces and was surprised to find some dry when they looked wet. She nearly tripped twice in her explorations because the flooring was overlaid in places with wooden planking and steps. Most of it was left natural or filled in with dirt, and Caffrey found those natural places much more fun.

In one winding corridor, everyone exclaimed as they came upon hundreds of pieces of paper, plaques, and posters covering the rough walls. They smiled as they read verses of Scripture, quotes, artwork, and poems. Vince informed everyone it was the Wisdom Walk, started by the proud parents of "Timmy."

Caffrey followed Vince's pointed finger to a brightly colored crayon drawing of smiling stick figures and the words: "Don't let something stew, between me and you, 'cause if you do, it will stink like poo." It was signed: "Timmy." An adult had written: "At age 5" underneath the signature.

Sharia chortled and read the next one, which was brown at the edges: "The essence of morality is that what you do, or don't do, *always* affects everyone else."

"Hmm, interesting. Oh, look at this one. 'If you haven't learned to forgive, don't bother coming down here. You'll never make it. Let it go and move forward.' Ooo, that one's sobering." Sharia frowned. "How long are we staying here?"

Mace ignored her.

Caffrey found several Scriptures from the book of Proverbs, which she tried to read, but she finally gave in to Mace's demands to move on.

His lectures became thwarted by passing residents, who wanted to stop and greet him, Vince and Gina. Several looked to be military people. Their respect for them was obvious as they made the strange hand-and-fist salute on their chest.

After several twisted turns, the group was pushed into a supply room and introduced to the Caretaker, who was a tall, feisty dark-skinned woman with curly black hair. With quick precision, she assigned Caffrey and Sharia to different bunk-filled "cabins." They complained at being separated but the woman explained there was room for only one more in each of the rooms. Barbara and Ron were thrilled to get a tiny, private cabin in an area for married couples.

The Foreman turned out to be an older, red-cheeked, grim man, who swiftly assessed everyone's training and talents, assigned tasks for the entire week, and ran through a long list of rules and regulations that made Caffrey feel like she needed strong tea. She groaned when Foreman scheduled her, Ron, Barbara, and Sharia for training and quiz sessions the next day on all tasks and duties required at the complex.

It was dinner that brought the greatest surprise. Expecting a decent meal and relaxation at a table in the massive cavern dubbed the "mess hall," instead, the newcomers were asked to stand against the wall, raise their right hand, and repeat a "vow of loyalty." The vow not only included secrecy of the location and its inhabitants, to uphold the rules of conduct, to salute and honor those in command, and pledge allegiance to the Underground and to the United States, but also a personal "dedication to the advancement and preservation of humanity and planet Earth." The muscular man who quoted the vow soberly ended with, "I accept a member's right to do whatever necessary, should these vows be compromised."

"What does that mean?" Caffrey asked.

Mace replied in a serious voice beside her, "That means, if I get caught by SAAFs and rescue doesn't look feasible, or security might be compromised, this gentleman right here...." He pointed to the muscular man. "Or anyone else, has my permission to shoot me if necessary, to keep me from revealing this location and these people. You have five minutes to decide."

Caffrey's jaw dropped. She was certain that, should she choose not to take the vow, getting shot, or locked up, would be her fate anyway, knowing him. Yet, in a world where Vhurruh mind control was as simple as touching a face, her life would most likely have already ended save for the daring actions of Underground members.

Caffrey did not need five minutes to decide. She proudly recited the vow, along with Barbara, Ron, and Sharia. Assuming that she was going to be allowed to eat, she was not prepared for the grueling ceremony that followed.

Every person in the entire complex who was available—89 at that particular moment—took a turn to stand in front of her, salute, give their code name, and ask her personally to promise them never to reveal the location, or persons within. By the end of the line, having looked into 89 faces, Caffrey was certain that physical torture could not pry the location from her lips. She and Barbara both asked if there was a stiffer drink available than sweet tea. Vince prompted someone to offer a special exception from storage.

A short, stout, silver-bearded gentleman, who gladly confessed to being one of the "seers," invited Caffrey, Barbara, Ron, and Sharia to his table to swap stories, since Vince, Gina, and Mace had become occupied in other conversations.

Later, other seers and links joined in the camaraderie, and they all moved to his cabin, shared with four other men. Fifteen people packed into the small, wood-covered space, some lying across bunks and others squatting on the floor, which had three carpets to keep the coldness of the granite out and the warmth of bodies and hearts in.

Caffrey listened with absolute fascination as the group discussed all they knew of the social and military structure of the Vhurruh, the violent takeover by several Gray drones, and speculations on their missions.

"So, they weren't just chasing the Z's, they were actually *looking* for another planet?" asked Caffrey, surprised that her Vhurruh had not elaborated on that agenda. She assumed he had told her everything, and here there were people who knew some things that she did not.

"Yes," said Parakeet, a brown-haired girl with a high voice, "but an uninhabited one. My link told me the *Nekkai* insisted on non-interference with a reigning, sentient species, so they would never be like the Zgeyyans."

"Well, messed that up, didn't they?" Caffrey muttered with distaste. "I'm not sure who is worse now."

"How can you say that?" asked another girl. "Our people meant well. They could not have foreseen what happened with the rogue Grays."

By "our people," Caffrey realized she meant "the Vhurruh," so she assumed the girl must also have a link.

After a gesture from Barbara, Caffrey told the group what she knew. There were cries of horror and disbelief around the room at the Vhurruh memories she described. Two of the links admitted that their Vhurruh had sent quick blips of Veerinay images in the last two days.

Learning that Caffrey was a new link, Parakeet proceeded to instruct her from a book she was writing, which contained details of Vhurruh life gleaned from all the links she had met.

Caffrey happily scanned the book while the others talked. She flipped to a page entitled "Castes."

> Vhurruh live in hives under the domination of queens, mated in some cases to a hundred drones, which can grow to huge numbers, not unlike Earth's bees. The main difference is that the other castes are not necessarily infertile females, but infertile hermaphrodites, which includes the towering, horned guards (or *kurnistarren)*, diminutive nursery aids called *sahmaen*, and workers known as *surranenn*. (Note that most Vhurruh terms are the same in singular or plural form, though occasionally they add an "en" or "an" sound to any noun to indicate plural.) They, along with the drones and queens, are created from the egg and larvae stage by being fed a mixture of special funguses, hormones and enzymes from glands of the *surranenn*, who have sole discretion on the creation of the breeder castes.

"Wow, this is great!" Caffrey exclaimed. "Can I borrow this tonight?"

"Sure. You have to promise to give it back tomorrow, though."

"No problem." Caffrey smiled.

The relief of talking with people who had lived through similar experiences was so overwhelming that Caffrey was nearly euphoric. She talked and listened for hours, sharing stories until she was both hungry and sleepy. Finally, they all dispersed to the mess hall to see what snacks might be left out for hungry raiders. The group stayed close together even in the narrow corridors, loath to disturb the unified energy.

Over the next three days, Caffrey had to admit that Barbara's edict was coming true. Scientists let her peruse their latest studies, delighted at her expressions of wonder and interest; contactees huddled with her in bunk-filled rooms to swap stories; and the two resident clergymen paused whenever she asked, to whisper a prayer for her family, and for her Vhurruh's safety.

In the science lab, Caffrey befriended Q, aptly named for his love of covert gadgets. Always completely entranced in some project, he was quick to smile and spare a moment of his time, especially to so rapt an audience. He was pleasantly plump, with an expansive middle giving him a shape nearly like an egg. His clothes and hair were wrinkled and disheveled as though he had slept in them, though he himself was fairly clean, even if his wire-rimmed glasses seldom were. Such personal tasks took time, and he had no time for frivolities when there were discoveries to be made and techno-toys to play with.

One morning he showed Caffrey his hummingbird, an alternative to the dragonfly. Caffrey begged him to fly it over and over, and he sent it down the hallways of the complex. It picked up conversations and frightened several unsuspecting victims. Q confessed that outside Remote, he worked for an innovative corporation which allowed him to come and go when he chose, since he had already made the company wealthy from his ability to transform discoveries into practical, money-making products.

"And these have cameras *and* speakers?" Caffrey asked him the third morning.

"Ha! Cameras are easy. I also get temperatures and all sorts of data. I even have detection of odors and chemicals. *And*, it can avoid obstacles and predators. An owl almost got one last night, though. Only saving grace is that he would have barfed it up."

Q pointed to a small squirrel resting on the farthest cluttered counter with Caffrey's digital smiling face blinking in a screen beside it. "There you are! I lose *some* clarity through heaviest metals, but check this out."

Caffrey squealed at the sight of her face looking like a screaming skeleton. "Ewww! Change it back. That's creepy."

Q chuckled gleefully. Caffrey laughed with him, entertained by his childlike demeanor. The squirrel continued to move as though chewing on an acorn.

Later that evening, a young woman, code-named Rapunzel because of her incredibly long strawberry-blonde hair, invited Caffrey to her room where others had gathered, and asked how often Caffrey initiated contact with her Vhurruh.

Stunned, Caffrey replied, "Never."

"Never?"

"He talks now and then, but...only for a few seconds. He's always running."

"Well, why don't you try now?"

"Now?"

"Why not?" asked Rapunzel, completely uninhibited. "Once he establishes the link, you can talk to him anytime. Well, not really *any* time, but if he's not mind-linked to his *rezefhen*, then you can get a few words in before he cuts you off. If the collective catches him, he's dead, but they're all too smart for that. Their minds are very powerful. They're split into several levels of awareness. He could talk to you on one level, and me on another, and his *rezefhen* with another. Most of the *Varraay*—the Blues—are part of a *Nemeygenyah*."

A young man with striking dark hair and eyes spoke up. "It's kind of a spiritual, telepathic discipline given by the elders, you might say."

"Oh, I remember that term! *Nemeygenyah*." Caffrey pronounced the humming Vhurruh tones.

"It's a mental karate club," jovially suggested Parakeet, and everyone chuckled in agreement.

"It's more than that," Rapunzel protested. "They're people of faith. They have all sorts of moral codes and beliefs."

Caffrey took a deep breath and closed her eyes, completely at ease with the intimate, aware group, and concentrated on her Vhurruh.

"I think I feel him, but...I...."

"Call his name lightly in your mind."

"I don't know his name."

"If you don't know his name," instructed Rapunzel, "you can't be precise. A name is an address. With it, you zoom fast in telepathy. Like a phone number. Focus on him. Only him. *Don't* focus on the area around him or on anything he's experiencing until you *know* it's safe."

Caffrey felt a strange pressure in her skull. It expanded like a small cloud around her head. Before she could clarify the sensation, she had locked onto the Vhurruh. Surprisingly, she felt his presence as well as his consciousness, his familiar warmth and masculinity. He was not alone.

"He feels me," she spoke in an awed whisper, her eyes still closed. "But...he's got people around him. I've surprised him."

"Break the contact!" Rapunzel snapped.

Caffrey popped open her eyes and gasped in fright.

"Sorry," Rapunzel apologized, laying a hand on her arm. "I didn't want you to get him in trouble. Any time you reach for him and you sense others, break the contact. He'll probably call to you when he's alone, or in a meditative state."

Caffrey heaved a voluminous sigh. Later that evening, as she lay in her bunk in a small room that contained three others, she wondered how in the world sailors ever slept deep in the hull of a submarine, knowing that thousands of pounds of water squeezed in on them every moment. A sudden feeling of etheric pressure enveloped her.

Wuvena, said a friendly, rich voice into the center of her brain.

Caffrey gasped in surprise and recognized the greeting she had read from Parakeet's book. *Oh, it's you! Hello.*

Are you safe?

Yes, I am safe now. Thank you for warning me on the mountain.

My delight, Amvezu. Have zizza netae?

Yes, we have it. But...we can't send it yet, we don't....

Cannot stay, will be detected. I am Mhetrrian. I come to you.

Oh, can't you stay for...! The protest went unheard as the connection snapped shut like a plastic lid. Some pressure remained in Caffrey's head, like an echo of his consciousness. His parting comment clearly warned her to let *him* initiate the contact. Caffrey sighed and flopped her arms onto the pillow. She smiled. Now she knew his name.

"Rapunzel?"

"Hey Fire, how's it going?"

"Good. Um, I know *Wuvena* is like a hello, but what does *Amvezu* mean? I don't remember reading that in your book."

"Oh. It's like a term of endearment. The drones use it for a young queen that they love and adore. And, are probably hoping to mate with."

Caffrey's mouth fell open.

Rapunzel smiled in a mischievous way and lowered her voice. "Did your Vhurruh call you that?"

Caffrey nodded.

Rapunzel giggled. "How adorable! I got to learn a lot of the language before my *Khrennam* had to limit our contact. I'm the only human linked to a *kurnistarr.*"

"*Kurni*– oh, a guard."

"Yes, everybody else is linked to drones, and some workers. But, don't let anybody know he called you that."

"Why?"

"Because guys get weirded out by it, and they won't ask you out."

Caffrey's eyes widened. "Seriously?"

"Well, think about it. How does a guy compete with a male alien that whispers endearments in your head?"

For a moment, Caffrey was stunned, then she guffawed. "I guess I didn't think about that way."

"Seriously, keep it a secret. It weirds them out, big-time."

"Fire." Gina addressed her in an admonishing tone. "You have *got* to be very, *very* careful. You could completely blow this location if he is caught. The rest of the links should know this. Don't try to contact him yourself. He will know when it's safe. I can't *believe* those girls told you how to contact him. And I can't believe he gave you his name without time to instruct you on the dangers. He is definitely young."

"He's not *that* young. And...I think he's pretty brave." Caffrey crossed her arms and stiffened her jaw. How dare Gina insult her wonderful Vhurruh!

Gina caught the subtle body language as she checked her inventory of medical supplies.

"You should talk to Eagle about this some." She softened her tone. "He had a lot of experience with *Herrengae.*"

Yes, well, Herrengae got caught. Caffrey berated herself for the judgment, and felt sorry for Vince. She *would* be careful.

Mace marched straight up to her in one of the main corridors, took her aside, and rested one foot on an outcropping of rock. She had seen him often, but mostly glances in passing, except for questions he and Vince came to her with about the new planet. She had gleaned all she could from the images *Mhetrrian* had given her and was not in a mood to be pushed for more.

"I told you everything I know about the planet."

"It's not that. I understand you're communicating with the Vhurruh again."

"Yeyyys." Caffrey drew out the word. The red flannel shirt looked dashing against his dark hair and skin. He seemed rested, happy, in his element, but still distant. She took in his firm, muscled arms and stocky profile in one fell swoop. "Is there *nothing* you don't know in here?"

"No," he answered shortly. "Know his name yet?"

Caffrey glanced downward and felt oddly self-conscious. "*Mhetrrian.*"

Mace took a deep breath and let it out slowly, as if resigned to something he could not prevent. "Be careful." He switched to his teacher persona. "If you're not, you could become a security risk. When he talks to you, block out all sense of where you are, and focus only on his words. Do not hold a picture in your mind of the room you're in, or location you're in, or any person beside you."

"What, he's supposed to see through my eyes like Q's squirrel?" Caffrey asked with sarcasm.

Mace glared at her. "How do you think you were found?"

Caffrey dropped her smirk, dumfounded. "What do you mean?"

His gaze traveled to her hair, as though taking it in, and returned to her eyes. "Charlie was linked. Your face, and your building, even the lay of the street, were obviously passed on from Charlie's Vhurruh to your Vhurruh. Otherwise he couldn't have found you at the office."

Caffrey stared at him for a long moment. She had never known how *Mhetrrian* found her and did not want a reminder of the frightening accident, or him unexplainably in a human skin. Was he part of something unthinkable, or was he forced to do what he did? Her heart could not go there.

"When you went down that night in the alley, your Vhurruh got desperate. He sent your face and your general direction to two other links. They reported to us. We were told to find you at all costs, but not told why, or who gave the order. We knew that you were in Atlanta, were Caucasian, and had red hair. That was it. We had no idea where to start searching. Vhurruh don't understand street signs. They only understand visuals from the air."

Shocked and silent, Caffrey forced herself to breathe steady and evaluate the revelation. Watching her, Mace's expression softened for a moment as though concerned that he had upset her.

He had never displayed much concern over what he said to her, and it lightened her mood. "So...how do *you* know all about the Vhurruh...and what they can understand and all?"

He smirked. "I read a lot."

Caffrey smirked back at him and rolled her eyes. Truthfully, she was stunned he had actually attempted a joke.

"Eagle told me," Mace admitted. "And, every other contact we have that's linked."

"Well, you really check everybody out, don't you?"

"Damn right. That's why I'm large and in charge."

"Ha!" Caffrey laughed at the playful glint in his black eyes. "Nightingale said you could actually be funny, but I didn't believe her."

"Yeah, well, there's a lot about me you don't know." His smile fell. Caffrey felt an odd sensation like warm gelatin filling her chest.

"Anyway," he continued, "that's why I say don't be visual with him. One face passed on, and his mind gets probed, then this place is history—and so are you. Got it?"

"Mmm-hmm." Caffrey wished he hadn't switched so fast to being "in charge" again.

He glanced absently down the corridor, then his eyes shifted to her face and neck and the blue shirt Caretaker had given her. "How *are* you?"

Caffrey froze, stunned by the change in his tone. "I'm...okay."

"I know it's...probably hard in here." He cleared his throat uncomfortably. "It's kind of a different world."

"Are you kidding? I love it here! Bernie's going to let me help with an experiment tomorrow, I mean Q, sorry."

"How do you know his real name?"

"I heard somebody say it."

"Who?" he demanded.

She frowned. "Chill out, Mace."

"Fire, that's a security breach. I need to know who's doing it. Besides the fact that *my* name is not Mace down here, you should not know *his*."

She rolled her eyes. "Anyway, Mr. Wolf, *sir*, I'm supposed to help with the sweeper detail and KP for lunch, which is no biggie. I get to help in the botany lab with the experimental seeds. Frosty is going over the alert drills after that, and I have gun safety with the rifle unit in the afternoon, with yours truly." She nodded to acknowledge his teaching assignment. "Or maybe not until tomorrow, Moose said, if it rains. And, Mama and Spice are going to let me help them make cheese. I've always wanted to do that, and...."

"Who said you could go up to the house?" Mace stood up straight, and his brows furrowed with disapproval.

Caffrey clamped her lips tight, unwilling to implicate Rapunzel, who had purposely asked the Foreman to schedule them both to work with Mama. Caffrey had been so thrilled for the chance to work with Mama, the most favored person at the complex, she had not disclosed to Rapunzel Mace's preference that she not be exposed above ground. Besides, Mama was rumored to always keep a kitchen full of delectable sweets and wonderful-smelling foods, which she would offer the whole time you visited.

Mace exhaled slowly, anger coloring his neck. "You *cannot* be exposed to the house. *Anyone* coming in is going to recognize you. You've been on the news." His jaw muscles contracted. "Do you want to jeopardize yourself, and all these people?"

Caffrey swallowed, and for a moment she did think of all the souls who had quickly become dear to her.

"Okay, okay, fine." She raised her hands in surrender. "I'll just rot away down here, me and Q's crickets. Just, you know, forget I ever knew what the sun was, or what air was, or clouds, trees...birds, moo-cows, corn quietly growing...." She had stepped closer to him with each playful word, hoping to dissuade his objection.

She squinted, and stopped inches from his face.

Mace frowned at her mischievousness, his head tilted to one side. Caffrey stared, and he didn't look away. The connection caused a great flutter in her sternum. She noticed him swallow as though it were painful. Strangely, he seemed not to want to move. She had forgotten how pretty his eyes were, beyond being piercing and panther-black. But, they were softer now, much more so than on a turbulent evening, a world ago on a mountain.

Breathing faster, his focus shifted to her mouth. As if a magnet was pulling him, his head bent toward hers. She raised her chin before the motion registered in her brain.

Just as his breath warmed her lips, he halted. His eyes closed tight and brows knitted together as though fighting some inner batter.

Barely breathing, she realized she did not want him to stop. Something powerful welled up inside her, stinging, burning in her veins like a fire that needed to be quenched. Unable to control herself, she brushed her lips feather light against his.

That was all it took. He grabbed her shoulders and covered her lips with his.

She melted into him, sliding her hands up his red shirt. His powerful arms engulfed her slight frame, one hand grasping her hair.

He kissed her with the wildness of a man starving in a desert. She reveled in the passion of his unrelenting lips, the hardness of his body pressing her against the tunnel wall.

Cackling laughter carried down the hall and they froze. Eileen's attention-getting laugh was unmistakable. Whether she was headed down the corridor or was at a junction immersed in jovial conversation, Caffrey did not know, but they turned to examine the corridor, expecting her to materialize. Other voices echoed in the tunnel, then grew faint as if traveling in another direction.

Mace relaxed his desperate grip, and placed his hands against the cold stone on either side of Caffrey. With his forehead against hers, he closed his eyes, then opened them, not focusing on her. "I'm sorry."

"You're...sorry?" Caffrey let her arms drop to her sides, unable to decide what to do with them.

"I shouldn't have done that. I...can't allow my...I can't get close. It's too dangerous." He straightened and took a step back as if he didn't trust himself.

"Dangerous? For who? What do you mean, dangerous?"

"I'm a leader, Caffrey. Damn, I mean Fire." He shook his head as if disappointed in himself. "In order to stay on top things, I have to be clear."

"And, I make you, what—*foggy?*" She blinked to enhance the sarcasm.

He exhaled loudly to convey his frustration. "You have to understand. I need to stay...objective concerning you."

"Objective? And, kissing me makes that impossible?"

"Yes!" He raised a hand and dropped it.

Stunned at the forcefulness of his answer, she narrowed her eyes and crossed her arms. "Fine. I'll be sure to stay out of your way. Since I possess some strange magic that makes your brain melt. I guess that also means the whole Underground would fall apart, too?"

Waiting for him to argue the point, she was disappointed by the distress in his eyes.

"Look...." His gaze fell to her lips, her eyes, then danced around her face as if avoiding temptation. "You are someone I need to protect. And...."

"And be suspicious of. Go ahead, say it. I can see it in your eyes. As long as I am linked to *Mhetrrian*, you will never trust me with...." She had almost uttered, "your heart," but could not finish the words.

Eileen's scornful laugh rose again as if she had paused and reentered the tunnel. They both looked away from each other.

Caffrey took a step toward the opposite direction, and stopped. They had not resolved the issue of her accompanying Rapunzel to the cheese room. She whirled, letting anger show in her face.

"If I can come up with an acceptable disguise, will you let me go upstairs? Or, at least, in the cheese room? They say it's a separate building off the kitchen."

Mace's demeanor shifted from distraught to concerned as he debated the suggestion.

"I'll talk to Cardinal." He sounded as if this went against his better judgment. With one last overall glance at her, he turned to trudge back the way he came.

"Mace," she called out.

He rotated, his lips thin with disapproval, though for a moment Caffrey fancied he was pleased by the sound of her voice calling his name.

She raised both hands. "Wolf, I mean. "I, um...I *really like* gardening...*a lot*. I couldn't have one in my apartment." She repositioned her stance, embarrassed. "Can I have a work detail in the garden?"

His black eyes narrowed, accompanied by a rise of his chin.

"Come *on*," she urged, rolling her eyes. "If there are others out there *with* me, and the place is constantly under surveillance, and I'm wearing a good disguise, and one of those stupid...grandma floppy hats, what could it hurt?"

Though his lips were still pressed in displeasure, she watched the lines of his face relax.

"I know it's upstairs," she pushed, her words stiff. "But, I have to have *some* time outside, and...I do love gardening. You can post someone as watch for me if you're that suspicious." She raised both brows.

"All right." He glanced up the corridor again, hearing reverberations of Eileen's raucous tones. "I'll assign Mink to you. She's due for a garden detail."

Caffrey groaned. *Mink* was Eileen's code name. *Weasel would be a better fit*, Caffrey thought, since the woman invariably made a slinky spectacle of herself any time Mace was near. With her model-perfect body and single status, every male in the complex vied for her attention. Caffrey could only watch with disgust as Mink manipulated and controlled them. The worst part was Mink's habit of making snide comments about all the other females in order to hold sway over the interest of the men.

Caffrey enjoyed referring to her as Scarlett O'Hara whenever whispering to Gina or Barbara, and on occasion, to Ron. Somehow, Sharia had become as innocently naive as everyone else, commenting that Mink "just has a *big* personality," so Caffrey no longer chanced the reference with her.

"Is there a problem?" Mace asked, curious.

"No, it's just...." How could she explain to him why the girl was so irritating? "She's...." Caffrey halted, then sighed. Mace placed his hands on his hips in anticipation. Caffrey mirrored his movements. There was no time like the present to stand up for herself. "If there's anyone else, I'd appreciate it."

"Why?" He narrowed his eyes.

She dropped her arms and glared. "It's *not* something I can discuss with you."

He stepped closer, his brows knitted together. "Is there something I need to know here?"

Caffrey folded her arms again. "She just gets on my freakin' nerves. I'd appreciate someone *else*."

Afraid he might force the two together to work out their differences, Caffrey was surprised when he said, "I'll see what I can do."

"Thanks," Caffrey offered, her voice cool.

"Com to Wolf," said a scratchy voice from Mace's shoulder unit. Mace sighed and strode back up the stone passageway. "Wolf. Go ahead."

Caffrey watched him walk, and placed a hand against her stomach to calm the fluttering inside.

It did not take long to reaffirm her anger toward him the next day, when Eileen marched up to her and declared herself ready to escort Caffrey in half an hour to the "top."

Caffrey nodded and said, "okay, thanks," but inwardly she fumed. She could not decide whether to give Mace a piece of her mind or not speak to him with any civility for the rest of her natural life.

After two glorious hours in the sunlight, even with Eileen flirting with members on field and garden duty and her amazing talent for talking about everything she did without actually doing any work, Caffrey felt tired but pleased to have experienced warm sun on her arms.

"He's a stud, ain't he? So cool." Eileen cocked her head in an artful, dissembling way that irritated Caffrey. "There is absolutely *nothing* he can't do."

"Who? Mace?" Caffrey added sarcasm to dispel the assault.

"Wolf," Eileen corrected her. You must think so. You haven't taken your eyes off him for more than a few *seconds* lately."

Caffrey rolled her eyes. "Give me a break. I notice him because he always gives me a hard time. *You* know him." *What is wrong with this woman!* In a location where seventy percent of the population was men, it wasn't enough that they all forgot what their discussion was whenever the dark-haired vixen walked into a room. She had to be certain the leader had eyes only for her. *Well, one of the leaders,* Caffrey corrected herself. Mace and Vince worked together as an inseparable team. Everyone in the complex was loyal to both of them, as well as "the Colonel" and "Bulldog," two military leaders.

"Ha." Eileen was not easily thwarted. "He only gives people a hard time when they're not toeing the line."

"Mmm-hmm, well, *that* he better get used to," Caffrey grumbled, more to herself than to Eileen. Caffrey flipped the hoe over her shoulder. "This *isn't* the Marines, and there are a lot of good people working very hard. Some of them are good leaders, too."

"Oh, you don't think he's a good leader?" Eileen feigned shock.

Oh, you would love to go tell him that one, wouldn't you? "Sure, I think he's a very good leader," Caffrey countered. "And I'm sure he'll save us all. When his heart isn't in the way. Or, I guess I should say, when his 'bad mood' isn't in the way, which he seems to have had ever since *I've* known him."

The correction did not escape Eileen. She raised her chin and cast lovely amber eyes down at Caffrey as though some internal war had been silently declared. "Yes, well, the Wolf...puts all of his *heart* into his missions, for sure." Eileen absently panned the vast cornfield beyond the garden. Her left leg vibrated rhythmically with irritation.

Caffrey stared at the girl, and felt a touch of sympathy toward her for the first time.

"So...." Eileen viciously shredded a long, green corn leaf. "You're not interested in him?"

"Oh, for heaven's sake!" Caffrey whirled. "You know what? This is really getting old, okay? In the first place, he is *way* too busy. And in the second place, he's in love with the Underground. And, if there was a third, it would be *none of your business.*"

"A simple 'no' would do." Eileen feigned wide-eyed innocence.

"Since Mr. Wolf isn't exactly my favorite subject, let's just drop it."

Eileen's stiffened body exposed her desire to push the issue, but Caffrey walked purposefully in the direction of the main house. Eileen switched gears and pretended the conversation had never taken place. Instead, she launched into animated "aren't we buddies?" prattle by taking jabs at various Underground members for their personal quirks.

Caffrey offered occasional smirks as if she were listening, but she was smiling to herself, thinking that beneath the dirt on which they walked, under immense veins of granite and Georgia red clay, were tunnels housing people no longer able to show their faces in the world above. And she was one of them.

"Bet you girls could use some lemonade," suggested Mama, who was drying her hands on a white apron as they entered the spacious kitchen. Caffrey wondered how Mama kept the apron so white since she was always preparing food.

"Oh, wow, that'd be great Mama," Eileen commented expressively. "You're always doing the *nicest* things." She grinned as if auditioning for a tooth-whitening commercial, and reached for the pitcher of lemonade.

Mama glanced at Caffrey with a subtle raise of her brows, and Caffrey smiled secretively, immensely relieved to find someone else aware of the vixen's attempts to manipulate and charm.

"Oh, goodness, child." Mama responded to Eileen, in a slow, Southern drawl, waving aside the compliment. "I just like hearing everybody tell me how wonderful I am."

Caffrey laughed at that. They visited for a short while; Eileen continued to flatter Mama by recalling past meals and celebrations, as if re-establishing her supposed place in everyone's heart. Several times, she started sentences with "Wolf and I" for an added touch.

It was Caffrey who finally rose from her chair and thanked Mama warmly, anxious to return to the subterranean world and any assignment that did not include Eileen. Concern for being late was a valid excuse. Not showing up for the next assignment was not taken lightly at the complex, since other members on that duty were required to find the missing person.

Grateful to be rid of Eileen, Caffrey descended once more into the maze of stone, fans and wires. She nearly ran into Crow in the east wing.

"Hey, Fire, wassup?"

"Hey, Crow." Caffrey smiled amiably. "On my way to the botany lab. Cleaning detail. Then I'm growing mushrooms. Or was it tomatoes?"

"Ew. I don't like either. Did ya like gettin' some rays, girl?"

"Oh." Caffrey sighed wistfully. "Was that great. Except, I got sunburned. Forgot sunscreen."

"Girl, I got my own sunscreen." He curled both hands toward his chest and grinned wide.

Caffrey laughed as she walked backwards. "No fair."

He stepped forward and slinked a long, brown arm around her shoulders. "Any time you need protection from the sun, honey, just let me put my lovin' arms around you."

"Oh, will you stop." She swatted at him, and he jumped away, laughing. He had brazenly flirted with her since she arrived at the complex. It was a disappointment to discover he did so with all the girls, and was completely shameless. She had to admit she didn't mind since he was so much fun. Sharia swatted at him daily every time he made kissing noises at her cheek. She didn't think Sharia minded either.

"Yeah, I probably shoulda gone up there instead of lettin' Mink trade, but she whined that you guys were good buddies and all." He gyrated playfully with his hands, as he usually did to make people laugh. "Said ya'll hadn't had any BFF time, so...."

"What?" Caffrey stopped walking.

"Me and Mink...traded, you know. Didn't she tell ya?" He paused in the tunnel. "Wolf assigned me to ya, but, like I said, she wanted you guys to have some time, so she asked me to trade. But that's okay—I'll get me some time in the sun tomorrow."

"Oh," Caffrey responded slowly. "I see."

19

HIDDEN MESSAGES

"When you aim, don't feel anything except the desire to hit your target—focus...focus...focus." Mace drawled out the last three words for emphasis. "Missing is *not* an option. Open your ears to commands and instructions, in case someone calls a cease-fire. But, for that split second of time, turn everything else off. There's no pain in your body. There is no one around you. Nothing exists. There is only you, the weapon, the target."

Mace's voice was soft and low beside Caffrey's ear, so close she could feel the warmth of his breath in the chilly spring air, which reminded her of their encounter in the tunnel and made it difficult to concentrate. He had been instructing five of the newest people, with others coming along for the practice, but he had lingered beside her.

She took a deep breath and obeyed his instructions. Concentrating on the red soda can, she lined up the threads. The gun became increasingly heavy every millisecond that she hesitated. Her arms began to shake. She held her breath and squeezed the trigger. The explosion jarred her shoulder and nearly knocked her over. Mace had warned that this would happen, but she had no idea it would hurt so badly. To her surprise and delight, the soda can on the farthest stump flew up in the air, flipped like a football, and landed behind it.

Mace cursed.

"I hit it! I hit it!" Caffrey chanted, jumping up and down like a child.

"Well enough of *that*," Mace said angrily, and turned toward the next trainee.

"Hey!" Caffrey protested the dismissal. "I need more practice than that. Come on." She was anxious to do it again, even though her shoulder throbbed and she had to rotate it to make sure it was still intact.

"You don't need any more practice. You shoot like a damn Marine."

Caffrey glared at him as he passed Crow a look she didn't appreciate, stealing away what should have been a compliment. Though she had given him every reason *not* to be suspicious of her, he seemed determined to be.

"Look, I've never shot a gun, okay?"

"Sure you haven't," he commented without looking at her.

Caffrey stomped away. She could hear Crow whispering, "Ooo, girl, you betta' come back here." But she ignored him.

She had been thrilled that morning to learn that Mace had accepted her request to ride with others to a nearby target range. She should have known he would ruin it for her.

"Hey, I haven't dismissed you yet," Mace warned.

"I don't give a friggin rat's butt if you haven't," she retorted, still stomping toward the truck. She would walk back to Remote, by God.

A vice-like hand snared her upper arm and whirled her around. "Don't *ever* disobey an order in weapons training, or *any* training," Mace said through gritted teeth. Though he had attempted to lower his voice, the others surely had no problem guessing his tone. "If we don't function as a team, *we don't function.* Leadership and subordination is part of that function. You got that?"

"Then don't," Caffrey protested, "insult me in front of everyone. Why do you always have to *do* that?" She jerked her arm free and desperately blinked back tears.

"Fire." His eyes darkened, though his tone softened at the sight of her glistening eyes. "Insults are part of the game. Stiffen up. What do you think *you* did just now but insult me by challenging my authority?"

"*You* started it. I have *never* shot before...."

"As—far—as—you—*remember*," he insisted, broaching the real issue.

Caffrey felt a tear fall down her cheek, but brushed it aside with a sleeve and stiffened her jaw. "My entire life is not some program that is subject to *scrutiny* every time I do something right. Everybody else gets to do something right, and you don't suspect them."

"Do you have any idea how many people ever get their first shot a dead bulls eye at thirty yards?"

"No, but..."

"I am the only person I know who's ever done it. I was eight years old."

"So, because...oh, let me get this straight." Caffrey felt heat rising in her neck. "Just because *you* did it, no one else could possibly be as good, right?"

"No. But it's rare. I lived it. I loved guns, and I loved hunting. I grew up in a military family. I couldn't wait to shoot." Again, he paused. "And I would be stupid not to consider all that's happened to you."

"You're stupid anyway!" she assaulted through clenched teeth. "Do *I* get to assume you were visited by aliens when you were eight and they taught you how to shoot? I *know* what I didn't *know*. My whole life isn't a program."

A gray pallor fell over his tanned face and she wondered if something *had* happened when he was eight. He swallowed, then shifted to an angry, tight-lipped glare and exhaled in frustration.

Caffrey blinked furiously to clear her eyes. "When that disc opened," she pointed a finger at him, "I knew that was the last of the programming. *I knew it*, deep down inside me, except for something important about their...ships. Something...I don't know what that is yet. But that's *it!*"

He rolled his eyes in disgust.

"I have always wanted to shoot a gun. I've always wanted to learn this. My grandfather died before I got to learn. He was the only hunter in the family. I followed your instructions and I got it right. And now, you treat me like I'm some...alien terrorist."

"Okay, fine. *Fine*," he held his hands up in surrender. "But, this is a military training exercise, and I am your superior officer. *You* took the vow. Either play the game right, or go sit in the brig." Abruptly, he turned, but it was Caffrey this time who grabbed *his* arm.

"Okay," she responded angrily, not backing down when his body tensed, "but just because you hate me is no reason to treat me differently. That is a true leader, *mister* military." She released his arm and tramped back to her place in line.

"I don't hate—" Mace halted and composed himself with a heavy intake of breath. He turned to address the entire group, who had been busy pretending they were busy.

"About-face!" he commanded. The small group straightened itself into a neat line, with the newest ones copying the motions of the alumni. Mace crossed his arms and addressed all present. "All right. Could you kill someone if ordered to?"

Several sets of eyes widened. One grim-faced man boldly answered, "yes, sir."

Mace nodded to acknowledge the answer. "In the service, you're taught to fire on command. It's based on training, and trust that your commander would have a good reason to order it. And you don't question that, aside from the fact that live action will change you real fast, especially when your life's on the line, or your buddy's life. In this unit, you have to learn to trust my judgment. If I ever tell you to shoot, you'd better believe there's a good reason." He glanced at Caffrey, and she flicked her eyes forward.

"But, if your conscience *cracks* at that moment, shoot to injure. Don't be the weak link in your unit. Go for the shoulders, arms, legs. They're harder to hit, but you can still disable your opponent, and more than likely they'll survive, unless you hit the main artery in the leg. Your conscience will live—that is, if *I* let you live. Remember, if your enemy's still holding onto his weapon, he can still shoot you, or the buddy beside you."

He cleared his throat. "You're civilians, but not you're not blind and dumb civilians any more. While you're under command on a mission, you're part of a team. Know where to hit, so you won't be a handicap to your group."

After an hour of lecture, target practice, and basic gun safety lessons, which the trainees gruelingly repeated until they made no errors, Caffrey joined another group of trainees, several fairly new like her, who had signed up to review all the basic military commands in order to be useful in the event of a full raid. Since such an exercise would be questionable out in the open, they returned for drills conducted in the cavernous mess hall.

The Colonel insisted that the Pledge of Allegiance to the United States, as well as the Pledge to the Underground, be recited before the exercise. Caffrey's eyes welled up with tears as she repeated the pledge; it had been so long since she had been given opportunity to recite it. An older man Caffrey had befriended whispered that he heard the Colonel's life had been endangered by his discovery of the Vhurruh faction's slow infiltration of military hierarchy. Two of his closest friends, both high-ranking career officers, had disappeared six months before, without a trace.

"Right face!" he yelled with a voice Caffrey was sure would bring down the cavern spiders. "If I give you an order to face right, that doesn't mean look at me! And don't memorize this face, while you're at it. You never saw it, and you never will. If this face passes you on the street, it won't give you the time of day.

"I'm here to whip you soft, cushy, civilians into *something* that resembles a team of soldiers, and that's what I intend to do. If you want to quit and be Vhurruh bait, that's up to you. But know that it'll be a cold day in hell if any of you get that far. I'm either gonna take a piece of your butt turning you into a usable soldier, or blow it apart with a plasma pulsar when I find out you're a worthless, lazy piece o' chicken meat that's been lucky enough to have real soldiers keeping your butt safe all these years. Now...."

Caffrey found herself smiling and worked facial muscles hard to erase the smile lest she be royally bawled out. A thrill rushed through her heart and spine with every barked command, and she darted her eyes often to make sure her actions duplicated that of the alumni around her. Two years earlier, she had attempted to join the National Guard, but after disclosing scoliosis in her back, the interviewer promptly stated she was not a viable candidate. Had Caffrey realized one had to have a *perfectly* healthy body to be accepted, she would have lied.

"I have never had so much fun in my life!" Caffrey burst into the medical lab, where Gina was busy sterilizing instruments. "What a rush! Left face—forward march—sir, yes, sir! I have *always* wanted to do that." She peeled off her hoodie and tossed it haphazardly onto a chair. Then she froze and blushed.

Mace stood leaning against the opposite counter, decidedly amused. Caffrey could not believe she had not noticed him. Awkwardly, she glanced at Gina and hoped she would make some comment.

"So, you thought that was fun, eh?" Gina said, rescuing her with a smile.

"Yeah," answered Caffrey, subdued. She wished Mace would leave.

"How about gun safety and target practice? Did you dislocate your shoulder? Can you still hear?"

"Almost." Caffrey felt more awkward as the seconds ticked by. Mace made no effort to leave but watched her with a fixed expression.

"So, how'd you do? Did you hit anything?" Gina asked.

Caffrey took a deep breath and frowned. "We won't go there."

"Bulls-eyed it," Mace interjected. "Flipped the soda can right up in the air like it had her name on it. Thirty freakin' yards."

Caffrey glared at him, confused by the hint of pride in his voice.

"Good for you!" Gina congratulated with a small clap.

Caffrey managed half a smile. "Yes, well, it should have been. Excuse me." She grabbed her hoodie and exited the room.

Lunch was a welcomed diversion. The line was already half the length of the cavern, since it was past noon. She exchanged pleasantries with her line mates and caught a wave from Barbara at a nearby table occupied by Ron, Sharia, and other familiar faces.

"Did ya hear what George's saying?" asked Barbara, as Caffrey approached with tray in hand.

"George?" Caffrey questioned. She twisted her legs to fit into the narrow spot at the bench.

"Oh, sorry," Barbara amended with a wave of her hand. "I mean Dream Master. I met him before, at a convention. Don't tell Mace—

I mean Wolf. See, there I go again. Dream Master's the one who sees visions in his dreams, ya know. He keeps having the same dream with people leaving here for another Remote-type facility, but one above ground."

"*Lots* of people," added Sharia, tearing a garlic roll in half. "Rows of 'em—all leaving in a hurry. And he hears an explosion."

"Anyway, he's got all the leaders banging heads for a new location," Barbara continued, happy with her juicy, inside scoop. "Eagle says they have two in mind. One's in South Carolina. The other is closer to Bigfoot, in eastern Tennessee."

"Bigfoot?" Caffrey questioned with a chuckle.

"Oh, Patrick. Sorry," Barbara whispered. "I chose it so Dancer and I could talk about him."

Caffrey snickered. "Wonder what he'd have thought of *that?*"

"Have you ever seen his feet? They're size thirteen!" Barbara exclaimed. "Anyway, the Tennessee location is in the mountains and it's a bunch of cabins supposedly rented out to vacationers. They all have interconnecting tunnels."

"Tunnels." Caffrey groaned.

"I wanna go there," Sharia mumbled with a wad of garlic roll in her cheek. "I like Tennessee."

"Well, I can't say *I'm* happy about it." Barbara frowned. "I was just getting to like this place. Poor Trainman can't sleep at all, though." Ron nodded in agreement. "That bothers me." Barbara watched him sip his soup. "Trainman's very sensitive, and when something keeps him from sleeping, something's afoot. Guarantee it. It's a sign."

Ron looked blankly at his soup. "Yep, I reckon it means something. Probably the lumps in that old mattress."

Everyone chuckled heartily while Barbara playfully swatted him.

"If I looked at all the signs around me," Caffrey spooned her soup thoughtfully, "I think I'd just shoot myself and get it over with."

Sharia blew a sound of exasperation from her lips, while Ron looked up in astonishment.

"Why?" asked Barbara.

"Oh, I don't know." Caffrey dodged the question.

"What?" Barbara demanded in a sing-song voice. She and Sharia exchanged a quick glance.

"Aaugh, it's nothing. Suffice it to say I won't be looking at every sign in *my* life right now."

"Oh, come now," Ron offered in respectful compassion.

"What happened?" Barbara asked bluntly. "There's anger all around you."

"Just...I'm tired of being suspected for stupid things. If I accomplish anything here, it's because I was programmed to. I am so over it. And anyway, you can get caught up worrying over little things meaning something."

"Oh, I don't know," Barbara disagreed. "All signs are important. I have learned that everything means *something*." Not getting a response from Caffrey, she pressed further. "Messages are in everybody and everything, Fire. Every conversation you have, every odd thing that happens. Everyone gets and transmits information in some way. Psychics learn that a bee buzzing around your head, or a dog barking, or a book dropping off a shelf, is a message in some form, often from your loved ones on the other side who are allowed to help you sometimes. When you learn to understand that, every moment becomes an adventure."

"Oh, come on Barb, uh, uh, Capricorn!" Caffrey shook her head as everyone laughed. "These code names are only fun if you don't know the person's real name. Then it gets on your nerves."

"Well, think about it: ninety percent of the people in here you only know by their code names, right?"

"Yeah."

"Then it's done its job."

Caffrey waved it off. "Anyway, so what you're saying is, the fact that I tripped on the stairs before going to target practice was supposed to *mean* something? The fact that I rammed my shoulder on the secret tool shed door meant something, other than I'm not paying attention to where I'm going? Or, the fact that Mr. Wolf treated me like dirt, as usual, was supposed to *mean* something? Or...."

"So, *watch* where you're going," Barbara interrupted, with brows raised and a slight smile curled at the corner of her mouth. "*Stand* your ground. *See* what's ahead. Are you tripping yourself up? Is someone tripping you up? Like maybe Wolf? Sometimes what happens is a sign for *movement*. What do you need to do? Do you need to draw the line on someone's behavior? Do you need to apologize for something you did that hurt them? Or, do you...."

"Stop!" Caffrey blurted.

"Let experiences *move* you, speak to you," Barbara continued, unhindered. She glanced secretively to her left and right, then leaned forward and lowered her voice. "Take what we went through the past few weeks. I've felt for a year that I should change my eating habits and lifestyle, but in the past couple months it got stronger. I kept getting all these signs. You know what? I ignored 'em all. I love food. I love having a good time. I'm a busy person, and I hate chopping vegetables. But, guess what? When I needed my body to be there for me, it wasn't. It wasn't fit, it wasn't slim, and it became my handicap in that awful tunnel. Now, if I was truly handicapped, that would be different, and I'd work around it. But, I had the power to *change* my body, and that could have been an adventure. Instead, I was crying the whole way through. The message was to *be prepared*, and I wasn't."

The three listeners stared at her.

"Hey, you weren't the only one cryin' in that tunnel," said Sharia.

Caffrey laughed outright. "*I'll* go along with that." They exchanged a high-five. Ron chuckled, too, but suppressed it when Barbara frowned.

"Mark my words. You'll see," Barbara added with a nod.

Caffrey noticed Mace entering the far end of the room with Gina beside him. Arms went up at various tables near the entrance to greet them. Slinking like a snake, Eileen casually withdrew from another table to saunter in Mace's direction. She stopped to greet others and laughed absurdly until Mace and Gina hurried through the buffet and approached a table with trays in hand. Eileen timed her addition to the table they chose with perfect timing.

"Unbelievable." Caffrey shook her head.

"What?" asked Barbara, trying to follow her line of sight.

"That Mink. No matter where Wolf is, she slithers over to park beside him. Like she's really fooling anybody."

"Oh, she can kiss that goodbye. He can't stand her."

Caffrey straightened. "Really?"

"Oh, I don't know," Sharia objected. "They're so much alike. I think they should get back together."

Barbara and Ron glared at her.

"*Back* together?" Caffrey asked, in complete shock.

"They were an item once." Barbara tossed both hands outward as though it were unimportant. "*Very* short."

Caffrey stared open-mouthed, and returned to spooning her soup, much slower.

"It could still happen," said Sharia defensively. "Don't they *look* like they're meant for each other? Besides, she told me they're already, uh...." Sharia paused, then picked up a cracker and began munching on it.

Caffrey busied herself with sipping more soup to deflect anyone from thinking this bothered her. The disturbing thing was that it *did* bother her.

"Don't you believe it for a minute," Barbara snapped at Sharia. "I don't believe half of what comes out of that girl's mouth."

"Well, I do." Sharia gathered items onto her tray, then threw a stiff, "Gotta run" to the group before abruptly departing.

Barbara glared darkly at Caffrey. "Mink's been sidling up to Dancer since we got here. She thinks Dancer's close to us, and to you, and to Mace, and she can get inside information. That's what that's about."

Mortified, Caffrey stared at her soup. Bluebird, another seer, quickly took Sharia's place at the bench. Bluebird leaned in to visit with Barbara but offered toothy smiles to everyone.

Caffrey liked the woman, though there was something disconcerting about her. Perhaps it was the many rings, necklaces, and bracelets she wore, always jingling and clinking with every movement; Caffrey wore little jewelry except earrings, and she found necklaces and bracelets cumbersome and uncomfortable. Or perhaps, it was that Bluebird always seemed to be completely aware of what Caffrey was feeling, which was unnerving. Caffrey lazily crumbled her last cracker into a million tiny pieces.

"He hasn't gone anywhere," whispered Bluebird.

It took Caffrey a moment to realize Bluebird had addressed her. "Who?" she asked, feeling her cheeks warming.

"The guy you've been watching for the past five minutes."

"I...I haven't been watching him. I'm watching that group over there, and the...wiles of someone." She stole a glance at Barbara and Ron, who were both looking smug.

"Then how'd you know who I was talking about?" Bluebird repositioned an arm to rest her chin on, which released countless fairie-like jingles from cascading bracelets.

"Look, I just like to know where he is so I can know if he's going to pick on me anytime soon." Caffrey noticed other acquaintances at the table were turning to listen because of her tone.

"He? He who?" asked Bluebird, wide-eyed.

"Hmmm, signs and messages," said Barbara, daring Caffrey with her eyes.

"Oh, stop it. I'm not listening to you guys anymore." She flipped her legs over the bench and grabbed her tray.

"Hey, Fire, Sunday evening, seven o'clock, come to my room," Bluebird called after her. "We're going to do something special." She winked.

Caffrey frowned and disposed of her tray. She felt Mace and Eileen's eyes on her as she approached the archway of the cavern. A blurred figure ran into her and immediately recovered by encircling her waist with a long brown arm and turning her in a complete circle.

"I'll do a ballet on the table top," sang Crow as he tilted her back and whirled her again.

Caffrey laughed and pushed him away. Crow continued to sing and dance toward the food line with a flourish of lanky arms and legs, blowing kisses at her. She snorted and giggled. Her eyes flicked toward Mace as she turned back to the cavern arch, and caught him staring with a fork suspended halfway to his mouth.

Caffrey exited into the adjoining tunnel and smiled. Maybe it was time to enjoy the flirtations of other men. Men that were not worried about their brains melting.

20

EASTER

Caffrey flapped her hands in fright and smacked her head and elbow into the stone wall adjoining her top bunk. "Ow! Oh." She rubbed her forehead, wondering what creature had landed on her face and if it was still in her blankets. She clicked on her flashlight.

China Doll giggled below. "It's Holy Saturday."

"Excuse me?" Caffrey rolled over to find a long branch, with feathers attached to the tip, dangling beside her nose.

"What the …?"

"I'm asking blessings on the room," China Doll explained.

Caffrey waved the branch away. "Go bless somebody else's. Did Bluebird put you up to this?"

"She's all about Native American stuff. She doesn't know anything about Sweden."

"Sweden?"

"Yes, we bless houses on Holy Saturday. My parents are from Sweden."

"China Doll," Caffrey began in a grumpy voice, "I appreciate your heritage, but if you try to bless everybody else's cabin you're going to get thrown out."

"Ha! They can't throw me out. I know too much."

Caffrey slid to the floor. "We all know too much."

"Oh, come on. It's Holy Saturday, and Mama's preparing the meal. I told her what to put in it. Eagle and Wolf won't let me have a bonfire, though. I'm going to miss that."

"You guys have bonfires the day before Easter?"

"Yes. I love Easter! We have festivities all weekend."

Caffrey rubbed her eyes. "I could use a festive weekend."

"It will happen!"

True to her word, China Doll badgered the leaders into allowing a small bonfire out in the farthest field Saturday night after the teenagers left. Word spread fast, and many joined her with marshmallows. Invites to special services spread around the ring of fire until they were all ordered back to barracks.

By late Sunday afternoon Caffrey had attended a Catholic mass, which she had always wanted to do, then joined a Protestant Easter service with communion, where she grew misty-eyed at the familiar hymns. Then she sang a mantra with a Hindu, who had accepted her dare for him to attend the Protestant worship service if she would attend his.

After that, she participated in a healing meditation, which did wonders for her back, had lessons in dowsing until she was giggling with the fun of it, and contributed to an illuminating discussion on alien communication with a group of contactees and links.

In the evening class that Bluebird offered, Caffrey found her animal spirit guides to be wolf and bear, with additional guidance from horse and spider. The last one she had trouble with, although she loved horses.

In contrast, the week that followed was overshadowed by a heightened sense of foreboding. Dream Master's vision had spread. Steps were being taken to box equipment and plan for a possible evacuation. Caffrey's assignments were frequently interrupted by requests to attend meetings concerning the mission to the Telenex facility.

Mace still found time to plan two more training sessions on assault tactics. Despite their earlier altercation, Caffrey signed up for both, determined to learn skills she might need from someone who was an adroit master, and to whom she wanted to prove she could do anything. Thankfully, tarps had been erected so satellite photos would not reveal the type of training being conducted. She hooted with pleasure at not having to wear much of a disguise, except for her hair being braided and covered.

"Where's the hat?" Mace asked at the start of the first session, his face stern.

"Aw, come on." Caffrey grumbled. "They're hot. And I'm under a tarp. And there's clouds."

"Hat on, Fire. Or go back in."

"I'll get 'er one." Crow volunteered, turning toward the barn.

"She can have mine," said Sha-me, a young man of Asian descent who worked in the Communications room.

"Thanks." Caffrey grinned and donned the cap.

"Aw, *you* can f'get it," said Crow, gyrating with his arms at Sha-me as he returned. "She's gonna be my wife."

Sha-me threw his head back and guffawed. "In your dreams, dude."

"Gentlemen, is there a problem here?" Mace's fierce glare made both young men stand straighter.

"Just my home-boy here checkin' my future wife, sir," Crow mumbled, holding his expression serious.

Sha-me snorted.

Mace gave Crow a long, hard look. Crow raised both brows and appeared unfazed and irreverent.

"All right," Mace called out to the group. "Pair up."

Crow and Sha-me jumped to either side of Caffrey. She giggled.

"You two," Mace pointed at Crow and Sha-me, "partner up. Fire's with me."

"Hey!" Crow and Sha-me both protested.

"Do we have a problem here?"

"No, sir," Sha-me replied, looking mutinous.

Crow sniffed as he passed by Mace, and mumbled low, his lips barely moving. "You leave it, I retrieve it."

Caffrey gasped softly, expecting Mace to take offense. Instead, he pretended not to hear and commenced with instructions to the group on defensive moves in a physical assault. He used a man his size to show several techniques. Everyone was ordered to try all of them.

Mace stepped toward Caffrey. Her emotions were whirling so fast it was hard to concentrate as Mace instructed her how to compensate for her small size against a tall, heavy man. After successfully managing two of the easier disabling methods, she groaned in frustration at her inability to dislodge him or flip him.

"Come on, you can do this," he urged when three tries did not succeed in knocking him off balance. "Focus on the key points. Make my size work against me."

Caffrey growled out loud and followed his instructions with more strength than she had ever used, which resulted in Mace landing on his back and her landing on top of him. He laughed, and she laughed with him.

"Okay, that was not the plan," she managed to say.

"I'm not complaining." He chuckled. "All I have to do is grab you in this position, though. You're supposed to follow up with a blow or kick. Or, run away."

Caffrey was hesitant to move and disturb the flirtatious moment, but she slowly stood. When she straightened, she found herself staring at an irate Eileen with nostrils flaring and hands on hips.

"I'll be her partner," Eileen suggested as Mace rose to his feet.

"Oh no, you don't," said Caffrey, surprising both of them. "Besides, we've got more to do. And *you're* late."

Eileen stared at her, wide-eyed, unused to Caffrey standing her ground. "I got my assignment done early. Wolf, you know I could teach her a lot." She offered him a dreamy smile and tilted her head coyly. Mace watched her for a few seconds, then glanced at Caffrey. Caffrey glared at him with an unquestionable threat.

"Wolf, I don't get this part," said a plump man. "Neither one of us has flipped the other."

"Excuse me, ladies." Mace nodded and walked over to the two men.

Eileen ignored Caffrey and followed Mace. "Here, use me. We'll show them how it's done."

Caffrey rolled her eyes. "Chicken," she whispered softly toward Mace's back.

Mace posed Eileen like a mannequin, flipped her, then allowed her to wrestle him off balance. Eileen grinned at the two men. "It's easy. It's all in breaking the stance and shifting the assailant's body weight." Her eyes flashed in Caffrey's direction, but Caffrey pretended to be watching two other trainees.

Mace used Eileen as a model for a second pair. He glanced at his watch and then at Caffrey, who stood with her arms folded as if merely observing the others. To her complete shock and delight, he abandoned Eileen while she was giving instructions to the second pair, unaware he was no longer beside her.

"Come on," he said to Caffrey. "Let's give it one last shot."

She smiled and backed up several steps to gain momentum.

"No," he instructed. "Whether I come at you from the front or the back, you don't have time to plan a run. I'm going to grab your shoulders and neck. Remember what I taught you."

She took a deep breath and was ready when his hands landed with vice-like pressure. She gave a yell, kicked his leg, elbowed his side, twisted one of his arms, and flipped him. Unfortunately, she slipped on the grass, somersaulted in the air and landed with her back sprawled against his chest.

Eileen let out a shrill laugh. "Wow, have you got a long way to go."

Caffrey opened her mouth to return the insult, but was interrupted by Mace. "All right, that's time. Let's go in." Caffrey felt his hands on her waist as he lifted her to her feet. She began straightening the front of her shirt, and realized Mace's hands were still lingering on her waist.

Eileen had taken several steps toward the tool shed entrance, assuming they had followed. She turned and froze.

Emboldened, Caffrey took a half step backward so that the length of her body was now against Mace's. To her surprise and delight, he did not move. Instead, he pulled dried grass slowly from her hair. His left hand tightened around her waist as he murmured next to her ear, "You okay?"

Eileen scowled at both of them with absolute hatred and pivoted on her heel.

Caffrey smiled wickedly, a rare expression for her. She turned her cheek toward Mace to respond, but the moment was interrupted by two men asking Mace questions about the next exercise. Mace dropped his hands.

Caffrey tried to stay close to him as they walked toward the shed, but lost track of him in the press of bodies descending into the corridors beneath the ground. Amidst all the conversations, she heard Vince's electronic voice requesting Mace's presence at a meeting. Hearing Mace's deep throated response, she slowed to wait for him at Spaghetti Junction, but he did not materialize.

Mhetrrian?

I am alone.

Yes! Caffrey mentally exclaimed with clenched fists. She had been resting on her bunk, unable to fall asleep after staring at a black spider hovering several feet above on its ghostly web. *How are you?*

I am fatigued. Much work.

Me, too. Wow, you really are tired. I can actually feel it. Are you okay?

He deflected her probe of his health and threw up a psychic block. She wondered how he created such a strong wall, but he asked a question as a further diversion.

Are you distressed?

Caffrey sighed. *There's a female, Mink, who's driving me crazy. She is jealous of me, I think. For some reason she considers me a threat. Why, I'm not sure, because I'd have to be seriously crazy to want someone as difficult as him.*

Mhetrrian gently flickered over her emotions to assess the dynamics of the conflict. Caffrey smiled at his lightning-quick ability and did not try to block him. Although it would serve him right if she knew how. She should make him stop and instruct her how to do it.

He bristled with displeasure at the scene she was recalling. *The drone Mace does not show proper respect and should not be considered for your hahmah.*

What, you mean as one of my mates?

Yes.

We're a long way from that, trust me. Though *Mhetrrian* had often voiced his displeasure at Mace's treatment of her, his reaction was stronger this time. Vince had said *Mhetrrian* was near the age where young drones are often kicked out of the hive by the older drones. On his planet he might wander with bachelor drones until young queens leave nearby hives to start a new ones. Caffrey wondered what his fate would be now.

We, too, have conflicts between same-hive queens, Mhetrrian responded, *but only serious if they are of the old ways. In my hive, the two sozuul are modern.*

Caffrey chuckled inwardly at his pride and focused on the new word, letting its meaning come to her. *Sozuul sounds like it would mean princess in my language. Fertile child of queen, unmated, is that right? That's a princess to us.*

Princess, he mentally repeated. *A strange word. However, my hive will allow the running sozuul to live nearby and converse with the queen-mother.*

Running sozuul?

Mating run. After that, they find new cave.

Oh. Like when they go into heat and the drones run after them?

Yes. If they stay, surranenn may even determine the dominant queen.

Why would the workers get to choose?

The surranenn always know the success of the hive. But, in other hives, there is still battle if the young queens do not escape. The victor rules or leaves. If the queen-mother is already dead, the young sozuul will battle.

Hmmm, Caffrey considered, *wonder who our queen-mother would be? I guess Mama, or maybe Gina, or Caretaker, and the rest of us would be princesses. That would be a lot of princesses.*

You have so many females! he exclaimed with thought patterns of wonder. *Your conflict with the one called Mink continues unresolved. Why do you not discuss this, or fight until there is a victor? Can you push her out to live in another cave?*

Caffrey chuckled at the thought of her and Mink having a catfight in the mess hall, and trying to push each other out of one of the secret doors. *I'm afraid that would only result in extra latrine duty. No, thanks. We do things a little differently, okay?*

So I understand. It is somewhat...interesting, though.

Nice save. But I think I like your way better. One female to a hundred drones? I could deal with that. Just make me a princess and run out the door with a hundred randy drones vying for my attention. Is the queen limited in how many drones she can choose?

The numbers are different with each queen, Mhetrrian instructed, happy to offer any information about his society, but unable to hide his displeasure at the visualization she presented.

Honey, when the numbers are that high, it doesn't matter. It's good for me! So, when are you old enough to chase after a princess? She was not prepared for the fierce rush of emotion that exploded from him. She was certain if she could see *Mhetrrian*, he would be blushing under all that blue skin.

Not yet time. But soon. When we return. She felt his frustration that many older, larger males were in the way of that future opportunity. Yet, he also conveyed a strange worry over his future, as though uncertain he would have one.

As soon as she questioned his concern, he deflected her with an arrogant confidence that when his chance came, he would win.

Caffrey searched for a new subject and felt an old question nagging her. *Mhetrrian, I need to ask you something.*

His guard came up instantly. *What is question?*

How did you...what happened to the man whose skin you were in? Caffrey swallowed hard against her fear of the answer. *I know that was you.*

Human Benjamin was linked to Herrengae. He was a nephew of one of your leaders. He was one who battled.

Battled? You mean, like, a soldier or a boxer? Caffrey sent *Mhetrrian* a mental picture of a square wrestling platform with ropes. He surprised her by sending an image of a circle in sand.

Oh! He was a sumo wrestler? In my hive-land?

Yes. We liked him to visit ship. He was big.

Caffrey's mouth fell open at the semblance of a smile attached to his statement. She supposed the huge man was more like them than the usual spindly humans. And he was respected as a fighter.

When Benjamin discovered he was dying, he asked us to heal him but we could not. Only queens can heal serious illnesses. He wanted to be of assistance to Nekkai before his death. Herrengae considered his frame could hide me among humans to fly to facility. I could send report. Our teknahts were guarded. Benjamin fell into an unbreakable sleep.

You mean a coma? Did he have machines around him?

Yes. We extracted his body on the pretense of conducting an experiment to preserve humans in stasis chambers. Human Charlie tried to send disc but was chased and killed. We decided you must be contacted. I devised a bold plan. The others were frightened of my possible discovery, but I was willing. It was difficult to move in human frame properly. More difficult than I imagined. Recovery took much time. But I found you.

Relief washed over Caffrey. She did not realize she was holding her breath until her chest muscles relaxed.

Thank you. I...needed to know.

You questioned my intention.

Caffrey knew he had read her fear of the answer, but even worse, she could read his bruised ego. *I am so sorry,* she crooned. *Truly. I think you are wonderful, and so very brave.*

A rush of pleasure and pride reassured her he felt vindicated. Abruptly, his mind pivoted. *Detection!*

Caffrey closed her mind without saying goodbye. She had grown used to it from their secret exchanges. Though she longed to talk more, she dared not risk anyone in his battalion getting suspicious. The consequences would be grave, especially since she was known to be wanted by the faction. She could not imagine losing *Mhetrrian's* marvelous exchanges or his alien wit and charm. Their daily stolen conversations had become dear, though most of the time they lasted less than a minute.

Caffrey sighed and remembered the spider, a black dot only four feet above her now. She wondered how disrespectful it would be to kill a member of one's animal spirit guides. She decided she would risk it and deftly slapped him with a shoe, then apologized profusely to the air around her. One thing was certain: if she spared his life and woke up to find him missing, she would freak thinking he was in her blankets. It had to be. She made a mental note to ask Bluebird what the message of the spider was, for she had already forgotten.

"Eagle?"

"Yes, Rapunzel." Vince looked up from the electronic tablet he was reading, concerned by her alarmed expression.

"*Khrennam* contacted me last night. He said *Mhetrrian* isn't looking good. He thinks he's being poisoned. He doesn't know how they're getting it into the food, but the *suurranen* feed the drones, so...."

"Oh, no." The loss of *Herrengae* became a hot pressure in his chest. He did not want Caffrey to have to feel that horrible emptiness. Plus, *Mhetrrian* was an asset to the Underground, and would be a great loss. "Are you sure?"

"It's what he said. The two of them have been playing along, you know, obeying the faction leaders, but *Vrenenjurr* has many spies."

Vince shook his head and ran fingers through his hair. He raised concerned eyes to Rapunzel, who looked stricken.

Rapunzel licked her lips. "You think I should tell Fire?"

Vince placed a hand on her shoulder. "No, no. She'll be overwhelmed with worry and start contacting him every hour to check on him. It will just put him, and her, in jeopardy. Of course, if he's being poisoned, he's already compromised." He heaved a heavy sigh. "Fire will start to sense it after a while. I did." Vince swallowed. His throat grew tighter. How he missed *Herrengae.* Such a dark vacuum remained where he used to be. His guide. His confidant. His friend.

Caffrey set out at a fast pace after breakfast, thrilled to have been granted another garden detail. She stepped carefully around sword-like stalagmites at a treacherous bend in the tunnel, and realized she could hear Mace and Eileen in a heated discussion. She halted and glanced behind her. She would be embarrassed if her garden-mates found her nonchalantly standing in the bend, listening.

"You *know* better than that," Mace admonished. "We *have* to keep things tight here."

"I had my assignment." Eileen snapped. "I just wanted to reinforce the relationship." In a low and seductive voice, she added, "He can't resist me."

"That assignment ended two days ago, and you know it. He's smart enough to have you followed, and he's got the resources."

"I know, I know," Eileen responded in a honey-sweet tone, "but my mom wasn't well, and I *had* to see her for a while. Plus, I had you on my mind an' all, you know."

Mace expelled a heavy sigh. "Don't worry me like that again. You weren't heard from for *sixteen* hours."

"You going to give me demerits?" Eileen teased. "Hmmm?"

"Mink...."

Caffrey felt a bubble of air catch in her throat, and she had to clear it with a brusque cough. There was nothing to do but continue around the corner after the escaping sound.

Eileen was sliding fingers around Mace's neck. They turned toward her in surprise. Mace straightened and removed Eileen's arms with his hands. Eileen glared at him for the briefest second, but recovered with a sneer of satisfaction toward Caffrey. She added a seductive hand rub to her hip as she repositioned her stance closer to Mace.

Fortunately for Caffrey, whose throat was threatening to close up, other trainees could be heard approaching from behind. She turned, stiff-lipped, to wait for them.

The arriving group threw jovial greetings to her, Mace and Eileen. Mace surveyed the various disguises, including Caffrey's loose-fitting clothes, bound hair, and her floppy hat.

"Looks like everyone's geared up. Let's go." Mace looked angry as he led the group up the stairs to the secret tool shed entrance and across to the barn for a short update in evacuation procedures before the garden detail.

Eileen sidled up to him and draped a hand over his shoulder while he read from a tablet. Instead of immediately removing her arm, he gave Eileen a hard look that was more an entreaty than a command. She grinned wickedly and slid her gaze through the group until landing on Caffrey.

Caffrey took a deep, disgusted breath. *Looks like your brain's not melting with Scarlett hanging all over you, huh, Mr. Wolf?* She turned away and paired up with Sha-me, who had requested a gardening detail for the first time. He smiled and offered an elbow. She took his arm, not looking back. She decided she needed to cancel the afternoon lesson with Mace. Other instructors had as much knowledge to share.

Don't think about him. Don't be stupid, she repeated angrily to herself as she headed to her next assignment.

Stupid, stupid, stupid, she chanted. What a fool she was for allowing her heart to be open to an impossible idea.

After requesting changes in her schedule, she found herself disappointed at seeing little of Mace except for glances across rooms or passing once in hallway full of people. Each time, his eyes would land on her and remain as if some pressing question were on his mind. Caffrey felt a strange flip-flop in her stomach and fancied he was making a mental assessment as to her well-being.

She also fancied he was making an effort to sit near her at meals, since he always ended up one or two seats away from her. His focus appeared to be on every conversation she had, regardless of who she chatted with. *Ignore it, ignore it,* she intoned repeatedly to keep herself on track.

Toward the end of the week, she noticed the lines of his face becoming shadowed grooves, his stance more intense and alert. "Mission mood," Gina called it, when Caffrey asked. Gina gave her a long, side stare.

"Don't." Caffrey held up a hand.

"You don't know what I'm thinking."

"Yes, I do. And don't go there."

"Hmm." Gina arched both brows. "By the way, we need you at the meeting on tonight."

"Meeting?"

"Break-in to Telenex. To transmit the disc you so bravely carried around in your gut. Be there."

When Caffrey entered the mess hall, she was surprised at the number of people seated and looking serious. All the links and seers were there, the senior leaders, and the mission members. A few people she did not recognize.

Vince was more excited than usual, though there were gray circles under his eyes. He placed his arms behind him and cleared his throat.

"You all know why we're here. We are going to attempt the impossible. However, one of the things we do here is laugh at the impossible. Don't we, Q?"

Q raised his head and waggled a hand in the air. He went back to tapping on an electronic tablet as several people hooted their support.

Vince smiled. "We believe that *Nekkai* is on the way. We need to give them every piece of intel they need to right the wrongs of the mission commanders who went rogue. I believe we will succeed.

"Every one of you who has volunteered for this mission has our hopes and prayers behind you, as well as our undying gratitude. In addition, the hopes of people all over this planet, and the hopes of Vhurruh trapped in a war for freedom, rests on you.

"We have discovered there is nothing we cannot do if we set our minds and our will to it. We have done meticulous planning. But even more than that, I believe in the talent and bravery I see before me. I could not be more proud, and more honored, to serve with you."

The room erupted in applause. Caffrey felt her eyes burn at sight of Vince's eyes and nose reddening.

Vince swallowed. "I am going to defer to the Colonel for the remainder of this meeting. Please accept my thanks for the privilege of being a part of this incredible mission."

Caffrey blinked back tears as Vince side-stepped to allow the Colonel to take his place and begin relaying plans.

Anxious to hear the plans, Caffrey was surprised when Mace took her elbow, and called the links aside for questioning. He was brusque and efficient as he posed questions from different angles until he was satisfied, which Caffrey and the others allowed, resigned to his interrogation tactics. But something indefinable teased her senses. Perhaps it was a new eagerness in his restless, ebony eyes, and the way he seemed to be scanning her body unless she was talking about *Mhetrrian,* when his gaze would focus on her face. Or, perhaps, it was the way he constantly shifted position, ever closer, as though he wanted to be near her.

She bristled when she and the other links were dismissed from the meeting.

"I know you were asked to be here," said Mace. "But we decided the situation on the two mother ships has deteriorated to the degree that, at any moment, any of your links could be compromised. This mission is too important for that to happen. Thank you for attending. You are dismissed."

Parakeet walked beside Caffrey in the corridor. "Once a link, we're never completely trusted, are we?"

"It's ridiculous," said Caffrey. "We are an asset in every way. My Vhurruh has sacrificed so much."

Ahead of them, Rapunzel turned. "I mean, I get that they're all afraid our links can be compromised. Maybe they *could* influence us. Personally, mine would die first."

"Yours is a kurnistarr." Parakeet smirked. "He probably would. Although, I think mine would, too."

"Mine, too," Caffrey added. It was refreshing to hear the anger in their voices.

She had grown fond of these enchanting and quirky people. Many who remained in the meeting were dear to her as well. What if they did not return? What if they were captured? Her stomach began twisting in knots of concern for her comrades.

Bluebird invited them all to a meditation session, but Caffrey opted for the special prayer meeting. Though she loved meditations and affirmations, she wanted the highest power she knew behind her request.

"Well, a penny for your thoughts." Father Daniels halted as Caffrey gasped and flailed arms to keep from colliding with him in a corridor.

"Sorry!"

"Don't mention it. I always pause at this bend in the tunnel. I've been accosted many times."

Caffrey chuckled. "Wait a minute, aren't you supposed to be at the prayer meeting?"

"No, I'm afraid I have urgent duties at my parish in Five Points."

"Five Points?" Caffrey asked, wide-eyed.

"Yes, why?"

Cold water seemed to be pouring over her body. She placed a hand to her mouth. "Near Marietta Street?"

He nodded, puzzled at her alarm.

"Oh, no. I was there. Right in front of your church. There were lights on. If I had gone in...I would have found you. You would have directed me to the Underground. Maybe...Maybe I wouldn't have gotten shot. Maybe it could have gone down a different way. Maybe...."

"Hold on there. Take a deep breath. You look very pale."

Tears welled in Caffrey's eyes. "It...it would have all been different. If only I had...."

"Child, it's dangerous to fret too much over what *would* have happened. That's a vicious circle that only ends in guilt. The kind of guilt that never goes away. Guilt needs resolution. You can never know what *would* have happened. Deal with what *did* happen. Accept it and move on. That is what forgiveness is for."

Caffrey looked into his gray, comforting eyes, and nodded, swallowing back tears. He gave her a warm smile and continued up the corridor.

"Father, wait. Before you go, I don't know much about Catholic traditions, but can you spare a minute to pray with me about the Telenex mission?"

"Of course. What do you want to ask for?"

Caffrey was surprised by the direct question. What *did* she want? She started to say "success of the mission," but she realized her fear wasn't that simple. One fear was greater than the others. A fear she couldn't push away.

"I want to ask that God send an angel to keep...keep...someone safe. All of my friends here, of course—and success of the mission. But...there's someone...." She bit her lip.

"You know, the good thing about my job is that I am the one person people will be completely honest with. They step into the confession booth, and it all spills out. Words they never intended to say. Sometimes I think it is not only forgiveness they need, but that moment when they come to terms with what they truly feel."

Caffrey swallowed and stood straighter. "I want to ask God to send an angel to keep Wolf from harm, to keep him alive."

Father Daniels smiled with a twinkle in his eye. "Let's pray."

21

MISSION TO TELENEX

After midnight, Caffrey awoke. Anxiety surrounded and pressed in on her like a heavy cloud of doom. She sat up in her bunk and searched for some explanation for the unease. Instinctively, she reached out for *Mhetrrian*. But, he was closed, so closed he was perhaps asleep.

Thoughts of Mace loomed in her mind. She pushed them aside from habit. They returned, fierce and strong. She lay back down and turned on her side, worried Mace would get caught, or injured. Burning pain stung Caffrey's left shoulder. She rubbed it and pressed all around. She pulled back her shirt and clicked on her flashlight, fearing a spider or a scorpion had stung her. Nothing was there. The pain grew, and she grimaced at its intensity. She threw off her blankets and climbed down.

China Doll had some psychic abilities, but she appeared to be asleep. Stardust was as well. Caffrey chose not to wake them. She donned jeans and a light blue hoodie. Gina was involved in the mission to Telenex. It would have to be Barbara.

Caffrey tramped down lonely, sparsely lit stone and sand hallways, her footsteps dulled by the hum of dehumidifiers and fans reverberating in every direction. Turning into a small, dry cavern where seven wooden rooms had been built, she rapped on the second door. The air was heavy with sage and incense, as it often was in any section where seers were housed.

"Capricorn?" Caffrey whispered.

A sleepy Ron opened the narrow, wooden door. Several pieces of his graying brown hair stuck out on one side. He smiled warmly and mumbled, "Hey, Fire."

"Hi, Trainman. Can I talk to Capricorn?"

"I'm awake," whispered Barbara's familiar voice. Clothes rustled in the dark. "I can feel your anxiety all the way over here."

"I couldn't sleep, either," added Ron. His brows were knitted in concern. "'Course, I don't sleep good in here anyway."

"I just...." Caffrey drew her hoodie tighter around her. "I feel like something bad's happening. I don't know...."

"What comes to your mind?" asked Barbara, to the point.

"Well... um... it might be...." She licked her lips, trying to pick her words carefully.

"Honey, close your eyes," Barbara commanded. "Clear your thoughts. Be very still. Breathe in deep and slow through your nose. Now breathe out through your mouth. Ask a question. Hear the answer. Let it come. Don't force it. Don't question it. Breathe again and ask another question. Don't hear your emotions. Hear only the answer."

Caffrey did as instructed. People were running. She felt their sharp urgency and fear.

"That's it," Barbara encouraged. "Don't put anything into it. Don't assume anything. Let the answers come to you."

Caffrey breathed in her connection to the pain. Where was it from? Who was feeling it? Like a grey blur, Mace appeared rushing, fighting, hiding—in terrible, burning pain. Caffrey's left shoulder mirrored the burning sensation, and she winced.

"Well?" Barbara prompted. "What do you see?"

"Mace is in trouble," Caffrey admitted. "Something about a... fight. It's like he's been detected, discovered. Something's... *hurting,* burning his shoulder."

"Uh-oh. Here, take my hands, and let's focus on him together, see if I can pick this up." Barbara grasped Caffrey's hands firmly and closed her eyes. Caffrey did the same, but it was difficult to focus with Barbara's overwhelming energy.

Barbara chuckled. "Girl, you're too much of a receiver. You're like a mouse cowering in the corner. Learn to hold strong. I got him, honey. He's definitely in trouble. Whoa, big boy got hurt." She opened her eyes. "And I think I got something else." Her chin went down and brows raised.

"What?" asked Caffrey, mystified.

"What kind of seer are you turning out to be, if you can't even read your own feelings?"

"What do you mean? You can't read yourself."

"I can't always see my future, yes, but I'm good at analyzing my feelings. I see an electric field between the two of you, like a cord of energy stretched across a distance."

"Oh, no, really." Caffrey dropped her hands. "I'm just concerned about him. I can't... he doesn't... I don't...."

"Get the phone, Ron," Barbara ordered. Ron fumbled on a side table and handed her what looked like a thin watch. "I've got one of

Q's wrist phones," Barbara explained, bright-eyed. "Mace gave it to me yesterday. I tried to tell him psychics can't wear watches. Com? This is Capricorn. Mace is—uh, Wolf is in trouble. I think he's injured." She paused. "Because I'm one of the seers, you idiot. If you already know about it, fine. But if you don't, consider yourself informed." She paused again. "Are you in contact with them? Well, why not? You know what, we're coming up there."

"Come on." Barbara whisked past Caffrey and marched up the corridor, her robe flying.

"You want me to come?" called Ron.

"Nope. Get some sleep, hon."

"I wasn't sleeping before," Ron called after them. "How am I supposed to sleep now?"

Caffrey hurried to keep up with Barbara over creaking wooden planks and up stone stairways. Barbara was huffing by the time they stopped at the security camera outside the Com door, but Caffrey noticed she was thinner and in much better shape than weeks before.

The overly cautious young recruit on guard had to endure a choicely worded berating from Barbara, who wagged a finger straight up at the security camera when he made the mistake of "respectfully" declining her access to the Com.

Bulldog, an older, burly man with a scowl permanently etched into the drooping lines of his face, opened the three-inch steel door and frowned with disgust at Caffrey and Barbara as though they were flies in his soup. Barbara whisked past him into the interior room full of wired panels, keyboards, dishes, and display screens. Of the five men in the narrow space, Caffrey recognized Bulldog, the Colonel, Roadrunner, and Sha-me, each tense and keenly focused on his equipment.

Sha-me turned and did a double-take as Caffrey stepped into the forbidden room.

"And why do you need to be in here?" growled the Colonel, with an unlit cigar protruding from his mouth.

"Because this girl...." Barbara pulled Caffrey forward. "Has a tap on Wolf. She can see him wounded and in trouble. Sometimes you boys need communications of a different kind, you know?"

The Colonel glowered at Caffrey. He picked up a microphone and temporarily removed the cigar. "Watchdog, this is Com."

"Watchdog here," answered a curt female voice.

"We have possible intel that Eagle One is under fire. The Wolf may be down."

"Understood. Do we engage Game Play?"

The Colonel took a deep breath and exhaled. "You have a go, Watchdog. Approach with all caution. Report status of Back Door or Eagle One."

"That's affirmative, Com," the female responded, as if delighted.

After a short silence, with the other men glancing at the Colonel, Barbara, and Caffrey, Barbara asked, "What happened to Back Door?"

The Colonel squinted at Barbara, then raised a questioning eyebrow to Bulldog.

"She was consulted by Eagle and Wolf," Bulldog said. "She has a red clearance."

The Colonel pointed at Caffrey. "What about her?"

"Roadrunner, what's her level?" asked Bulldog.

Roadrunner tapped several screens and replied, "She has yellow level, sir, and a link. But security warnings are to be given red status."

The Colonel grunted and pushed the cigar to the other side of his mouth.

A buzzer sounded. "Aw, heck, what now?" Bulldog growled. Caffrey could see Bluebird and several other seers on one of the view screens.

"We're all concerned about the mission crew." Bluebird looked up into the camera.

"We're on it," said Bulldog. "We got two of you already in here. Can't fit any more. Keep us posted if you get anything specific. 'Preciate it."

Caffrey could see Bluebird glowering with both hands on her hips.

"Com, this is Back Door reporting," called a male voice over the speakers.

The Colonel pressed his headset microphone. "Back Door, this is Com, what's your status?"

"A local badge stopped to help us out with our 'flat tire.' Had to go silent. We're at a shopping center now. Has Eagle One reported?"

"Negative. Watchdog is approaching Game Play."

"Understood, sir. We're good to go. Say the word."

"Hang tight, Back Door."

"Yes, sir." The young man sounded disappointed.

After several minutes, Roadrunner spoke up. "Colonel, Eagle One's signals could be jammed. Snoopy told Wolf yesterday that the last time he pulled up to Telenex his radio and cell went out."

"Why weren't we told this yesterday? Q's equipment was supposed to get past all that!" the Colonel roared.

"Q was consulted, sir, and said the rotating signal interruptions are broadcasting outside the building but not in. To his knowledge, it's only a short distance. The devices are in the lamp posts in the parking lots, with a specific trajectory."

"Back Door, this is Com. We may have signal interference. Seer intel says Eagle One may be under fire."

"Understood, sir. Give us a go, and we're there."

"Com, this Watchdog," the female voice returned. "We are on approach, and headed for site North-Cat. I repeat, North-Cat."

Caffrey knew this meant the opposite of north, so she wondered if the girl meant the south parking lot of Telenex. She had seen the maps in the room where Vince and Mace had asked her questions.

"Understood, Watchdog," said the Colonel. "Back Door, approach Game Play. Report when you are approaching target."

"Affirmative, Com."

"Com, this Watchdog," said the female, but her voice was crackling. "We are approaching...Com, we see laser fire! We are en..."

The female voice did not continue.

"Watchdog, what's your status?" demanded the Colonel. He waited. "Watchdog, what is your status?"

With no response, the Colonel sat back. Several times he called again as minutes ticked by.

"Com, this is Back Door." Static made the voice almost unintelligible. "We are approaching the target. Please advise."

"Back Door, hold your position." The Colonel turned to Bulldog. "We need more intel. Why didn't Q program modulating communications?"

"Um...." Roadrunner's eyes darted.

"Roadrunner?" The Colonel barked.

"Eagle said they didn't have time to wait, sir."

The Colonel shook his head. "I'm going to slap his butt in the brig if he survives this."

Bulldog paced behind The Colonel, then abruptly glared at Barbara and Caffrey. "What about you seers? Can *you* give me a status?"

Barbara spoke up. "We'll try." She stepped to the monitor still displaying the seers gathered outside the metal door. "Roadrunner, let me speak to them." Roadrunner pressed a button, and Barbara instructed the corridor group to join forces and focus on Eagle and Wolf for an update. Bluebird complied without hesitation and formed the group into a circle, hands clasped.

Barbara grasped Caffrey's hands and moved her against the door. "Fire, close your eyes and block all this out. No emotion. Be completely calm and focus on Wolf. Think of him, and wait for it to come to you. Keep saying his name in your mind. Don't just *see* him, *feel* him."

Caffrey did as instructed, though it was hard to block out the heightened energy in the Com room. She breathed slowly and pushed everything away until she felt calm. *What's going on, Mace? What are you doing? What's happening?* The sensation of fear hit her, but also a focused sense of gritty, angry determination. He was running again. Others were with him, running past trees, away from Telenex. Flashes of light erupted from all directions. The pain in his shoulder was unbearable.

"I think they're running outside the building," she whispered, fighting to keep her emotions calm. "In some kind of woods. Someone's firing at them from all directions. Somebody else got hit, too."

Bluebird suddenly spoke up. "Com, we see our people running. A small group. I'm seeing two injured. Weapons firing. A second group is covering them."

"Back Door, you have a go," barked the Colonel into the microphone. "I repeat, engage!"

"Affirmative, Com! We're going in."

After nearly a minute, a faint voice crackled into the speakers. "Com, this is Back Door. We have a visual on Watchdog. They're taking fire and approaching us."

"Back Door, cover their butts!" yelled the Colonel.

"Affirmative!"

Everyone in the room seemed to be breathing in short shallow breaths.

After nearly twenty minutes, during which the Colonel paced back and forth across the short space, the female voice spoke: "Com, this is Watchdog. We have Eagle One. Every one of 'em, sir!"

Cheers rang throughout the room. Roadrunner and Sha-me had their arms in the air and were hooting.

"Good job, Watchdog," bellowed the Colonel. "What's your status?"

"We have two injured, sir. We are headed for the Fender Bender. Back Door is behind us. Game Play is probably in pursuit, but we do not have a visual. I repeat, we do not have a visual on pursuit."

"Watchdog, do you see birds in the sky?" asked the Colonel.

After a pause, the female replied, "Not a one, sir. We took out several enemies."

"All right, Watchdog, keep me posted."

"Yes, sir."

"Eagle One, you got a horn workin'?" asked the Colonel.

"We do now, sir," came Vince's voice.

Caffrey caught her breath. Barbara grinned and shook her arm.

"Was the package delivered?" the Colonel asked.

"Affirmative, Com, package was delivered," Vince replied. The men in the Com cheered again. "However," Vince added, "we did not get a duplicate." His voice was sad. "I repeat, we did not get a duplicate."

The room went silent.

"What's that mean?" Caffrey whispered to Barbara.

Barbara answered softly. "They got the disc sent through that subspace wave drive thing. They expected it to disappear. But Vince wanted a copy of it first. You said it contained star charts and stuff to find the new planet."

"Oh, yeah."

"Understood, Eagle One," said the Colonel, his voice dejected. "You accomplished the main mission and didn't lose a man. That's a job well done."

"Thanks, Com," said Vince. "You're right, of course. Still, it would have been great."

"It ain't over 'til the fat lady sings." The Colonel shifted the unlit cigar to the other side of his mouth.

Vince answered in a tired voice. "Remind me of that in the morning."

"Will do, Eagle One. Watchdog, you still clear?" The Colonel asked.

"Yes, sir," the female replied.

"Back Door?"

"Affirmative. No visual pursuit."

"Com," Vince spoke up. "I know we planned this when we knew Vhurruh air traffic would be light, but that was the most overconfident security I've ever seen. Cameras and two dozen guards? For *that* place? They had us surrounded, but still, I expected more. An alarm was triggered with the transfer. We took out a SAAF inside. When we took out the second one, he hit the floor, and alarms went off. Must have a device that registered his proximity to the floor. Brilliant strategy. They barely caught us leaving before firing on us. Unless we're missing something."

"Could you have a tag?"

"I don't think so. We didn't touch anything."

"That's a copy, Eagle One," the Colonel replied.

"I think we should risk a satellite link," said Bulldog to the Colonel.

The Colonel glanced at him thoughtfully. "Who we got that's close enough to hijack a signal?"

Bulldog rubbed his chin. "Tooth Fairie might be close enough."

"Get 'em on the horn," said the Colonel. "Let's see if our people are being watched."

Bulldog turned to Sha-me. "Sushi, boost signal eight for me."

"Sir, my name's not Sushi, it's *Sha-me*," said Sha-me as he typed with blurred speed into a keyboard.

"Then why's everybody calling you Shushi now?"

"'Cause Crow started it. He got jealous. Don't worry, I'll kill him later." His eyes flicked toward Caffrey and back to the screen in front of him.

Bulldog guffawed, but his face became serious as he dialed into a cell phone. "Hey, Sam, Bulldog here. How're the kids? Yeah, that's great. They still into Fairie stories? Uh-huh. They got Fairies flyin' around? Yeah? Well, all my kids are doin' good, too. They're kinda' sick tonight, though. Mmm-hmm. Yep, they don't need any Fairies flying around in their heads tonight. Oh, sure, I'll hold." Bulldog looked knowingly at the Colonel.

A female voice spoke. "Com, this is Watchdog. Two scouts ships flew right over us, headed back toward Game Play. We're mixed in with late night traffic. I don't think they know we're here. I'm going to cut off the signal. We'll report when we get to Fender Bender."

"That's a copy, Watchdog. Back Door, you got that?"

"Yes, sir."

"Com out," said the Colonel, removing his cigar.

Caffrey leaned over to Barbara and whispered, "What's Fender Bender?"

"A junkyard where the owner has cars waiting, ready to exchange," whispered Barbara.

"Hey!" Bulldog exclaimed into his phone. Then he paused. "Just four? Two headed east? That's great, man, I owe you one. Everybody in your family doin' okay? That's great. Listen, we'll have to get together soon and do some grillin'. Yeah. Take care, man." Bulldog closed the phone and spoke to the Colonel. "He picked up four scout ships but shows no surveillance aiming for our people. Chatter is starting to rise. They'll be lookin' over recordings shortly. They could have eyes on them right now and be waiting for a location. We're not out of the woods yet."

The Colonel took a deep breath. "All right, let's sit tight. They've got a diversion path mapped out." He shoved the unlit cigar back in his mouth and chewed on it.

Nearly an hour later, Caffrey's throat caught at the sound of Gina's voice reporting that the Wolf caught a cold, along with the Squirrel, but they would recover. Return to the den would probably be after sundown-cat.

Since this meant the opposite, Caffrey assumed they would arrive shortly after dawn. Her stomach knotted with anxiety.

When dawn came she was waiting outside the Com room. She had dozed off and on in her bunk for an hour, but finally she had given up and grabbed some juice and a day-old biscuit from the mess hall; on second thought, she turned and grabbed more for the Com watch, along with packs of butter and jelly, then headed up the connecting passageways. The burly Bulldog was still there, the skin under his eyes hanging lower than it had hours before. He nodded and grunted for the gift of biscuits but refused her entrance into the room. Sha-me leaned past the door frame and gave her a thumbs up.

Half an hour later, the Colonel came through the door looking much more affable, though his 6' 5" height and yard-wide shoulders were as imposing as his disapproving glare for her presence outside his Com room. She ignored him and nibbled on a biscuit.

Another hour and a much bigger crowd later, after word had spread, Eileen was camped near the secret tool shed entrance. When the trap door opened, Vince and Gina stepped down the wooden stairs, and the crowd exploded into applause. Vince smiled famously and raised his hands as if in humble but grateful surrender. Squirrel, a short, spunky young man appeared behind him, limping, and the crowd exploded again. A woman with cropped red hair, whom Caffrey vaguely recognized, came down, and Mace appeared behind her. The crowd roared even louder.

Mace smiled, clearly warmed by their welcome. His left arm rested in a gray and white sling. White bandages showed under the open V of his black shirt. Eileen quickly draped herself like a sweater onto his free arm and walked him through the cheering crowd. Applause continued as other comrades descended. Instead of turning down the adjoining tunnel, Mace headed straight for the Colonel and Bulldog. Caffrey slipped behind their towering frames.

"Mornin,' Colonel," said Mace, as though they were trading pleasantries.

The huge man shook Mace's right hand firmly, dislodging Eileen. "Mornin,' Wolf," the Colonel responded in a graveled voice, then replaced the crumpled cigar back in his teeth. "You slip and fall there?"

Mace grinned wider, and several people chuckled. "Got me with a damn plasma pulsar." He shook his head. "Man, them things hurt. Like being splattered with hot cheese pizza that you can't peel off."

The burly man roared with laughter and slapped Mace on the un-wounded shoulder, which caused his eyes to pop open, revealing the pain he was still feeling.

Mace jerked his head toward the pressing crowd. "I understand those whiny seers saved our butts again?"

Without turning his head, the Colonel reached around and grabbed Caffrey by the back of her light blue hoodie, nearly lifted her feet from the floor, and dragged her in front of him as though she were a puppy. "This one started it, got the others all riled up. Little pests, those seers are. Can't live with 'em, can't live without 'em."

Caffrey was not sure whether to kiss or kick the Colonel.

Mace's smile dropped. He swallowed. Color drained from his face. Caffrey straightened her hoodie self-consciously.

"Oh, where would we be without all those *crazy* little seers?" chimed Eileen with a flagrant chuckle. She glanced for support at those nearest her. "I felt something, too, ya know. It just came over me, and I started worrying about you—all night!" She squeezed tighter on Mace's arm only to find his eyes unmoved from Caffrey's.

"Were you informed?" Mace asked Caffrey in a still voice. Eileen glared at Caffrey, clearly hoping she would give him whatever answer he did not want.

Caffrey realized he referred to *Mhetrrian*. "No. I just...." Caffrey lifted her shoulders apologetically, *"Knew*. I felt you. You were in pain."

Mace averted his gaze downward and rubbed a hand across his weary face.

"You're tired, Wolf. You need some rest," Eileen crooned, and she flashed a scathing glare toward Caffrey for holding him up. Several people shouted questions at Mace over the clamor of many conversations and cheers, anxious to hear the story. Mace glanced back at Caffrey, his dark eyes flashing with an odd blend of delight and sadness. Caffrey swallowed, embarrassed.

Voices and slaps on the shoulder diverted Mace after he shook hands with the Com crew. Without another glance at her, he turned and moved through the crowd. Caffrey gritted her teeth and forced her way past him and Eileen, scraping her back against stone walls to push between bodies. She scrambled out of the cramped corridor, down the stairs, and along the many passageways to her small room. Like a monkey, she hurled herself up the top bunk and flopped onto her back. Alone was what she wanted, as was apparent by anyone who happened to pass her, tight-lipped and silent along the way.

Why couldn't he have said, "Thanks," or at least nodded with a, "Well done," and clasp of his hand to her shoulder, like he did the Com crew? Instead, he was uncomfortable and hesitant to acknowledge her help in front of the crowd.

Caffrey remained fixed on the stone ceiling until several of her linked friends came looking for her. They begged her to come to the Cavern and tell her part of the story at the celebration going on. After she politely refused to go or to disclose her reasons, they glanced silently at each other and left. Caffrey waited until their voices died down, leapt off the bunk, and escaped down to the botany lab to avoid any further probing questions.

She liked the lab. It was peaceful: nothing but growing plants and the restive sounds of waterfalls from drains and recycling areas. This was the one place inside Remote where she could take an oxygen-rich breath of air.

In the center rested a fountain, complete with the donation of a plump alien statue, a Blue drone with its fluffed mane meticulously carved and back fins and tail splayed, sensuously curving and reaching for some unknown spot in the sky. One of the artists had dreamed the Vhurruh likeness, and Caffrey often visualized *Mhetrrian* in the image, fighting to stay alive.

Her favorite pastime was to rub the soft, cool leaves of the many plants with her fingers, to send and receive love, as the gardener had taught her. "At least you guys like my love," she whispered. Then her smile dropped as she realized what she had said.

22

HEART OF FIRE

"Vince?"

Vince waved a long arm to acknowledge Caffrey's approach. Gina was leaning her light frame over the stair railing. Caffrey felt a lonely stab in her heart, watching the two smile for a fleeting moment and kiss each other as though no one else were on the planet. Gina threw Caffrey a friendly smile before skipping happily up the stairs.

Vince seemed taller as he mounted the first step, holding a cup of steaming coffee. He watched Gina disappear around the curved staircase.

Caffrey cleared her throat. "Vince, I need to talk to you."

Vince pretended disapproval. "I know we're close to the one of the entrances, but the Wolf'll kill us for not adhering to regulations." His quick smile let her know he was partly in jest.

"Sorry, Eagle, sir." Caffrey grinned and saluted.

Vince smirked and lazily returned the salute. "What do you want to talk about?"

Why he looked so worried, Caffrey did not know. Perhaps he was tired from a day of making decisions. She plastered herself against the iron spindles of the staircase. Vince casually leaned against the cold stone wall on the other side as he sat, balanced one long leg on a step, and propped the cup of coffee on his bony knee. Something in the set of his brows worried her. She straightened her jeans and cleared her throat.

"I heard you've been avoiding everyone all day, said you weren't feeling well," Vince stated.

Caffrey focused on her shoes. "I need to leave." She blurted the words, lest they choke her.

Vince suspended his coffee cup halfway to his lips. His brows were raised in surprise.

"I need to be...away from...someone in this group." She cleared her throat again. "I can work and be a part of *any* other location. But I just...I need to be away from this one."

Vince's blue eyes narrowed. "Why?"

Caffrey felt her throat constrict at his squint of suspicion and concern. "I can't tell you."

"Excuse me?"

"Look, I can be of help to the Underground anywhere, can't I?" Somehow, she had envisioned him being more sympathetic and amiable. "You've got *all* I know. There isn't anything else hidden in here." She knew this was not entirely true, but hoped he believed it. "And, you could put me anywhere, really...another state. Actually, another continent would be good. I've learned a lot of skills, and I can be a great help to any division. Besides, the group might be safer."

Vince set his coffee cup down. "Do you have reason to believe this group is in danger?" His face and neck flushed red.

"No, *no!*" She realized her mistake.

"Has *Mhetrrian* said something? Is anything compromised?"

"No, nothing like that." She reassured him with a cutting motion of both hands.

Vince breathed deeply but held her gaze. "Okay. I remember over a month ago, you said you were getting away from everything you knew and wanted to stay with this group. Am I remembering that correctly?"

"I know. I know. I've...changed since then."

"*What's* changed since then? Do you have any idea how suspicious this sounds?" Anger colored his voice.

Caffrey let her head fall back, then forward with frustration. "Eagle, come on. Somebody in here's got to trust me. Look, there is someone here who I do not get along with, okay? And I...need to get away from him, and clear my head." She took a deep, shaky breath.

"Let me get this straight." Vince clasped both hands together, his lips a thin angry line. "You've got someone you can't *get along with*, and I'm supposed to make some very difficult, and probably dangerous, arrangements to move one of the most *visible* people in the Underground?"

Caffrey glanced up at the ceiling. "Okay. Eagle, I think I deserve better than that."

Vince eyed her, incredulous. "And I think *I* deserve better than that! We've got some of the best people on the planet for helping with conflicts and relationships here. Rev's team does nothing *but* that." He shook his head. "Request denied."

Caffrey placed both hands on the sides of her head and balanced her elbows on her knees. How could she tell him? What could she do to convince him? "Eagle, don't cut me off. I'm too embarrassed to go into this."

"So be embarrassed." Vince's gruff manner softened, but only a touch. "What's going on Caffrey? You're tougher than this."

"Ha, you used my real name."

He waved a hand. "Forget that. Come on. What's up?"

Caffrey rolled her eyes. "I can't."

"Now."

Caffrey exhaled sharply, then swallowed. "Fine. I *care* for someone in this group. I'm in love—I don't know why, but I am. That someone does *not* care for me. I need to get myself diverted by...*something* else. It's too close here."

The strange curiosity in his eyes made Caffrey realize something she hadn't thought of. "It's not you, Vince."

A broad smile spread across his face. He slapped a hand to his heart. "Well, that's a relief. My heart's broken, but, hey...I'll get over it."

Caffrey snorted. "Your heart's not broken. Your heart's well taken care of. But how would you like it," she continued quickly, "if Gina suddenly stopped caring for you? And you had to work side by side with her every day, feeling what you feel and knowing...that she didn't love you." Caffrey swallowed to avoid losing the tight control she was exerting on her emotions.

"Who is it, Caffrey?" Vince asked with the edge of command. "That's an order. Besides, I'm not doing anything until I know." He stood.

Caffrey steeled her jaws to keep from responding but her throat muscles were quivering with the desire to answer. How *Mhetrrian's* suggestion to obey Vince's orders still had an effect on her, she could not fathom.

Her shoulders drooped. She closed her eyes. "It's Mace."

When Vince did not respond, she stole a quick glance at her leader and friend.

Every muscle in Vince's face seemed frozen. "You're kidding."

"No, I am not kidding. And it makes no more sense to me than it does to you, believe me."

"Well, I'll be darned. That Indian was right."

"Don't even mention that prophecy thing. Just because I have red hair. I didn't even get to choose my own name because of that stupid prophecy."

"Hey, ever since you came into the picture, there's been a fire under our butts. The name just fits now. And, you have grown a bit of a temper."

"I have not." She drew back, angry.

"So many times I felt that I saw something between you and Mace, and then you guys would get into one of your hate matches, and each time I would think, *Nope, that Indian's gonna be wrong this time.* Barb said, 'You just wait.' Should have known she'd be right."

Caffrey groaned and rolled her eyes.

"Caffrey, don't you think...? Does Mace know?"

"No, of course he doesn't know! He still thinks I'm the same...link to be suspicious of, who's going to bring down the whole Underground. Besides, maybe he's got Mink."

"Mmm, I think that ship has sailed. Not my place to say. Regardless, Caffrey, he needs to know how you feel if it's this serious."

"Vince, don't you dare tell him."

Vince avoided her eyes.

"Vince, I swear, if you...."

"Calm down." He placed a broad, warm hand on her arm. "I'm not going to go run off and tell him. But, we have to work this out...do what's best for you, and for him." He paused in reflection. "Don't you think it would be a good idea for me just to hint at this and see what his reaction is? Maybe he's...."

"No! Absolutely not. I'll kill you."

"No, you won't," he jested. "I'd kill you first, or Mace would...or Gina would warn me I was in danger, or...."

"Oh, cute. Very funny."

"That's what we have them 'whiny seers' for." He squinted. "That's why you saw Mace the other night. In that vision. Gina said you must have been thinking about him."

Caffrey heaved a sigh. "I can't *stop* thinking about him."

"Caffrey, to move you I'd have to make some incredible arrangements, and how do you think I would accomplish that without Mace? He's my right arm."

She sighed and rubbed her temples. "I need more time to think about it 'cause I haven't come up with anything really good. I've only heard about a few of the other keeps."

"You're not just anybody. You're hotter than me. You'd have to wear a complete facial and body disguise to go anywhere, including fingerprint caps and digitized contacts." He frowned, but his eyes warmed with pity. "Don't you think you ought to talk to Gina about this some, maybe Barb?"

"I think they already know." Caffrey answered ruefully.

He tried to suppress a smile. "They usually do. Did it ever occur to you it might be *good* for Mace to know this?"

"No." Caffrey shook her head resolutely. "You know how he is. He'd use it against me. He'd just think it was some kind of plot my

Vhurruh set up to get intel out of him or something. You know that's going to happen. Besides, he thinks I'm a danger to him because he can't *think clear*. As long as he's in the Underground, that pretty much means forever."

Unconvinced, Vince nodded as though in agreement.

"Crow!" boomed Mace's deep voice from the southwest corridor. Caffrey and Vince locked eyes, surprised not just by Mace's unseen approach but by the shuffling of feet and squeaking of wooden planks around the corner. Vince leapt across the stone floor and disappeared beyond the archway just as Crow responded to Mace with, "Hey, man," in an obvious attempt to keep his voice low.

"Crow?" Vince demanded an explanation with his tone.

Crow's arm gestured past the edge of the wall. "Man, I wasn't tryin' to listen, I swear. I was just comin' up the hallway, man, an' waitin' for Wolf. But seriously, this is cool. I ain't kiddin' wit' you." He rounded the corner and flashed a silly grin and wave at Caffrey for an apology, then turned back to Vince. "I'm totally down with this. Even though she's *supposed* to be my wife. But, y'all be cool, seriously."

The firm, crisp footsteps advancing up the stone corridor were unmistakable. Caffrey's heart beat wildly, and she backed up the stairs. Mace's voice joined the other two. The edge of his shadow cleared the corner. His voice halted as Vince started berating Crow.

Caffrey turned and ran up the stairs. Her only choices were the corridor to the right, which led to the secret tool shed entrance along with the side tunnel to the Com room, or the winding branch off to the left, which led to Mama's kitchen. She would have to explain her presence in either corridor, and there would be monitors. She turned right.

Deep male voices echoed up the tunnel. Caffrey skirted past the walkway that led to the tool shed. The voices moved closer. At a bend in the passage that led to the Com—a dead zone between security cameras—Caffrey froze. Louder and louder the voices rose, and Caffrey's heart thumped louder with them. She closed her eyes. *Not this way, please.* She listened intently for any sign that Crow was telling Mace. Would Vince stop him? Caffrey's stomach churned.

Caffrey, are you in danger?
No, I'm okay. I'm just…worried about something.
If you are sure, I will go.
No, stay and talk to me.
I cannot. I am watched now.
What? You're not discovered, are you?
I go.
No! Ugh. Caffrey sighed in frustration. *Just great.*

The echoing voices changed abruptly and became muffled. To her incredible relief, the men had advanced up the secret tool shed ramp. Mace's bass tones reverberated off the walls. Even now, she loved the sound of his deep, rich voice.

Caffrey forced herself to breathe and be calm. She did not know whether Vince had surmised the direction she had headed and steered them away on purpose, but she was eternally grateful. As quietly as possible, she tiptoed back toward the "Y" where the two tunnels connected. Her plan was to turn down the stairs to Spaghetti Junction, not far from where she and Vince had been sitting. But as she passed the tool shed tunnel, her body slowed of its own accord. Words registered in her tense brain.

"You've got to tell him, man!" Crow implored.

"Tell me what?" demanded Mace. "Is this a security issue?"

"I have a responsibility to the disclosure, Crow." Vince was angry.

"Is somebody gonna tell me what's going on?" Mace asked, annoyed.

"Byron," Vince blurted in disgust, dropping Crow's code name, "I am going to lock you in the brig."

"He needs to know this!" Byron insisted. "I *know* him. I would never say anything if it was anybody else, man. But, I know him!"

Caffrey gasped and vaulted down the corridor, terrified her footsteps would be heard. But Ghost Walker had taught her how to walk with light steps, to be one with the air. Breathing in through her nose and out through her mouth to focus, she headed lightly down the stairs and across the wooden planks, barely making a creak. With a sudden burst of energy, she ran down into the earthen maze and cursed the distant location of her personal quarters.

Offering a quick, fake smile to those she passed in the tunnels, she finally reached her room and hurled herself onto the top bunk for the second time that week. She let her head drop back and closed her eyes.

Mhetrrian? She called out. *Can you talk?*

Only silence greeted her. She pushed and reached for his mind, but when he sent a barely perceptible touch of alarm, she retreated, discouraged.

Sadness rolled through her, making her body ache. She prayed silently, but not knowing what to ask for, other than Mace losing his fear of getting close to her, she settled for the word "help." When she opened her eyes, two new spiders came into focus on the ceiling above her. She sighed in irritation.

Voices echoed from the corridors over the hum of the fans and dehumidifiers. Doors opened and closed, and footsteps thudded on wooden walkways at various locations. A sudden burst of laughter rose through the air outside Caffrey's narrow, wooden door. The happy sounds seemed strangely unnatural while her mind whirled in troubled thoughts.

A light rapping on the doorframe jarred her awake. She held her breath and searched for the battery-operated clock. Half an hour had passed. "Who is it?" she called out, terrified of the answer.

"It's Nightingale," came Gina's voice.

Caffrey yanked open the wooden door and stuck her head out into the hallway past Gina to be certain no one else was around.

"Oh, you're not going to believe this!" Caffrey grabbed Gina's sleeve and pulled her into the room.

"Calm down." Gina surrendered both hands into the air. "I already know."

"*What?*"

"Eagle told me."

Caffrey's mouth fell open. "Well...well, that's okay. I don't care about you. I mean.... No, I don't mean that." She shook her head.

Gina smiled tolerantly. "I know what you mean."

"Thank God somebody knows what I mean."

Gina stood with both hands on her hips, cocking her head to one side. "Are you so sure people don't ever know what you mean?"

"Well, *some* people don't. The ones who count. Oh, I don't mean that."

"I wouldn't be too sure about that, either." Gina smirked and crossed her arms.

"Okay. What's up?"

"Well...." Gina leaned on the bunk's bedpost. "I know that you're in love with Wolf. But then, I've known that for a while."

"Well, you knew it before me." Caffrey began to pace in frustration.

"Probably true." Gina watched Caffrey pace.

"And do you know *everything else*?"

"I know everything Eagle knows."

"That figures. That's okay." Caffrey bobbed her head in mild sarcasm. "Do you also know about Crow wanting to tell Wolf? About him eavesdropping on me and Eagle?"

"Yep, know that part, too."

Caffrey froze. "What happened? Did he tell him?"

Gina hesitated. "Yes. He told him."

"Oh my god!" Caffrey wailed, covering her face. "This is worse. I've got to get out of here. I am leaving tonight."

"You are *not* going anywhere."

"Oh, yes, I am. I am going to...." Caffrey whirled on one foot. "What did Wolf say? Tell me what he said."

"From what I understand, he didn't say much, other than, 'What?' and he looked confused. Then he turned away and rubbed his face. He wouldn't answer any of their questions."

"Oh, no. I am dead. I am absolutely dead."

"Fire, get a grip."

"You get a grip! You know how he is." Caffrey circled the small room again. "Nightingale, if you knew I was...in love with him, then...then you know how *he* feels." She looked hopefully at Gina.

Gina shook her head. "Not completely. Sometimes I do, but that is only because I've been around him so long. Some people can block me. It's rare, but it happens. Sensitive abilities aren't fail-proof. You have to *want* to know things before they come to you. And the other side has to, sort of, consent. You're reading energy in another form, like pheromones. Besides, what's going to happen is always changing based upon the simplest decisions that people make, *and....*" She paused. "Wolf himself doesn't want to know."

"What do you mean?"

Gina sighed. "He doesn't want to deal with a relationship right now. He sees himself in a war. He has a way of clamping down the energy around him so tight that it's like hitting into a brick wall."

"Just like *Mhetrrian*." Caffrey frowned. "Figures. Both of the men in my life have erected brick walls."

"Mace was attracted to you from the beginning. And, he is very concerned about you. He asks about you all the time."

"You're kidding."

"No. I can't believe you didn't *see* any of this!"

"Didn't *see* any of this? He chewed my face off every time I saw him! Well, except for in the tunnel once. And, class once. Maybe twice. Training got...nicer. And he...talks nicer now. But..." she shook her head, "what about *Mink*? She's all over him."

"Mink is a clever soldier to him now, nothing more. They were an item a while back, but he withdrew when she became too demanding. Besides, I've got my own ideas as to why he puts up with her."

"Well, he seems to *put up with her* very nicely."

Gina smiled tolerantly. "Fire, he's been completely crazy ever since you came into our lives, displaying a more...aggressive side of his personality than any of us has ever seen before. I mean, he's nuts when you're around!" She flapped her arms. Then her expression turned dark. "But, I also know that he doesn't *want* to care for you, or for anyone else. You probably sense that, too. He doesn't want the liability of a relationship. He believes he'll think clearer without it."

From somewhere inside, Caffrey knew Gina's words rang true. "Did he act crazy when he and Mink were together?"

Gina pursed her lips, weighing the disclosure. "Yes. But, he didn't trust Mink. Plus, she wanted a permanent relationship, and he wasn't ready. So, he backed off. I don't think she ever got over that."

"Oh, I can *tell* you she didn't. Most definitely not. She's always in my face about him."

"Well, he didn't show quite the craziness for her that he does for you."

Caffrey dropped her shoulders and sighed. "I can't face him." Gina opened her mouth to speak, but Caffrey asked. "Where is he now?"

"He's out walking."

"Oh, no." Caffrey closed her eyes.

"He's out *thinking*. I know that's what he's doing."

"He's going to come back here and *kill* me." Caffrey threw a hand into the air. "One shot, and it'll all be over with."

"You are as bad as he is! I've *never* seen you be such a...*drama queen*." Gina grabbed her shoulders. "He is not coming back here to kill you."

"And how do *you* know, since you can't read him?"

Gina smirked. "'Cause I don't see you *dead*."

Caffrey snorted. "I feel so much better now."

Gina gave her a sarcastic frown.

"So, he gets to go out and wander all over Georgia and *think*, and I'm stuck down here with cameras around every corner?" Caffrey fumed.

"Eagle called him on his cell, but he's avoiding him. Com says he's still out on the hill. They've got him in their sights."

Caffrey covered her face with one hand. "Oh, that's just great. All of Com knows. He's going to think this is the best ploy yet. I am getting out of here."

"Will you stop with that?"

"Don't you see? He thinks this is a ruse of some kind. He's out there right now trying to decide what it means. I'm a link that wants to get in with him so I can get the inside scoop and report back to the enemy." The flicker in Gina's eyes told Caffrey she was right.

She whirled and yanked out her sparse clothing from the dresser. "He is *not* going to do this to me. I am not going to let him make me doubt my own self one more time."

"And just where do you think you're going?" Gina folded her arms.

"I'm going to walk straight out onto the road and keep on going, in the opposite direction from where he's headed."

"Oh, right. He'd really come after you then. Not to mention the entire Remote militia. I don't guess anyone in the Com, like, might *notice* you on the screens?"

"Look." Gina firmly grasped Caffrey's shoulders and turned her around. "This is not getting us anywhere. Eagle is going to talk to him. I am going to talk to him. Let—us—handle this."

Caffrey glared at Gina defiantly, but tears welled up in her eyes. "I can't *face* him. I feel so stupid."

"Why? Because you love him?" Gina raised both arms. "He should be *glad* someone loves him. It's more than anyone can hope for in the Underground. We don't even know who's going to be *alive* the next day."

Caffrey knew Gina was right, but she needed to get away—away from a life of hiding, away from her beloved Underground, away from *him*.

"Look, come on over to the guest room," Gina urged with fondness in her voice. "Vince and I were going to stay there tonight to be alone for a while. Laronda said the house is empty and feels funny with nobody in it."

"Over at the Soul House?"

"Yeah, you met Laronda, didn't you?"

"Oh, yeah. In Mama's kitchen once. How come she doesn't have a code name?"

"She does. It's Jelly Bean."

"Seriously? Why?"

"Because she loves Jelly Beans." Gina shrugged. Her face grew serious. "Come on. Wolf'll never look for you there. Stay put and *chill*. Can you talk to your Vhurruh?"

"No, I tried. He checked on me a little while ago. But he's scared. And...he feels funny."

Gina froze. "What do you mean?"

"I don't know. He just...feels tired, and...it's like he has the flu. It's a weird feeling."

Gina cleared her throat. "Let's go up to the house. I am going to go find Wolf and talk to him. Eagle and I will both talk to him. This is going to be okay. I can feel it."

Tears escaped from Caffrey's eyes. Gina hugged her. She let the tears fall, but only for a minute. Anger and pride welled within her, and she stiffened. She stuffed her backpack with eleven meager pieces of clothing, two of them socks.

"Make sure he doesn't come there and bother me. I'm going to rest. Gosh, it'll be nice to see stars again. I can look out the window. I'll have myself together in the morning. He won't see *anything* in my face, mark my words."

"Now, Fire."

"I'm serious. I'm not going to let him make a fool out of me."

Gina sighed. Together they marched up many interlocking passageways. Caffrey avoided everyone's eyes. Finally, they traversed the longest, most treacherous passageway to the secret basement entrance of the Soul House. Gina pulled on a cord, and it was only a minute before Laronda gave them a smiling welcome at the grate of an old coal bin. Gina politely asked if Caffrey could spend the night instead of her and Vince. Laronda flashed cocoa-brown eyes at Gina, curious as to the real scoop, but she was graciously accommodating.

A favorite television show of hers was playing, and she invited Caffrey to watch. Caffrey accepted the welcome diversion. But soon, the program became an emotional tale of rejected love. Caffrey tactfully claimed a headache and hid away in the upstairs room to be with her depressing thoughts.

Donning a blue lace nightgown Laronda had lent her, she sat on an old brass bed. Amber and pink hues from the fading sun glistened on a hanging wind chime, unmoving and silent outside the window. Caffrey noticed a few birds fluttering past to settle in for the evening and wished in vain that she were one of them. She wondered idly if the old Cherokee woman could truly change shape. How wonderful it would be to have the freedom of the sky.

Slowly, a parade of stars winked in and out of passing clouds. Stiff from sitting, Caffrey shuffled lazily to the windowsill. Out of habit, she scanned the heavens for any dots of light that might move.

The sky had darkened to a rich purple-black. Above her, the full moon broke free from a string of clouds to pour creamy white satin into the room, outlining everything around her. Sadly, its mystic beauty held nothing for her. She moved resolutely to the edge of the antique dresser and lit a thick, vanilla-scented candle. Its tiny flame caused the darkness to retreat only as far as it had to.

Low voices mumbled outside the door, and it creaked open. Caffrey turned, expecting Gina. She took a step back and hit into the dresser, nearly knocking over the candle. A familiar dark figure quietly walked in.

23

NEVER LEAVE ME

Candlelight silhouetted Mace's frame, making him appear large and dangerous in the elongated shadows. Without speaking or looking away, he closed the door behind him and turned the lock until it clicked.

Caffrey took a deep, calming breath. "What do you want?" Whatever he was going to say, or accuse her of, she was not going to give him the upper hand.

Slowly, Mace stepped toward her and she felt her heart pump faster. "To talk," he answered. His eyes shifted briefly to the revealing blue nightgown.

"Ha." Her voice sounded oddly squeaky. "You? Talk?"

He scanned her face. "Mmm-hmm. This time."

Caffrey swallowed and readied herself to reply to his accusations. She had learned a few lessons in standing up for herself. Hadn't he painstakingly taught her?

Mace bridged the gap between them with one last, careful step. Caffrey searched his face as it came into the meager light. This was not the Mace she knew. No suspicion or anger radiated from the hard lines of his face, not even his familiar air of control. Instead, there was a keen, expectant observation of her, as if he was waiting for something.

Caffrey boldly returned the scrutiny. Seconds ticked by. She found herself searching his fathomless black eyes in a way she'd had the chance to do only twice before.

"Why do you really want to leave, Caff?" he asked in a still, deep voice, a ghostly echo from the depths of a bottomless well.

The reverberations sent chills through Caffrey's veins and confirmed her worst fears. So many words swelled into her throat at once, she nearly choked. She turned toward the window, no longer caring to hold his gaze. "I explained it to Vince. I don't want to explain it to anyone else. Please, just go."

"I'm not anyone else."

"You are now. You proved it with your question." When he did not comment, she turned back to him. An explosion erupted in her heart at his expression of surprise and confusion. The familiar rush of fire in her veins at his proximity did not help. "Mace, just go. I don't want to talk to you."

"That's not what I was told."

"You don't believe what you were told. Besides, I make your brain melt, remember?"

After a roll of his eyes, he sighed audibly.

Caffrey stepped away from him. "You're making me miserable staying here. I know you don't care what I'm feeling, but...."

"Where did you get the idea that I don't care?"

Caffrey opened her mouth to speak but lost the words as she wrestled with the possibility that he meant he was to her a leader, a close comrade, even a friend.

"I care about everyone here." His voice did not match the statement. She watched him swallow nervously, something he had never done. "People don't always reveal the real reasons for their actions. I grill them until they blurt it out. I think you know that."

Caffrey lifted her chin, surprised by his honesty. "Yes, I remember. But I have my reasons, and they're personal." She cursed Crow mentally for putting her in this position. "I just... need to get away from... from here. From you." Embarrassment suddenly overwhelmed her, despite her efforts to steel her emotions. She edged her body to the right to put more space between them, no longer able to bear his scrutiny. "You wouldn't understand."

He side-stepped so that his movement halted her own. "How do *you* know I wouldn't understand?" He sounded insulted.

"Because I know *you*. You probably think I made the whole thing up, right? Or better yet, I've been *programmed* to...." she halted and rolled her eyes. "It's all part of a plot against you, I'm sure." She waved a hand for emphasis. "It's obvious. Go ahead, you might as well tell me what conspiracy theory you've got."

He was motionless.

"Go ahead," she urged. When he did not answer or move, she rubbed a hand over her eyes. "Mace, please go."

Torturous seconds passed before he spoke. "You don't know anything about me. You don't know what I feel, or what I think."

"Are you kidding?" Caffrey almost laughed. "You are *incapable* of love, Mace. You've closed off your heart completely. You have no idea...."

Mace turned away from her as if struck. Caffrey halted mid-sentence, unable to fathom the hurt in his face.

"You think *you* have some corner on the market?" Mace implored. His eyes drank in hers fiercely. "You think you're the only one to ever know pain? Heart pain? I knew pain inside and out before you were even born." His voice became a rough whisper. "You don't know anything about me...*anything*." Almost as if he could no longer resist it, he reached a hand toward her face. His fingertips brushed a wayward hair from her cheek. Caffrey felt the shock of his touch race through her body.

"I've been in love with you since the first moment I saw you, Princess, lying in a pool of blood in an alley."

Caffrey's jaw dropped. She felt suddenly unsteady on her feet. "W-what?" she asked, incredulous, her voice unrecognizable to herself.

"I don't know what happened...that night. I wish I did," Mace continued in a daze. His dark brows knitted together. "I still remember that night. Something hit me when we went to pick you up. I felt it before I even got there. There you were, lying in the mud, a complete mess. But you were so...beautiful. And your hair. God, I love your hair." His eyes roamed over her hair. "I prayed you weren't dead. I would have killed somebody right there if you were dead. I don't know what it was. But...." He paused, and his eyes narrowed. "Hid it pretty good, didn't I? Even from me. I don't need love, Caffrey. It just gets in the way. I have things to do. The very sight of you...most of the time...makes me angry."

Caffrey couldn't move. Mace was breathing fast. He reached for her shoulders and curled his thick fingers over her tender skin. "I even wished you'd get killed in the beginning, even though I was trying to keep you alive. I had to keep from feeling anything for you." He shook his head. "You were all I could think about." His grip tightened. "Every person I *ever* cared for, Caffrey, was taken from me. My whole life! I don't need that kind of liability right now. I don't *need* love." He mumbled a curse as if arguing with himself. His fingers dug into her shoulders. "Don't you understand? If I love you, I'll *lose* you!"

"Mace!" Caffrey entreated as his grip became too tight. He let go, and they both stood still, gasping.

Suddenly, he pulled her to him and pressed his mouth firmly against hers with the passion of a man possessed. Caffrey's knees gave way, and her body fell limp against his. He curled strong arms about her and held her tight.

Liquid fire raced through Caffrey's limbs at the sensations his hungry lips ignited. Of their own volition, her hands reached under his jacket and slid upward across his muscled back. She was actually touching him. The moment was real, but not real. The warmth of his mouth and his firm body against hers fired every nerve ending she possessed. Her arms tightened around him, and she kissed him eagerly with long-suppressed desire. Again and again they kissed with unbridled passion, pouring their souls into each other, as though the chance might be stolen away from them.

Then Mace's amorous kisses slowed, and he reluctantly hesitated an inch from her lips. He cupped her face with his hand and scanned her eyes as though assuring himself that she was responding of her own choice. Caffrey's body tingled at the look of love and desire in his gaze.

Relieved, Mace pressed his cheek endearingly against hers. She squeezed him tightly and sighed.

"Why, Mace," she implored softly, "why did you wait *so* long?"

"I had to, Princess. I...I had to be sure. And I didn't... I tried to fight it." He pressed his face into her silken hair. "I felt like I was cursed or something."

Breathing in unison, they held each other in silence. Mace kissed her cheek and perused every inch of her face as though having never really seen it before. Silently, the edges of his mouth curled into a gentle smile. "At least now, I'm sure." Then his black brows knitted in concern. "But, you were going to leave me."

"I *had* to. I couldn't stand it. It was too painful. Every time I saw you I...." Caffrey faltered, and saw only his rich, ebony eyes. "I *hurt*. I wanted to touch you. To be with you. To kiss you. But I couldn't."

Bending slowly, savoring the moment, he kissed her lips gently, expertly, one hand exploring her lithe frame and the other slipping through her thick mane of hair. Willingly she melted into him, letting him have her. No more pretending. No more holding back. She wanted to experience the touch of his lips and his hands again and again.

She curled her fingers around his neck and into his hair, surprised at how thick, coarse, and yet sleek it was, unlike any hair she had touched before. How many times had she wondered what the feel of his hair would be like, his skin, his body meshed with hers? For what seemed an eternity, they touched and kissed and caressed, gently then with passion, letting their hands feel and absorb each other, in relief as well as delight.

With his every touch, Caffrey shivered as exquisite currents of raw energy transformed her limbs into an inferno. Her feet felt as though there were no floor. Their loving souls and excited bodies were all that existed. Mace kissed her lips, her eyes, her neck, and Caffrey sighed. She tried to push his jacket out of the way, to be closer. Mace tore the jacket from his body and dropped it to the floor. Then he wrapped both arms around her, nearly throwing them both into the dresser.

She ran both hands up his chest and halted at the thickness under one side of his black T-shirt. *Bandages.* She remembered how she had felt his pain. Tenderly, she kissed his shirt there.

He sighed, kissed her cheek, and murmured into her ear, "Thank you, by the way."

"For what?"

"For saving my life."

She pulled back to examine his face. "I saved your life?"

"We were surrounded in a small strip of woods. There were only five of us and the SAAFs had three weapons a piece. The disc transfer set off an internal alarm. All our electronics went out. I had taken out three SAAFs guards when a fourth shot me. He was aiming for my head but got my shoulder when I moved. They had cut us off from our vehicle and were closing in. If the second team hadn't showed, we might not have made it."

"I...." Caffrey stuttered. "I thought the second team just helped."

With tenderness, he pushed several strands of hair from her face. "A minute longer could have been too late."

Shocked and relieved, she smiled. "I'm glad I saved your life."

"You are?" He returned the smile and rocked her gently. "Why are you glad?"

"Because you wouldn't be here kissing me right now."

"And I'm never going to stop kissing you." With that, he kissed her lips and moved downward to the hollow of her throat, where he buried his face into her soft, satin flesh. A moan escaped her. Eager hands ran along her back and pressed her supple body into him as though he could not get enough of her.

Everything about him felt right. She wanted to let go, to let him have all of her. She drank in the hardness of his body and matched his every movement, fueling desire between them as they reveled in the newness of love.

Tenderly, Mace curled his fingers into Caffrey's thick, silken tresses, and pulled her head gently from him. "Caffrey," he whispered softly, his eyes deep pools of shimmering black, full of tenderness and desire only for her. "Stay here with me tonight. Just be with me. I'm not asking for more. But, we haven't much time. We may have to move tomorrow. The seers are all worried. Two of them were frantic an hour ago but couldn't give us a timeline. I know this is too fast. But...what if something goes wrong? What if I lost you tomorrow?"

Fear danced through Caffrey's heart. What if she lost *him*? She touched his cheek with her fingertips, and he pressed his face against her hand. His skin was rough with the growth of his beard after the long day, but Caffrey didn't mind. The thrill of being able to touch him freely was intoxicating and sent shivers through her body.

Of course she would stay with him. Not only all night, but forever. Would that they never had to sleep, or eat, or have to think of anything else other than experiencing each other. Yet, as she felt this, another part of her, the thinking part, began to push for space.

"Mace, I...." Caffrey stammered. "I want to stay with you. More than anything. It's just...what about...well, what will people think? What will Laronda think? If we...I mean...?"

A slow smile spread across Mace's face. "Well, aren't you an old-fashioned girl?"

Caffrey felt her cheeks flush. "Well, I am, but, I think we should...maybe wait."

"You sound like a virgin," Mace said with a teasing grin. Abruptly, the grin dropped and his eyes widened as he watched red color fill Caffrey's cheeks. "Oh, my god," he whispered. "You are."

Caffrey pushed away from him, embarrassed and angry.

"No!" he implored, tightening his hold on her. "No. No." His voice softened. "Don't push me away. Not now, Caffrey, not ever. Not after I've found you." He surveyed her face with adoration. "How did anyone as beautiful as you manage to stay a virgin until you were twenty-one?"

"Hey, my parents were strict and watched me like a hawk. And besides, I wanted to save something for my wedding night. Let's just say I came *very* close with my ex-fiancé. I won't say how close."

Mace's expression darkened for a moment. Caffrey knew he had done an extensive background search on her and probably knew everything about her relationship with Brian.

"But, I'm glad I didn't." Caffrey spoke with tenderness. "Because you're the one I truly want to be with."

Mace hugged her fiercely and pressed his face against hers. "I love you," he whispered softly into her ear. Caffrey felt weak.

She smiled and whispered, "I love you, too."

"Caffrey, don't ever leave me," he implored. "Marry me."

"What?" Caffrey's head was spinning.

"I mean it." His voice had become deadly serious, a tone she recognized. "We may have to leave tomorrow. Heck, we could be dead tomorrow. I'll get Reverend Brinks to do it, in the morning," he said excitedly. "Before the shifts. Say yes, Caffrey, please. Let's just do it." He watched her incredulous face and grasped her arms. "I love you," he said with absolute finality. Then, to her utter shock, he dropped to one knee and gripped her hands.

Caffrey's mouth fell open. "Are you crazy?"

"Yes."

Caffrey smiled and giggled. Tears filled her eyes.

Mace forced his face to be serious. His voice softened. "Caffrey, marry me." She had to chuckle at what was worded as a command rather than a question, though he gazed up at her face with heart-wrenching sincerity.

Caffrey felt her legs turn to butter. "Yes." The word escaped her.

Mace brightened with disbelief only for a moment. He stood and embraced her so tightly she couldn't breathe. Before she could protest, he flinched, grimaced, and rotated his shoulder, but did not let her go.

"You're still hurting."

"Not so much now," he insisted. With a happy growl, he whirled her in the air. Caffrey squealed and laughed, though she worried he would damage his wound. Abruptly, Mace stopped turning. His face became stern. He repositioned his arms around her possessively and gazed into her eyes. "All I ask is that you promise you'll never leave me. No matter what, we find a way, we work it out."

Caffrey gazed into his dark, beautiful eyes, and whispered, "My heart will always be yours."

With deft movement Mace picked her up and carried her easily to the bed.

"Mace, your shoulder!" she protested.

"It doesn't matter," he replied, and gently lowered them both onto the patchwork quilt.

Caffrey curled her arms possessively around him as he laid his heavy body lovingly against hers. "Mace," she asked, "won't someone come to...?"

"Shhhh," he entreated, pushing back a lock of hair from her eyes. "I told Crow anyone coming through that door is dead meat. Don't worry."

"But won't Vince...?"

"Vince knows." Mace moved to take possession of her lips once more, but she resisted.

"Knows what? That we...?"

"That I'm not going to kill you."

She raised both brows, and his followed in mock incredulity. "Well, you're still alive, aren't you?" he asked with a slow smile. Lovingly he touched her cheek with his fingers, enjoying the softness of it.

"Yes, but...stop that. Are you going to let me finish any of my sentences?"

"No." He covered her lips to prevent another interruption. Tenderly, then aggressively, he kissed her with the passion of a man who had no tomorrow.

Moving as one, they caressed and made love through the night, reveling in the simple joy of discovering each other's bodies, hearts pounding against each other until they throbbed in unison. Every movement joined them together forever, each thrust blending their souls into pure energy. Fire enveloped them as they merged to a sweet oneness neither had dared to believe possible.

24

CAPTURED

Caffrey listened to birds chirping with delight outside the window and moved to stretch. She was stopped by a heavy arm that rested possessively across her chest. She slid her fingers tenderly up and down the hair-covered arm and turned to see sleepy ebony eyes awaken.

Mace lay perfectly still and gazed at her face. He smiled slowly and Caffrey felt her heart leap.

A sharp pounding on the door caused them both to jump.

"Hey!" yelled Vince from the hallway. "We got dead people or live people in there?"

"There's going to be some dead people out there in a minute!" exclaimed Mace as he and Caffrey both sat up.

Several snickers sounded through the door. "Well." Vince tried to sound serious. "If you don't get out here soon, I'm eatin' the rest of breakfast."

Mace flopped backward onto the pillow and stared up at the ceiling. "I got breakfast!" he mocked, with a smile at Caffrey.

"Mace!" Caffrey cried in protest, and slapped him. A roar of laughter erupted from the hallway. Judging by the voices, Caffrey was certain it was Vince, Gina, Crow, and Roadrunner. Mace turned suddenly to tickle her, and she screamed.

"Somebody need rescuin' in there?" called Crow.

"Not if you want to keep living!" Mace yelled.

"Well, what if we want the other party to keep living?" queried Vince.

Caffrey struggled and broke his grip twice, only to be recaptured each time.

"She's alive and kicking. Trust me." Mace chuckled through gritted teeth.

"Come on," they heard Vince command lightheartedly to the small group.

"Mace!" Caffrey scolded in a low voice. "I want breakfast. I'm starving."

"Why?" he mocked. "Did you use up some energy?"

Caffrey reached with both arms to tickle him in response, but his arms were faster, and she only managed one jab to his side.

Half an hour later, hand in hand, they rounded the entrance to the huge dining Cavern. Everyone in the room froze, some with forks halfway to their mouths. As if on cue, three tables of Mace's militia friends leaped up and began cheering, clapping, and whistling. Other tables followed in a massive wave.

Caffrey covered her face with one hand and curled her body into Mace's. Mace slipped his arm around her shoulders and hugged her to him. Caffrey peeked through her fingers and saw that he was sporting a wide grin.

"All right, knock it off!" he called out to his comrades. Caffrey was certain she could never show her face again. Her cheeks felt as if they were on fire. The clapping died down, but jovial laugher, whispers, and a few late whistles flew about the massive room.

Caffrey passed Crow, who was rocking back and forth on two legs of a folding chair. He grinned from ear to ear and reached out a long, brown arm as if to stop them. "'Sup girl, you mad at me?" He chuckled at her scathing glare. "I mean, I did give up my first wife an' all."

Caffrey grabbed the back of the metal chair and pulled.

"Aaauuugh!" Crow yelled and fumbled desperately for the edge of the table as the chair collapsed. He swiveled to get free and simultaneously grasped Caffrey's shirt, which pulled her to the floor.

Mace yanked Crow up by the shoulders and feigned anger. "Get your hands off my woman," he threatened in a mocking voice.

"Wooooo!" came a chorus of voices from the nearest table.

"Hey, I'm the reason you *got* that woman," Crow teased. Mace let go of Crow and deftly pulled Caffrey to her feet.

Crow grinned and pointed. "You owe me, dog."

"Yeah, yeah," Mace taunted.

"For the rest of your *life.*"

"Don't push it." Mace replied as they stepped away.

The grizzled Colonel approached them with a cup of coffee in hand and an unlit cigar in the other. He looked from one to the other. "So, Wolf, you got somethin' to report here?"

"That's affirmative, sir. This...." Mace wrapped one arm around Caffrey's shoulders while pointing at her with his free hand. "Is *my* woman."

The Colonel stuck the unlit cigar in his mouth. "'Bout danged time. I'll make a note of it in the log."

Mace nodded. "Thank you, sir." He pivoted toward the buffet line but bent his head toward Caffrey and kissed her hair. Nearby hoots and whistles followed. Caffrey watched Mace glance at their comrades and smile with reckless abandon and felt a surge of inner joy, knowing it was she who made him smile.

How long had she spent endless nights alone mourning Brian, stoking her blazing anger at God for tearing him out of her life? Now, she could not imagine a life *with* Brian. Not when she had found the man who completed her, who always surprised her, who knew what sacrifice, responsibility and dedication truly meant.

"He who?" came a chiding voice nearby, and Caffrey turned to see Bluebird grinning and winking on her way to visit another table. Caffrey winked back, then panned the room in time to see a slim figure stomp purposefully through the stone archway, her long, dark hair flying. Caffrey felt a sting like an insect bite on the back of her thigh. She slapped a hand to it and rubbed the strange spot, worried it was from a bug. A sense of alarm snaked through her veins.

By the time they obtained their ration of breakfast and chose a table, most people had finished eating. Many of their friends gathered around to have a second cup of coffee and raid any food left in the buffet line. Everyone seemed to be in the most lighthearted mood Caffrey had seen since arriving at the complex, with the exception of the morning after the disc transfer at Telenex.

Caffrey left Mace at a table while she entered the kitchen on a search for mayonnaise, since she was the only one who used it on her egg biscuit. A quick "hey" caught her attention. She turned to find Vince casually leaning against the cabinets, a cup of coffee in hand, keeping Gina company as she wiped up counters.

"You okay, babe?" he asked with a smile.

The endearment warmed Caffrey's heart, and she felt her cheeks redden again. "Yeah, I'm okay," she answered in a soft, timid voice.

Gina shot a coy glance at Vince and leaned toward Caffrey. "Told you it'd be okay." She smiled as she carried the last tray of steaming honey rolls. Vince quickly took it from Gina and deposited it on the buffet as the three strolled out in unspoken unity to the table where Mace sat surrounded by friends and admirers. Like a small wave, his friends moved back to give Vince, Gina, and Caffrey space, but they quickly closed back in as the three sat down. Mace linked a finger into one of Caffrey's and gave her a quick warm smile. She couldn't get enough of that smile.

"What's that frown for? I know that frown," Vince demanded, and Caffrey realized he was addressing Gina. Several men ran past their table, having noticed the last tray of honey rolls.

"I'm not sure," Gina replied. "Something is definitely up. I didn't sleep well, haven't for three days, and this morning I had a foreboding feeling right when I woke. It's back now, and I don't know why. It's getting stronger."

"Why didn't you tell me?" Vince asked, his voice serious.

"Well, it's happened before, like when that bad storm came through and destroyed a lot of crops, and the time the northeast tunnel flooded, so I thought I'd ignore it until it got stronger. There's only so much you can do if it's Mother Nature."

Barbara approached with a decidedly "I told you so" grin and swagger. She rocked on her heels and offered Caffrey a heavy wink. Caffrey smiled with embarrassment and returned to eating her biscuit while there was still some warmth.

"Feel anything odd this morning?" Barbara asked of Gina.

"Yes, definitely." Gina frowned. "Have you checked with anybody else?"

"Yep. Just got through talking with Stardust. She's had a stomachache since four this morning. Didn't know what to make of it. But now she says it's definitely a premonition."

"*Now* you tell me?" Vince scolded.

Barbara scowled at him. Gina scrunched her shoulders in apology.

Mace swung his legs over the bench and dusted crumbs off his hands. "What's this I'm hearing?"

"Trainman and I woke up with a bad feeling this morning," said Barbara. "But we kind of forgot about it when we heard about... uh...." Several people snickered as Barbara cleared her throat and raised her brows.

Mace frowned sideways at Barbara. "Man, I get away for one night, and nobody tells me anything."

"You were busy, big boy," Barbara admonished. "Even *you* need a break. But seriously, I'm getting concerned now. Hate to break up the happy party, but every seer I've talked to *is* feeling this. Something is not right, and it's getting worse."

Mace turned to Vince, and Caffrey watched the carefree joy of the morning leave his face. He stood. "All right, let's consider this a drill." He gazed down at Caffrey with such intense worry that her heart thrilled and clenched at the same time.

Vince nodded. "Let's go yellow first. Then blinking."

Mace tore his gaze from Caffrey and strode toward a box on a nearby wall where he punched in a code. A yellow light came on in the cavern and in the adjoining corridor.

"Awww, *man*," came a chorus of protest.

"Do we suddenly have a problem with self-preservation?" Mace called out, adding a reproving glare at the remaining faces in the room.

Several people stuffed a last bite into their mouths as they reluctantly rose from their tables.

"Ladies, I'd like to see *you*," Mace stiffly addressed Gina and Barbara. "I want Dream Master and Bluebird in here, too." Even in his most demanding voice, Caffrey could see the difference in him. There was a glow in his eyes, and his face seemed altogether younger.

Not wishing to make a spectacle of herself with the gathering unit leaders and seers, Caffrey turned toward the archway. She knew she should head for her first scheduled post to wait out the drill, but her entire being ached with sadness at having to walk away from him so soon. Each slow step tore at her heart.

Brusquely, an iron hand grabbed her arm, and she was whirled to within inches of Mace's stern face. He kissed her quickly but soundly. "*You...*be careful," he commanded, with a slow smile.

"Okay," Caffrey managed to say.

"You know, we may go to red," he said as she turned away. "You could just skip your garden detail and hang out here."

Touched by the worry in his wrinkled brow, she smiled and gave a soft shrug. "They'll have to come look for me if I don't show up. Why don't I just go hang with my detail at the Junction? If it goes to red, I'll meet you back here."

His brows furrowed deeper as he took a slow breath and looked over her face with longing. "Okay. Deal."

She hovered at the cavern arch for one final glance at him. Vince and the Colonel were beside him, all with heads down in concentration. Gina, Barbara, and Bluebird joined the huddle.

Leaving him with the business of command, Caffrey strode down the corridor and passed several people who called out greetings or nodded, most looking dutifully serious. Half an hour later, Caffrey's familiar gardening mates were still sitting on the stone floor at Spaghetti Junction, some on the wooden sidewalk, all listening to the sparse commands traveling via one Q-altered radio.

Suddenly, the yellow light began to blink. "Aw, *dude*," complained someone in the group. "There goes my sunshine." They all hustled to their feet. A sense of concern tingled in the air.

"This one feels different," said Moose. His chubby brown hand rested on his chest while he stood and frowned.

High-Five, a young man of Mexican descent, snorted. "What, you turning into a seer now?"

"Heck no," said Moose. "I don't ever want to know what's runnin' around in your head."

High-Five roared with laughter and slapped Moose on his broad back. "You know that's right. I'm goin' to get my pack. They'll probably make it red, just to keep us on our toes."

Several people agreed with him, so the group tramped in the direction of the living quarters to pack their few precious belongings and be ready.

"Fire!" Eileen called behind Caffrey. Caffrey bristled and turned but kept walking to show she was keeping with her group. Expecting some tart comment, she was surprised when Eileen closed the gap and leaned close as if to whisper. "We need to get some ammunition that's buried in the edge of the cornfield."

"What?"

"Yes, come on. Wolf said to. If we have to leave tomorrow, he wants to take it with us."

"He does? But, we can't go through in a blinking yellow drill."

"They've already checked everything," Eileen insisted. "Blade just told me it's all because of bad storms coming in. Tornadoes. It's been all over cable news. Com says the storms are moving fast. We don't have much time." Eileen placed a hand on her hip. "You know Wolf likes to take advantage of a drill. Blade says they're probably going to change it to red if a tornado gets close, so we may only have ten minutes."

Caffrey listened to the shuffling of her group disappearing around the bend of the tunnel.

"When Wolf said he wanted the ammunition," Eileen continued, "I suggested you to help. He agreed, since you're going to miss your stint in the garden because of this. Come *on*," she urged, and tugged authoritatively at Caffrey's sleeve.

Caffrey groaned as she moved reluctantly with Eileen, knowing this was surely the girl's attempt to grill her for intimate details concerning her and Mace. In desperation, she tried to think of an excuse not to go. She would have to run all the way to the mess hall to speak with Mace, or grab the guy who had one of Q's phones. Or, she could go to the Com.

"Mink, I'm going to step in and check with...."

"We've only got ten minutes, remember? He's notified Com. I *don't* want to disappoint him." Eileen climbed the steps to the hidden tool shed entrance.

Caffrey knew that was true enough. She was secretly pleased that Eileen was at least measurably pleasant after her exit from the Cavern. It puzzled Caffrey that the girl no longer appeared upset. Eileen's cheeks were flushed, but she was focused and calm.

"We've got to hurry so we can beat the red drill, *and* the tornados." Eileen punched a code and pulled the lever to the tool shed door.

As Eileen stepped up into the dusty shed, Caffrey wondered why the guard hadn't arrived, since it was a blinking yellow drill. She glanced worriedly down the steps they had climbed and remembered the security camera. Com would know they were here. She pulled herself up onto the wooden floor of the shed, dusted off her jeans, and realized red light covered her arm. She whirled as the floor panel slid shut and an old radiator pivoted across it to completely disguise the entrance. The dull clunk of an iron bolt slid into place with leaden finality.

"Mink! That was red!" Caffrey yelled.

"I told you they were going red. Quit worrying. We'll go fast. What if the storm tears this stuff up and hurls it across the field? The neighbors might find the guns. Come on." She gestured with an impatient roll of her eyes. "You're so new here. Blade's in the Com room. He'll let us back in. Hurry. We can do it in less than five minutes, I'll bet you."

"But...." Caffrey followed the running girl as she lifted two garden shovels from their hooks and leaped out the door toward the cornfield. Caffrey knew how competitive Eileen was and how she relished any assignment from Mace.

A strange tingling began to dance across Caffrey's skin. She had only experienced one red drill, but it had made her nervous for hours afterward.

Mhetrrian? Caffrey called out. *Mhetrrian?* A strange unbalanced feeling was all she could get from him, like unbridled energy in a formless storm. She had never felt that exact sensation before and did not know how to interpret it. Perhaps he was merely asleep and dreaming. Did Vhurruh dream?

Clouds rumbled above the fields in menacing, boiling circles, a sure sign of a brewing tornado. Wind tore at Caffrey's hair and reached icy fingers into her cotton shirt. Toward the largest barn, Caffrey recognized the tall, dark-skinned man that Eileen, Hank and Cameron had greeted on her first day at Remote. He was releasing horses from their stalls.

Caffrey ran to keep up with Eileen. The merciless wind ripped at the young, green corn plants. Caffrey cringed at the thought of a tornado tearing up the fields over which she had labored.

Eileen rounded the far end of the field closest to the wooden gate, and stopped. "Okay, uh...Wolf said to look for three rocks along the edge of the field."

"I thought you knew where this was!"

"It's been a while, okay? He only showed me once."

The sky darkened, and Caffrey considered returning to the tool shed despite Eileen's prompting. As Eileen stumbled aimlessly, fighting the wind, Caffrey realized Eileen had handed her a fairly small garden shovel, a tedious tool for unearthing a buried cache of weapons.

"You look over there." Eileen pointed to the east side of the corn rows. "And I'll look down the west side. Remember, he said it'll be where three rocks meet in a triangle. *Hurry!*"

A definite feeling of warning assaulted Caffrey with an aching pressure in her skull that traveled into her chest. Still torn with the desire to run back into the safety of the caverns, she searched for the pattern of stones. There were few stones of any size. Most had been removed from the field. The apprehension could not be ignored as the hair of her arms stood on end. She turned toward the main house. Several dark cars with tinted glass, followed by two white vans, sailed up the graveled driveway.

Caffrey dropped to the ground. Gasping in fear, she crawled quickly into the dark green plants, which were still only three feet in height. She raised her head a few inches and watched with horror as black-and-gold-clad figures in helmets and field gear jumped out of the vans. On hands and knees, Caffrey snaked as fast as she dared along the rows of corn. The plants would hide her until she came out closer to the back door of Mama's house. Would there be time to make it into the kitchen entrance?

"Halt!" called an incredibly loud voice from her right, obviously through some kind of speaker.

Caffrey ran stooped over, knowing she would be exposed. Broad green stalks slapped at her face and pulled at her clothes. As she cleared the field's edge, she could see Eileen turn to look at her from the back kitchen door, pale and wide-eyed, but not surprised. A horrible, leaden feeling exploded in the pit of Caffrey's stomach as Eileen disappeared into the house and slammed the door.

Swallowing back panic, Caffrey struggled with the decision to run for the house or retreat through the cornfield toward the woods and the hills. It would be hard to scale the six-foot fence. Still, the woods were a better choice, since she would otherwise lead the intruders straight to her comrades. If they were after her, they would only get her. Those inside were probably already going down the northeast escape tunnel, warned by the Com's surveillance cameras.

With a quick intake of air, Caffrey pumped her legs along the edge of the corn stalks toward the woods.

White-hot pain stabbed into her right thigh as a loud "bang" resounded. She tripped and fell hard into the dirt. "No!" She groaned, thinking she had been shot again. She examined her throbbing leg but was surprised to find a red-feathered dart lodged deep into the muscle. Grabbing a firm hold, she yanked with all her might and screamed aloud as flesh ripped. She threw the dart to the ground next to her and eyed the cruel, barbed tip with horror. Gritting her teeth, she slapped a hand to her bleeding thigh and crawled toward the woods.

Gunfire erupted from the direction of the house, and she flattened to the dirt as she had been carefully taught. She recognized the *rat-a-tat* and boom of assault weapons, rifles, and handguns. Underground units had scrambled out of the labyrinth, out of safety, to fire on the SAAFs. Surely, Mace would be among them.

All around her in the field, cars slid to a halt and crushed the carefully tended corn plants. More gunfire exploded with a deafening roar through the air above her, and she knew that SAAF officers were firing on Underground units at the back of Mama's house. Desperate to get away, she crawled as fast as she could, but a great, fast heaviness washed over her. Her mouth felt dry and strange. She willed her arms and legs to keep moving, but the drug was too powerful, and her head dropped to the dirt.

Strong arms pulled her body up, and she felt the drizzle of rain on her face. Her head lobbed to one side like a rag doll. Military-like commands issued around her. "Fall back! Fall back! We have the package. Repeat, we have the package!"

"Lieutenant, fire when ready. Target that building." A metallic voice issued from an electronic device.

With indescribable horror, Caffrey heard a deep *pfffftttt* sound and then an explosion, which shook the feet of her bearers so that the vibration carried to her limbs. She was dumped across a backseat and double seat-belted in. Plastic ties were strapped onto her wrists. Amidst the distorted chaos around her, Caffrey focused enough to pray silently for her friends, hoping against hope that they survived, especially one.

25

NEMEYGENYAH

Caffrey sensed the Vhurruh before the airtight metal door came into view. While one of the SAAF officers busily tapped in a code on the lighted numeric keypad, Caffrey analyzed the strange pressure of *presence* that tingled in her arms and legs. This Vhurruh was undoubtedly gifted. A green light on the panel flashed, "ENTER," but it was the *"Enter"* formed clearly in Caffrey's mind that caused her body to move. She glanced at the SAAF officers. They made no special movement that signified they heard the summons one way or the other.

With a distinct *swoosh* the door opened, and Caffrey flinched from the dank, musky odor that assaulted her. A prod from an officer propelled her over the bottom edge of the capsule-shaped airlock into the dimly lit quarandome. The officer bowed slightly and stood at attention beside her. The door closed behind them.

Sharp hisses emanated from humidifiers and oxygenators in the far corner. Not ten feet from Caffrey, a pallid form lifted the front half of its heavy body with ease from the smooth floor to the top of the twenty-foot ceiling.

As often as Caffrey had seen Vhurruh in media clips, nothing had prepared her for this massive, slimy, gray hulk of rippling flesh that towered above her like a mythical snail from an ocean's forbidden depths. The creature's two large forearms, broader in circumference than Caffrey's torso, stayed folded against its body, almost retracted into the gravestone-gray underbelly. Several fins protruded like wet wings over his strong, finned legs. Around his head was an immense silver mane of hair. On his back, a thick mantle resembling a hooded cape appeared shellacked with shimmering bands of black, orange, and white that ran from his head to his curled, pumpkin-orange, gill-tipped tail.

Beside the broad, seal-like slits of his nose, long, gray whiskers were the only indication of where his mouth resided. Several of the whiskers extended to the floor like thin, oriental mustaches. In sharp contrast, four brilliant, black, gray, and orange striped eye antennae fanned upward to their fullest height; their feather-like fronds quivered slightly as though forever searching for more information about her in the air.

Two smaller Vhurruh of a darker gray color were on either side. Their presence seemed insignificant next to the pallid, slick giant in the center. Twelve bulbous, frond-covered eyes pointed in Caffrey's direction. From the pressure in her head and the sense of unified intention, she was reminded that the Vhurruh minds in the room were linked. Her every emotion and opinion was an open book to their formidable abilities. She breathed slowly and calmed her thoughts to a controlled blankness.

The huge Vhurruh enveloped her mind with vice-like pressure and easily read her mixture of fear, rebellion, and respect in mere seconds. He gloated, mildly pleased that she respected Vhurruh rather than loathed them.

Caffrey realized she had been standing with her mouth slightly agape. The Vhurruh were to be feared but there was no denying their incredible, unique beauty. She clipped her mouth shut.

Wuvena, Caffrey. So glad you join could us. I am Tarrek Wysstangrr. We will be glad to discover how we can help alleviate the feeears of the Underground Rebellion.

Though he conveyed amiable intentions, *Wysstangrr* spoke entirely from a surface level of thought, Caffrey noted, his mental English expended with absolute perfection.

No, thank you, Caffrey thought dryly back to him.

And why not, concerned and devoted one?

Because you're not on the side of humans anymore.

Wysstangrr conveyed veiled surprise. *And whose side do you think we are on? What have we to gain here? Your planet is still not safe to us. We do not have immunity to all of your bacteria and viruses. Our mission was one of aid, and that aid we gladly gave. Similar to what your own hive-land often does. Is that not so?*

Caffrey raised her chin *Sure, my country gives aid to other countries. But, if things ever get out of control, who screams the loudest? We do. So,* she added coyly, *who screams on your planet?*

The barest flicker of hesitation in the great mind gave Caffrey a moment's satisfaction. Her comment had hit its target, though it was a minuscule victory in light of the absolute power of the practiced, careful mind that held hers.

The rogue Underground is a hindrance to much that has been accomplished. Earth cannot stay united if factions of disrupters are allowed to continue to spread fear and defer the flow of purpose. That is also true on our planet. The Vhurruh evaded her question as smoothly as any human politician. *We used to war like you. Now, we link minds and purposes.*

Your queens link minds and purposes. You, however, trap minds and force your purposes. And look who's talking about 'factions.' We know rogue Gray drones took over, and you have your own secret agendas. Lots of them, in fact.

We have studied much of your world's hives, Wysstangrr replied, his manner calm. *Drones in power, ruling with fear and intimidation, was often the state of your existence before the invasion of the Zgeyyans. How long do you think your hive-land would have lasted if your excesses had continued as they were? It is a great source of pride to us that we succeeded in helping another race defeat a common enemy. Creating mind links was necessary to stop your wars, to build tolerances, and to unite your hives so that their focus was in defeating a common enemy. Do you not know of this?*

Caffrey felt an odd, pin-like probe in her mind that become painful. She quickly answered to defer his progress, lest she betray thoughts of *Mhetrrian. Yes, I do. Absolutely. And I was happy about your assistance. Many are grateful for what you accomplished. But, who draws the line if the Vhurruh have 'factions of disrupters' that 'defer the flow of purpose?'*

The drone paused at the question, and Caffrey sensed him holding back.

We were invited to help.

You are invading now, Caffrey responded. *And you know it.*

Aside from the Zgeyyans, your planet was becoming a refuse. Now, with united Human and Vhurruh interests, the planet is slowly restoring. There is a chance for your offspring.

Caffrey nodded, thin lipped. *Okay, environmentally, that was true. I do not deny it. And I generally* like *Vhurruh. But, something is wrong now. What about the continued disappearances? What about the humans being brainwashed and programmed? What about...?*

Did it ever occur to you that the Underground orchestrated the appearance of continued abductions and fabricated the stories of 'brainwashing?' Or that there are simply more players in the celestial arena here? We have observed many silent visitors here. Your skies were full. Our presence now maintains balance above and below. Something all hives here wanted. There are always sacrifices to preserve peace. Your race has great visions and possibilities, but also great destruction and denial.

We believe you mean well, Caffrey. We read no greed in you. This is not true of many human leaders. Perhaps you could learn to understand us after all.

I would like that, Caffrey answered honestly. *But right now, we have the right to evolve and control our own planet. Your help is appreciated, but let us grow. Let us find the best in ourselves. All by ourselves.*

Your race has outgrown its nursery, said the Vhurruh, tiring of the banter. *Life can only survive when there is balance. You destroy life's balance here. You have become the outsiders.*

Look, maybe we've screwed up a few things here, but we *belong here, not you,* Caffrey insisted. *This is where we were born. We had a great awareness growing on the preservation of this planet, and we would have done just fine....*

It was out of control, and you know it, interrupted the Vhurruh.

Caffrey knew verbalizing anything else was fruitless, since he was reading her feelings, not her words. Her honesty betrayed her. She breathed deeply to focus her response. *You are trying to justify the extent of your control here, but you have not said anything that reassures me. No amount of philosophizing or programming will deter a mind that sees. I have experienced abductions of people close to me. Your plans are no secret to me.*

Sometimes Tarreken have to keep secrets for the good of the hive.....

No. I disagree. It is never good! Caffrey shouted with her mind. *To foil an enemy, sure. Weapons, communications, yes—hide them so the enemy cannot discover them. But, sometimes commanders just want to preserve their ability to make choices without anybody raising questions or getting in the way, which is exactly what you and the other Tarreken have done.*

I see the group you resided with has damaged your sensible thinking. The Vhurruh grew impatient. *We can remedy that. We have been very successful in restoring humans to more logical thinking.* The broad, silver-and-black-striped head lowered toward her. All four orange-tipped antennae moved with anticipation. *And while we are restoring you, we will discover what has been going on in your rogue faction, so that a better balance can be restored for all.*

I don't think so! Backing up to the airlock, Caffrey squeezed her mind to keep him out. Knowing she was losing the battle, and vividly recalling her vow the night she had entered Remote, she dropped to the floor, kicked the back of the SAAF officer's knees and dove for his weapon. Like a wildcat she fought him as Mace had taught her. She surprised the officer by head-butting him and pulling the lethal end of the weapon to her forehead.

No! commanded the Vhurruh. Strong forearms pushed her head away and seized the weapon. One arm curled around her waist like a snake and lifted her off the floor. With paralyzing pressure, the alien mind deflected her concentration so she could not move her limbs.

One of the smaller Vhurruh appeared beside Caffrey, holding a tubular, metallic-looking device. *Wysstangrr* allowed her to see his thoughts. The device carried a drug that would cause her to tell everything she knew, so they did not have to damage her mind. She only had a moment to consider why they would bother preserving her mind before a cold, tingly sensation washed over her. She felt sleepy. The source seemed to emanate from above, but she could not look up to see what produced it.

Leave us, the ghostly Vhurruh commanded to the SAAF officer. Panic gripped Caffrey as the SAAF straightened, retrieved his weapon, and obediently left.

Tmeerah, Hmraay, assist me, called *Wysstangrr*.

Certain she would strangle to death with fear before she could determine a way to injure *Wysstangrr*, the paralyzing chill left Caffrey's body, and she fell to the floor. With a shake of her head, she became aware of a gurgling sound emanating from the large Vhurruh. His bulbous head lowered toward the metal floor as though he were falling asleep. Locks from his silver mane fell perilously close to her eyes, and she turned her face from the pungent, moldy-clay scent. The smaller Vhurruh still holding the metallic device appeared frozen. He had closed opaque sheaths on his eye antennae, as did the other.

With a heaving intake of air, the gigantic Vhurruh rose to full height, though his four eye antennae sheaths remained closed. A wave of cool energy washed through Caffrey, as if a breeze had suddenly blown into the room. Somehow, the Vhurruh's mental touch was different—lighter, yet more complex. Caffrey sensed a mental smile.

Wuvena, brave one, came a strange, multi-voiced pattern into her mind. *We are the Nemeygenyah.*

Caffrey brightened but projected confusion for an answer. *I thought you were a movement...a belief.*

We are elders, they clarified. *Some physical, some not. We are the Manarenen order of Nemeygenyah. Though we are now three orders, we can function as one.*

Where are you? Caffrey asked, mystified.

We are everywhere. Wysstangrr does not hold a surface-level awareness of our presence, as is his choice and his training. In a very deep place, he is aware that we communicate through him and even feels touches of it when he is safe. But he also chooses to be as unaware as possible to allow our existence and communications. Our race lives in a one-mind world. There are no secrets unless one learns how to cloak them. These two devoted surranenn are assisting in masking this transmission so that souls outside these walls will not be aware until they choose a greater path that will give them the ears to hear.

Swaying slightly, the two small Vhurruh appeared in a trance-like state, with tense wrinkles etched across their facial areas and eyelids closed on their unmoving, orange-striped antennae. Caffrey considered the possibility that this was an illusion.

Do not be afraid. You have done well. We thank you for your perseverance. It is good to see how you chose. There is much more for you to do.

Caffrey's mind whirled. Suspicion colored her every thought. *How do you know what I've done?*

We have only to read the energy about you. And, young Mhetrrian has devoted himself to our order of Nemeygenyah. He is well-taught. But, time is short. Your human-hive obtained the disc and crystals. We cannot give them more. They will have much to do, since your presence here means that what you knew before is now known to Wysstangrr and our rogue brothers. Young Mhetrrian had the forethought to give you some extraction protection concerning levels of information. We will not fracture you. We may have need of you, yet. We intercede now only to see that you are put back where you belong, so the balance is not jeopardized.

Where I belong? Caffrey asked. *Are you going to put me back with my friends?*

Where you have chosen to be.

I did not choose to be with them.

Did you not?

No, I...I stumbled into them, and then...got caught there. I mean, I'm glad I'm there now, but....

Every decision, every thought, every opinion you made was a choice within the energy of your path. You could have created another. We are glad you chose the one you did.

Whoa. Wait a minute, Caffrey protested, confused by the Vhurruh's logic. *All right, forget about that. So, whose side are you on? The rogue faction or Nekkai's mission?*

We are on the side of wisdom. We are old ones. Our mission is not to judge but to retain balance within our world, which now must extend to yours. Perhaps, since we are still in a state of self-distinctness, there can be a remnant of self-interest. However, we move toward unity and devotion with Rahzukai, and so at some eon will know true selflessness. We must hurry now or risk discovery. The block cannot be maintained for long.

Caffrey stared at the tranced Vhurruh in wonder. She knew from the links at Remote that *Rahzukai* was one of several Vhurruh names for God. Puzzled at the message and the many thought patterns linked in the communication, Caffrey again questioned whether she was in some dream state the Vhurruh had put her in.

The Vhurruh's hand was on the side of her head before she could duck. With searing pain, a tremendous pressure enveloped her mind, and her last thought was that her brain had exploded.

26

MISSING TIME

"Come on, honey, wake up."

Caffrey forced heavy lids to open and viewed a blurry, blond-haloed face. She blinked forcefully to focus. "Evan?"

"Hey, I knew you'd come back to me. Life's pretty dull without you." Evan's voice was like the warm coo of a dove.

"What are you doing here?" Around her were sterile pastel walls and a TV suspended from the ceiling. She was resting in a metallic bed covered in warm, white and blue blankets. "Where am I?"

Evan enclosed her right hand in both of his. "You're in Emory Hospital, hon. You were in a really bad car accident. Got quite a bump on the head, and a couple stitches, but it's all gone down now."

"Stitches?" She rubbed her forehead in alarm and felt a bandage. "Ow!" There was definitely a raised bump under it. "I remember having stitches, I think." Behind the sore area, a great pressure throbbed within her skull as though someone had wrapped it tightly.

"You've been here for a week. How do you feel?"

"I feel...week? Did you say week?" Caffrey moved her jaw from left to right in an attempt to throw off the stiffness in her face.

"Uh-huh. Relax," Evan urged. "Not *too* much, though. I'm glad to have you back." He reached for the call button, and a bland female voice responded.

"Please tell Dr. Roley that Caffrey Hanson is back in the land of the living."

"I'll inform him right away."

Caffrey raised her left arm to inspect her aching hand. She groaned. She hated IVs in her hand.

"Are you okay, babe?"

"Yeah...I think I'm okay." *Did he say, "babe?"*

"Something wrong?" Evan brushed a lock of hair from her face and possessively took her hand again.

Caffrey peered at him in surprise and resisted pulling her hand away, touched by his tenderness. "My head hurts. And my hand hurts."

"Well, that's understandable, but we'll talk to the doctor about it when he comes in. You gave me quite a scare, you know. Hey, if you're up and about soon, we might even be able to attend the Governor's Gala in a couple weeks. It'd be great to have you with me again."

"Governor's Gala?" Caffrey searched her memory for such an event. A sharp sting seared through her brain like an invisible ice pick.

"Don't you remember? Coming to stay at the Harvey mansion after the accident at your apartment? I told you about the banquet."

Caffrey stared at him in shock. "No...I...when did that happen?"

"A few weeks ago." Disappointment lined his handsome face. "The doctor said you might have some...memory loss. You've been through a lot. The doc said not to talk too much about everything that's happened, so we'll deal with that later, okay?" He squeezed her arm.

Memory loss. The thought sent a chill up her spine. Evan's take-charge attitude, warm green eyes, and concerned tone eased her fears, somewhat. She massaged her aching temples. "Mansion...I remember something about being in a mansion. Man, I've got to have something for this headache. This is like the mother of all migraines."

"Why don't I call the nurse and see what she's authorized to give you?" Evan patted her side. "Hey." He leaned closer. "You haven't forgotten *us,* have you?"

Caffrey's eyes popped open. "Us?"

"Yes, us. Me and you. I was afraid you wouldn't remember. You do remember, don't you, honey?"

Flinching from a new eruption of pain behind her eyes, Caffrey held both sides of her head and felt the familiar surge of nausea. Oddly, she wondered what her hair looked like. "I remember feeling...I don't remember a real, I mean, *close* relationship. What happened?" Needles seemed to be sticking into her eye sockets. "Why don't you tell me about us?"

"Wehhhhll." Evan explored her hand in his. "Maybe that's not such a good idea. Maybe you need to discover what you feel on your own, or rediscover. I was so afraid this would happen." His sandy-blond brows were wrinkled in anger, which surprised Caffrey. He seemed to be gritting his teeth. "The doctor said I needed to be patient. Why don't I call him again, so I can get you some medication for that headache?"

Caffrey nodded, and then regretted the movement. Admiring his body as he exited the room, she had no trouble remembering attraction for him. She searched her aching brain for the missing time, confused that everything seemed awkward and out of place, yet oddly correct.

After a deep, cleansing breath, she pinched the bridge of her nose between her brows, which used to relieve her migraines somewhat. A painful stab reminded her the IV was there. She grimaced. Her skin would be a mess from allergy to the adhesives after a week. The blue mesh tape around the needle showed swelling but no rash. *Humph, must be a new kind of bandage.*

As she dropped her aching head to the pillow, a kaleidoscope of images flashed by with nonsensical scenes and faces she could not put names to. The car accident was a blur, with running people appearing and disappearing. Her family came to mind. *Okay, I have parents,* she thought with relief. *I know my parents. I have a brother.* She tried for other details. *Job. Do I have a job?* Slowly, the pristine lobby at Property Resources came into focus, along with the smaller lobby of another past office. Kimberly came to mind. Caffrey smiled and breathed a sigh of relief.

"I don't like my job anymore." She frowned, but quickly realized it was mostly her boss, and some indefinable secrets the office harbored, something that haunted her. Most of her co-workers were amiable and talented, and she enjoyed office work. But painting, gardening, and scientific research were what she really loved—and volunteer work.

A memory of singing with a church youth group at a nursing home and giving out Christmas gifts flashed like a media clip. It took her a moment to realize it was from five years earlier. Other images of people and places scrambled together, including feelings she could not connect with experiences.

Frustrated, she pulled back the covers and swung her legs over the bed. The chilled air of the hospital gave her goose bumps. She reeled with the quick movement and grasped the metal frame of the bed and the IV stand to steady herself. The IV stand turned out to be flimsy. Working to control her body, she breathed in and out. This was familiar, this breathing and focusing.

A curtain swooped back, and it frightened her so that she lost her balance.

"Hey, girl, what're you trying to do?" Evan's quick arms caught her by the waist and guided her back onto the bed. He chuckled endearingly, his hands lingering "You're such a little bitty thing."

"Only in size, buddy," she retorted, then swallowed to dispel nausea.

"Don't I know it. Now, *that* sounded like the real you!" He laughed.

"Evan, I need a diet soda, two headache powders, and a honey roll."

"What?"

"I know what I need for this headache. A cup of orange juice would help, too."

"Ah, Dr. Broley, good to see you." Evan rose as the doctor entered.

Broad-faced and somewhat chubby, Dr. Roley welcomed Caffrey "back" with a firm but unemotional voice. A clinical, guarded expression never left his eyes, which made her feel as though she were a numbered folder instead of a human being. Caffrey mentally decided it would be the last time she ever saw him.

With professional detachment, Dr. Roley asked her several questions, scribbled simultaneously on a chart, and quickly prescribed two medications. To her dismay, he insisted that she stay there another day, since it was already nine o'clock in the evening, to which Evan heartily agreed, adding that he would be there in the morning to pick her up. Caffrey was irritated but in too much pain to protest. Part of her was touched by his generosity. She was still thinking about his light kiss on her cheek and heartfelt "good-bye" when she fell asleep with the aid of medication.

In the morning, Evan arrived after breakfast. Caffrey felt a thrill at sight of his handsome face and happy smile. Why had she waited all those months, and deprived herself of that smile?

"Brought you some coffee." He held out a Styrofoam cup.

Caffrey stared at him. "You know I don't drink coffee. I drink tea."

His smile dropped. "Oh, yeah, well, um, remember you told me you would try it? I thought...you were starting to like it."

He looked so sincere. How had he talked her into trying coffee? It did sound like something she would do for him.

"Tea," Evan said with a wink. "I'll get you some."

When he left, she spotted the phone on the side table. She dialed her parents almost in a panic, wondering why she felt like someone might stop her. Her mother cried when she heard her voice, and the two cried together as Caffrey joked that now she was going to leave the hospital with a red, swollen face. Her father was greatly concerned over her lack of memory and spoke of the trauma the whole family had gone through. Reporters had camped out on their lawn before SAAF officers had cleared them away. Horrified, Caffrey barraged him with questions until she heard her mother in the background, fussing at him for talking about events the doctor had said not to mention.

Caffrey whirled on Evan as he entered with the tea. "What's this about reporters on my parents' front lawn? What the heck!"

Evan sat the tea on her tray and took the phone from her. "Mr. Hanson? Yes, she gained consciousness late last night. She's doing fairly well. Some memory loss, like the doctor thought, but he says to take it one day at a time. Don't worry, I'll take very good care of her. You can count on me. Say hello to Mrs. Hanson for me. Take care now. Bye."

Caffrey's mouth was hanging open. *He knew her parents?*

Evan sat on the side of her bed. "A lot has happened. Your doctor says to take it slow. I don't want to...."

"I want to know now!" She groaned and held her head as the statement caused renewed throbbing. Evan gently removed her hands. His green eyes danced as he gazed into hers with concern and devotion.

"What you need is some rest—*and* some good times. I'm going to make sure you get both."

The sun shone golden in a beautiful azure sky as the two arrived at the stately, pink-and-beige-bricked mansion. The massive front of the building with rounded steps was familiar, but Caffrey found herself greatly disturbed when she walked into the foyer. It felt foreign yet familiar.

Panning the six-sided room, she looked up, and her mouth fell open. The domed ceiling rose two and a half stories high and was covered with beautiful paintings of biblical scenes. Cherubs danced along the edges. Several lovely images of robed people and angels cascaded down the walls, even between the pillar-like supports which met in separate tear-drop points like an East Indian palace.

Caffrey could not help the smile that spread across her face. How could she forget anything so beautiful?

"Evan, this is gorgeous. I could stand here all day."

Evan brightened with a wide grin. "I knew you'd remember it. You loved it the first time you saw it. I've had a lot of work done— repairs, mostly—so some areas may not be the same. The kids who inherited this place didn't know what they had, and didn't care about anything. They must have partied the whole time. They had *motorcycles* parked in here."

"You're kidding!"

Evan shook his head, and Caffrey rolled her eyes.

"I remember the mansion, but...." Caffrey's smile fell. "I don't remember these paintings, or those doors there, or...."

"Hey, hey." He curled a strong arm around her protectively, and she felt reassured by his tall, virile body. The wonderful smell of his cologne warmed her. How she had always loved that smell.

"Remember what the doc said: 'Take it moment by moment, memory by memory.' Let's go to the library. I know you love libraries."

He led her through ornately carved double doors, and she gasped in wonder at the expansive library. With the exception of the bay window seat ensconced by tasseled burgundy curtains, every wall was covered with shelves of books of every size and color, rising nearly to the ceiling.

"Wow! I'm never leaving this room."

Evan chuckled at her delight.

"This feels so familiar." She sighed. "Wasn't there a section over here with lots of religious books, and one to the right with some nature books that were old and tore up?"

"Oh, I've had them moved all around. They won't be the same."

"Oh," she commented, feeling a bit sad. A memory of her sitting in a cushioned chair perusing the books flashed for a second.

"Come on." He took her hand. "Let's look at the rest of the house. Maybe you'll feel better. You'll love it, again."

After exploring the main-level rooms, Caffrey begged to lie down and relieve her aching head. Evan guided her to an upstairs room and opened the door. Tears filled Caffrey's eyes at sight of her dream catcher from a fair she had attended with Kimberly. And there were her horse statues, her easel with the half-finished painting of a blue unicorn...even her bonsai tree, which wasn't faring well. Several small pictures adorned the marble fireplace mantle, and two sat on her nightstand—one of Evan. She explored the room with stomach-tightening wonder and smiled at the picture of last year's Christmas party at work. Everyone had silly hats on and even sillier grins on their faces. Mary had a rose in her mouth. And there was Jim, holding that green concoction that he had mixed himself and nobody liked.

Caffrey heaved a deep breath and blew it out slowly. "This is really upsetting."

"Why, hon, these are all your things! I thought you would feel better in *here*, at least."

"I do, I do, but...having no memory of this room is really disturbing. I don't remember hanging my dream catcher there. I don't remember having a fireplace. This is my bed, but...did I arrange it there? You can't imagine what this feels like."

"Look." Evan held her shoulders. "What matters is that you feel safe and comfortable now. Don't worry about what happened before.

Let it come back in its own time." He cupped her chin in his hand. "Do you feel good now? Do you feel taken care of?"

"Yes," she answered softly. "I *do* feel better—*and* taken care of. And thanks. I think I owe you one."

A smile spread across his face. His green eyes squinted hungrily. "Don't mention it." For a moment his face leaned close to hers, and she stiffened. He turned his head and acted as though the moment had never happened. "Hey, you want some of your medicine so you can rest?"

"Yes, I would like that. Thanks."

"Okay. I've got Marianna—you know, the maid—here from eight to three today, so if you need anything, just call her. I've had an intercom put in, so you've got one here by the light switch. She'll hear you anywhere in the house."

"Okay. Thanks."

"Stop thanking me," he chided.

"Why?" She flapped her arms. "You're doing *everything* for me. I appreciate it. I really do."

"Remember me. That's all I ask." His voice was gentle, pleading. With tenderness, he brushed a lock of hair off her face.

Caffrey gasped at the familiarity of the motion and took a step toward him. She reached up and ran her fingers through his sandy hair experimentally. She had always wondered what his hair would feel like. It seemed thinner and silkier than she had expected. Black hair and mahogany eyes flashed before her. She flinched and tried to retrieve the wisp of memory, but it would not surface.

"What's wrong?" Evan rubbed her shoulders and looked disappointed.

"Nothing...nothing. It's just...I'm really tired. I need to rest my head. I've got so many things flippin' around in here."

Evan searched her face with a worried brow. "Okay. I'll be right back."

She sighed as he left the room. Her stomach churned uncomfortably, and she rubbed it. Tentatively, she surveyed the room again, but as she tried to reconnect with each item, her head began to throb unmercifully.

"Ugh! Stop." She rubbed her temples.

She stretched across the bed. It was soft, comfortable, and familiar, and she nearly fell asleep before Evan brought the medicine and a cup of water. She thanked him, and they laughed together as he wagged a finger at her. He rested his hand on her thigh. It felt comforting there, but Caffrey hesitated to respond to him. He smiled, squeezed her leg, and left.

She awoke, uncomfortable in her clothes and in the strange dark room. The clock beside her read 7:33 PM in orange neon. Her stomach growled as she sat up. Food was definitely the priority. She entered the hallway and for a moment was disoriented. Remembering, to her delight, that the kitchen was on the first floor and to the left, she headed across the carpeted hallway and down the beautiful curved oak stairs. She ran her hands along the railing and smiled at such luxury and beauty. She could get used to this.

Evan had only briefly shown her the dining room before she had felt ill, so she looked it over now in detail as she walked through. It was a cozy room, with many green plants and ornate hutches spaced around a long, shining, golden oak table. Hunt scenes decorated the walls. *Just great. Hounds pouncing on a fox while I'm eating. I can't believe I put up with that.*

Pushing through the double doors to the huge kitchen, she went straight for the first of two white refrigerators, where she found little to eat. Only a couple items occupied each shelf. *Well, either I haven't been here in a very long time, or he doesn't know me very well.* Spying two red tomatoes, she decided on a tomato sandwich. She grabbed the condiments and could not find cheese. At least there was lettuce.

Searching all the drawers for knives, she grew frustrated and gazed about the foreign kitchen. "Two refrigerators," she said out loud, and squinted at a vague memory. "I think I remember two refrigerators." She panned the room for a giant freezer but did not see one, which seemed odd.

Turning away, she spied a wooden block with ten or more knives imbedded in it. Grinning sheepishly, she grabbed one and went about the business of creating her sandwich. Building it to perfection, she turned to the glass table. Glass tables made her uncomfortable.

Grabbing the plate and a soda, she headed out a side door. She could see the massive foyer down the hall, but as she walked on the cushy carpeting, she became aware of an angry, low voice. Quietly passing a room where the door was slightly ajar, she peered in and spied the back of Evan's head from a brown leather sofa. A black cell phone was at his ear.

"It was the *only* thing I asked for. And it wasn't like it should have been that hard. We did feel something for each other. All it needed was a push." After a slight pause, he continued. "Yeah, well I finally had to block that vixen from my phone she called so many times—just a *little* pissed. I'm going to need extra security against her. She's probably stalking me right now."

Another silent pause.

"Because your boys got a little out of control, that's why. *Bombing* the freakin' place? What the heck was that? I don't care who fired first! You guys are so trigger-happy it's pathetic." Evan sighed and rubbed his eyes. "Yes, of *course* we'll be there. I'm not going to miss it, either way. You do know Margaret Bancor and Senator Fincher are coming? Congressman Baker, too? Yeah, I just heard about it. Well, listen, I gotta run. She'd better not remember you. She doesn't take things sitting down." He exhaled in exasperation and changed his tone to a sarcastic one. "Yeah, she *is* beautiful, and it's none of your business. All right. See you then."

Caffrey hurried past the door, terrified she would not make it up the stairs before he came out of the room. Her heart pounded wildly in her chest. In her haste, she nearly tripped on the top step, caught herself, and thanked God she had not opened the soft drink. On tiptoes, she ran to her room, placed her snack on a small, round, cherry wood table which had two matching chairs. She stuffed two bites into her mouth. Her mind raced with possibilities and denials as she chewed.

She grabbed a small pillow to mask over the sound of the soda can while she opened it, and felt silly: the *shhhuck* seemed loud anyway, and diet soda sprayed the underside of the pillow. Panicking, she dropped the pillow down by the side of her chair. She forced herself to be calm, and sipped the cold liquid, feeling it run down into her body. The chilling sensation caused a violent shudder. Fear almost choked her, causing her to breathe in gasps.

What is wrong with me?

Knuckles rapped lightly on the door.

"Come in," she offered after a calming breath.

"Hey." Evan was dressed in a blue T-shirt and khaki shorts, which looked bright against his tanned, well-exercised arms and legs. "I was coming to check on you. You've been asleep for hours. I didn't know you were up."

"I got hungry."

"I see that."

"Evan," she admonished, "how could you possibly have so little food in this house? And, excuse me, *two* refrigerators?"

He laughed with a handsome smile that *was* familiar. "They were left over from the previous owners, and I haven't done anything about them. You can't leave them unplugged, you know, or they stink. And I'm never really here much to eat. I rarely grocery shop. I eat out a lot. *We* ate out a lot. Mind if I join you?"

"Please," she offered, motioning with her hand. "I can't eat the other half, anyway."

"That's okay. I'm not really hungry. I just thought I'd sit with you. Although, ice cream sounds kind of good."

Caffrey widened her eyes and added a teasing smile.

"You're going to eat ice cream after a tomato sandwich?" he asked.

She grinned a challenge.

He nodded toward the hallway.

She grabbed his hand and pulled him playfully down the stairs, to his delight, then headed for the dining room entrance across the tile foyer. He raced her instead of being pulled. With a burst of speed, he hit the dining room doors, shouted "I won!" and danced around, miming boxing with an invisible opponent.

Caffrey rounded the other side of the long dining room table before Evan realized the race wasn't finished. He took off toward the kitchen doors, his long legs carrying him swiftly, but not before she pushed through the swinging doors with pure momentum.

"I won!" She jeered back at him, and he reached out to tickle her. She squealed and squirmed away lest the moment get too intimate, then grabbed the left handle of the first refrigerator. To her delight, there were three containers of ice cream.

"You *do* know me!" she exclaimed. "Nope. Wait a minute. There's no chocolate chip."

"Yes, but there is Neapolitan, which I *know* you like." He snatched two of the boxes. "Let's see, I've got chocolate syrup here somewhere, too." He scanned the kitchen, trying to decide which cupboard it might be in.

Caffrey laughed. "You don't know this place any better than I do."

"Well, I'm never *here*. I just got back from Washington four days ago, and before that I was in North Carolina, and before that...."

"While I was pining away in the hospital?"

He dropped the ice-cold containers onto the counter. "Hey." He grabbed her waist before she could protest. "I still have *work* to do. And you were *well* taken care of. I would have stayed if I could. They had strict instructions to call me as soon as you...came to."

Caffrey swallowed, reassured and mesmerized by his entreating voice. She was tempted to run her fingers up his arms, but turned toward the counter instead.

Together they decorated their bowls of ice cream like children, with chocolate syrup and a mixture of nuts and M&M's from a bag of trail mix. Evan led her to the small den where she had observed him earlier on the phone, which made her feel guilty and uneasy. Curling up on the leather couch to face the television, they chose a movie to view as they ate.

"I'm so glad you're here." Evan watched her spoon the last bit of melted ice cream from her bowl. "The place is complete now." Reaching his arm along the couch back he grasped a lock of her hair and twisted it in his fingers. She threw him an endearing gaze but dropped her eyes, wondering if she would hesitate to cuddle with him if not for the phone call.

"Come on." He took her bowl and placed it on the coffee table. "Sit close to me."

Caffrey hesitated. "Evan, I don't want to rush anything. I mean, being with you is wonderful, but...."

"It's okay, it's okay," he murmured, with a wave of his hand. "I know you will...one day soon." His flat smile made her feel guilty. She looked back toward the television and wished she had moved beside him.

"Um, Evan?"

"Mmm-hmm?"

"I...uh...." She snickered nervously. "I'm kind of embarrassed to admit this, but I passed by here earlier, when I was getting the sandwich. And I overheard a bit of a conversation you were having. I mean, just for a minute. I was trying to find my way around. What was that all about? If you don't mind my asking. I don't mean to pry, it's just...." She bit her lip, glanced at the television, then back at him.

He appeared frozen. "Well, I had several conversations in here. Which one are you talking about?"

Caffrey swallowed. "It was something about a girl, who was...angry with you. And about a bomb."

"Oh...oh," he said, with a slow nod. "Well, there's this girl...she's a bit on the psychotic side, who's been...stalking me. The police are onto the situation, and they're trying to keep tabs on her. She's been through a...conflict with a militia group, and never quite got over the experience." He shifted his position on the sofa, his warm demeanor gone. "I'm beefing up the security here around the house, because I think she could be very dangerous. If you see her, stay clear of her. She's got long black hair. Pretty slim, nice-looking, probably in her twenties."

Caffrey looked down at their empty bowls on the table and felt guilty.

"And the other thing...the building that got bombed." His brows knitted together in concentration. "That is...I am connected with a lot of classified operations with the government, and there was a...situation with a militia group we're having to, uh, control. They're working on stockpiling weapons. You know, a lot of people still want to be in militias because of the Zgeyyan Invasion. Well, a building got bombed that our military thought housed a terrorist militia, and...." He shrugged his shoulders. "I felt they should have waited, you know. It really wasn't necessary. There could have been just regular people in there, unknowing of the militia's plans on their property."

"Oh. Wow."

"It wasn't the kind of thing you should have overheard. It's not that it was anything really bad, but some issues I'm involved in are...classified right now."

"That phrase sounds familiar."

"It does?"

"You must have said that a lot to me."

"I'm sure I did." A shadow seemed to pass over his eyes.

She regretted doubting him. It had been so enjoyable to see him happy. "I'm really sorry."

"Thanks. Of course...you've got to pretend you don't know anything, okay? Because nobody's supposed to know about all of that."

"Absolutely." She nodded, a bit sheepish.

For a while, neither spoke. Evan scratched the back of his neck and peered sideways. "Do you always go around spying on conversations?"

"No! Of course not," Caffrey stammered. "I told you. I...thought it was odd and didn't know what to think, and...." Caffrey shook her head and stood up. "Look, I didn't mean to eavesdrop, okay? It's just that I went down this hallway instead of the other way, and was disoriented, and...."

"Hey, hey." He stood and closed the gap between them. "It's okay. Really."

Caffrey curled the corners of her lips in a semblance of a smile and debated whether or not to return to her room. Nowhere else in the mansion did she feel comfortable escaping to, except perhaps the library. But, she also needed to re-familiarize herself with the house, and with him. "Why don't we forget about it and watch the rest of the movie?" she suggested.

"Great idea."

Evan fell into the couch and stretched his arms across the back, his face silent and thoughtful. The old black-and-white movie was intriguing, but his words continued to dance across her mind. Classified information could easily be misconstrued. Besides, when she did not question him, when she thought kindly toward him, her head hurt less, and she felt more at ease. Surely, that meant something. She dosed off somewhere during the end of the movie.

A loud snoring woke her. She was in a dim room lighted by a television screen. Burgundy paint covered the bottom half of the walls, while a rich, tapestry-like wall paper decorated the upper half. Several large paintings adorned the walls. Overstuffed brown leather chairs sat on either side facing the television, matching the sofa she had fallen asleep on.

Beside her, Evan lay snoring, his mouth partly open, his face handsome even in the dim light. She remembered having misgivings when she saw him in the past, mixed with attraction. But the feeling of misgivings was no longer there.

"You snore," she accused, as he groggily opened his eyes.

"I do not," he argued sleepily. Stretching long arms and legs until the bones in his back popped. He reached for her—too late, as she jumped away.

They walked up the stairs together, too tired to talk. At her door, he leaned down, kissed her lightly on the cheek, and murmured "goodnight." Part of Caffrey wanted to hug him, to make everything all right. Instead, she watched him amble down the hall and stop at the door on the other side of hers. Earlier, he had shown her the master suite down the hall, which she had assumed he was using.

Puzzled but unconcerned, she entered her own spacious room and pulled open several drawers before finding an oversized T-shirt. The items in the drawers were reassuring, and she felt through them with her hands, reconnecting. Everything was in the right order. She smiled with relief and snuggled into the bed, emotionally and physically exhausted.

Caffrey sat up straight, barely able to breathe.

Her bedroom door flew open, and Evan rushed to her side, his body naked except for light-blue boxers. "Are you okay?" he implored.

"Yeah, I think so," Caffrey answered, her heart pounding. "I have the most awful dreams. They're so confusing."

"Hey, it's okay," he reassured her, gently pulling her to him. "What do you mean? You had one last night, too?"

She nodded. "And the night before."

"Why didn't you tell me? I could've called the doctor."

"What can *he* do? I don't like him anyway."

"Well, he could at least give you something to help you *sleep*. I don't want you having these dreams. I want you to be happy. Why didn't you tell me you were having them?"

"I don't know. Felt stupid, I guess. So much doesn't make sense." She rubbed her forehead. "My dreams are so bizarre. I'm always in a cave and...."

"Why don't I lie down with you?"

"Okay."

Like a warm blanket, he lay behind her and enveloped her with his arms. His cheek snuggled against hers.

"Mmmm," she responded, allowing stiff muscles to unwind. "I feel better already."

Tenderly, he kissed her below her ear. His lips were warm and inviting against her skin, and she smiled.

"You were yelling something in your sleep when I woke," he whispered. "Sounded like 'vase' or 'ace,' but I wasn't sure."

"Hmmm." She pondered. "I don't remember. There was something falling into the darkness, and I couldn't save it. I was trying to grab it. It was important, but a Vhurruh, of all things, was chasing me, trying to swallow me."

"A Vhurruh?"

"Yeah." She chuckled nervously. "Go figure."

"Yeah."

"There was someone there, fighting the Vhurruh. She had red hair and looked like me. I called out, but she couldn't hear me."

"She looked like you?" Evan asked. His body stiffened.

"Yeah. Weird. I was so scared."

"Shhhh, don't worry about it now," Evan soothed. "Forget it. Leave it in the past. I'm here with you, and I'm not going to let anybody hurt you now. Just relax and rest."

And she did.

27

A NEW LIFE

"*Caffreeey!*" Kimberly screamed as she hugged Caffrey's neck. Caffrey embraced her warmly and looked over the lobby as though a year had passed. It was hard to shake a foreboding feeling at being back at the firm, but she had insisted, against Evan's wishes, that she needed something productive to do. She needed to choose her life.

"Just for a couple of days," Caffrey had argued earlier that morning, flapping the arms of Evan's thick white bathrobe she had confiscated, her damp, red hair cascading all over it.

Briefcase and cell phone in hand, Evan had been pacing to and fro, gathering several items and explaining where he would be. "It's not a good idea. It's too soon."

"But, I remember it! I remember everybody there. I realize I'm not really crazy about the place, but I feel like it's unfinished business or something."

"Why don't you just stay here? You said you wanted to redo the old garden—go for it. I know you love gardening. I'll even rent some equipment for you."

Caffrey frowned, but not unkindly. It was difficult to explain that she did not *want* to be indebted further to him. She wanted to be free to *know* that she was choosing him. And, she missed being around people, being productive, having her own money to do with as she pleased.

"Maybe we should talk to the doctor first." He dropped his briefcase onto the ornate side table and began dialing into his cell phone.

"Evan!" she yelled. "I do not need any doctor to tell me how I'm feeling."

"And what about Dr. Pensce? What did *she* say?"

"Dr. Pensce is a schizoid. She thinks everybody who experiences anything beyond her concept of reality is schizophrenic. She's like half the psychiatrists out there—probably *causes* more depression than she'll ever prevent. 'Here, you're nuts. Let me give you some meds.'"

Evan dropped his shoulders, leaned his sandy-blond head to one side, and frowned in protest. "Caffrey, these people are trained professionals."

"These people are *trained* in a one-sided reality. They don't use any intuition."

"They are trained to *listen*."

"Oh they listen, then decide what meds you need. I need my old therapist. She understood *real* reality. She was open to things. I could say anything to her. And she gave me advice, *not* meds. She gave me…tools."

"She moved, remember?"

"Yeah, and left no forwarding address. Now, that's too weird."

"I'm sure there's a good reason."

"I need to go back there, Evan," Caffrey insisted. "I know it's not what I really want to do for a living, but…it's like…I don't know. Something's missing. A piece of a puzzle or something. Maybe I'll find it there."

"Give it a few more days, okay?" He implored her with handsome, concerned, green eyes. "We'll go to the Governor's banquet this weekend and have a great time. Meet some movers and shakers, people who are trying to make a *difference* in the world. Then think about going back to a place you're really not crazy about. I'll speak to one of my constituents and see what openings they might have. You could for work for a cause that really matters to you."

She smirked sideways, unable to resist him. "All right."

His enticing lips widened into a smile.

"But, maybe just for a day," Caffrey amended.

"You are the stubbornest thing!" He waved his cell phone. Caffrey smiled and reached out to hug him, surprising them both. With his face so close to hers, he lost no opportunity, and covered her lips with his.

Warmth rushed through her body. His lips were sensuous and full, and he tasted wonderful. Why had she waited so long to get close?

Evan kissed her with greater passion and longing. He curled his arms about her slim shoulders. Caffrey felt herself letting go, letting the rush of energy excite her. Her senses drank in the depth of desire he had for her, the aura of power and sensuality emanating from him; his strong hands pressed against the small of her spine. Desire grew, but also a tiny voice of caution in the midst of their passion. Mixed emotions crowded into Caffrey's brain, each vying for space. She reluctantly pulled back lest she become too intoxicated with him to think clearly. She was ready, but she wasn't ready.

"You're going to be late," she whispered, and rested her cheek against his, smoothing down the hair on the back of his neck with her fingertips.

"I'm my own boss, remember? And right now, I've got better things to do." He kissed her neck, sending delectable shivers down her spine. But if she remained in his arms, he would stay.

"Go on, get out of here," she whispered, and tried to calm her own breathing. With effort, she pushed him gently and stepped backward. "We'll have more time later," she added to soften the sting.

Though he was clearly defiant, the hint of a future rendezvous caused his expression to alter to hopeful victory. Reluctantly, he grasped the ornate brass handle of the etched glass door. She blew him a kiss as he exited, then stood in the doorway to watch him walk to his red convertible, admiring the way his body moved.

In the driveway he turned back and broke into a smile as he realized she was watching him. "One thing I'm going to do is get a garage built here. I hate all this yellow pollen getting on my car."

Caffrey smiled, then gasped as she spotted her blue car off to the right. "Where did that come from?"

She raced past him. He sauntered over to join her.

"Was this here all the time?" she exclaimed.

"Noooo," he taunted musically.

"When?"

"I got it for you yesterday."

"Where? How? I mean, I thought it was crashed."

He tilted his head to one side with a cocky, self-assured grin. "I can do everything," he teased, and flitted his thick, brownish-blond eyebrows. Caffrey crossed her arms and pursed her lips.

"Okay, I know someone who knows someone, etc. I had it fixed for you. Although, really, you should get something a little more saucy. It's too plain and practical. Maybe I'll surprise you one day."

"Don't you dare! Hey, where's the keys?"

"Hey, you made me a promise."

"No, I didn't. Where's the keys?"

He squinted reproachfully.

"I might want to run out to the store or something." She threw both hands in the air.

"Everything you need is *here*. If you need something, send Marianna for it."

"Evan." Caffrey's voice darkened. "I'm not a bird in a cage. We need to get something straight. I need to be free."

"I'm not keeping you here." His voice had turned angry. Averting his gaze to the grass, he stepped close and bent his sandy head beside hers. "Was what happened a moment ago not of your own free will?"

Caffrey glanced away as well. She felt her resolve dwindle as she breathed in his enticing cologne. "Yes. Of course, but…."

"Did I not get your car for you?" His voice was quiet and firm.

"Yes you did, but…."

"Your keys are on the little table in the foyer. Had to have some made." He turned to leave, and she reached for him.

"Don't leave me angry."

His face was stern. "I'm not angry. I just want to make sure you're okay, all right?"

She watched him for a moment. "I believe you."

A raven squawked and caused them both to jump.

"Hey, you, get off of my car!" Caffrey yelled. The bird continued to maintain its perch on the blue hood, its eyes fixed keenly on Caffrey.

"Shoo!" Evan waved an arm. "I just had this thing cleaned!"

Caffrey laughed as they both waved arms to scare the bird away. At the last possible moment, the scraggly bird flapped large black wings in a slow beat and veered off to a nearby branch, as though it was determined to reclaim its prize once they left.

"What's wrong?" Evan queried.

Caffrey continued to stare at the front seat. "My head's hurting a little. Something…it's a dark, scary feeling from the last time I was in the car, I think. I don't know. Maybe from the crash."

"It's okay, Princess," Evan murmured reassuringly and squeezed her shoulder.

"What did you say?"

Evan shrugged. "Just 'it's okay, Princess.' Why? Did that bother you?"

"No, it's…Did you used to call me that before?"

"I'm sure I probably did." He wrapped an arm around her. "You *are* a princess to me." Curling her against his chest, he kissed her with such longing that she considered asking him to stay home.

"Rest, remember?" He released her.

Caffrey smiled and watched him rounding his car.

"Please, be a good girl. Take it easy today?"

"I'm *always* a good girl. That's what's *wrong* with me!"

"That's what I like about you. You're a lady. But you're also strong. And smart. And beautiful." He started the engine.

She called out, "And since when did *you* go after the good girls?"

"I was *always* after you. You know that."

"Yes, you were," she said to herself as he drove away. Then, smiling mischievously, she sprang like a deer back through the house.

The drive to the office nearly gave her a migraine with the traffic and unfamiliar route from the mansion. She had planned her way with a map on the phone he gave her, expecting all the while for memories of the route to materialize, but to no avail. At least the drive down Peachtree Street *was* familiar. She was relieved to turn into the dull cement parking garage.

Martin White appeared shocked but pleased to see her and gladly agreed to her working for the day, since they were busier than ever. Kimberly whispered that he had not been happy with the two temporary assistants who had tried to replace her. Caffrey smiled in satisfaction.

An hour after she arrived, Martin called her into his office and grasped one of her hands with both of his. Caffrey nearly flinched with shock. With a smile he suggested she might be ready for the more challenging position of say, Office Manager, overseeing the general run of the office and freeing Mary to do more research. "Certainly a bit more prestigious," he added. "And, I think a salary increase is in order."

A thrill of excitement ran though her, but also concern. Martin had never treated her as a professional. He had always been overbearing and judgmental. It was his plastic smile that gave her pause. He wanted to make her happy. Why did he want to make her happy?

She had worked hard and did deserve a promotion. She had learned every aspect of the business and could run the office without him.

Then it came to her. Being Evan's presumed partner was changing the way she was viewed. It was disheartening to realize Martin wanted to please Evan, not her. Was this a good thing, or a bad thing? Maybe she should be smart and ride the wave.

"That sounds like a wonderful idea, Martin. Can we talk about it tomorrow? Give me time to think?"

"Sure, sure. Take your time." He rocked on his heels. The plastic smile seemed frozen on his face. Caffrey smiled graciously, and could not exit his office fast enough.

"I'm so glad you're okay!" shrieked Kimberly again, bouncing up and down. Kimberly had cut her hair to shoulder length, and she looked wonderful to Caffrey The familiar hallways and rooms were both reassuring and disturbing. Though still fighting an odd regret at being back, Caffrey knew as she greeted and hugged each person that it was a good idea for everyone, as well as for her. There was relief in their eyes to see her healthy and doing well. There was also a strange mixture of curiosity, pity, and distrust, which she didn't fully understand until she went out to lunch with Kimberly and Jim.

"So, how crazy were the Underground people?" asked Kim, barely able to contain her excitement. "They didn't do anything bad, did they?"

"Kim!" Jim chastised, though curiosity was in his eyes as well.

"What do you mean, Underground people?" asked Caffrey, puzzled.

Kimberly and Jim exchanged worried glances.

"Well..." Kimberly faltered. Her eyes darted. "I meant...."

"Never mind," said Jim quickly. "Let's talk about something light. You're going to stay, aren't you, Caffrey?"

She stared at him. "*What* about the Underground people?"

Jim's shoulders seemed to drop. "Sorry, Caff. We were told not to mention anything so that we wouldn't mess up your getting your memory back. I guess we goofed already," he said, with a hard glare at Kimberly.

"*Who* told you this?" Caffrey asked, furious.

"Well, Evan did," said Jim. "He said your doctor had strictly advised against it. Hasn't he tried to talk about any of this to you?" Jim waved his fork in the air.

Caffrey gritted her teeth. "He doesn't even know I'm here. He thinks I'm at the mansion resting today. Look, there is *nothing* wrong with me. I can remember on my own. But, I'm not somebody who likes to be in the dark. You guys are my friends. Don't treat me any differently than you did before. If something's too much, then we'll both know it."

There was a long pause while Jim and Kimberly stared at her. She returned the stare.

Jim cleared his throat. "You know, you're a little different."

"What do you mean, different. *What's* different?" Caffrey fumed.

"Why don't we talk about something else?" Jim suggested.

"Jim!"

"Okay, okay. You're just a little bolder than I remember. You never...raised your voice at me before."

Caffrey blinked. "I didn't?"

"No. Never."

"I'm sorry."

"No, no. Don't be sorry. I think I like it. You were much too shy and...and...I don't know. You *needed* to be more aggressive." His smile appeared genuine.

A waitress interrupted them to refill their glasses. A silver chain swung free as she leaned forward to refill Kimberly's iced tea. On the end of the chain rested a silver oval ring housing a rhombus diamond shape of the same silver metal. Caffrey froze, spellbound.

"Caff? Caffrey!" Jim demanded.

Caffrey jumped. "What?"

"She was asking if you wanted more tea." Jim looked alarmed. Kimberly's eye were wide.

"Oh, uh, sure. Thanks."

The waitress glanced at her while she poured, as if she had a question. Caffrey took a deep breath and let it out.

"So," Kimberly began in a nervous voice, "tell us about the mansion. I couldn't get anything online about it.

Caffrey described the vast rooms and décor to them while Kimberly battered her with questions, as she usually did when she was nervous. Caffrey sensed a touch of jealousy from Kimberly, but not to the degree she remembered it. She ate while Kimberly and Jim talked about several clients and properties involved with the firm.

"Kim, are you seeing anyone?" Caffrey dared to ask, afraid that Kimberly would be insulted at her lack of memory.

Kimberly smiled secretively. "Well," she said, glancing at Jim, then back at Caffrey, "actually, I've been seeing Vinny, Frank's brother. You remember Frank, from the club?"

"Oh, yeah. I *remember!*" said Caffrey, relieved. "He was sort of Italian-looking. Lots of rings on his fingers. We were at The Brim." Caffrey's expression dropped suddenly. "I can't believe you got me to go out to The Brim."

"You asked *me* to go, remember?"

Caffrey found only a blank space in her brain, and she shook her head.

Kimberly swallowed. "Well, me and you were—and Evan too—at The Brim, gosh, *weeks* ago, and we met a guy named Frank. We left because of the fight, you know, and me and Evan went to another club. Frank's brother, Vinny, met us there and...later called me. You never met him. We've gone out every weekend since." She glanced at Jim, embarrassed by his chiding smile, and cleared her throat.

"I can't believe I can't remember him, or you guys dating," said Caffrey. She shook her head in dismay and looked down at her half-eaten food.

"Hey, forget about it. You remembered most of it," Jim said authoritatively. "That's what's important. So, let's not talk about too much right now. And hey, we need to get back to work anyway. By the way, how's it feel, being back in this crazy place?"

"Very strange, Jim," Caffrey responded with a heavy feeling in her chest. "I think I was beginning to dislike my job. Not the people, of course. I enjoyed being part of the team. I like doing a good job, and keeping everything organized. I mean, when I was here, I was totally devoted to it. And sometimes I *did* enjoy the hectic pace. But, I didn't like the secrecy. The questionable practices. Skirting around laws. Doing something with abandoned property is a good thing, but not because someone disappeared in the night against their will. And, the government always denying it happened."

Looking up from her plate, she found both of them watching her with strained eyes. She knew then that they felt it too. That question deep in their soul: "Am I doing something bad, or something good?"

"Well," she brightened, "maybe I'll move on to something else. To what, I don't know. Plus, everybody's acting strangely around me, looking at me like I'm a lizard or something." She snorted. "And Martin wouldn't let me into the cash box earlier to exchange five dollars for soda money for that old clunker machine. How weird is that?"

Jim and Kimberly both stared at their plates. Jim broke the silence. "Just take it one day at a time, kiddo. You know I'm here for you. You can count on me."

"Me, too!" added Kimberly, frowning at Jim for leaving her out.

Caffrey smiled, warmed by their friendship. "And you won't dance around issues like everybody else is?"

"No." Jim shook his head. "I won't dance around anything. I think."

"Hey!" Caffrey protested as he rose from the table, grinning but avoiding her.

With renewed camaraderie, they told jokes all the way back to the office, and Caffrey began to feel that she might have found the missing link she was looking for: the old sense of family and dedication to her work at the firm, things that she was almost ready to give up.

Kimberly manned the front desk while Caffrey headed for the rest room in the communal hallway between offices. She laughed as she eyed a familiar, light brown Georgia cricket on the white tile inside the ladies' room. How many times had she called building management about the silly creatures? The more the large, spider-like insects jumped to avoid a passing body, the more they seemed to jump *at* the passing body, causing many a shriek to echo down the corridor.

Uneasiness came over her as she washed her hands. She stared at the sink, a flash of memory afflicting her. She, Mary and Kimberly had been in here together, concerned about something.

Caffrey smirked at the thought of Martin's indignation at finding the "girls" missing all at once.

Careful not to trigger one of the crickets to jump, Caffrey exited the cold bathroom, and gasped. Leaning against the opposite wall, not six feet from her, a dark-haired man with a frighteningly deadly gaze stood perfectly still, as though he were waiting for her. A tingle, like hot electricity, zapped through Caffrey's entire body as she gazed into the shiny, piercing eyes, dark brown—almost black—against his tanned face.

His body did not move, but his eyes watched hers, unblinking. Had the man moved a single muscle toward her, she would have turned and run, screaming for all she was worth. Yet, since he made no move of any kind, she was uncertain how to react. He was dressed in blue jeans and a white T-shirt, accompanied by an orange safety vest and white hardhat. *Okay*, she thought, *he's obviously from the construction crew outside, working on the adjacent building.* Except, his demeanor was not that of a worker focused on some errand.

"Hello, Princess," he said in the deepest voice she had ever heard.

Caffrey stopped breathing for a moment, puzzled by the familiar term, thinking perhaps he was merely flirting. The sound of his voice shivered through her, and she wanted to hear it again. She reminded herself that he did not look safe. He looked powerful and deadly. She considered backing up into the bathroom, but she feared getting trapped into a room with no escape.

She managed a small, noncommittal smile and moved slowly to the right so that he would be unable to push her back into the rest room. "Can I help you?" she offered, taking several more steps to her right. "Are you looking for a particular office?"

The man's dark brows knitted together in disturbed confusion. "Maybe," he answered quietly. A great familiarity surrounded him, as though he were someone she had known in school or from some obscure meeting.

As she stood staring, the familiarity seemed to grow, causing a great, heavy pressure in her chest—a lonely, throbbing ache—matched by a steady pounding in the center of her skull. The lights in the hallway were way too bright. Growing sick to her stomach and feeling needles attacking the back of her eyes—the onset of a migraine—she moved again one step to her right to indicate she was headed in that direction. The office door was only ten yards away, around the corner. She hoped someone else would come out from the other offices.

"You don't know who I am, do you?" he asked. He knotted his dark brows together as though the idea unsettled, shocked and angered him at the same time.

Nausea threatened to overwhelm her. She rubbed at her temples, squinting against the bright lights of the hallway. His keen eyes focused on her fingers pressing against her temples, and his face grew angrier.

"You seem... familiar to me," she answered truthfully. "But I can't quite... place you. Should I *know* you?"

"Oh, my god," said the man slowly, almost in a whisper. His face lost its tanned color. "They took you."

Caffrey stared at him, horrified. His words echoed in her head like a strange death sentence. Unnerved, she brushed along the wall faster toward the corner.

"They took you from me!" he roared. He pounded a clenched fist into the wall beside him and broke through the sheetrock. "I'll *kill* them! I'll *kill* every last one of them!"

Caffrey hit the corner of the wall as she ran. A female voice from somewhere in the corridor called out, "Let's go! Now!"

Caffrey flung her body into the wooden office door and ran hard into Jim, nearly knocking him over. Before the door swung shut, Caffrey heard the woman call out, "There's nothing we can do here. Let's go!"

Caffrey was so terrified the man would follow her that she continued trying to run past Jim, dragging him with her.

"Hey! Hey! What's going on?" Jim demanded. He grasped her arms firmly and glanced back at the slowly closing door.

"There's a crazy man out there!" Caffrey cried. "Call security! Lock the door!"

Jim stared at her, eyes wide and mouth slightly agape.

"Jim!"

Moved by the panic in her voice, he turned the lock on the door and ran to bolt the front glass doors. Then he grabbed the phone. Kimberly and Mary ran out of their offices, anxiously yelling questions.

Jim gave building security a quick description from Caffrey while Mary put an arm around her, alarmed by her distress, which felt oddly familiar to Caffrey.

She continued backing up, pulling Mary, and glanced from one door to the other. "He won't give up," she said to Jim and Mary. Jim hung up the phone.

"What?" Jim asked.

"Who are you talking about, honey?" asked Mary.

"He won't give up, he'll...." Caffrey halted, and gasped for air. "How do I know that? Oh, my god, Jim, how do I *know*? How do I know what he would do?" She backed into a shelf of books. Tears were streaming down her face.

Jim took hold of her. "Shhh. Shhh. Calm down now. Here, let's go in my office. Mary, get Martin and Don out here to guard the doors. Tell everybody security's been called. I'm taking Caffrey to my office."

With a firm grip on Caffrey's shoulders, Jim escorted her down the oak-paneled hall before anyone could protest and shut the door behind them. "Let's sit down, okay? I've been wanting to talk to you alone anyway."

Caffrey sniffed, and breathed in shaking gasps. Jim snatched several tissues and handed them to her.

"Jim. I am so scared. Why do I know this guy will come back again? I mean, where did that *come* from? Who...who is he?" Her own voice sounded hysterical.

"You're going to have to take this one thing at a time. Maybe one *person* at a time," Jim instructed. "He's obviously someone you met within the last month. Maybe he's one of them."

"Them?"

"The Underground people."

"But, I don't *remember* that. I mean, I remember almost everything else." Caffrey waved an arm. "I remember everything from before. Except for the last month."

"Or, except everything about the Underground," Jim suggested.

Caffrey stared at him.

Jim sat with one hip on his desk. "Caffrey, we were told you were kidnapped by the Underground."

"What?" Panic gripped her again.

"Okay, be calm, okay?"

"What...what else happened?" She gripped the armrests of the chair.

Jim licked his lips. "I don't know if I should tell you."

"Jim! Please, don't do this to me. Not you." Caffrey shook her head and felt her eyes burning.

Jim exhaled and looked down at the carpet. "Okay, do you remember the night you disappeared?"

"I disappeared?"

"Oh, good grief." Jim covered his eyes.

"Okay." Caffrey breathed deeply. "Just...tell me what you know. I am calm. I...am totally calm." She stretched out her hands for emphasis, then drew them back when she realized her fingers were shaking. "Evan told me I was in a car wreck." She glared darkly at Jim, anger beginning to replace fear.

Jim swallowed. "I don't know if I'm helping you or hurting you."

"Jim." Caffrey grasped his hand, not caring if he thought it against protocol. He looked at her then, as a caring friend. "I would do it for you," Caffrey insisted.

"Okay. If it were me, I'd want the same from you," he agreed. He squeezed her hand then let it go as he sat in the guest chair beside her. "All I know is that you were missing after the accident at your apartment. The gas main break. Then, it was said that you had joined the Underground. And even stolen...well, we'll go into that later. Then, we were told you were kidnapped by the Underground because you worked *here*, and they wanted to know about all the property arrangements and missing people. 'Cause, it's their thing,' the investigator said. Most recently, we were told you were in an accident when the police were chasing the Underground. You were supposedly in a car with some of them, and it crashed. Three of them escaped, but you were injured. That's the last we know, except that you had lost your memory."

Caffrey stared at him, open-mouthed. "Jim, I don't remember *any* of that." Tears fell unchecked down her cheeks again. "How could all that have happened to me, and me not remember any of it? Where did I *put* it?"

Jim sat in silence. "Where did you put it?" he mumbled, more to himself than to her. His eyes rose to meet hers. "Was it ever there?"

Caffrey sniffed, not caring as tears fell onto her suit. "Well, I remember an accident. But I remember it being *here*."

"Oh, there *was* an accident here."

"There was?"

"Yes, out front. You were helping someone, and you got blood all over you."

"Oh. Wow." Caffrey felt a stab of pride for helping someone. "I don't remember that. Well, I remember going out there, I think. Next thing I remember is dancing with Evan at The Brim." She waved her hands. "I don't remember *why* I was there. But, when Kimberly said it earlier, I remembered pieces of it, just parts with Evan. That's only a little thing. But...Jim, I don't remember moving in with Evan."

"But that's a recent event," he said, and glanced away from the intimacy of the subject. "Right after you were with the Underground people in the police chase."

"How long ago was that?"

Jim thought a moment. "That was a week ago."

Caffrey's jaw dropped. "Jim," she whispered, "Evan told me I moved in with him after the gas main break at my apartment, a month ago. He said I was in a recent accident and was in the hospital for a week, unconscious."

Jim frowned. "But, Caffrey, you were *missing* for weeks. Is he saying you were really with him at the mansion?"

Caffrey shook her head. "I don't know. Why would he tell me something different from you?"

"Maybe he thinks you can't handle the trauma of being kidnapped by the Underground."

"But Jim, if that's true, why was all my stuff already at his place?"

"How do you know?"

"Because it was there when I got there! My pictures, clothes, statues, everything."

Jim looked down at the floor, then back at her. "What if it was moved there?"

"What do you mean?"

"Maybe...." Jim scratched the back of his head worriedly. "Maybe he was talking about the accident out here. Maybe we're just misunderstanding him."

Caffrey watched him for a moment. "You don't believe that."

Jim's heavy sigh answered for him.

"Where was all my stuff after I supposedly got kidnapped by the Underground? Was it still at my apartment? What about the fire? Kim says my building burned. Was that before or after I moved in with Evan?"

Jim blew air out slowly. "I don't know. I just...he's got a lot of connections, Caffrey. And we obviously aren't being told the same story. I think...I think you had better pretend you don't question any of this."

Caffrey felt an icy chill trickle into her chest. "Okay, tell me this. I woke up in the hospital with my head aching. I had a lump, and two stitches. I've got some scars on my stomach that I have *no idea* how I got. They look like they're still *healing*. And I've got two stitches on the back of my thigh. Those are recent."

She inhaled deeply to steady her nerves. "I didn't discover them until I took a shower at Evan's. And, my stomach muscles are so shaky. I can feel the difference when I do my exercises. And, supposedly, I'm *living* with him, and have been since the apartment fire? I remember absolutely *nothing* about any Underground. I don't even have little pieces of memory. Nothing. Nada. If I had been through some traumatic event, I would have *pieces*, at least. Especially if I *want* to remember. Wouldn't my desire to pull all of this up *mean* something?"

"I don't know. I just don't know. But, Caffrey, I think you could be in danger if you remember."

She stared at him, breathless. "Why?"

"It's the smell of it. First, what you're being told and what I'm being told doesn't match. And, ever since the accident that happened out here on Peachtree Street, SAAFs have been crawling all over us. We were all required to get Top Secret clearances the very next day. They haven't all gone through yet, but...heck, my office could be bugged, for all I know."

Caffrey looked around at his familiar office, the furniture, the pictures, his drooping corn plant. "I remember talking to you about things like this."

Jim smiled. "Yeah, we could always talk about stuff like this. Caffrey, what if someone has actually messed with your memory? I know it sounds crazy, but.... What if the Underground group did it? Or, what if the government did it? I mean, I don't mean to scare you, but you're not entirely the same person. You remember some things from before and after, but not everything in between. And, some very strange things happened the night you went missing."

They jumped at a loud knock on the door. Martin White let himself in before Jim could answer. Two tall, stocky men from building security sauntered in behind him wanting more information from Caffrey about the intruder. They had found no trace of the man, even after checking every person in the construction crew. As she exited, Caffrey threw a look to Jim that begged further discussion at some later point.

After questioning Caffrey for several minutes, the security officers finished writing up their report. Only by standing on either side of her were they able to persuade her to re-enter the hallway to show them exactly where she had seen the man. They examined the hole in the sheetrock.

As the men left to scour the remaining floors, Jim suggested to Caffrey that she return home, or stay with Kimberly. Before Caffrey could decide what to do, Kimberly noticed two SAAF officers passing by the windows, heading for the front entrance. Everyone moaned as if tired of the process that would follow. Caffrey stiffened at sight of the black and gold uniforms; her entire body turned ice cold.

"Caff, it's Evan," said Kimberly.

"What?" Caffrey whirled.

"He's on the phone." Kim gave her a brief, envious smile.

"Oh." Caffrey sighed in relief.

"She'll take it in my office," said Jim. He ushered Caffrey back into his office to the curiosity of Mary and Kimberly. Caffrey's arm shook as she picked up the receiver.

"Caffrey Hanson," she stated in her professional voice.

"Caffrey, *what* are you doing there? You told me you would wait!"

"Stop yelling! My head hurts. I wasn't really planning on it. It just hit me."

"Honey, *why* didn't you wait?" Evan wailed in frustration. "Martin told me what happened. Are you okay?"

"No, I'm *not* okay!" she cried, shaking. "There's SAAFs out here, and I'm scared to death."

"Listen, honey, listen. Just calm down. I'll come pick you up, okay?"

"No. My car's here."

"We can take care of your car later," Evan suggested, with an edge to his voice.

Caffrey gulped a breath. 'No. I want to drive my car back. I...I should finish out the day. I don't want to quit, but...I can't face those SAAFs." She sobbed. "I don't know why they unnerve me so."

"Honey, I know you're not a quitter, okay? You've had a very rough experience. I know this guy frightened you, but rest assured, *that* won't happen again. You need to relax and take this thing slowly. And let me take care of you."

"Evan, I...I didn't tell you about the guy."

After a moment of silence, he replied, "I called Martin about some property, and he told me."

"And what's all this about the Underground? Why didn't you tell me?"

Evan exhaled and cursed under his breath. "Caffrey, if you had just given me time, I could've explained it all to you. Dr. Roley said not to tell you too much, but to tell you only as you remembered and asked. You didn't remember, and you didn't ask!"

Caffrey considered this a plausible explanation and felt somewhat guilty for her suspicions. He had done everything to help her, and here she was, accusing him again.

"All right, I'm coming home."

"Good. I've got one more appointment this afternoon, but I can cancel it."

"No, don't do that. I'll...come home. Man, I don't want to have to pass those SAAFs. Just the sight of them terrifies me."

"Don't worry about them. I'll talk to them."

"How can you talk to them? You're not here."

"I know lots of people, remember?" he said with calm satisfaction. "I know the head of the Georgia Bureau of Investigation, and also a few folks at the SAAF division in Atlanta. They're probably just checking things out because of the Underground factor, which...you obviously know about now. I want you to hang up the phone, and I'm going to make a couple of calls, and everything will be fine. Okay?"

"Okay." She couldn't help but be reassured by the wielding of his power. It felt good to know the ally wielding it was hers. She sat at Jim's desk and waited. Jim had been called into Martin's office. As much as Caffrey wanted to confront the SAAF officers bravely, she could not muster the courage to do so. Her stomach and ribcage quivered at the thought. She had always thought them quite dashing before. What had changed?

Jim entered the room, wrung his hands, and jerked his head toward the hallway. Caffrey heard the faint creaking sound Martin's glasses made when he took them off and realized Martin was actually hovering there, listening. With a masked face, Jim informed her the SAAF officers were gone. Then he tactfully escorted her toward the door and wished her a better afternoon.

Caffrey's heart wrenched as she left the office with a parting glance at Jim, who stood mutely in the hallway, concern etched across his wrinkled brow.

28

ILLUSIONS

Sandy-haired arms curled around Caffrey and squeezed.

"You know, it's really not that bad that you're remembering the Underground now," Evan whispered in her ear.

Of the mansion's five balconies, the small east balcony overlooking the rose and lily garden had become Caffrey's favorite. Cool, rose-scented breezes danced around them and brushed her loose hair gently across Evan's face. The day had been unusually warm for late April.

"Maybe you could be the voice that people need to hear." He smoothed her hair. "You could tell them what you experienced with the misguided Underground and steer them toward working to help the Alliance. Space is our future, Caffrey. It's only up and out from here. The Vhurruh are a smart race, and they are our answer to the health and prosperity of this planet. *And* future investments."

Caffrey ran her hands over his strong arms and let her head rest back against the crook of his neck and shoulder. The white rattan lounge chair creaked under their combined weight.

Why he felt so right, she did not know, but the more she touched him, the more she cared for him, the less her head ached and the more her body relaxed. "I believe that, too. But, Evan, what if the Underground isn't all wrong?"

"What? *Honey*," he implored, turning her around to face him, "you can't be serious."

"Well...." Caffrey examined her conflicting feelings concerning the Underground. The dull ache in her skull rose with the slightest effort at recall. "I don't remember much about them, just feelings. But, I understand what they have stood for, especially after Brian disappeared."

Evan stiffened. "Kimberly told me about him. She said you were still...stuck on him."

Caffrey snorted. "Sounds like something Kim would say." She could sense Evan waiting. "No. I put Brian behind me. Don't remember when, exactly."

Evan smiled in relief and pulled her close. The sensation sparked warmth in her limbs and dissolved fears that had nagged at her for nearly two days after her visit to work. He had been sweet and attentive since that day, and she felt better the more time she spent with him.

"You know," she said, "I always thought you were someone who was out to get all you could, and didn't care about real issues, or people, or the charities you supported."

"Caffrey! I can't believe you thought that."

"I'm sorry. It's just that...I remember you always being hungry for property. You love acquiring property."

"For the charities, for the good of society. Now, to you, I will say, yes, I do love the acquisition." He grinned wickedly and gazed toward the setting sun. "I like the challenge of winning people over. And, in order to have the power to change things that need changing, I also need credibility. People need someone they can trust, someone who knows how things work with handshake deals and closed-door politics. My father took me everywhere. He could talk his way in or out of anything. My brother was an idiot—joined Earth-Sentinels. Said he was going to change the world. What a dreamer." He smirked. "But, *I* understand hungry billionaires, always wanting 'a little bit more,' or that special admiration for taking on a new charity—or, maybe a nice tax write-off. I understand the little people, too, living from paycheck to paycheck. I'm perfect. I bridge the gap."

"I already voted, dear," Caffrey taunted.

Evan frowned but was undeterred. "Okay, I guess I'm a natural campaigner. You going to be my first lady?" His fingers rubbed the straps of her loose, yellow cotton sundress as though itching to move further.

"Hmmm," Caffrey teased. "Sounds like an offer I can't refuse."

"Mmmm," he crooned happily, and kissed her neck.

"So, Mr. President, what great things are you going to do for the country—no, for the world?"

"Ah, just you wait and see." He lightly kissed her cheek. "The timing has to be right. Our environment is being restored, but I want a moratorium on keeping parks intact. Ninety percent of all trash will be *required* to be recycled, instead of voluntary, like it is now. And, as more and more farmland is being sold to developers, I want at least a tenth of it to be turned into new parks, maintained by state and local funds, so there will be lots of parks between subdivisions. And..."

"Hey, those were my ideas!" she protested, and glared at him.

"I stole them. They're brilliant." He laughed while she squirmed away in anger. "Oh, I'll give you credit, too, dear." He latched his arms tighter to keep her from escaping. "We need to build up your following as well." She opened her mouth to protest but he continued. "Natural resources, like oil and trees, will be required to be sold here first—say, ninety percent of it—to prevent so much being shipped overseas along with our jobs. All illegal drugs—and the ingredients and processes needed to create them—will be regulated, taxed out the wazoo, and treated just like alcohol."

"Seriously? You think that's a good idea?"

"Crime bosses and black markets all but disappeared when alcohol was made legal and regulated years ago. If the government can control it, get revenue from it, everything will change. The DUI rules will broaden and 'designated driver' will take on a whole new meaning. Instead of breathalyzers, we'll have bloodalyzers and people will get their fingers pricked every time they're pulled over for erratic driving."

"Hey, that was my idea, too!"

"Honey, we're a team. Don't get angry." He tried to pull her closer but she stiffened her body. "I promise you, I have no problem giving you credit. It works perfectly into my plan. Besides, we don't have to worry about politics getting in the way as much now. The governments are under control—I mean," he corrected himself, "they're all working together for once."

"I think you got it right the first time," Caffrey replied. *"Controlled."* She squinted as the familiar dull throb behind her eyes spiked.

"Look," he argued, with a touch of frustration, "somebody has to take control, or there is chaos and anarchy. We say we're a free people, but we're really just free to choose our own controls."

"Agreed, but don't you think it should be 'by the people,' as in *humans*—not aliens?" she asked.

"It is by humans. Humans *and* aliens. There's no stopping that now."

Caffrey raised both brows. "And who tells the ones in control that they're right? Who keeps them honest?"

Evan frowned. "Alliances with aliens are the future for this world. Let's make sure we ally ourselves with the ones who hold the *power.* One day, the Underground will be remembered as nothing more than a cult-like militia group that couldn't see the big picture."

At her disapproving expression, he softened his voice. "Look, I realize they had you believing they meant well. But they don't know what they're dealing with. *Look* at what we've accomplished with the help of the Vhurruh."

"Yes, they did good things." Caffrey nodded. "But Evan, the existence of the Underground also proves that people are scared."

"You know," Evan said softy. "You could be a voice to the world about these fears. The Underground has tried to bomb embassies, caused major brownouts, raided corporate offices, even killed two SAAF officers. Plus, they kidnapped *you!* I'll never forgive them for that. We have a lawful means of making changes in this country. They think they're *above* that." He cupped his hand to her chin to force her eyes to look into his. "We *need* someone who's been with them and can discount their claims. You are the perfect person for that."

"I didn't realize I had a job assigned to me." Caffrey raised one eyebrow. She found the idea both tantalizing and conflicting.

"I know you want to help your country, if not your planet. This is an exciting time in history. We're *living* the Age of Contact!"

"*Televised* contact, *admitted* contact," she countered.

"Okay, Miss Picky," he chuckled. "Officially sanctioned contact. How's that? The Underground will eventually disappear. Oh, there may be a faction or two—just a place for the crazies."

"I don't know, Evan. Sometimes it's good to have watchdog groups around. Granted, they're always full of eccentric people. But maybe, they'll keep the crazy politicians on their toes."

He squinted in mock insult and waved an arm. "The Underground just hates the Vhurruh."

"They don't *hate* them. They are responding to inconsistencies and cover-ups—and don't tell me they're not there. Why not propose a new program to establish checks and balances in the Alliance—a committee, maybe, made up of people from special-interest groups, scientists, civic leaders, clergy, representatives from other countries—a group that does nothing but investigate how the Alliance is being run. Something that calms people's fears and makes them think, *Hey, somebody's checking on it. We're okay. There's oversite.*"

A slow smile curled at the corners of Evan's mouth. "See, I knew you were right for me. You are beautiful and demure, but your mind's always thinking, challenging. And you ruffle your feathers for the really admirable issues. You defend 'the people' as though you were the First Lady."

"Flatterer. Really are shooting for President, aren't you?"

"Not this year," he countered. "Haven't been Governor yet."

Caffrey laughed outright. "I'm sure your adoring fans are waiting for your announcement."

He smirked. "So, you think I have adoring fans?"

"Oh, come on, hot-shot. Every girl who gets near you is practically slobbering."

He chuckled and encircled her waist with one arm. "But, they're not *you*." The depth of desire locked within his piercing green eyes nearly burned a channel straight to Caffrey's heart. "They all *want* something," he continued. "I'm a luxury car they want to be seen riding in. But you...." Admiration colored his intense gaze. "You don't want anything from anybody. Not my connections. Not my money. You're just you."

With so much longing it frightened Caffrey, Evan's greedy eyes traveled over her face, her body, and then lingered on her lips. "I can say anything to those other girls," he added, "and they smile like robots and kiss my feet. You challenge everything I say. You push me to question why I do what I do." His lips curled into a smile. "And it seems I still have to work to get you."

"Hmmm." She squinted her eyes teasingly. "Another acquisition?" The question had popped out of her mouth before she could stop it. At so rare a moment as Evan Parchek baring his soul, insulting him was not her intention. Still, it was what she had always done: question his every word, goad him into admitting his intentions, always searching for some kind of reassurance she could not define.

For a moment, he looked affronted, but after a wry smile, he slowly shook his head. "The *only* acquisition."

Caffrey felt her body turn to warm butter. This was what she had been waiting for: an unmasked honesty that would reassure her she was not just his latest catch, was not a challenge unmet, but truly mattered for who she was. Elated, she kissed him back and forced her fears aside.

As though it was a signal he had been looking for, his hands roamed over her back and shoulders, urging her soft, willing body against his. Of their own volition, her hands slid up his white tank shirt and felt his lean muscles tighten under her touch.

His tongue slipped into her mouth to caress hers. Electricity raced through her body. The fierceness of it both frightening and exciting her. The pounding behind her eyes began to recede, replaced by the pounding of her heart.

Evan pulled her leg across his lap. She sighed as he pressed hungry lips into her neck. The more he caressed her, the more she could not seem to get enough of him, as if some spell made it so. She reached one hand into his sandy hair to guide his head and felt surprised that his hair was wrong. She froze, confused by the thought. How could his hair be wrong?

His hungry lips halted at the bodice of her dress. "You want to go inside?" he whispered, misunderstanding her hesitation.

She wanted to say yes. Of course, his hair felt new, different, she argued with herself. They were learning and exploring each other's bodies. Touching him, caressing him, loving him, was the *right* choice.

"Hey," he whispered, shifting position so his eyes met hers. Immediately, she became lost in his emerald-green gaze, so full of passion and love. She brushed fingertips into his hair, and the odd sensation of *different* returned, like a coat she had put on up by mistake.

"I'm sorry," she murmured. "Maybe we're moving too fast."

He rubbed her arm softly. "We'll go as fast as you *want* to go."

"You don't seem to have any doubts."

"You know how I feel about you. You've always known."

She smiled, averted her eyes for a moment. "You know, you never answered my question about the committee."

"Committee?" he queried, mildly annoyed.

"Mmm-hmm. Remember?"

"Ah, yes. Committee." He planted several small kisses on her neck and mumbled, "We'll talk about the committee tomorrow."

"Are you evading me, Mr. President?" she said softly.

"I'm practicing for press conferences."

"You're something, you know that?"

His hand slid into her hair. "No," he insisted. "*You're* something." His warm lips closed over hers once again. Caffrey's headache began to recede. That was a good sign, wasn't it? And, he was wonderful to her, wasn't he?

She explored the taste of his lips and the feel of his aroused body against hers. It felt good to be loved, to be desired. The rattan lounger creaked in protest as their bodies shifted for more desirable positions.

"Let's go inside," Evan crooned. Together they stood and linked hands as they sauntered through the sliding glass door.

In unison they claimed each other's lips and fell onto the bed. Wanting to feel more of him, Caffrey's hands roamed up his spine to his muscled back. He was too thin. Caffrey froze. Panic made her heart skip a beat. How could he be too thin? She shook her head to dispel what must have been a leftover memory of Brian, who had a chunkier frame and thicker hair on his chest. More like.... more like.... A shadowed face hovered in her brain but became a blank space when she reached for it. Dull throbbing filled the empty space the shadow vacated, and she pressed a hand to her head.

Evan's lips faltered. "What's wrong?" He was breathing fast, worried but still hopeful.

"Nothing. I just...."

A definitive buzz reverberated close to Caffrey's ear, and she turned to find a huge dragonfly suspended above the white comforter mere inches from her face. She squealed and cowered.

Evan frowned when he spotted the intruder. "He'll go away. Don't worry about it."

The green, bulbous-eyed creature did not go away. Evan pulled Caffrey on top of him. The dragonfly made a flagrant pass at her head.

"Evan," she cried, "get it!"

Evan threw out his arm, but the shimmering insect neatly avoided his reach and returned to dare him again. "Hey, get your own!" Evan yelled.

"It's a warning," whispered Caffrey, mortified. The faint voice of a pretty, almond-eyed girl reading from a green book floating up from the depths of her memory. "'Don't give your power away to an illusion.'"

Evan looked at her, puzzled.

She chuckled nervously. "Where in the world did *that* come from?"

A veil seemed to pass over Evan's eyes. "Been hanging out with some tribe?" He swiped angrily at the insect as it dove at him.

"Tribe?"

"Yes. Belief that God uses animals as messengers is something a lot of native tribes swear by."

"Oh." Caffrey reached for the memory of the girl, but it had evaporated. "Well, I can't say I've been anywhere lately." As soon as she spoke the words, they both became uncomfortable. "Maybe it was my friend, Maiba. That's odd. This is the first I've remembered her. Dear Maiba. She came from Africa, and she used to tell me all sorts of wild stories."

"Ah." Evan nodded. "I'm sure that was it."

Nausea whirled in the pit of Caffrey's stomach at further recall of Maiba. She groaned at the piercing assault in the center of her head, and rubbed her temples.

The dragonfly began to dart in and out of the open glass door to the balcony. Leaping off the bed, Evan slammed the door shut. "Ha!" he exclaimed. "Get your own girlfriend."

Caffrey's brows raised. "Girlfriend?"

Evan flashed his most charming smile and closed the gap between them. "Don't you want to be my girlfriend?"

She tilted her head sideways. "I think I could get used to it." With the absence of the breeze, the vast white room seemed too quiet and still. "Although, I still feel like a stranger in this house. I mean, who would decorate an entire room in white?"

"Honey, this house— is *our* house." He kissed her cheek and then nuzzled at her neck. "Change it any way you like."

She inhaled at the warmth of his touch. "I always thought when they were ready for the first colony on Mars, I'd be the first to volunteer. And here I am feeling odd and dislocated in a place I've already been in for several days."

Evan brushed the loose strap of her dress off her shoulder and smothered the spot with a kiss.

"Think we'll get there?" she whispered, then swallowed.

"Caffrey?"

"Umm-hmm?"

"Stop asking questions.

"Evan, I want to be with you. I do. You kiss me and I feel warm and wonderful. Then, when I'm ready to let go and push all fears aside, weird flashes keep...disturbing me. I feel like it must be a message of some kind, and I just...."

"It's okay," he said sadly, and wrapped his arms around her. They held each other for a moment. "I remember you saying you were going to live on the first Mars colony someday. At the firm you said that. Kim used to roll her eyes, remember?" They smiled together at the memory.

Evan eyes sparkled as he gently pulled her down to the bed. "How about Veerinay?"

"What?"

"You must not divulge this to *anyone*," he said with a serious tone. "The Vhurruh were so determined to catch the Zgeyyans, they *found* the planet where they were dumping the humans."

"What? Wait a minute. I thought they were still *looking* for it. That was one of their missions."

"Yes, it was. But, they found it already. They have complete control over it, and they're building a weapons system around the planet, like the one they built here. They can broadcast their synaptic blast against the Zgeyyans. The need us to build more machines that help them do that. And...this is classified, okay?"

Caffrey nodded compliance.

"Everyone will know eventually, of course. They can't bring the people back yet because of contamination reasons. It's a different ecosystem. They could bring back all kinds of diseases, or spores. Some plants are dangerous. So, once you go, you have to stay. For now."

A horrific scene of dead bodies covered in plants flashed across Caffrey's brain and made her gasp. She rubbed her temples.

"You okay?" Evan asked.

Caffrey nodded. "Horrible picture."

Evan continued. "The Vhurruh keep the Zgeyyans out, and everybody has everything they need. They call it Veerinay." He spoke the word with mystical reverence. "If everything works out, we'll soon have a place where people can transplant to. They're building huge quarandomes there. They've even placed two quarandomes on Mars for research. Kind of an Ellis Island transfer point. The beginnings of a colony, Caffrey. With the Vhurruh, we have the chance to fix things here *and* start over somewhere else, and do it right. Not to mention the subspace drive to get there."

Caffrey stared at him wide-eyed and felt the hair rise on her arms. "*Mahyen nde-dehye.*"

"What?"

"Travel. It means travel between. You're serious about all this."

"Yes, I am." Excitement grew in his face.

"But, what about those people, Evan? So many people—so much pain. And what about the other liftings? I worked at that office. I *know* they were still happening. Don't even try to tell me they weren't."

"Honey, any liftings that happened *beyond* the Vhurruh stopping the Zgeyyans were groups given the chance to relocate and have a life somewhere else. That's why you heard so much about prisons and such. If you were in prison and were given the chance for life somewhere else, even on an untamed planet, wouldn't you take it?"

"Maybe. I don't know. But, murderers and rapists loose somewhere? I mean, some of those people just made big mistakes, but some are sick. Oh, my gosh. They were right all along," Caffrey whispered gravely. "All those reports, the chat rooms, the protest marches. Evan, how do you know all this?"

A slow, secretive smile curled at one corner of his mouth. Caffrey shivered. The sun was nearly gone beyond the horizon. The falling temperature in the room chilled her skin through her sun dress.

"We've got everything under control. Don't worry." Evan stroked her arm. "Doctors, builders, lawyers—well, not so many lawyers since we don't want them in the way—but psychiatrists, therapists, teachers, clergy...medicines. Everything that these people need to rehabilitate, to start new lives. We're doing humanity a great favor. A lot of people were asked to go, to help out. That's why you kept hearing rumors. The deal was that they couldn't leave any explanation for why they were gone."

"Okay, that's just wrong."

"No, it's a great plan." His green eyes flashed. "Imagine all the people complaining that we're not doing it right, that we're exposing people to this or that, or that we should let the man-eating plants run the planet because they were there first. Once it's already done, it'll be a moot point to say, 'Wait, let's do an impact study.' Possession is nine-tenths of the law. And, think about all the vultures wanting a piece of *that* planet."

Caffrey blinked at his reference.

"Yes." He eyed her. "I know about your little term at the office."

She grinned sheepishly.

"Imagine all the countries fighting for a piece of this," he continued self-righteously. "We need to do this right."

She stared at him in amazement. "We?"

"Yes, *we*. And *we* can be a part of it. You and I. What a team we would make! They need leaders, governors, mayors. I would love to run for Governor of the first Veerinay colony."

The thought of going to a new planet, beyond Mars, was exciting. She had always talked about being a colonist, and here was the opportunity being handed to her. Then, her heart constricted at the memory of Brian and her three friends. "But, what about all the grieving families?" She scolded. "My fiancé was lifted over a year ago, Evan. He did *not* choose to go. He was *taken!*"

Evan eyed her carefully. "I thought you put him behind you."

"I did...I just...." She floundered. "Well, I wasn't given a choice, was I?" In righteous fury she stood and paced about the room. "He was taken, Evan! *Nobody* contacted him. He would have told me."

"Hey, hey. Don't get upset, sweetheart." Evan crossed the room and captured her shoulders. "Remember, we've got another species involved here. The Vhurruh have a stake in the planet, too. Its atmosphere and sea caves are perfect for them. Their home planet is getting overrun, now that their hives don't fight. This one's a little thinner in air, and the gravity's a touch lighter. A lot needs to be worked out. People will have to acclimate."

Caffrey exhaled slowly. She needed to get away and think, and take something for this never-ending headache. "I still disagree on keeping so much secret."

"Caffrey, people in high places, making tough decisions—the money decisions—always have secrets, and always will." He massaged her shoulders and cupped her face with his hands. "You're either out front, or straggling along behind, wondering what's going on. Information needs to stay secret in order to stay secure. Sometimes you have to make deals with the devil."

Caffrey examined his determined green eyes. "Did *you* make a deal with the devil?"

"Depends on the devil. But, I do it for good reasons." His eyes glistened with self-confidence in the rising moonlight as he stroked her shoulders. "And I am *good* at it."

"Yes, you are." Of that, Caffrey was certain. Emotions and decisions whirled around her. Having inside knowledge of political events was irresistible. The security of the mansion, with the money and lifestyle, was available to her for the taking. But, could she handle Evan's brand of politics and his unquenchable desire for power? What of her suspicions and uncertainty about his involvement in the last few weeks of her life? And, why couldn't she stop thinking about the man in the hallway at Peachtree Towers?

A sharp pain seared the center of her skull. She groaned and rubbed her head.

"You know, you really are bothered too much by those headaches," said Evan. "Why don't you call the doctor tomorrow and see what he can do. Why be bothered with them?"

"I guess you're right. I *am* tired of it. I want it to be over. I don't care what meds I have to take."

"Hey, we could make some good memories and take that headache away." He touched the softness of her cheek and urged her chin upward. He kissed her lips, lingering. Waiting.

"That sounds like a wonderful idea," she whispered, noting the pressure in her head lightened. "Maybe you're the best medicine for these headaches after all."

He smiled and reclaimed her lips.

At the edge of a nearby wood, two men lay in complete camouflage, motionless except for occasional readjustments of their binoculars.

As a light went out in an upstairs room of the mansion in the distance, the younger man turned to the older one. "You going to tell him?"

The older man shifted his wad of chewing tobacco to the other side of his mouth. "Nope," he murmured without moving his eyes from the binoculars.

"Me, neither," said the other.

29

SYNAPTIC BATTLE

Caffrey sat up straight on the couch. The newscaster was relaying the hottest story of the day, a film clip of Vince Mansfield in a secret interview with Holly Dunn's sister, Ivy, proving he was alive and well, and still running the Underground.

"These recent rumors of kidnapping and 'bombs' at embassies are the work of a militant group," claimed the late senator's son, "and we suspect the Vhurruh faction has encouraged it." His demeanor remained poised and confident, though his piercing blue eyes flashed indignantly. Caffrey watched him, mesmerized, and began to feel ill.

"The Underground is a non-profit organization of concerned citizens that is forced to remain hidden because of rogue drones within the Alliance that have become corrupted. Left apart from their ruling queens, drones attempt to take over other hives. To them, we are just one giant hive. Important rulers from Hurratt are on their way here to clean up the controlling faction and restore the Alliance to its original mission. We are here to back them up, and we don't need bombs to do that."

As Ivy nervously asked Vince questions, unused to the role of reporter, the station newscaster muted their dialog and resumed his outline report. At a point where Vince Mansfield looked straight at the camera, the clip froze.

Bile threatened to force its way up Caffrey's esophagus. Her entire nervous system seemed to explode. She bent over, curled her arms protectively over her chest, and rocked to dissuade the assault. Fear closed in on her like a heavy blanket made of stone, so that she could scarcely breathe. She sobbed in terror and glanced fearfully around the room, not understanding. Suddenly, in horror, she knew. This sensation was familiar. She was *remembering*.

Instinctively, she fought to suppress the memories and gain control over the suffocating fear. But another side of her wanted to know. No matter how traumatic or gruesome, she yearned to see so it would be out, not hiding away in a moldy dungeon of her brain, capable of haunting her dreams. Sobbing and rocking, she opened her mind. Her body shook with the effort. Nausea made the room move. Would she be able to keep from vomiting in Evan's den?

Like a newsreel in 3D, she saw herself take a small object from a bleeding man. Moments later, a towering, obese man, her Vhurruh, in the skin of a human, touched her face and quickly whispered instructions as he placed wired crystals into the holes of her earlobes under her hair. She saw how he functioned in the human skin, felt the incredible, nerve-searing strain of his gelatinous body to keep the form. With a surge of ecstasy, she blended with his soul, felt his desperate mission to conquer the rogue drones and restore the Alliance. Lights reflected around her at The Brim. She was dancing with Evan. A deathly quiet scene at the front lawn of her apartment. A dark city street. Her heels clicked on concrete as she walked, alone and desperate, toward two girls. Finally, in a dismal, muddy alley near Five Points, a gun fired, and the impact threw her to the ground.

Tears poured down Caffrey's face as she relived the events. She kept her mouth open so her heaving lungs could breathe. It was as though she were in two places at one time: in the plush, dimly lit den at Evan's mansion, and in a dark, cold alley, writhing in pain. In horror she watched herself reach a tired finger into mud and blood and write a last message: *Get my body to the Underground.* She could hear her unknown Vhurruh's pleas for her to live, to keep breathing, to survive.

An entire, hidden life progressed before her like a dream in fast motion. Caffrey relaxed her body onto the sofa and closed her eyes. Her head throbbed without mercy at every pulse beat. It seemed an eternity she lay there, shaking, afraid other images might pop out at her through the walls. Slowly, carefully, she made her way to the medicine cabinet on the second floor. With every step, she began to loathe and fear the house that had been her home for nearly three weeks. Had it only been three weeks?

The name of every acquaintance raced through her mind like a computer search in a frantic effort to decide who to contact. She swallowed ibuprofen and lay down on her bed. *Her bed,* in this foreign place. Warring emotions danced around each other and vied for supremacy as she willed her body to stop shaking.

She knew now that she was more than a messenger; she was a decoy. Charlie had sent an earlier report from *Herrengae* to a queen on Hurratt months before. It was the second report, along with the star charts and coordinates to Veerinay, he had attempted to send when Telenex security had detected the unauthorized use of the forbidden transfer device and caught up with him. The disc Charlie had allowed the faction to believe in, to chase feverishly after, the one she had carried in her body, had bought the *Nekkai* delegation time.

Charlie had died so *Vrenenjurr* and the faction commanders would believe they still had time to further their plans, still had sole knowledge of the location of *Veerinay*. The date *Mhetrrian* gave to Caffrey was an additional decoy in case she was apprehended. The *Nekkai* Vhurruh had left the Hurratt solar system after they received *Herrengae's* first message. They were traveling in the only remaining functional mother ship captured from Zgeyyans. The *Farrekhren*.

Though Charlie had successfully completed the impossible, he and his linked Vhurruh had wanted to give *Nekkai* the star charts to the new planet in hopes of rescuing the stranded humans, and letting out the secret. The mission to Telenex had accomplished that.

Caffrey breathed and rocked and thought. There was one more task left to do. One more task—and she had no idea what it was. She could feel it in her subconscious memories, just on the other side of a door, an elusive ghost waiting for the right moment to appear. She had to make sure she survived, and was ready. She could lie low and wait. No, she quickly amended, she wanted out of that house.

Placating her body, forcing her emotions back into check, she began calculating her responses and movements. Her mind focused with crystal clarity.

Mhetrrian? She concentrated harder. *Mhetrrian!*

I hear. His warm mental projection poured into her mind, but it felt oddly distorted and stressed. *I only have moment.*

Are you okay? You sound strange.

I function, for now. You are open.

Yes, I know everything. I remember. Are you sure you are all right?

I am not well. I hope to be well soon.

Please take care of yourself. I could not bear to lose you.

She felt affection and gratitude from him. *Be careful. Be safe. Must go. Love and devotion, Amvezu.*

No wait! Prickles of fear raced up her arms and the sides of her neck. Illness. That was the strange energy she had felt weeks before. *Oh, no. Just like Herrengae.* She reached again for *Mhetrrian* but he resisted. She could detect the edges of his presence, but the wall he projected held firm. She sighed in frustration, but not defeat. A plan began to form in her mind.

Dipping her head into the hot spray of water, Caffrey reviewed the previous hour. She had carefully timed running out for the postman as he drove up in order to mail some pictures and small things of importance to Linda Brinks, a friend of Brian's from his former employer, who had often asked Caffrey if there was anything she could do after Brian's disappearance. A few changes of clothes were stuffed into a many-pocketed khaki jacket and placed under her bed. In the strange event that the landscapers working the front lawn were more than they seemed, carrying the jacket would not appear as odd as a suitcase.

Finding the Underground again would be the time-consuming part. With her knowledge of the secret symbol, she could search quilting sites and look for it. She debated driving to the restaurant to find the waitress that was wearing the symbol. First, she would send an email to several militia websites that would prompt the receiver to get the word to the Underground. She wished she could contact Father Daniels at his parish, but feared *Wysstangrr's* probe of her mind might have jeopardized the priest.

She had to admit the wisdom of restricting code names at Remote made perfect sense now. *Wysstangrr* would have limited his exploration of her memories to Underground members.

Withdrawing a significant amount of money could trigger any internal tags to her account, but a withdrawal of $200 cash would add to the $225 in her purse that Evan had given her. It wasn't much, but it would take her to North Georgia. Mama's house had been attacked. Laronda's had not. It was two hours away, but it was a place to start.

She found herself shivering, even in the steamy water. She dialed it hotter, and the slippery liquid served to cleanse her mind of jitters and fatigue.

Caffrey, time is moved. They arrive tay-nuniz.

What? Translate that to my time.

In five of your hours, near dark over your hive-land.

Tonight?

Both mother ships are here. It must be now. Tell others. Be warned. Take cover.

Why?

Some destroy what they cannot have. They fear punishment and reintegration. Do you know of 'Cry?'

Cry?

Remember, Caffrey. From a deep part of his mind a snippet, a mere moment in time, flashed into hers.

A quivering sensation filled Caffrey's chest at the revelation. *Yes. I see it. I remember.*

Wear the necklace. We can find you, too.
What necklace?
I go.
No! Dearest, wait!

As the window of thought slapped shut, Caffrey caught wisps of other minds having touched his. She felt certain he had closed in time and the others had not detected her. Immediately, she shut down, lest they follow the energy trail. She busied herself with scrubbing her body and blocked all thoughts from her mind but the soap and the scrubbing. After a few moments she relaxed. She was still careful not to think of *Mhetrrian*.

"Hey, sweetheart!" Evan rapped lightly on the door.

Caffrey slipped on the bathtub floor and grabbed for the safety bar. "Evan, you scared me half to death!" she screamed.

"*Sorry,*" he called out, not sounding repentant.

Caffrey could hear him stifling a mischievous chuckle. She gritted her teeth. He was not supposed to be home for at least two more hours. She groaned inwardly. She would have to go to the Governor's Gala after all. Being around Evan that long would be impossible. How could she do it? How could she pretend? Perhaps she could escape after the banquet, later, during the night. She would have to be very, very careful.

"Are you okay?" he called, when she did not berate him further.

"Yes. *No!*"

"I'm going to hit the shower, too. See you in a few, hon!"

"All right," she muttered.

Caffrey's mind whirled. Could she get to her car without him seeing her? Even if she made it, he could alert the police, and there would quickly be nowhere for her to hide.

If she was caught, what was to stop Evan from having her forcibly taken back to be reprogrammed? It wouldn't matter if she screamed or fought all the way; it wouldn't matter what she knew about him. She wouldn't remember it later. Suddenly, she realized the absolute power the faction had—and any human in league with them. She could be anyone they wanted her to be. She would never know the difference.

Seething with anger, she took her time getting ready. Though Evan tried to enter her room and speak to her, she locked the door and refused him on the excuse that she didn't want him to see her before she was completely ready.

Twice his cell phone rang while she put the finishing touches on her red hair, piled high with a few loose wisps at the sides. She thanked God profusely for giving Evan a diversion, and prayed for a way to escape. Finally, there was nothing else she could think of doing to herself. Regret overwhelmed her as she gazed at the beautiful green dress for which she had shopped nearly two days. How she loved it, and loathed it.

She inhaled resolutely and descended the stairs. Evan's voice echoed from the den, still engaged in an affable phone conversation. Laying her purse quietly on the hall table, Caffrey gazed across the vast, plush foyer, and repressed the desire to run to her car. Sadly, she raised her eyes to the magnificent ceiling paintings and enjoyed them one last time.

Evan stopped in the hallway. To Caffrey's surprise, he froze like a mannequin in a store window, his mouth slightly agape. Only his eyes moved. He blinked suddenly and recovered his normal suave persona. "You look absolutely fabulous. Am I ever going to be the envy of the party."

Caffrey mustered a smile. "Thanks. I think."

He swaggered toward her. She swallowed, desperate for something to divert him. Her heart pounded. Grasping the sides of her skirt, she whirled away from him. "The dress turned out better than I'd hoped, and...."

"Oh, it's not the dress," he interrupted with a short wag of his head. "I mean, the dress is great, but...it's the whole package." He mimed an hour glass with his hands.

Caffrey cleared her throat. "You look quite dashing yourself, sir." She feigned a desire to step back and look at him. The rugged tan of his handsome face added a touch of virility to the tall, lean picture of tuxedoed perfection. Caffrey turned to the hall mirror and fussed at an invisible stray hair. "I'm so glad the weather turned out great. It's going to be a beautiful night, don't you th...."

Arms grasped her waist and rotated her. Before she could protest, Evan's lips claimed hers possessively. For a fraction of a second she attempted to kiss him back, but had to stop. She pulled away and chuckled. "Hey! You'll mess up my makeup!"

"So? We have plenty of time. You can fix it again." He moved to demand her lips once more.

"Oh, no, you don't." Caffrey turned her body and giggled nervously. She gave him a firm push.

Evan laid a hand on his heart. "Always pushing me away—the man whose heart is captured."

"*You're...?*" Caffrey stopped short. She had almost blurted angrily, "You're captured?" She turned back to the mirror and bit her tongue.

"What?" He coaxed her to finish, closing the gap between them. He ran yearning hands along her shoulders and forearms.

Caffrey coyly stepped away from him again.

"Hey, are you okay?"

"Of course I'm okay," Caffrey sputtered. "We need to go!"

Evan tilted his head back. "Did something happen today?"

"No. Why?" Caffrey brushed at a curl she had worked on for 20 minutes, and willed her hands to stop shaking.

"You seem...tense."

"Oh, come on, Evan. Just because I don't want to ruin my makeup? Today's been...pretty dull. Hey, I thought you weren't going to be back until 4:30."

He examined her reflection in the mirror. "Bill got a call about his mother. She's real sick. They've got her down at Grady Hospital. He and his son were half the game, so Rob and I decided we'd finish another day. We thought about playing cards for a while at the clubhouse, but decided against it." She watched him scan her body with longing. "You sure you're okay?"

Caffrey rolled her eyes. "I'm *fine*. You know, this is a big change for me. I'm fixing to go to a banquet with the *Governor,* for heaven's sake, not to mention all the state senators and representatives. I don't know any of these people. I probably won't know half the subjects they bring up. I've got a lot to be nervous about. I want to look fresh."

"You don't need to be nervous." He relaxed somewhat with the explanation. "Stay right beside me, and you'll be fine. Smile one of those beautiful smiles, and everyone will be charmed."

Caffrey whirled. "Evan! This is the 21st century. I'd like to be appreciated for *more* than a pretty smile."

"Oh, here we go. What, pretend you're not pretty?" He waved his arms. "Pretend it doesn't matter? Did you spend two hours getting ready for nothing?"

Caffrey folded her arms. "There are plenty of people in politics who are not good-looking."

"True enough. But a tool is a tool, Caffrey. Use every one that you have. People are sexual beings first—at their most basic, animal level. *Always* remember that."

Caffrey wondered that she had ever seen him as anything more than a slim, sophisticated Attila the Hun. His phone conversation she had overheard that first night snapped into her brain with piercing clarity. She swallowed hard and averted her gaze. On the tip of her tongue were the accusations she longed to throw at him.

"So, if I ever have something go wrong with my face, or body, am I no longer a tool for you?"

He was visibly taken back. "How can you say that?" He stepped toward her, more angry than she had ever seen him. "Do you think that's what you are? Just a tool?"

Caffrey lifted her chin in defiance.

"I can't believe, after *all this,* that you don't see how much I care for you. What do I have to do, announce it on cable news?"

After a moment, Caffrey swallowed. "That would be good."

Staring at her in shock, he roared suddenly in respectful laughter. "You *are* tough, you know that? That's what I've always liked about you. You're sweet, but you catch me off guard. Well, Miss Hard-to-get, just to show you how much I *do* care, I have something for you. I want to be sure I don't lose you again."

From his tuxedo pocket he produced a rectangular, midnight-blue velvet box. Hesitant but enchanted, Caffrey slowly opened it, then gasped at its contents. A brilliant, rainbow-swirled opal glistened in a gold-filigree locket, encircled by alternating peridot gems and sparkling diamonds. Two smaller replicas of the locket were set in earrings beside it.

"Evan." She gasped. "It's beautiful."

"I knew you'd like it. Those green gems are your birthstone, you know—oh ye of little faith."

A nervous smile escaped her. "I know, I mean, I figured those were peridots. Nothing else is that same color green. Evan, it really is beautiful. I've always loved opals. This is the biggest one I've ever seen! And, it has such wonderful green and blue and pink in it. It's perfect with my dress."

He grinned and rocked on his heels. "I had it made when I heard about the dress you picked out."

Caffrey's smile dropped. "Heard about it?"

"You know...uh, when you told me about it that night."

So, you had me followed. "You got this made in one day?"

"Well, no, I actually inquired about the design a few days ago, and I had thought about rubies, but when you said you were going to find a green gown or die trying, I decided on these stones."

Caffrey swallowed hard and forced a stiff smile. "Thank you very much. So, why did you say something about not losing me?"

"Oh, this has a GPS locator, inside the locket. With a little help from some friends, and a few satellites, I can find you anywhere on the planet." His eyes twinkled with self-satisfaction.

The sensation of bitterly cold water trickled over Caffrey's skin. The chill carried to her stomach and she suppressed the sudden urge to vomit. Then she remembered *Mhetrrian's* cryptic message. *Wear the necklace. We can find you, too.*

"After that guy showed up at Martin's firm, I wanted to be sure nothing could happen to you. Well, don't you want to put them on?"

"Oh. Of course," she mumbled.

His hands rested on her neck as she fumbled with the latch. He took it from her and latched it himself, then pressed warm, eager lips into the side of her neck.

Breathe, she thought. *Just breathe. You can do this.*

She squirmed and moved to collect her purse. As she straightened, Evan's arms encircled her waist, but his hands did not stop moving. They roamed hungrily over her curves.

"Honey," she whispered, "the time for that is later. Let's go schmooze with the Governor." She took his hand firmly, and led him toward the etched glass doors.

"Promise?"

She answered in a low, sensual voice: "By then, I won't need to promise."

Evan's entire face glowed with anticipation.

During the drive she queried him regarding each attendee and what she should talk about with them. Since this was an area where he prided himself in excelling, it was easy to keep him talking.

They arrived at the hotel amidst dignitaries and wealthy patrons dressed in their finest. Police and security guards stationed at various points in the street and around the hotel maintained a pronounced atmosphere of control, which added to the air of celebrity. Caffrey saw several men and one woman in crisp SAAF uniforms enter the hotel. Anger welled within her, and she had to remind herself they were people—programmed, but still people.

After lingering in front of photographers long enough for Evan to be certain enough pictures had been taken, they entered the lavishly decorated hotel, and paused, to her surprise, for a retina scan.

Evan greeted every person they passed on the way to the banquet area. Charmed by Evan, as usual, many of the older women raised questioning eyebrows toward her, though not all unkindly. Their looks seemed to ask, "Is this the one?" With him at her side, Caffrey found it easy to mingle.

After brief remarks of appreciation and mention of several distinguished guests, a councilman offered prayer, and the meal thankfully began. Caffrey managed to down small bites of filet mignon and boiled shrimp, followed by a few spoonfuls of rice and steamed vegetables. When Evan joked she was eating like a bird, she smiled and whispered she was nervous about meeting so many new people and making a good impression, which pacified him.

Dessert was placed in front of her, and Caffrey managed several nibbles of what was surely the most delicious peach cobbler she had ever tasted; her jittery stomach would not allow more than a few bites. Instead, she downed her entire cup of hot tea and combed the room for the hundredth time, hoping against hope that she would recognize someone, anyone, from the Underground.

A woman introduced the Governor at the podium, and he spoke for half an hour, first on the various charities for which the proceeds of the evening would be donated, which drew several rounds of applause, and, second on his accomplishments over the past two years and his plans for the next. During his speech, those responsible for the banquet, and those deeply involved in the charities, which included Evan, nodded graciously as praise and applause were directed toward them. Caffrey smiled winningly, certain her cheeks would ache for days.

The Governor also spoke of his hopes for the future of Georgia, and briefly mentioned that federal funds had become available to expand a nearby military base with proper landing facilities and quarandomes to accommodate Vhurruh visits, and ended with sincere thanks to all who attended. After mention of a surprise special guest to arrive later, he bid everyone enjoy the door prizes, the dancing, and the remainder of the evening. The entire, shimmering audience stood and applauded him. Obligingly he waved and nodded, and he did not get far before being surrounded by those vying for his attention. The music began.

Immediately, Evan took Caffrey's hand, determined to make a first entrance onto the dance floor amidst smiles and admirers throughout the room. Many people took his lead, and the open area was soon filled with dancers. Caffrey could have kissed Mary for bullying her into the ballroom dance classes months before. Thankfully, Mary had not wanted to go alone.

Halfway through the song, an older gentleman asked for a dance with Caffrey, and Evan gracefully acquiesced, smiling with approval at the gentleman's importance. *Always political*, thought Caffrey. To her relief, the gentleman was charming, though his face was red from too much wine, and he became a bit too flirtatious. Still, she enjoyed the dance and his conversation.

While they clapped, another couple beside them recognized her partner and joyfully engaged him in conversation. Others offered her curious nods and handshakes of introduction. The musicians began a slow tune. The man and the couple headed for a table so they could renew their acquaintance. Caffrey politely excused herself to rejoin Evan. Before she reached him, a firm hand grasped her arm and whirled her about.

"May I have this dance, Mademoiselle?" The dark-haired, bearded man had an incredibly deep voice and thick French accent. While Caffrey stuttered a response, he deftly captured her hand and waist with strong, determined arms and drew her into the crowd of dancers. Caffrey gasped, moving out of sheer momentum. Though the man was neatly bearded and dressed in a luxurious black tuxedo, the fierce mahogany eyes were unmistakable.

"Mace?"

Losing his footing, Mace grasped her so tightly he nearly bruised her arms. "You remember me?"

"It *is* you! Oh, Mace." She broke into a tearful smile. Then she faltered. How desperately she wished to embrace him. "Keep moving," she pleaded, realizing they were standing still. Mace resumed the dance, though his arms were nearly shaking.

Caffrey stole a glance to her left. "Evan's watching," she whispered.

"I see him." His eyes narrowed, but the sharp look left his eyes as he scanned over her face with longing. Caffrey's heart lurched painfully in her chest as she realized he was actually blinking back tears.

"Oh, I want to hold you *so* badly!" she cried.

Mace closed his eyes and pressed his cheek against hers. "Caffrey." He spoke her name imploringly.

"Move further into the crowd," she urged.

With the appearance of casualness, he turned them several times between numerous bodies to block Evan's curious gaze. Unable to resist, Mace drew Caffrey tightly to him, nearly squeezing the breath out of her, his cheek pressed as close as he dared against hers.

"Oh, Mace." Caffrey sighed, furiously blinking back her own tears. His body felt wonderfully strong and fierce against hers. If only they could stay that way.

"I thought I'd lost you forever." He kissed her cheek.

With great effort, they slowly relinquished their embrace and continued moving further into the mass of silk and sequined bodies, loath to take their eyes from each other.

"What are you doing here?" Caffrey asked, fearful.

"I had to see you. We...watch you. Plus, there are friends of ours here. Something's up. The seers are all in a tizzy. They say something big is going to begin here, and get bigger."

"Vince and Gina are here?" Caffrey could barely contain her joy at the thought.

"No, not Vince. He's good at camouflage, but they're using retina and fingerprint scans. I didn't want to risk him. His leadership is too important. It's others you've never met. Sympathizers. They're well hidden and unsuspected. Politicians and rich people know how to play along."

Caffrey chuckled. "That sounds like something Vince would say. Are you *all* okay?"

Mace hesitated before answering. "Yes, we're fine."

"But, the explosion! Was anybody hurt?"

Mace swallowed. She watched his face change into the familiar mask to hide his pain. "Roadrunner, Mama, and Laronda were killed."

Caffrey gasped. "Oh, no." She squeezed her eyes shut as her stomach coiled into tight knots of grief. She had found joy in Laronda's house.

"Laronda was visiting Mama," Mace continued in a strained voice. "They were back in the sewing room. Laronda's grandfather had arrived at the Soul House, and he had a heart attack when he saw the explosion through the car window. He tried to run across the fields. He's still in the hospital. They say he'll make it."

Caffrey swallowed hard and breathed in short gasps as they kept sway with the music. And here she had been thinking of running away to Laronda's house, not knowing Laronda would not be there to greet her.

"Crow got shot in the leg. Panther was hit in the chest, and Moose got his legs burned. They're all recovering. A rocket hit the house," Mace continued in a strange voice. "Nearly burned the clothes off my body. We were still rolling down the stairs before the metal door closed. Everybody's out now. We're relocated. The SAAFs left after firing on the house. They showed no knowledge of the underground base. They never even went down. All they wanted was you."

Caffrey stared at him, her lips apart. "That's crazy, Mace. I didn't even have what they needed."

"Apparently...." His teeth clenched and his face flushed with rage. "*You* were what was leaked, not Remote."

Caffrey blinked, confused and overwhelmed. Comprehension dawned on her. "It was her."

"Yes." Breathing hard, he glanced carefully around the mass of dancers to divert the intensity of his emotions. "Sha-me called me from the Com when he saw you two leave during the drill. Then they spotted the dark cars and the vans on their way down the road, and changed the alarm to red. I was headed for the northeast corridor, the farthest branch. I ran up to the house. I knew something was wrong, but I had to make sure everybody was getting to the exits. I told Vince to take over. Crow and I, and the others, engaged the soldiers. Mama and Laronda were going to play innocent and try to stall in case the SAAFs came to the door. I kept yelling at them to go down inside, but they wouldn't. Once the firing started, they just hit the floor. Roadrunner got hit several times. When we saw the missile being launched, Moose grabbed Panther and I grabbed Crow. We all dove for the secret door. Mama and Laronda were in the front living room. They never stood a chance."

He cleared his throat and glanced about the room with righteous anger fixed on his face.

Caffrey blinked back tears.

"Mink's being held someplace where I can't get to her," he added in a deadly whisper. "She had volunteered to foster a relationship with Evan Parchek, to get intel. At first he seemed interested, but then he cut off contact with her. We think she called him that morning. She tried to tell me the whole setup was your idea, that you were trying to get back to Evan. That you two already had a relationship going, and she had figured it out. Gina said no way. Once we were clear, Barb and Gina and Groundhog meditated on the event. They told Vince what they saw. Groundhog's the one who gets 'motivations,' you know."

Caffrey nodded.

"Vince moved Mink someplace secret. Made two of my best friends promise not to tell me where she is." He gritted his teeth. "It's a good thing."

Caffrey moved with him in silence and held him as close as she dared.

He sighed. "It's the first time they've ever kept something from me."

Realizing they had slowed to nearly a stop, they both renewed their concentration on staying with the dance.

"How did you remember?" Mace asked, the edge of uncertainty in his voice.

"I saw Vince on TV. He was my trigger."

He blinked twice. "What do you mean? Who gave you a trigger?"

"*Nekkai*. Well, sort of. I was programmed by a Vhurruh drone they don't know is really in with *Nekkai*. His mind is amazing. Levels upon levels. And there's a group called the *Manarenen*. Part of a *Nemeygenyah*. It's a long story."

Confusion and suspicion flickered in Mace's eyes. "That's too perfect, Caffrey. Don't give me that look. Think about it. A Vhurruh that is secretly with *Nekkai* gets ahold of you, programs you, but makes sure you're not damaged. Now you're in cahoots with movers and shakers. What if that *is* the program? It would be so perfect. And now, you're in contact with the Underground. Heck, they could've made me right now, and I wouldn't know."

"Mace!" Caffrey hissed through clenched teeth. "You weren't there when the trigger hit. You weren't there when I almost threw up while remembering an entire hidden life. You weren't there when Evan was kissing me and I had to pretend I wasn't *revolted*."

Mace's hands tightened against her as though he wished they were around Evan's neck. His jaw constricted.

"The perfect program?" Caffrey continued, barely able to contain her rage. "My whole life was stolen from me. *You* were stolen from me. I've been through hell—twice! Mace, don't you *dare* start doubting me now, not after all I've been through. Don't you do this." Caffrey brushed a tear from her cheek and sniffed. "If you don't believe me, I am walking away right now. I swear to you, I am walking away right now if you do this to me. I will not...."

"Shhhh, shhhh," he soothed. "It's okay." He held her tight and swayed with the music.

Caffrey's breath came in rough gasps, and she felt her chin shaking as he hugged her close.

Mace kissed her ear and cheek and whispered, "It's okay, Princess. I'm with you. For better or worse, remember?"

Caffrey chuckled, then sniffed again. "We didn't get to marry." Suddenly, her face dropped. "Mace, I have things to tell you. But, first, do you remember I said once there was something about their ships I'm only supposed to remember at a special moment?"

He nodded with concern.

"I'm clear. I want you to understand. I'm clear of everything. Everything, except that. It's still there, buried. I felt you should know."

He searched her eyes. "I understand."

"I guess I'm only in danger if I blow my cover with Evan, or if I'm with another Vhurruh. Of course, that's not going to happen."

"Caffrey, don't you know there's a Vhurruh here tonight?"

"What?"

"A military chopper lowered the quarandome earlier. We had someone verify it with the detector to be certain. Their pheromones spread through the air every time they open the door. You weren't told?"

"Oh, no, the *special guest!*" Caffrey lamented. "I can't believe Evan didn't tell me!" She inhaled sharply. "Yes, I can. He didn't want me to know. He wants me reprogrammed." She grasped Mace's arms tightly. "Mace, whatever happens, don't leave here tonight without me."

"I won't. I promise." Desire to kiss so overwhelmed the two that they had to look away from each other. The song was nearly over.

"Mace, listen." She spoke fast. "*Mhetrrian* spoke to me earlier today. The arrival of the *Nekkai* delegation is tonight. The original date he gave me was false, to buy time if I was caught. They know the faction has a plan called 'The Cry,' where all SAAF officers will be triggered by a signal—I don't know what kind—and they'll all start shooting civilians. They tried to undo some of it, to alter the command, but it could still happen. It's to keep any *Nekkai* spies from moving on them to take back control in case they show up. If they get wind of *Nekkai*'s arrival tonight, they'll broadcast the signal immediately."

Shocked but quickly digesting the information, Mace asked, "What time?"

"I don't know. Soon. Maybe within the hour if I understand their time system."

"Is there anything else?"

"No, that's it. I think."

Mace exhaled. "With you I never know. I gotta get you out of here. If that Vhurruh reads this, it'll blow everything." A look of pure hatred came over his face, and Caffrey turned as a familiar long-fingered hand gripped her shoulder.

"My date's getting stolen away from me tonight." Evan was jovial, but there was a hint of challenge in his eyes. The last few notes of the song ended, and the dancers began to clap.

"Indeed, Monsieur," Mace responded in a perfect French accent, though his eyes were not in harmony with the amiable smile. "But she is a beauty, and we French cannot rrresist beauty."

Evan smiled and placed a possessive arm across Caffrey's shoulders. Caffrey watched Mace's body stiffen. "I don't believe we've met."

"Ah, Jean Martin," said Mace, and shook his hand firmly. "The Consul General of France asked me to come in his place. He is a great supporter of the Fulton County Foster Center."

"Oh, yes, I've spoken with him several times." Evan flexed his hand after the too-firm handshake. "Evan Parchek. State Senator, Alpharetta district. I support the Fulton County Foster Center as well, and the Atlanta and Cobb County Foster Centers. Also, the Atlanta Children's Home, the Alicia Parchek Special Needs Center, and the Harvey Rehabilitation Center," he boasted. "We're working on it now. Good to meet you."

"The pleasure is mine, Monsieur." The bearded man gave him a curt nod. "If you will excuse me." Before Evan could prod further, Mace disappeared through the milling bodies on the advent of another song.

Caffrey quickly fell into a monologue of delight over the Frenchman and her earlier dancing partner. If Mace could give such a magnificent performance, so could she. Evan barely had a moment to speak as they made their way back to the table.

"See," he gloated, "and you were all worried about being among dignitaries. I knew you would learn how to be charming, with the right teacher." He raised his chin in self-satisfaction.

Caffrey gave him a winning smile that was a complete fabrication, and turned toward the dancers returning to their seats. All she could think of was the man she had just left, how talented and quick-witted he was, how courageous and beautiful he was, and how desperately she wanted to run through the crowd, throw caution to the wind, and wrap her aching arms around him.

"I have a surprise for you," Evan announced in a teasing voice. "The special guest is one of the Vhurruh Commanders. A *Tarreken*, they call him. I've arranged a special meeting with the Vhurruh, all for you. I know how badly you've wanted to meet one. And...perhaps he can help with your headaches, and the memory trauma. They're good with things like that."

Caffrey steeled her nerves to keep from shaking. "Yes, I have wanted to meet one. But, why did you keep this a secret?"

"Honey." He took her hand, noting the suspicion in her eyes. "I wanted to surprise you."

I'll bet you did. She downed the remainder of a glass of wine and excused herself to the ladies' room. Evan called after her, commenting she would have to hurry, clearly dismayed she might be stuck at the back of the room. Caffrey knew that Vhurruh custom dictated no one move or walk around when a drone *Tarrek* was speaking at a special gathering, especially since it was a great effort for Vhurruh to speak human languages. It would be perfect.

"I'll hurry," she called back, then grabbed her skirt and shuffled quickly through the crowd. Pausing at the banquet room entrance, she heard an official begin the announcement of the special guest.

The rest rooms were down an adjacent hallway. Caffrey glanced around for Mace but was woefully disappointed. She kept walking.

Inside the rest room, Caffrey was nearly overrun by women rushing to get back to the ballroom. She washed her hands and tried to look in a hurry. Regaining her poise back in the hallway, she was unnerved to find a SAAF officer stationed at each end of the hall.

Trying not to appear the only person unconcerned with time, she scouted for exits at windows and doorways she passed. Would it be obvious if she chose another direction? Reluctantly, she neared the crowded entrance. People were clapping.

A familiar figure stepped casually out into the hall. Caffrey's heart raced. Mace smiled and nodded amiably in his role as Frenchman, then offered her an arm, which she gladly took.

"Why Miss Hanson, how are you?" A portly man beside them asked as he paused in conversation with several people also stuck at the entrance to the room.

It took Caffrey a moment to recognize him. "Oh, Dr. Roley. How are you?"

"I'm doing fine. How are *you*? Evan said you were having more headaches every day. Why haven't you come to see me?"

"I've...uh, been busy. And, really they're getting better now."

Mace tugged at her arm.

"We'll talk again later," she added. "I need to speak with…uh…Monsieur." The doctor eyed Mace as she turned away.

"Doctor, how are you?" Evan's voice called out behind Caffrey. She and Mace stiffened but kept walking.

"*Caffrey?*" Evan called to her in a puzzled voice.

This time, there was no escape. How could she explain heading away from the banquet with someone else?

"Be a hostage!" Mace commanded in her ear. With lightning speed, he pulled out a gun, placed it at her neck, and whirled to face Evan. "Try to stop me, and I'll kill her."

Several women screamed and ran.

Evan put out an imploring hand. "Don't hurt her."

Attendees scrambled in all directions like mice. The nearest SAAF officer pulled out a gun and yelled for Mace to drop his weapon.

Mace pointed his gun straight at the officer and positioned Caffrey directly in front of him. "Drop it!"

When the officer did not comply, Mace shouted, "Drop it! Or I start shooting people!"

"Do what he says!" Evan yelled at the SAAF officer.

Nearly choking her, Mace dragged Caffrey down a side corridor. Hysterical voices and frantic bodies ran from the banquet area and main hallway. The SAAF officer continued counter-commanding Mace to drop his weapon. Another officer appeared and aimed for Mace's head.

Evan continued to follow, adding his own commands to the SAAF officers not to risk hitting Caffrey. In a low, threatening voice he added, "Don't let that man out of this building alive."

Officers shouted to each other and into com units, vying for positions from which to shoot Mace and secure the building. One of them fell to the floor, and Caffrey noted a dart in his neck. Another dropped.

Mace continued to move purposefully down another corridor. It was easy for Caffrey to appear an unwilling hostage while Mace roughly dragged her and painfully gouged the barrel of the handgun into the flesh of her tender neck. His arms were so strong she could not have budged them even if she had been truly fighting. Choking and coughing, she grabbed at Mace's sleeve.

"I can't breathe!"

"You can breathe later!" he said through gritted teeth. He fired his gun down the corridor to force additional SAAF officers back.

A great weight encompassed Caffrey's brain, moving in like the leading edge of a thunderstorm. This was not the caring telepathic sensation she was used to. A Vhurruh voiced no statement of greeting, only exerted tremendous pressure and confusion.

To her surprise, two SAAF officers shook their heads. Mace groaned. He stumbled and struggled to keep standing. This was a powerful mind, more powerful than *Wysstangrr*. Terror gripped Caffrey at the possible discovery of her knowledge of *Nekkai's* plans. It could not, must not happen.

Detecting her fears, the Vhurruh probed deeper and chuckled at his unexpected treasure. Caffrey screamed as the bulk of the Vhurruh's mind assaulted her desire to hide secret knowledge.

Filling her with the sensation of searing pain every time she tried to divert him, the Vhurruh pushed her to remember why she was fighting him. *Who are you protecting? Who is so important? Let me see.*

Underground members surfaced, their faces popping up one by one as though she was viewing a photo album. Vince, Mace, Sharia, the Colonel.

Stop! Stop it! She strained to suppress the images. How could he do this without touching her? They were not linked! Caffrey could hear him mentally laughing.

With each revelation he pulled from her, he locked their minds tighter together and caused her to cry out again. He continued the skillful pounding until he glimpsed the faces of the linked humans from Remote—and the names of their secret Vhurruh.

Caffrey's soul screamed in horror, but there was no stopping him. For a split second, she was filled with sorrow and compassion for the Vhurruh on the ships, especially the *surranenn*, fighting against such a battering of their spirits for months.

Which surranenn? Show me.

Caffrey gritted her teeth and clenched her fists, fighting to suppress the names of every Vhurruh that was discussed by the links at Remote as being part of *Nekkai*.

No, you can't have them!

Mace was shaking her and yelling her name, but she was straining every muscle in her body with the effort to block the Vhurruh, and dared not focus on anything else.

Overwhelmed with physical and emotion pain projected by the Vhurruh to punish her, Caffrey frantically reached for the Vhurruh's mind and tried to pull information from him in a desperate attempt to put him on the defensive.

Amused at her admirable attempt, he allowed her to read him. Caffrey gasped. This was *Tarrek Vrenenjurr*, the most powerful mind of all the Commanders on the mission. She experienced his frightening, dictator-like need to control, his drive to succeed, his sarcastic arrogance at his ability to control her mind even from his remote position in the quarandome adjacent to the banquet room.

Oh, no. You have a teknaht. The device enhanced his mind like a synaptic megaphone. With it, he could envelope her consciousness and extract what he desired. He allowed her to see the portable amplification devices he had forced humans to create throughout the building, giving his machine unprecedented power. He chuckled at her probe of him and made no attempt to hide any information, as though this were a game.

Tiring of her inconsequential efforts to dissuade him, the crafty *Vrenenjurr* diverted Caffrey's mind into separate trains of thought, as his mind was capable of doing.

I am you. What are our secrets? What are our plans?

As though she were recalling a blip in time, the secret messages she had been given replayed with perfect recall, followed by the contents of the disc and the crystals.

Vrenenjurr delighted at each nugget he pulled out of her, like a child running wild in a candy store.

Caffrey was crying and sobbing. Her heart was breaking as she tied to pull back the information that spilled like water. *Vrenenjurr* redirected her thoughts to what she was wearing, who she came with, what she ate. While her mind pivoted between questions, he perused every memory she tried to protect, which caused the horrific scenes of Veerinay she had been given to appear like moving photographs.

Who gave these to you?

No! Nobody did. They're mine.

Gunfire pounded Caffrey's ears like never-ending fireworks, booming and crackling. She was peripherally aware that SAAF officers were falling and darting away, and that Mace and two other people were firing weapons together.

"Caffrey, come out of it!" Mace was shaking her violently, his voice desperate.

For a moment she tried to work her legs and stand, but the concentration on movement took energy from her grueling attempt to halt *Vrenenjurr's* progress into her soul, and she refocused her energy to thwarting him. She knew on some level that she was being roughly dragged by the arms, but she could not spare thoughts to address it.

Kaleidoscopes of images assaulted Caffrey so fast her brain became fractured and disoriented. Serenity snaked like humming electricity through her arms and legs, but she recognized the sensation and forced her body to stay in fight-flight mode.

Do not resist. Feel serene, relaxed, release your worries. Come with me....

Like a hand through gelatin *Vrenenjurr* reached into Caffrey's confused mind, and touched her meeting with the *Manarenen*, surprised by the hidden elders assisting *Wysstangrr*.

"*Nooooo!*" Caffrey screamed, mentally and verbally.

She nearly lost her dinner as Mace flipped her over his shoulder and continued shooting to hold the SAAF officers at bay. "Scorpio! Now!" he yelled. An explosion thundered with ear-splitting resonance, followed by another, causing the entire building to shake around them. Water immediately fell on Caffrey.

Mace was carrying her.

He is your attacker, isn't he? He is hurting people, he is dangerous. We need your protection. Protect the people in the hotel.

Nooooo! I won't listen! Caffrey cried. Snakes were crawling over her body as the sprinkler system continued to shed water over her skin. *Vrenenjurr* intensified the sensation. Caffrey squirmed to get the snakes off, only to find more were falling on her.

Mhetrrian! Caffrey screamed with all her might. Instantly, the young Vhurruh was with her, groggy and disoriented as if newly awakened. Swiftly detecting her terror and the intrusion of *Vrenenjurr*, he viciously attacked with the ferocity of a jealous male, hurling synaptic sensations that felt like bolts of electricity.

Get away from her! I will kill you!

The jolt nearly exploded Caffrey's brain. It had not occurred to Caffrey that her gender would be a factor, but she remembered even in the midst of mind-searing turmoil that Vhurruh society was based on one female to many competing drones. Though he was not yet of official drone age, *Mhetrrian's* instinct was powerful: protect the queen at all cost.

Surprised by *Mhetrrian's* presence and invasion, the older Vhurruh retreated for a split-second, then retaliated, embroiling the three in a battle for control on a level of synaptic energy so deep and sophisticated, that Caffrey nearly lost all sense of herself.

Astounded at the incredible ability *Mhetrrian* possessed, Caffrey attacked with him. She *was* him. His intentions and emotions she mirrored and amplified. They were powerful.

Other minds joined the fight like an avalanche rushing and expanding into a fierce, tumbling wall of energy. Minds poured into the connection, some workers, some drones, following their links to *Mhetrrian* in his *Nemeygenyah*. Most were in a heightened state of alarm, as if somewhere, in their physical circumstances aboard a mother ship, they were fighting to survive against imminent discovery as well as attempting to augment *Mhetrrian* and Caffrey against *Vrenenjurr's* mechanically enhanced and vicious mind. *Vrenenjurr* had forced links with many of these, and now they had access to his mind.

One of the drones sent a sudden, piercing instruction into the link, alerting the *Nemeygenyah* members that he had acquired the *teknaht* aboard the Blue mother ship. *Mhetrrian* and his *Nemeygenyah* merged together into a greater, stronger force, letting go of any need to hide or be separate. The sudden fullness became an eruption.

The collective threw their entire enhanced, synaptic weight against the older Vhurruh and attacked the primordial essence of his brain with high-pitched, searing frequencies of light and sound waves on such an otherworldly level that Caffrey lost all sense of space or time.

Like a swarm of bees, they dove into every emotion, every memory, every fear *Vrenenjurr* possessed, with stinging precision. Caffrey understood it, saw it in the mind-link of the sect, and felt its wonder, its design, its deadly force.

Enmeshed in the collective of souls, Caffrey believed herself one of the Vhurruh and reveled in the brilliance of her race. This was how they had defeated the Zgeyyans years before. Led by the powerful queens, they had struck the Zgeyyans with synaptic pain, controlling them to land their ships, then exploding their brains.

Crumbling under the assault, *Vrenenjurr* attempted to separate parts of his own mind to contact others for help, which he had not immediately done out of overconfidence, but *Mhetrrian* zoomed in to block the tight channel, pulling every resource of psyche he possessed to such a strain that Caffrey felt it killing him, and her as well. Knowing the fate of Earth and the arriving emissaries, none in the link debated the issue. They would die if they had to.

Something phased in Caffrey's brain. They were all outside their physical bodies now, a mass of whirling, struggling energy, focused on a single goal. With one final, scorching surge from the *Mhetrrian-Caffrey* link of united minds, *Vrenenjurr* let out something of mental-soul scream, and darkness engulfed them all.

30

A CHOICE

Re-sensing her body, Caffrey marveled at what a heavy, cumbersome vessel it was to house her soul. Her skeleton possessed such gangly, bone-heavy limbs, ones that would not cooperate. Blurred shapes and colors began to assault her pupils. Gravity held her in place. She had never truly appreciated its necessity. A Vhurruh body was so flexible, so versatile, so *meaty*....

And she was alone. So alone in the universe without the other minds touching hers.

A strange vibration was rocking her. It registered that she was in the backseat of a car. Mace was beside her. His black hair and tuxedo were soaked. He appeared backward until she realized he was turned around and scanning out the back window with alert, tense eyes.

Caffrey closed her eyelids and called. *Mhetrrian.* She winced as the telepathic attempt caused incredible pain.

No response.

No other mind spoke to her. Were the others unconscious, or could the unthinkable have happened? She dared not press further. It hurt too much, and she feared the answer.

Rhythmic pressure and churning assaulted Caffrey's midsection. She was going to throw up. Knife-like stabs in her ears and skull throbbed without mercy and distorted her sense of motion. She kept wondering why her arms and legs would not respond to her brain's request to move. The car swerved, and her torso slid on the seat. She groaned.

"Caffrey? Hey, you okay?" asked Mace relieved and fearful.

Caffrey swallowed and concentrated on moving her mouth. With effort, she was able to mutter, "I gotta throw up."

"Oh, boy. Jimmy, we'd better pull over. There's some room up there to the left. Wait, let's get under that bridge."

"We'll still be easy to spot!" the young man in the front seat warned.

"Yeah, but we'll be real sorry if she throws up in this car."

"All right, no problem," Jimmy agreed. Caffrey felt the car veer to the left and screech to a stop.

Mace cradled Caffrey's head out the back door while she vomited. Jimmy offered him a couple rumpled napkins to wipe her face. Ten car-filled lanes of I-85 traffic whizzed by with a terrific roar, rocking the car and whipping dust around them. Red and pink hues tinted the windows as the sun descended beyond the horizon.

"Princess," Mace queried, "do they know everything?"

Caffrey straightened herself in the seat before answering, not quite capable of doing two tasks at once. Even so, her movements were jerky and delayed. The electric responses to her muscles would not completely connect. Jimmy swerved suddenly, then apologized as he hurled the car back into the fast lane. Something cold fell to the side of Caffrey's neck. Evan's necklace.

"Almost," Caffrey answered finally. She did not offer an additional explanation, first because it took too much effort, and second because she had to think, and thinking was unbearably painful. *Mhetrrian* had said he could find her with the necklace, too. But, as damaged as he surely was, what good could he do?

"The necklace," she tried to mumble.

"What?" asked Mace.

"Necklace...locator...GPS."

Mace cursed loudly. He yanked the necklace from her neck. "Jimmy, we gotta get rid of this. We're being tracked."

"Throw it out the window!" Jimmy exclaimed. "Wait! Let's find another car—a truck bed or something—and throw it in."

"Great idea, but if I miss, it hits the road. Let's stop at a gas station or something. Nope, I ain't waitin' that long." Mace opened the window and threw out the necklace.

"Oh, my god!" Jimmy shouted, his eyes bulging in the rearview mirror.

Mace whirled to look behind him. "Man, two seconds—*two seconds,* and he would have had us."

"What is it?" Caffrey managed to ask.

"Scout ship."

Tires squealed around them. "Watch out, Jimmy. Stay cool, stay with the flow."

"Everybody's stopping! No, no, no!" Jimmy yelled in an effort to guide the car.

"I need to see," said Caffrey weakly, and she reached for Mace's shoulder. With one strong arm he lifted her to shaky knees on the seat. His face was lined with worry as he watched her marionette-like attempt to move. She could feel her head bobbing strangely as her neck muscles faltered.

She squinted past him at a thin beam of violet light that emanated from a small, circular scout ship hovering over the emergency lane where the necklace had landed. Had it not been so unnerving, it would have looked beautiful, with the last pink rays of sun glinting off the ship and darkness closing in.

The sleek, smoky-gray hull shone like the surface of a compact disc. The violet light snapped off, and the vehicle turned. As though pulled by a magnet, it began to skim over the traffic, heading toward Caffrey. Two helicopters followed.

"Get in the floor!" Mace commanded.

With every muscle jerking fiercely, Caffrey crouched into a frog position. She felt a jacket drop onto her. She also felt something else: a tingling energy.

"Got your guns hidden, Jim?"

"Yep."

"Make sure they're beside anything hot. Doubt if it will help."

Ten torturous seconds later, Caffrey felt her limbs lighten, as if her bones had disappeared.

"We ain't workin'!" Jimmy screamed. His foot pumped at the floor.

Caffrey could hear the screech of tires and the horrible crunch of vehicles impacting beside them.

"Get past that truck!" Mace ordered.

"The motor's goin'. They're *doing* somethin', man!"

Mace cursed again. "They ain't takin' me alive." He cocked a gun and grabbed another from under his feet. Suddenly, he roared in protest.

Caffrey sat up, alarmed.

"Get down!" Mace ordered.

Caffrey could see he was having difficulty moving his arms, struggling as though he were under water. Their vehicle weaved and swerved. More cars slammed into each other around them, their crashes audible even above the roar of the helicopters.

Their car pivoted and came to an abrupt stop.

After hitting the window power button without response, Mace smashed the window beside him with his weapon. Straight up at the hovering ship he fired. The thunder of gunfire was deafening. Sirens wailed and blue lights flashed across his arms as a SAAF vehicle screeched to a stop in the emergency lane.

Caffrey groaned as her body lost its sensation of solidity and lifted from the floor. Before she could speak Mace's name, her body phased, bereft of weight or mass, and disappeared from existence. Certain she was dying, she screamed, but no sound came out.

Outside the roof of the car, she became solid again, still clearly defying gravity.

She could hear Mace scream, "No! You can't have her!" A volley of weapons fired around her, but her only option was to concentrate on not throwing up again.

Floating haphazardly, she found herself rising in a hazy beam of distorted energy. The slightest jerk of her arms or legs propelled her in odd directions inside the beam, ever upward. Droplets of water floated around her. She could not remember how her hair had gotten wet.

As if approaching a vacuum cleaner, she was sucked into an open black maw in the side of the scout vessel. Landing on a cold, dull gray floor, she slid to a stop as the energy source altered with a faint hum and variance in pitch.

Before she could sit up, a ten-foot long, glistening, silver-gray Vhurruh lifted her with its upper arms and deposited her into one of four elongated, dish-like couches. With the touch of a button, she adhered to the couch as if she were magnetized. Two of the other four couches were occupied by Gray Vhurruh, similar in size, deeply locked in concentration on the screens and controls in front of them.

We have the queen. Exiting to canyon. Caffrey heard the Vhurruh's telepathic broadcast. The ship lurched to breathtaking speed. All the organs in Caffrey's body shifted into her pelvis. Her lungs tightened so that no sound came out of her mouth when she screamed in fright.

She forced her eyelids to open. A glance toward the three Vhurruh showed their silver underbellies and leg fins in a slow ripple like unset gelatin. Along their backs shimmered brilliant dark-gray mantels, with the outer edges sporting vertical black, orange, and white stripes, resembling capes waving under water. They lacked the hairy neck mane and long, face whiskers of *Wysstangrr,* and were less than half his size. Their eye extensions sat tight against their heads like half-submerged bronze marbles.

After several seconds, the ship and Caffrey's body disappeared, and she lost all sensation of time or gravity, which was beginning to feel familiar. The pressure of movement had evaporated. A moment later, they regenerated into solid matter and slowed to a stop.

Providence Canyon. Caffrey's mind formed the words as she glanced at the screens. The white, sandy cliff formations were unmistakable. She and Brian had traveled here when their group of friends had decided to visit every state park in Georgia.

The three Vhurruh focused their attention on her.

Have we the honor to link with you? They slid toward her. Stiffening in fright, she felt them open their minds so she could perceive their intentions, which held no malice. Something about a ship, something they needed to know. They were of *Nekkai.* *Mhetrrian* had asked them to assist if he was compromised. A sense of urgency and worry colored their emotions. They waited for her permission.

Dare she believe them? They were Grays. Then again, *Wysstangrr* was a Gray, and he was a hidden *Nekkai.*

As she debated, she noted that for once, someone was giving her a choice. They would not beg her. They would not force her. She alone could choose.

Did she really have a choice? What they needed from her was so important they nearly shook with anxiety. Still, they waited.

Caffrey took a deep breath. *Yes,* she consented, praying she was making the right decision. Silver arms extended and touched her.

Like an invasion into the womb of her soul they reached, comforting and curious at first, then intent on their purpose. Softly, noting her synapses were weakened, the three Vhurruh minds shot past all her masks, fears, and memories, to the core of her being, the pure spark of her life force. Indescribable was the rush of ecstasy in which she-they floated in the quick fusion of souls. They were an etheric primordial soup rippling with joy under the life-giving breath of creation, happy to be part of each other for one brief moment before separating into individual entities.

Caffrey's entire existence was their united hearts, minds, energies, as if this was all she was, and all else around her was feeble illusion. So blissful and natural was the experience that, were it not for the religious discipline of the Vhurruh, Caffrey would have stayed indefinitely, unconscious and uncaring of time, content in the ecstasy of bodiless existence.

This was what *Mhetrrian* had done, plunged into her soul, planted a *m'hye*—a fusion of psycho-neuro connections—a private link for all time. Now, the four were linked together in a similar unbreakable, unreversable bond, one that Caffrey now understood would always be there, a touch away, for as long as each lived.

The three Vhurruh were overjoyed at the privilege of linking with her, a human queen. Their humble joy felt almost dignified, compared to the passionate, driving emotions of *Mhetrrian.* Then Caffrey realized these were *surranenn,* workers, asexual hermaphrodites who did most of the actual labor in a hive.

Flashing in hundredths of a second while they remained open to her, Caffrey viewed the *surranenn's* birth from their larval sacs, lessons with their hive mates, their queen-mother linking them to her, bonding with their drone-fathers, and their connection to secret *Nemeygenyah* elders and spiritual training. A connection that included forbidden links to Blue *surranenn* and to *Mhetrrian,* a young Blue drone. The Vhurruh jointly steered her from this, since time was of the essence. It mattered not to Caffrey. She went where they led her.

Swiftly, they shared their knowledge of three mother ships occupying the solar system. The original two, the *Hovuret* and the *Gherrenfae,* were still in orbit around Earth. They had come from the *Hovuret* which held many Blue Vhurruh still in stasis because they had refused to join the faction. The *Gherrenfae* carried the bulk of the Gray dissidents.

The third, the *Farrekhren*, lay hidden behind Jupiter, concealing an entourage of *Nekkai* members from Hurratt, still in stasis so their minds could not be detected. Three queens rested on board. Caffrey flinched at the visualization of the queens, who were twice the size of the drones, for she had seen a large drone. The queens were shielded with special metals and electromagnetic fields, since any fertile drone could detect the proximity to their female energy and telepathic vibrations. The incredible rush of information was conveyed in mere seconds.

The three Vhurruh waded through recent details of Caffrey's life and focused directly on the final hidden message from *Mhetrrian*—the trigger to release the incoming Vhurruh from stasis. It was thought-encrypted, and they telepathically chanted the Vhurruh syllables to open the sealed pocket of instructions. Carefully, their minds withdrew and released Caffrey.

She sat up, hobbled shakily to the control panel, and began keying in a sequence of numbers, pressing unfamiliar symbols. Searching the panel, she grasped a thick, dish-shaped object connected to a long rubbery tube of light connections—the *teknaht.*

The dish was small, no bigger than her palm, yet she felt the pulsing energy waiting like captured lightning, ready to zap through space and time toward another mind.

Against her forehead Caffrey pressed the sticky *teknaht*, with no consideration for the state of her sensitive brain. She focused on the *Farrekhren* and the three queens, until she was certain she had made the connection. With great care she thought eight notes and Vhurruh words into the mother ship's receiver, wired to the head of a single drone male on the incoming ship.

A slight backwash of energy resonated from the device, for which Caffrey was not prepared. Her fragile synapses were so sensitized and injured the effect was compounded. She dashed the slimy *teknaht* away from her skin and fell straight backward. The Vhurruh caught her and laid her carefully on one of the couches.

The Cry has gone out, said one of the Vhurruh. *All is detected.* Caffrey cringed as she heard through the collective mind their drone *Tarrek* advising them, and all in their unit, of the alarm signal being cast by a single faction scout ship. Agitated by

Vrenenjurr's interrupted call for help, the scout ship had launched away from the *Hovuret* into a wider patrol, and detected the incoming mother ship.

Is there anything we can do? Caffrey whispered with her weakened mind.

No, only the queen-mothers can force the rogue drones to contact their linked ones and control them.

Caffrey waited, listened, and prayed. Thoughts of Mace surfaced. SAAF vehicles had been gathering around him. They would now be shooting randomly and without restraint at everyone—at him. He had mentioned several weapons in the car, but how long could he and Jimmy hold out? She was confident of his resilience; however, stuck on a ten-lane, downtown highway, there was nowhere to run.

Plagued with guilt, Caffrey realized that from inside buildings, from vehicles, out of helicopters, even at military bases, programmed SAAF officers all over the planet were killing soldiers and civilians randomly. The panic, screams, and carnage were sure to be horrific; yet, here she was, thinking of one person.

The three Vhurruh turned to face a direction upward and east. Caffrey followed their awareness. Numerous drones, guards, and *surranenn* on the hidden ship were waking and linking swiftly with each other.

Hidden members of *Nemeygenyah* began linking together like stars appearing in the night, expanding to a consciousness that was calm and focused, dragging Caffrey with them. The drone Captain, *Arragall*, whom Caffrey had awakened, called upon links of *Nemeygenyah* sects from Hurratt itself, faint connections through time and space, but intact on a level of etheric communication for which Caffrey was certain humanity had no name.

Such powerful, disciplined minds, she thought in awe as she flowed with them, carried like driftwood on a growing ocean wave. Though their gargantuan bodies were sluggish to wake, their minds were lightning-quick.

Each *Nekkai* member called upon secret *m'hye* connections with each other across the mother ships, to every cruiser and scout ship, and finally to Earth, to connect with their human links.

Gathering strength and focus, building to a fierce power, the unified minds of innumerable Vhurruh and several thousand scattered *Nekkai*-loyal human links, nine of whom Caffrey recognized from Remote, reached out like flashes of lightning and touched the mind of every other Vhurruh around the planet one by one. Any resistance was an instant battle for supremacy. Most rogue *surranenn* needed little persuasion, being used to compromising to the will of the hive, but it took many *Nekkai* Vhurruh to occupy the mental battle for each faction Commander, which quickly split their defenses and began to weaken the immense allied mind.

Only the telepathically strongest Vhurruh had been sent on the original mission, including the faction leaders, and they had no intention of going quietly. Their fear of losing their self-imposed dominion, of not being able to make choices—even unethical ones—without detection, flared to a whirling, defiant storm. Caught off guard they would have been easily taken, but the few seconds of warning from the outer perimeter scout ship had given them time to link themselves into a mind-unit of their own, enhanced by the *teknaht* devices available to them. The two sides waged war, gathering recruits until all Vhurruh were in the battle, some changing sides to join the *Nekkai* link, relieved that they could.

A great power blasted through the links, encompassing the *Nekkai* collective and the entire battle it engaged. Caffrey reeled at the incredible force of the three fully awakened queens, feeling as though she had been physically flattened. Their touch was electrically charged beyond anything she could have imagined. With focused mental energy the queens reached out for the *m'hye* connections of every Vhurruh in the solar system. It was then that Caffrey understood. The queen-mothers held *m'hye* connections with every one of their offspring and with the drones of their hives.

Even though the Gray queen, *Mrennah*, had died, the rogue drones, led by *Vrenenjurr,* had forced links with the remaining crew in order to control them. There was no one that was not mentally connected to the others and therefore all were accessible to the queens.

Like wayward children, the faction members acquiesced as they were detected and caught one by one. There was no escape. They all knew from experience, it was futile to resist.

Caffrey could feel their shock and dejected surrender. They had not considered the possibility that any queen-mother, let alone three, would leave the home planet. The risk of interdimensional travel causing infertility had long been considered too great to allow any queen to venture into space. These queens were nearly past their prime and willing to take the risk.

To Caffrey's surprise, one of the faction drones, *Mekrenzett,* bolted suddenly, with a piercing mental roar, enhanced by a hidden *teknaht* device. The queens, drawing on the collective, filled the rebel drone's mind with searing wails of sound, and flashes of psychic energy powerful enough to kill. At the breaking point, the drone was soothed and redeemed with strokes of love and care, lest his mind be too damaged to follow his hold on his human links, since he had programmed more of the SAAF humans than *Vrenenjurr.*

Bathing *Mekrenzett* with persuasive affection was a good thing, Caffrey concluded, based upon a quick flash of emotion from one of the stronger-tempered females, *Ghissella*, from whom permanently silencing him was briefly considered.

With a great, triumphant surge, the unified queen-drone-human collective reached into the cowering faction minds and followed their *m'hye*-connections to each programmed SAAF officer scattered across the continents. The hive queens, accustomed to communicating with thousands, easily encompassed the numbers and gave a calm, instant command to cease firing all weapons, and surrender.

Caffrey felt her shoulders physically relax. The shooting, all over the planet, had stopped.

Unification does not mean absorption of self-distinctness, the joint female mind stated to the entire collective. *It is merely the ability to function as one when needed, to stop an enemy that would destroy us, to stop wars between hives, to address a wayward queen-mother lest she infect her hive and destroy peace, and to heal the mind that is disturbed, the heart that is wounded.*

Never again will we allow a mission without a senior queen on a vessel to guide and control. Your reign is over. Peace will be restored.

After a moment, several faction drone *Tarreken* spoke up, though Caffrey heard only two dominant voices. They asked for more queens to be born into the hives, to create smaller, more diverse hives, where a smaller number of drones shared a queen. Caffrey could almost hear the hush as the queens conferred with each other over the suggestion. The three pulled away to keep their deliberations private.

Caffrey listened to the amazement and speculations wafting through the collective. These were modern *Nekkai* queens who bred young queens often and tolerated their presence in nearby extended hives. *Non-Nekkai* queens would never debate such a radical change in their society

Your requests are heard and considered, addressed the three females. *At a future time, the Council of Queens will meet and discuss these entreaties.*

For now, while we reign within the Earth system, limited distinctiveness will be allowed within agreed safety parameters. For those drones who compromised peace, separation will not be permitted. Breach of cohesion will be instantly disciplined.

The agreement with humans has been violated and must be restored. Veerinay is available for a new hive, but drone tyranny has created many impediments. Our needs remain. If humans agree to share the resources, the new planet will be jointly

governed. A young queen will be planted. We meet again at Earth's moon rotation to discuss further. That is all.

Though Vhurruh thoughts flitted through Caffrey's awareness, she felt the emptiness of isolation as the multitude of minds retreated. The connection remained open like a megalithic conference call, with many small conversations buzzing in the background. Vhurruh and their links were giddy with the freedom to converse and reconnect.

About Mhetrrian.... she asked the three Vhurruh with her. *Is he all right? I did not sense him in the link.*

While Caffrey held her breath, the three communicated with various minds before answering. Caffrey could not travel with them; her mind had become too tired and weak.

Vinrrahi, the queen-mother, is reaching for him now, as he is her offspring, the three responded. *Our queen-mother, Ghissella, will connect us.*

Oh Lord, not her, Caffrey thought to herself.

After a moment, one of the *surranenn* replied. *He sleeps. He will take long to recover. She says he may yet survive.*

Caffrey's heart constricted in grief. *May yet survive?* At least he was not dead. It was little comfort, but it was something to hang onto.

I am so glad. He saved me, she responded. She wished she had the nerve to thank his mother personally, but after hearing horror stories about the unpredictable reaction of queens to perceived female intrusion, she decided against it.

Yes, he sacrificed much, the three *surranenn* agreed. She could sense that they considered *Mhetrrian* quite noble for saving his human queen. Though, with complete lack of emotion or prejudice, they questioned his decision to place the success of the incoming mother ship into a human's mind for safekeeping. Caffrey snorted and smiled sideways at their practical logic.

You're a little late on that judgment, guys, she thought to them.

She may accept you, they spoke with excitement. *You need to be announced.*

Before Caffrey could question them, their thought patterns changed, and a pressure nearly knocked her off the couch. She grasped the sides to steady herself, feeling the room spin.

I am Ghissella. I allow Vinrrahi to speak through me. The hot-tempered queen might as well have used a megaphone at Caffrey's ear, for the pain her mental voice caused. Tears fell from Caffrey's squinting eyes. As *Ghissella's* presence dissipated, a second voice emerged.

In silence *Vinrrahi* scanned Caffrey with such power that Caffrey almost lost consciousness. She could hear the queen assess her as fragile, sincere, intelligent, loyal, minimally psychic, non-aggressive—nothing to be jealous of. Caffrey was affronted by the quick assessment, not certain whether to be relieved or insulted. This was most certainly a female, regardless of the wisdom and strength behind the personality.

My gratitude flows to you for your assistance, Vinrrahi offered, sending a positive vibration that caused Caffrey's head to hurt less. *Vinrrahi's* thought patterns were so specific, Caffrey was not sure she even heard language. A purring sound emanated from the three *surranenn* in reaction to the queen's transmissions through their *m'hye* links.

It was my privilege to help, Caffrey answered with sincerity.

May you have a request, it will be considered.

Surprised, Caffrey moved to decline out of politeness, but she caught herself. To request anything of this powerful individual was unthinkable, but having learned not to let such opportunities in life go by, Caffrey strengthened her resolve.

Yes. I wish to know of Mhetrrian when he recovers. He is dear to me. He sacrificed so much to give me the code to awaken you. I have a human, a drone, who may have been harmed in the held ones assault. I wish to find him again. She sent *Vinrrahi* a visual of Mace. *If he is wounded, any healing ability you possess would be greatly appreciated. And, my human friends who risked their lives daily to fight against the rogue faction all this time—for them to be recognized by our governments, and by yours, for their efforts, and to be considered in all future plans for the Earth-Hurratt Alliance and the new planet, would be a fruitful choice, for humankind and for Vhurruh.*

Caffrey felt an inward smile from *Vinrrahi* at her numerous requests. The queen found it audacious of her and therefore commendable. Caffrey's requests were pointedly for other beings and not personally for her own advancement or power, which the queen also found to be meritorious.

We shall meet again, you and I, was the answer *Vinrrahi* gave her. *May you produce many, and rule wisely.*

31

UNITY

Vince Mansfield was announced, and cameras began flashing. Caffrey's feet ached in her new dress shoes. Time spent with the Underground in hiking boots, and later at Evan's in slippers, had spoiled her feet for good. The ceremony at the United Nations building was the culmination of an entire morning of meetings and private conferences. A Blue and a Gray drone *Tarrek* waited in separate quarandomes to the right of the main podium, a structure that had been built into the wall of the General Assembly Hall a year and a half earlier for the original Alliance ceremony.

Caffrey felt it should be one of the queens who should address the assembly. However, they were so large they could not fit into any known quarandomes, which was fine with the drones and the guarding *kurnistarr* who had caused a ruckus when the bold Gray queen, *Ghissella,* actually considered it.

Others had argued that the drones were the true salesmen of the species and therefore could win the hearts of human observers.

In the end, a Blue and Gray drone *Tarrek* from the *Farrekhren*, untouched by the faction, were chosen. Their slick, neon-blue and silver-gray colors, offset by black, yellow, orange, and white stripes, shone brilliantly under the many lights focused on the platform and the two misty quarandomes.

Vince stood tall and proud, with dark bags underneath his eyes from being up for nearly 48 hours, engaged in debriefings and negotiations, both human and Vhurruh. He had traveled by airplane and scout ship alike. Still, there was a triumphant sparkle in his eye and victorious lilt to his step. Caffrey was thrilled for him.

Determined and calm, he laid his hands on either side of the podium and spoke with slow distinctness, pausing every few words for emphasis.

"Ladies and gentlemen, distinguished guests, representatives of Earth's nations, and representatives of Hurratt's hives: Most of you are aware of the unfortunate events of the past few days. I have been asked to speak to you on behalf of those who have been voiceless for some time...both Vhurruh, and human."

He appeared surprised when the crowd broke out in applause. Caffrey knew the positive response moved Vince by the twitching of the corner of his mouth, but he maintained his air of dignity. A lump formed in Caffrey's throat. She had been granted a seat in the assembly but had refused any acknowledgment of her contribution to the success of the *Nekkai's* overthrow of the faction. It was enough that her request of Queen *Vinrrahi* succeeded in Vince's being chosen to address the nations of Earth at this moment. If only all her requests had been granted.

"What has taken place is a tragedy for us all," Vince continued soberly, "but one that we have *jointly* conquered. Conquered by determination, integrity, and honor...both from Vhurruh, and from humans.

"Our future is, firstly our home, Earth, and secondly, the vast universe before us. I believe together, we can explore new worlds and create unlimited opportunities for ourselves, our races, and our children. But, let us not forget that harmony begins at home. On Hurratt, a great movement began some years ago to unify all races in common goals and knowledge, while also addressing the concerns of individual hives. It is a great accomplishment for them and for their many societies and cultures, and I applaud them. May they rise to the challenges of a new generation of ideas.

"On Earth, we, too, have taken steps over many years toward similar goals, in our re-dedication to alliances between nations, and our recognition that all cultures and religions have the right to co-exist peacefully within a framework of equality, safety, and opportunity for all.

"And, like the Vhurruh, in the midst of such worthy goals, we also discovered that defense against foreign intruders of our beautiful planet was, and will forever be, of primary importance. We have known for several years that we are no longer alone in the universe. Some of us, I daresay, have known for decades. I believe the continued success of our defenses includes the restoration of trust and cooperation with our Vhurruh allies."

Several whispers and murmurs of dissent followed his statement.

"In the spirit of restoring that trust and cooperation," Vince continued, "human representatives from many countries, including scientists, physicians, therapists, spiritual leaders, military leaders, educators—and yes, *even* politicians—are being chosen for a panel to address the issues of mind control and infiltration, which are of great concern to many here today. The leadership of Vhurruh military, and our human military and political offices were most greatly affected by the rogue faction. We would be remiss not to consider the wisdom offered *by* those affected. We do not...*ever*...want this...to happen...again."

The crowd exploded in applause, and Vince waited patiently to let them express their support.

Caffrey noticed he had been careful to show both Vhurruh and humans as victims, and being similar in their endeavors and accomplishments. She smiled at his gentle brilliance.

"Before us is a most extraordinary, most incredible opportunity: the chance to explore and colonize another planet, capable of sustaining human life, and that of our allies, the Vhurruh." Low grumblings echoed in several spots throughout the room.

"Our *ally....*" Vince emphasized the word, "Hurratt, gave us a new technology to defend ourselves against a common menace, the Zgeyyans, who had the capacity and the will to destroy our life, our civilization, our world. We will *not* forget this great decision on their part, which was not an easy one for them. Having the same concerns of non-interference, which we ourselves have wrestled with in our contemplation of exploring new worlds—and will have in our future discoveries of new life forms and civilizations, the Vhurruh also debated such interference in our battle with the Zgeyyans. I, for one, am thankful they did not debate it for long.

"Let us focus now on repairing the damage done by another common enemy—tyranny—and let us go forth, together, to find and assist our loved ones on Veerinay. Let us create a civilization—a child, if you will—of ourselves, and teach it how to live and grow. This child, as most of you know by now, cannot return to the nest. DNA-altering organisms natural to the planet on which our beloved people reside are now part of *them*. Forever. Though perhaps not by choice, they are the new, the brave, explorers of a brand-new country, a brand-new world.

"With the existence of quarandomes, built in response to Vhurruh needs, we may have the technology to allow for visits on both sides. I realize this will create a great stampede, if you will, as many on Earth and on Veerinay will want the privilege of reuniting with loved ones. We must ask for your patience a little longer. Scientists have advised us that even the quarandomes themselves could attract and harbor dangerous microorganisms that could be transferred from one ecosystem to another. The safety of both planets must be considered. Suggestions have been made for satellites to be positioned around Veerinay, and a station be built on one of the two moons, so that electronic communications can be safely sent and extracted. Whatever we have to do, if there is a way, I can assure you, we *will* find it."

Explosions of cheers and applause traveled over the assembly.

"And, yes, as has been speculated, we have created an office, as part of the United Nations, housed here in this building, to address such issues. A phone number as well as a website will be available in one weeks' time. Anyone, from any country, can call or search the site, in their own language, for information on progress toward accounting for the missing humans, as well as progress toward visits—digital visits at first, but hopefully semi-physical visits in the future. On the day of the website launch, despite our programmers working around the clock, getting through the phone lines and the site may take a small act of God. However, our goal is to keep you informed. And, as before, it is also my personal goal that no government or military, *theirs* or *ours*, be allowed to manipulate, or stand in the way of, your access to the truth."

People stood in a wave across the auditorium, clapping hard and loud. Vince scanned the assembly, his face set. The applause continued for almost an entire minute. Vince nodded and smiled.

"We have also partnered with the Red Cross, since they already have a page dedicated to finding loved ones after a crisis. Countless thousands of you have been listing your missing loved one's names and pre-disaster addresses for almost three years. Members of the Red Cross—very brave members I might add—have volunteered to assist in a joint mission to Veerinay, along with a few members of human rights and watch groups. We hope to have a preliminary list, in 30 days, of survivors, and of the deceased. The first will be easier than the last, as we do not wish to make any errors and cause unnecessary pain. If you have not already done so, please post the most recent photos of your missing friends and loved ones in order to ensure accuracy. Your photos will remain secure so that companies cannot access them for any database or mailings. Facial recognition software will make note of duplicate listings."

Vince's brow furrowed as he looked down at his notes, and back up at the audience.

"We have faced two incredible planetwide disasters. First, the Zgeyyan Invasion, which was overcome with assistance from the Vhurruh. Secondly, the Vhurruh Faction Coup, which was overcome with assistance from the Vhurruh and humans working together." Vince gave the assembly a long, hard look. "I will not call it a war or an invasion as many of you have attempted to do. There will always be factions from countries, from groups, from belief systems, and from alien cultures, who will desire power over peace."

Vince cleared his throat. "Many people are focusing on the fallout from this most recent disaster instead of recognizing the incredible valor of those humans and Vhurruh who fought and triumphed. Because of this, we are now facing a third disaster. Prejudice on a galactic scale. Like lepers of the past who were kept outside city gates to fend for themselves, I have encountered people who have confessed that they would rather their loved ones be deceased, than have to see them genetically altered and unable to cohabit with...unaffected humans. It has even been suggested that any photo taken of such survivors should remain restricted. I respect their pain. But as for me, I will always want the truth, no matter how difficult, or painful."

Scattered clapping echoed in the room.

"There is also a growing prejudice against those humans still linked to Vhurruh. I can assure you, I know of many Vhurruh who fractured their minds to give the appearance of complying with the faction. They did what they had to in order to support *Nekkai*, and support us. Many humans are calling for justice against them. Do we have laws that fit their crimes? It may be that the only reason I have been allowed to stand before you today is because, firstly, I am trusted on both sides, but secondly, the Vhurruh I was linked to...paid for our freedom with his life."

He swallowed. Tears stung Caffrey's eyes as she watched him.

"So, am I deemed safe? Let us not rush to judgment with fear and bigotry. Let us be driven by our hopes and aspirations, by a sense of right and wrong capable of encompassing another race of creatures and the complexities of their culture."

Vince seemed to stare at the podium for several seconds, then raised his eyes with a look of conviction. "Someone asked me today where we were going to put the list of Vhurruh who lost their lives in the Faction Coup. I was ashamed to admit that none of us had discussed such a list. We were so busy focusing on the human disaster that we forgot the other victims who lost their lives. So today, we created a website called Nekkai.org. In a few days, we will post the list of those Vhurruh who fought against the faction and survived, those still in recovery, and those who have fallen."

Caffrey pressed her lips together hard in an effort to keep her face from scrunching into a painful cry. Still unable to make a connection with *Mhetrrian* that morning, it was she who had asked Vince where the list of fallen Vhurruh would be. She still remembered his widened eyes and paled expression at the realization that no one else had asked. She took slow, deep breaths to regain control, and glanced at the faces around her. All of them were still and pensive. Many had wrinkled, worried brows.

Vince scanned the crowd as well.

"Much work is before us. We have a lot of healing to do. However, I believe, together, we are up to the task of rebuilding.

The mission to Veerinay is a joint one. The Vhurruh have offered much in the way of supplies and technology, as they have a desire to help rebuild the Alliance and also because they have a stake in this new planet."

Vince stood taller and raised both hands to suppress the murmurs of protest.

"Let Veerinay *no longer* be seen as a place of tragedy. Let it also be seen as a place where two species from different planets, from different societies, found a way to exist and prosper, and accomplish great endeavors together—on different continents possibly, for now." He held up one hand for emphasis. "For safety concerns, of course. Perhaps, side by side in the future. Ladies and gentlemen, the greatness of the human spirit *has* prevailed. The greatness of Vhurruh *Nekkai* has prevailed. Truth, integrity, and faith on both sides has prevailed.

"My organization, AllianceWatch, will continue our efforts to bring matters of integrity and human rights to light within the Alliance, and our open-door policy for ideas and opinions will remain. Thashan Kumar of We-The-Humans and Yune Milan of Earth-Sentinels will do the same. Many have assumed that because of the joint effort of humans and *Nekkai*, and because of the newly created panel, that we would simply dissolve and become enmeshed in common purposes. I hope, and it is my plan, that this will partly become the case. However, I also believe that there is still a need for our voices.

"Watchdogs keep great houses guarded. A watchdog group we began, and a watchdog group we will continue to be. In addition...."

He waited a moment for hearty applause to diminish.

"Let there be no mistake that our purpose is to uphold the integrity of the Alliance, to further the prosperity and security of our planet, and to be a voice for the voiceless, be they human, *or* Vhurruh."

Vince offered a slight smile to the continued applause.

"*Veerinay Hodzu* in the Vhurruh language means 'new home of life-giving water,' so named for the many natural waterways and springs near the original Zgeyyan landing site. I believe it is aptly named. It *is* a new home. A new world. And, we are in a new dawn. The Earth-Hurratt Alliance has renewed its dedication, purpose, and mission. It is stronger now, and smarter. Let us dedicate ourselves, once again, to a new future, and to the preservation of life in *all* its many and wonderful forms."

As he stepped away from the podium, the applause became deafening. Attendees began to stand.

A tap on Caffrey's shoulder suspended her hands mid-clap. A clean-cut teenager in a Page uniform leaned down and dropped something cylindrical and brown into Caffrey's hand. "I was asked to give you this, ma'am."

Caffrey examined it, and gasped. It was a small, brown spice bottle labeled "Mace." She whirled to find the Page, but he had skipped up the isle and was disappearing into the mass of bodies and security guards at the doorway.

Caffrey shuffled up the steep aisle as gracefully as she dared in high heels while the introductions of the Vhurruh began. She regretted missing it, knowing she would not be allowed to enter the room in honor of Vhurruh custom.

Wrrynatt, Vrreemeh, Umurrgnn, did you find him? Is he here? Caffrey called out to her links.

We cannot tell.

What? Why not?

We are having a ruse.

As politely as possible, then with determination, Caffrey pushed through the crowd of reporters and observers in the hall. Like a cat, she weaved through them, nearly making herself motion-sick amidst a strobe light of camera flashes. Two men in suits and wearing earplugs followed her.

What are you talking about, "having a ruse?" Caffrey asked. There was a smug secretiveness in the *surranenn* minds. *You rascals,* she thought back to them. *You guys are spending way too much time with humans.*

After skirting down an adjoining hall, Caffrey slowed, not knowing which direction to take. She scouted every black-haired, tan-skinned frame in view as she walked. As she rounded the corner of an intersecting hall, a voice halted her movement.

"Hey, Princess."

"Mace!" She flew into his arms, knocking them both into a wall. She crushed her lips against his with ferocity, oblivious that she was in a building where dignity was the rule of the day. Cameras flashed and passersby smiled. The uniformed guards on either side of Mace ordered the reporters to step back. Caffrey halted when she realized the guards wore black and gold. Her smile fell.

"It's okay," Mace responded, reading her concern. "They're new and non-linked. And they're on orders to make sure *this* package gets delivered." He raised his brows and tilted his head in chastisement. "Some *friends* of yours talked to their buddies, who talked to their linked humans, who talked Vince into giving up our contact code in order to find me, if that wasn't bad enough." He frowned teasingly. "Then, they wanted to drag me halfway up the continent to *this* crowd."

Caffrey puzzled for a moment. "My Vhurruh? The three *surranenn*?" She thought to them quickly—*You guys are wonderful!*—and sensed them gloating.

"Mmm-hmm," Mace commented with squinted eyes. "Seems these 'friends' have been searching for two days, insisting they could not disappoint their queen-mother, or their *human* queen, by not providing me to you, even though I was fully prepared to blast their little scout ship right outta the sky. The thing hovered not twenty feet off the ground. I had a plasma pulsar by then, from a downed chopper. It's a long story. And, I was hiding out in a place only Vince knew about. Damned Vhurruh are lucky they're still breathin'."

Caffrey grinned. She had no problem picturing that scene. "They *did* it. I can't believe they found you! Are you okay? Were you hurt or anything?" She scanned over his wonderful body with her hands as well as her eyes, noting a cut above one eyebrow and a long burn mark on the side of his face where a lock of hair was missing.

"Well, like I said, it's a long story," said Mace in a tired voice. He ran his hands up and down her shoulders possessively. "Once they took off with you, all hell broke loose. I couldn't tell who was shooting at who."

"The counter-cry. *Mhetrrian* explained it when the trigger hit me at Evan's mansion. Did you actually see some of the SAAFs fire on people and then turn on each other?"

"Yeah." His expression turned sober. "One chopper fell right in front of me. Nearly blew me into oblivion, except for the car I dove into. Jimmy got out okay."

"The counter-programming was done from the beginning," Caffrey explained. "The hidden *Nekkai* Vhurruh did program many of the SAAFs in order to appear compliant with the other faction members, like the one that reprogrammed me. But, they made certain their linked officers would follow The Cry, with the added instruction to turn after a few minutes on their fellow officers to stop them—not to kill them, but disable them. Hundreds of people were still killed, and thousands wounded, I understand, but many were saved, too."

Mace nodded in acknowledgement, a sad frown creasing his forehead. "Well, anyway," he continued after a thoughtful pause, "this morning I refused to ride the scout ship. I'm not ready to trust a bunch of slugs. They are *not* touchin' me. I flew the 'friendly skies' once I talked to Vince and Gina on the phone. How'd you like Vince? After guarding him for nearly three years, I don't like letting him run loose and unprotected in there."

"You've been here all this time?" Caffrey protested, anger rising.

Mace chuckled, enjoying her indignation. "I've only been here for a little while, but I'm not much for crowds, or politicians. And, you were a *little* tied up. I'd still like to remain somewhat anonymous. Can't do my job if I'm not. Your three little 'friends' have been a real pain in the butt, keeping track of me for the past few hours. They even flew beside my plane. *And,* they're hovering out there at the landing pad now. Think the little buggers'll leave us alone for a while? Long enough for us to get some rest?"

Caffrey smiled. "They'll do whatever I ask of them. Did you see them? You know they're only ten feet long?"

He snorted. "Small beans compared to the big guys, huh?"

"You didn't see *Wysstangrr*. He's the stuff of nightmares. Although, I shouldn't complain, because without him I wouldn't be here with you now." Caffrey beamed with happiness. "Yes, rest sounds like a great idea. The *surranenn* volunteered to help me heal. They tried a little, but they need a queen. I still have a constant migraine that I can keep dulled by meds but can't get rid of. It hurts to think about anything important and I can't stand any lights. I had to sit through two meetings with sunglasses. I've just about O.D.'d on ibuprofen and headache powders. The *surranenn* said I'd probably sleep for two days after their hands-on healing process if the queen assists them."

"No!" Mace protested. "I don't want another one of 'em touching you."

Caffrey frowned. "Mace, these guys are okay, really. It doesn't matter, because I can't afford to be asleep for two days. I've got so much to do still."

"You do?" he asked, disappointed.

"Well, there're all these meetings taking place, and I know so much, and everybody wants to ask me everything, and I might get to meet the President...."

"Let's get out of here," he suggested in a low voice, and brushed a lock of red hair from her cheek.

"Yeah," she agreed softly. "If they need any more info, they can ask someone else. My brain's dead-tired."

Umurrgnn can we have a ride? she mentally called out.

Certainly. Our queen-mother commands we are here for you. Have not been called away. Where do you wish to go?

An island hotel I know about. It's in a place we call the Caribbean. She visualized the hotel and an aerial view of its beach location from a map she had seen in a brochure.

We comprehend the location. We can find. Your drone will not board our vessel.

Oh, I think I can persuade him. Just give me a few minutes.

The secret exchange occurred in seconds, but Mace had noticed when her eyes went unfocused. "You don't have anything else hidden away in that little brain of yours, do you?" he playfully asked. "No programs, no Vhurruh secrets, no triggers?"

"Nope," she answered with smiling certainty. Then she let loose a mischievous grin. "As far as I know."

www.ingramcontent.com/pod-product-compliance
Lightning Source LLC
Chambersburg PA
CBHW031133260626
47153CB00021B/124